The Coven

Magical mystery and mayhem based on the award-winning
series Maya's Magical Adventures

By Maya and Malcolm McCoard

Edited by Anne McCoard

For Maya and Anne.

Special thanks to:

*Granny Kerr and Grandma McCoard, in the hope of placating
some of the damage done by later references to 'cunning old
bats.'*

Edited by Anne and Elizabeth McCoard

First published in the United Kingdom in 2021

Written by Maya and Malcolm McCoard and based on the bedtime stories and illustrations of Maya McCoard.

©2021 e book and paperback on KDP

This is a work of fiction. Names, characters, businesses, places, events and incidents are either the products of the author's imagination or used in a fictitious manner. Any resemblance to actual persons, living or dead, or actual events is purely coincidental.

Except for the character of Aunty Dot, who sadly is that shallow in real life!

Part I - Missing and unhinged

Morning broke.

No, today it wasn't just broken. It had shattered, like a dropped mirror, fragmenting into a myriad of irreconcilable pieces. A mirror, which now reflected Maya's fractured world. One suddenly cast into disarray and despair, in the aftermath of one inexplicable event.

She'd tried in vain to fix it. Using pancakes and chocolate spread for breakfast, but stubbornly, it remained broken. Even her dad couldn't bring a smile to Maya's face today. She was miles away. Alone with her melancholy thoughts and tormented day dreams. His bad 'dad jokes', just faded away into background noise. Corny punchlines went unheard, dwindling away to nothing, like diminishing echoes, in the recesses of a cave. Nothing was the same now, not since her mum's disappearance. Not even pancakes.

Having pushed her breakfast around the pate for some time, without consuming a single mouthful. Maya thoughtfully left it for her dad to tidy up. Clearing up after her, she reasoned, would keep him occupied. It was the least she could do. Maya made her way wearily back upstairs to her bedroom. She passed Mischief, their rather lazy black and white cat, sleeping on the top step.

Mischief too, was unusually subdued these days. Ever since her mum had vanished, he'd slept there, in that exact same spot. Snoozing away most of the day and all of the night, every night. Abandoning his more customary position, curled up at the foot of Maya's bed. It was almost as if he was holding vigil. Waiting patiently for her mother's return, stationed like a sentry, outside Maya's mum's 'secret cupboard,' as if awaiting her return.

3

Maya's dad had christened it, 'Mum's secret cupboard.' A cupboard crammed full of 'her stuff' and coincidentally, the last place that any of them had seen or heard from her. Maya reflected now, on how her mum's 'secret cupboard' wasn't all that secret, after all. Although Mum had often warned, both Maya and her dad, within "an inch of their miserable lives and on pain of death or something far, far worse!" never to open it. Maya and her dad had, of course, often raided her secret hoard. Obviously, only when Mum was out working. The temptation to dip into her secret stockpile of chocolates and biscuits, or even just to see what she'd bought them for their birthdays and for Christmas, was just too great. The key wasn't well hidden either, stashed on top of the cupboard's deep wooden door frame. A hiding place, which was now well within Maya's reach, when she stretched up on her tip-toes.

Maya's weary eyes were now drawn to the task in hand. Dad had decreed, that it was high time that the pile of birthday presents, still littering her bedroom floor, was finally put away. It had been two weeks since Maya's thirteenth birthday. Two weeks since she'd last seen her mum. The longest and worst two weeks of her short life.

Maya bent down and picked up a bundle of new clothes and presents from the top of the pile. She dropped them wearily on top of her chest of drawers, then returned for another load. A tiny silver object, a neckless, caught her eye. Eyes which now filled with tears. Maya bent down to pick up the neckless. She'd all but forgotten about it, with everything that had happened since her birthday.

Maya studied it closely, her vision blurred through tear-stained eyes, as she held it in her outstretched palm. Mum had given it to her on her birthday, just a few hours before she'd vanished...

In a clumsy and obvious flashback, indicated by three small asterisks, the narrator took the few remaining readers back two weeks, to the day of Maya's birthday.

It was a windy Friday morning, thanks to one of Dad's curries, consumed under protest, the previous night. Maya had been ripping open presents enthusiastically, all morning. It had been fun, but Dad was in the dog-house again, as usual. This time, for forgetting to buy cream and strawberries and candles and indeed any kind of a cake for Maya's birthday.

"One job. Just one job!" her mum had ranted. "The only thing I asked you to do yesterday. You had the whole day off, lazing around, whilst some of us were out working our fingers to the bone, doing a fourteen-hour shift!".

You could usually gauge the degree of Mum's frustration, by the extent to which she exaggerated of the length of her shifts. She worked as a nurse, at the local hospital, caring compassionately for 'hypochondriacs and riff-raff', who didn't deserve any sympathy,' apparently. A fourteen-hour shift, probably meant Dad would be in the dog-house, for at least a week.

Dad quickly made himself scarce. Mum smiled and laid down a rather worn little red book, which she'd been reading obsessively, over the past few days.

"A miracle wouldn't you say?" Mum asked Maya, with a mischievous glint in her eye.

"Miracle?" Maya queried.

"How a man with no backbone, can still walk upright!" she explained, with a smile.

Maya smirked in response.

Maya's mum was now sporting a satisfied and rather devious grin, as if she'd been plotting how to get Dad out the way, for quite some time.

"I wanted to give you something. Something special. Keep this just between us girls though," her mum insisted. Then rummaged around in her pocket, before producing a small black velvet pouch and handing it to Maya.

Maya pulled on a leather bow, tied around the neck of the small black velvet bag, then poured a delicate silver chain, out onto the palm of her hand, accompanied by a gasp of delight. The neckless was beautiful, it had two small delicately hand carved silver charms on it. One a tiny, old-fashioned key and the other an equally petite heart-shaped locket. Maya looked up at her mother and smiled appreciatively.

"My little girl thirteen already, I can't believe it," her mum mused. "My mum gave me this neckless, when I turned thirteen too." Maya's mum reached around her neck and showed Maya her own neckless, which she never took off. It too, had an identical heart-shaped locket, a similar tiny key and a number of other delicate silver charms.

"They're family heir looms. Very precious," her mum whispered, as if conveying some great secret. Then she grabbed both of Maya's hands and looked her deep in the eyes, with a seriousness and intensity that Maya had never experienced before. Insisting:

"Keep this safe and use it well. Remember my words carefully. Whenever things look bleak or hopeless, the key is always to follow your heart."

Maya nodded and looked down at the delicate neckless in her hand, as her Mum finally relinquished her grasp.

"A key and a heart. Clever... the key is, to follow your heart. Got it," Maya acknowledged, as Mischief brushed up against her mum's leg, with a needy meow.

"Oh yes, sorry Mischief, and trust your cat. That's very important too. He's wiser that you'll ever know," she added, with a smile and a wink.

Maya gave her mum a big hug. Mum squeezed her back, then kissed Maya gently on the forehead, as she released her.

Maya had a good birthday. The last good day she could remember. She was allowed a pyjama day. Relatives, delivering presents, came and went and all complained bitterly, about the lack of cake. That would be her mum's cue to glare at Dad. Which in turn, was his cue, to suddenly think of something, anything, that he should be doing in another room.

Later that afternoon, Maya and her mum were in the living room. Mum was reading that boring little red book again and Maya was playing on her tablet. With an audible gasp, her mother sat upright abruptly, scribbled something in the margins of the book and left the living room, explaining:

"Won't be too long. Just popping out to the shops for a few birthday essentials. Oh no, actually, there's something else I need to do, I might be gone for a while. If Dad asks any questions, just say I'm away out to buy a cake and to cool off a bit. He'll think, he's still in the dog house. That should keep him stewing for a while," she added, with a wicked grin.

Footsteps made their way up the stairs, as if heading for her secret hoarding cupboard. Dad returned rather furtively, the coast was clear, so he turned up the volume on his old-fashioned CD player. It started to blast out some of his terrible 'dad dancing' music. Maya rummaged around for her phone and quickly engaged her ear phones, as a counter-measure.

But, as the afternoon wore on and it started to get dark, there was no sign of Mum or Maya's birthday cake. Teatime came and went. Eventually, Dad made something resembling a meal. More relatives arrived and left disappointed by the lack of birthday cake. Phone calls and texts were sent, but all went unanswered. Mum's twin sister, Aunty Dot had heard nothing either. Still no sign of Maya's mum nor of Maya's cake.

Something was wrong. As night fell, Dad sat her down nervously and explained that Aunty Dot had phoned the police. Apparently, she'd not held back, when it came to conveying, exactly who she thought was to blame. So, as a result, he'd been invited to assist them with their enquiries, down at the local police station.

Search parties were organised. They were no fun though, no balloons or games and still no cake. Just endless long walks looking for her mum, but still there was no sign. No clues to her whereabouts, nothing. Not that night, nor all the next day. She'd simply vanished, without so much as a trace.

Two weeks had passed now, without any sign, not a single clue or sighting, nothing. Shock and worry had now been overtaken by grief. Hope by despair. It was as if the sun hadn't risen above the horizon, since that night. Twilight replaced the dawn and a cruel ache clawed at Maya's heart, with every heavy beat.

Dad had lost his sense of humour too. He tried in vain to muster jokes and lighten the mood. Desperate to take Maya's mind off it, even just for a moment.

"When she comes back, this cake had better be worth...," but even with his notoriously poor taste, he couldn't bring himself to finish the jibe. Even his cuddles felt hollow now. They felt weak and apologetic. As if, he knew, in his heart, that he'd failed her. Unable to explain her mother's disappearance. Powerless to comfort his own daughter or bring back her mum.

Auntie Dot was a gibbering wreck too.

"Unhinged," Dad called it. "Even more than usual."

A shadow of her former self, even finding it difficult to exchange meaningless gossip. For the first time in her life, she was completely out of idle chit-chat.

Maya missed her mum, no that wasn't it. She was lost without her. Her heart had been ripped out of her chest using a blunt spoon, stomped on by a herd of hippo at an all you can eat buffet and fed mercilessly, like chocolate cake to a 5-year-old's birthday party.

Mischief, their trusty family cat, was off his food too and had seemingly forgotten how to purr. He rarely ventured out and slept by the door to Mum's secret cupboard, both day and night.

***

Another three asterisks indicated, not a sudden flurry of snow, but rather the author's clumsy return, from the previous flashback.

Maya gazed down at the delicate neckless in the palm of her hand, as Mischief brushed up against her leg affectionately. Her mother's words came back to her once more and she shared them with her cat.

"Whenever things look bleak or hopeless, the key is always to follow your heart," Maya snuffled out loud. Tears followed random tracks, down both of her cheeks, like drunken skiers on the piste.

"Things couldn't be more hopeless than they are now, I guess. But, how on earth do I follow my heart, when my heart is broken?" Maya asked her cat out loud.

Mischief brushed up against her leg, as if to re-assure her, then with his head lowered, nudged her solidly in the back of her calf.

"Oh, sorry Mischief. Mum also said, I should trust you too and, oh yes, that your wiser that I'll ever know," Maya laughed in response. Snorting back the tears and wiping a snail trail, all the way up her hoodie's sleeve.

Mischief nudged her again, as if encouraging her towards the door, but Maya was suddenly distracted.

It was glowing!

The neckless. Faintly, but distinctly. The heart shaped charm, was actually glowing. A faint green light, only just visible to the naked eye, but there was no mistaking it. The solid silver charm, was now inexplicably luminescent.

"That's weird!" Maya announced to her cat.

Mischief nudged her once more in the calf and instinctively Maya stepped forward in response. The heart pulsed with light, as if betraying a tiny heartbeat. Maya stared down at Mischief in disbelief, who nudged her once more. Maya took another step towards the door and the tiny charm responded with another beat and shone more brightly still.

"Follow your heart... trust the cat?" Maya whispered to herself in disbelief.

Mischief looked up at her, as if to say 'finally' and made his way quickly through the door.

"Where are we going?" Maya asked, half in excitement, half in scepticism, at her sudden delusional belief, that her scruffy black and white cat, was somehow showing her the way.

Maya followed Mischief through the doorway, the neckless continued to beat and glow more brightly, with every step that she took. Maya stepped out onto the landing, at the top of the stairs. There, Mischief stopped abruptly and sat facing her mum's secret cupboard door.

Mischief meowed. Mischief hardly ever meowed.

Maya looked puzzled, but there was no doubt, the tiny charm was still glowing. Its light appeared even stronger now, shrouded in the dim light of the stairwell landing.

Maya reached up on tip-toes and retrieved the cupboard key from above the door frame. Then, with her heart beating like a bongo drum strapped to a runaway camel, she turned the key in the lock and opened the secret cupboard door.

Maya studied the contents carefully. Could there be a clue in here, she wondered? Parcels, chocolates and guilty empty sweet wrappers lined the shelves. There were scented candles labelled, 'Dot's Xmas,' which Grandma had given her mum for her own birthday. But nothing unusual. Nothing at all.

Then it leapt out at Maya, a sudden realisation accompanied by crushing disappointment. Half a shelf, covered in catnip filled cat toys and feline treats. Tears of disillusionment, came once again to Maya's eyes.

"Oh Mischief, is this all you've been after?" Maya asked, snorting back the tears once more.

Mischief though, just plodded forward and disappeared under the bottom shelf. Maya waited for him to reappear. Then waited and waited. Maya let out an audible sigh, then popped the neckless over her head, and disentangled it from her long blonde hair, as she pulled it through the chain, at the back of her neck.

"Come on, out of there silly," Maya encouraged, bending down to retrieve her cat. But Mischief was nowhere to be seen. Even by the strange green light from her neckless, which now swung around her neck. He was nowhere to be found. It was as if he'd vanished or walked straight through the back of the cupboard. Maya checked the stairs behind her, but there was no sign of her elusive cat anywhere. He too had just vanished.

"Curious?" Maya announced to herself.

Out popped her tongue too. This was a reflex action for Maya, whenever she started thinking. A curious habit. Her dad often teased her about it. Observing, that whenever Maya's brain kicked in, it was as if it had swelled up, with all the effort and expelled her tongue, just to make room.

Maya felt something else now, there was something very odd here. As Maya rose to her feet slowly, her neckless tugged gently to one side. Like a magnet, drawn to an invisible iron bar. Maya straightened up in response and stared in amazement, at the tiny heart shaped charm, which now floated in mid-air and glowed with a dazzling green light. It pulled her neck gently towards a very old and sturdy black metal door hinge, inset to one side of the cupboard door frame.

Maya had never really noticed it before. There were three such hinges; top, middle and bottom. Much too substantial for such a normal looking cupboard door. They would look more at home at Hogwarts, or on a safe door from a Wild West movie. Not on a simple cupboard door, in her own house, Maya thought to herself.

Maya stepped forwards to inspect the middle hinge. There was a small matching metal plate next to it, engraved with strange symbols. None of which she recognised, except for a small heart shaped indent in the centre.

Maya studied it closely. She gave it a right good 'looking at' in search of inspiration. As Maya stared, she engaged her brain further, slipping it gently into top gear. She bit down on her bottom lip, then wiggled the tip of her tongue over her lips in deep contemplation. Oral gymnastics were an involuntary response, every time she started to concentrate. Tongue waggling, Maya really truly believed, helped her to think and as an added bonus, cut down on the need to wash her face after eating chocolate biscuits.

Then, as she leaned in closer...

Click-clunk-clunk-clunk!

The heart shaped charm found a home, drawn like a magnet to the matching indent in the metal plate. In that instant, the charm dropped free again and a loud clunk, came from each of the sturdy hinges in turn. Metal bolts raised out of each of them simultaneously and the whole cupboard shuddered back and forth alarmingly.

Maya stepped back nervously. She was feeling slightly unhinged herself. Slowly, very slowly the whole, now unhinged cupboard swung back into the wall to reveal a dimly lit room, hidden beyond.

Maya gasped, swallowed deeply and called out hopefully:

"Mum?"

What have you been up to Mum?

There was no reply. Maya's heart sunk once more. For a moment, just one brief moment, she'd dared to hope her mum would be in here. Waiting for her, with a big hug and some rotten excuse, but there was nobody there.

The room was empty, except for a few pieces of old-fashioned furniture. Maya stepped forward a few paces into the hidden chamber and surveyed the scene. As she did so, the inverted cupboard, which looked much like a normal door, from this side, closed gently behind her. Letting out another rather satisfying solid clunk, as it did so.

The room smelt musty and everything inside appeared aged and rather scruffy. Old-fashioned oak panels lined the walls and in the middle of the room, stood a sturdy, bashed and rather shabby looking dressing table. On top, lay a large open book and beside that, a brown paper parcel, wrapped in string. The dressing table mirror was discoloured and cracked. The floor, composed of uneven and well-worn wooden planks, looked as if it hadn't been swept in years. Everything in the room was covered in a thick layer of dust. That at least, Maya told herself, was a good sign. Her mum really didn't do dusting. So perhaps, she was finally on her mother's trail, after all?

Next to the dressing table, stood a full-length mirror and beside that, in the corner of the room, sat an old wooden chest. Perched on top of the chest, were three small sturdy looking triangular shaped bottles, each with a cork stopper and a label.

"What have you been up to Mum?" Maya whispered to herself.

Tentatively, she stepped forward towards the dressing table, to investigate further. There had to be a clue in here somewhere,

14

didn't there? Something to make some sense of her mum's sudden inexplicable disappearance. If there were clues here, Maya was determined to find them.

Lying open, on top of the dressing table was a very large, obviously weighty and well-worn leather-bound book. Its pages were covered in elegant old-fashioned and rather flamboyant writing, as if scribed from the quill of an old-fashioned ink pen. Maya's heart sunk once more. Her mum's handwriting was awful. This couldn't be a diary. Probably just another one of those weird local history books, her mum had taken to reading recently. Maya paid it no more attention and instead focussed on the brown paper parcel, sat next to it.

Tucked under a loosely tied string bow, was a small folded piece of paper with her name on it. Maya's heart missed a beat and started to pound in her chest, thumping against her rib-cage, like a guinea pig caught in a tumble drier. She recognised that painfully untidy handwriting this time, alright.

"Mum?" Maya gasped, frantically reaching out and unfolding the small scrap of paper. Maya read it aloud to herself:

"Maya my dear, you have come of age. I'm so proud of you. Remember, whenever things look bleak or hopeless, the key is always to follow your heart."

Maya paused. Tears filled her eyes once more. Then suddenly and rather angrily, she ranted:

"That's it? That's all mother, really?"

Maya pulled impatiently at the string bow, which bound the parcel and ripped away the paper impatiently. Inside she found another large leather-bound book. It matched the one open on the dressing table, beside her. Two sturdy metal cross straps locked it shut securely. Where the straps met, there was a square metal plate.

15

There were more of the same curious symbols, like those she'd seen earlier on the plate beside the door hinge. There in the centre, she could make out a delicate heart shaped indent. Maya had seen this before.

"Follow your heart, I wonder?" Maya asked herself aloud, as she pulled out the chair and sat down in front of the weighty tome.

Maya retrieved the chain, from around her neck, once more. Then, with a shaky nervous hand, she compared the heart shaped charm, against the recess in the plate on the book.

"It matches!" Maya announced, rather proudly to herself.

Without warning, Mischief leapt up onto the dressing table. Maya jumped out of her skin, then landed, quaking in a cowardly one, two sizes smaller. Still shaking, she mustered a nervous smile and scolded him, with an affectionate scratch under the chin;

"Where did you get to?" she laughed. "If I didn't know better, I'd swear you can walk through walls!"

Maya stroked the top of Mischief's head with one hand. Then, she placed the heart shaped charm gently into the metal recess on the book, with the other.

The delicate heart shaped locket clicked, rather satisfyingly, into place and instantly, the metal straps sprung apart. Maya sat back rather startled. Mischief though, didn't flinch at all. He simply yawned and stretched, as if he had seen this all, a hundred times before.

Maya however, now gazed, wide mouthed in utter amazement and let out an involuntary gasp of surprise. Her jaw dropped, bounced off the floor and slapped her firmly across the face on the way up, to check she wasn't dreaming. As the book opened slowly ... by itself.

"Wh...?" Maya heard herself not asking.

The pages were thick and made from old and slightly yellowed hand-made parchment. They were blank, but only for a moment. Now a voice spoke, as if coming from the book, in a gruff elderly tone:

"Hello little witchling."

Again, Maya jumped. Pushing the chair backwards several inches across the wooden floor, accompanied by a loud nerve-jangling screech.

Mischief simply ignored the book's antics and started to wash his front paw. Even more surprisingly, as the book spoke, its words were being written in neat and elegant prose. Black ink, started to write across the first blank page. Each word appearing, as if scribed from the nib of an invisible quilled feather pen.

"Me? I..., I'm not! Not a witch, that is," Maya stammered, her eyes open wide as crumpets. She stared, transfixed and bewildered, by the spectacle unfolding in front of her.

"Hmm..., no, not yet you're not, but we'll see?" replied the book.

Maya stared in astonishment at the book, then finally plucked up the courage to ask:

"How, eh..., how is it? Er, I mean?"

Maya was unnerved by the whole spectacle. Her brain had temporarily lost contact with her mouth. This wasn't possible. Was she dreaming? Unnervingly, she had also noted, with no small amount of discomfort, that as she spoke, her stuttering words too, were writing themselves across the pages of this strange book.

"Ah, little one," the book interrupted. "The answer to the question, which you are most eloquently not asking me, is that every witch writes her own story."

"Witch, story? I don't understand, what story? How do I start it?" Maya asked.

"You already have, little one. The moment you opened me," the book replied.

"My mum! I'm looking for my mum," Maya announced, suddenly changing the subject. "Have you seen her?"

"No little one. I am your record keeper. Your journal in the magical realm... your mother, as a witch, has her own."

"My mum's not a...," Maya started, but she couldn't finish her protestations.

Maya's heart missed yet another beat. Her eyes, now drawn immediately to the other open book, sat on the dressing table, next to her own. Somehow, all the strange talk of witchcraft and magical realms faded into insignificance, compared to the revelation that the book sat next to her, might be her mother's journal. A diary which may have recorded her fate.

"Is that...?" Maya started.

"Yes, little one. Your mother's book," answered the mighty tome.

"Will it...?" Maya started once more.

"Tell you where she is?" the book completed her sentence again, paused and confirmed, "Yes."

"Is she...?" Maya asked, this time much more meekly.

"Yes, little one. Her book is still open," the book replied rather more gently. "Her book is only half finished. If her story's still being told... then she's still alive."

Maya burst into tears. Tears of relief. Tears of joy. Tears on tears... things got wet!

"Steady on, little one. Some of us are made of paper and don't really appreciate a soaking," the book eventually interrupted.

"Sorry," Maya blubbed, wiping tears and snail trails from her nose, all the way up her sleeve.

"She's alive, little one. But something is wrong," cautioned the book, in a rather sobering tone.

"What? What's wrong?" Maya demanded, looking up in alarm.

"Her story no longer writes," replied the book. "I've never heard of such a thing."

Maya stared down at her mother's book. The writing was indeed static. Just as you'd expect, from any normal book.

Maya turned back to her own journal, which now wrote:

"Though obviously not the brightest... the young witchling was slowly catching on. The answers to the questions, which she most desperately wanted to hear, were probably written in her mother's magical journal. Yet here she sits, wasting time, reading her own story out loud to herself."

"Hey!" Maya complained, then bounced her chair across the floor, accompanied by further nerve jangling, wood on wood screeching noises. She pulled herself in towards the dressing table, with a further loud squeak, until she sat nervously in front of her mother's book.

Maya's hand trembled, as she followed the text with her finger and read aloud, from the last entry in her mother's journal:

She knew exactly what she had to do, no time to waste, it was midnight and she climbed by the light of the full moon. She knew in her heart though, that her magic would not help her now, not where she was headed, but she had to try. She stepped out slowly and carefully, summoning every ounce of her courage. Her mind was made up now, this was it, it had to be here. The stone crumbled beneath her feet, as she stepped out and fell...

It just stopped. Maya turned in horror to her own book:

"Is she?"

"No, I told you. Her story, it's not finished. Her book is still open," the book scolded, rather impatiently.

"But it just stops!" Maya complained bitterly.

"Yes, that is very strange. As magical journals, we record everything. Every thought and happening, whenever you're in the magical realm," confirmed the book. "In fact, the only time we stop..."

"Go on!" Maya interrupted excitedly.

"As I was saying," the book continued, obviously rather irritated by Maya's interruption. "The only time we can't record a witch's story, is when they're in a coven."

"A coven?" Maya interrupted once more.

"Yes... as I was saying, before again being rudely interrupted. We cannot see what happens in a coven," the book complained rather impatiently. "When the coven shield is raised, what happens inside, is hidden from all outside it. No witch, nor magic can cross that boundary. That's the only time a witch's journal ever stops writing, unless you leave the magic realm of course."

"What's a coven?" Maya asked excitedly.

"Really?" the book sighed in disbelief. "A gathering of witches. They meet every full moon."

"So mum, she's in a coven then?" Maya asked, her excitement growing.

"Sorry, little one," the book replied, rather more gently. "I'm really not sure. They don't last that long and from what you just read aloud. Your mum really didn't sound like she was joining any kind of coven. Not one, that I've ever heard of anyway."

"So, what's happened to her then?" Maya demanded, her voice breaking with frustration and disappointment.

"That's a bit of a mystery," the book replied.

Maya glared at the book in exasperation. Then the tip of her tongue appeared, to herald in a new line of thought.

"Maybe, if I read back a bit, in Mum's journal. To see what she'd been up to a couple of days before?" Maya suggested excitedly.

Maya didn't wait for the book to respond. She flipped back a few pages and started to read once more.

Her mother's previous adventure, into whatever this 'magical realm' was, had been a full week before. Her mum had apparently entered this 'magical realm' through Granny's…

"Granny too!" Maya announced in disbelief. "Granny's a witch?"

She'd heard her dad say it on many occasions, but she'd never believed him. But there it was, now written in black and white.

21

"Naturally," her journal confirmed. "You come from a long line of witches, on both sides of your family."

Maya shook her head in disbelief. Dad was never right about anything! Maya read on in a state of shock.

Her mum had apparently entered this 'magical realm' through Granny's secret broom cupboard, hidden under the stairs. Maya didn't even realise that there was a broom cupboard under Granny's stairs, but then, she was currently sitting in a secret room in her own house. One, that she didn't know anything about, up until a few minutes ago.

Her mum had taken the opportunity to read through some of Granny's book, which lay invitingly open and on its last page. Maya's journal intervened at this point, to explain that this wasn't really unusual behaviour. Apparently, her mum often took the liberty of probing into Granny's dubious past. Her life of 'scandal and impropriety,' as her mother called it, apparently. Maya had no idea what an impropriety was, but Granny had apparently had had more than her fair share, in her day.

There didn't sound like there was much of interest to read in Granny's journal though. Granny had been returning home from a nostalgic moonlight 'brush trip' to the house where she was born. But her Mum's book, had also divulged some of her mother's thoughts. Reading this, had upset her mum considerably, for some reason. A single tear had rolled down her cheek, as she read this, but infuriatingly, the journal didn't bother to explain why.

Maya read on. Her mother had then gone out flying with Evaline.

"Flying on what?" Maya asked aloud. "And who's Evaline?" She demanded, but Maya didn't even look up, to invite her own book to respond.

She read on in search of answers. Her mum had been out flying with the latest addition to the Prestwick Coven, a young witch called Evaline. According to her mother's book; "Young Evaline", as her mum referred to her, had just announced that she'd be leaving them, to try out for another coven. A much more powerful coven apparently. The Coven of Deeds, she called it.

This, had apparently, concerned the whole coven greatly. Evaline was easily their most talented young witch. It had come as a bit of a shock to everyone. Especially, as she had only just joined them and all the witches of the Prestwick Coven, were very taken with her. They all thought she was lovely, if a bit fearsome. Well, quite a lot fearsome actually. She was thoughtful too, and had even given Maya's mother a parting gift, for being so kind to her, since her arrival. A small scarlet-bound book on local history.

Maya paused. Somehow, the mention of that little book, made all these weird stories of witchcraft, feel much more real. She'd seen her mum engrossed in a tatty little red book, the week before she'd vanished. Could all this, actually be true? She had, after all, just met a talking book!

Maya read on engrossed. The High Priestess, whoever she was, was worried though. It was leaving them a witch short of the required thirteen. There would be an empty seat in the coven, and that left it weakened.

Granny had been drafted in to help, brought out of retirement, to take up her old seat in the coven. An under witched coven was vulnerable apparently, though her mother's book didn't say to who, or what.

In fact, it said very little else. After that last flight with Evaline, her mum had returned home and there were no further entries until Maya's birthday. The day her mum had disappeared.

Maya took a deep breath, as she turned the page and read on. Her mum had been excited and distracted, her journal recalled. Preoccupied and hardly even bothering to exchange small talk with her journal, before entering the magical realm, in the normal manner. That wasn't like her at all.

"What does that mean... entering the magical realm? What normal manner?" Maya demanded, looking up towards her own journal for answers.

"We'll get to that soon enough," the book responded, rather evasively.

Far from satisfied by her book's response, Maya read on regardless. Her mum had hurried through some sort of magical portal.

"Portal?" Maya enquired, but this time, she didn't wait for any half explanation from her journal. It was confusing, but compelling reading. Her mum had apparently mounted onto her brush, telling Mischief:

"No, not tonight, this I must do alone," and flew off through the night. She knew exactly where she was going now...

"Where?" Maya cried out in frustration, wrote her own book.

"And how does a brush fly?" Maya demanded once more, glaring at her cat. "And what my furry friend, do you know about all this?"

With no explanation forthcoming, from either her new rather vocal journal or disinterested looking sleepy cat, Maya continued reading.

Her mum had flown inland, until she came across a river. Then with the light failing, she followed its banks, as the swollen waters meandered their way through the countryside. Finally, she reached her destination, guided now by the light of her faithful wand.

"Where? What destination? What wand?" Maya cried out in frustration once more.

There she landed and rested by the banks of the river to prepare herself, as night fell. It was getting cold and she conjured a fire to keep warm. This was the place, she was sure of it now, but she'd have to wait for midnight. She wasn't sure what concerned her more... the test to come, or coming up with a plausible explanation for walking out on her own daughter's birthday. So, there she waited, alone with her thoughts, watching the stars slowly appear overhead, until the time came.

"Test... what test?" Maya pleaded in frustration, as she turned the next page.

"No!" Maya cried in exasperation. "It can't be!"

Maya rubbed the edges of the page with her finger in desperation. Hoping against hope, that she'd turned over two pages at once, but no. This was the final page. The same passage she'd read earlier. Maya read it through once more, with tears of frustration swelling in her eyes:

She knew exactly what she had to do, no time to waste, it was midnight and she climbed by the light of the full moon. She knew in her heart though, that her magic would not help her now, not where she was headed, but she had to try. She stepped out slowly and carefully, summoning every ounce of her courage. Her mind was made up now, this was it, it had to be here. The stone crumbled beneath her feet, as she stepped out and fell...

The portal

There was a protracted silence, as Maya reflected on what she'd just read. There was a lot to take in. Could all this talk of witchcraft, actually be real? What had her mum been looking for? What could possibly be that important? So crucial, that she'd even forsaken Maya's birthday cake for it?

"So?" Maya's own journal, finally broke the silence. "Are you ready to follow your destiny?"

"My what?" Maya replied. "Your destiny. I told you. You come from a long line of witches. You're thirteen now, it's time that your training began."

"Training?" Maya asked curiously.

At first, there was no response from the book. Mischief though, suddenly sprang into life, dropping down from the dressing table to cross the room, over to the old wooden chest, which sat in the corner.

"It appears your cat is eager to lead the way," observed the talking journal. "So, why not choose a potion and we'll see what sort of a witchling you can become?"

"Witchling..., potion. What potion?" Maya stammered, unusually lost for words.

This time, there was no reply from the book.

Maya, sensing that the book was not in any mood for unnecessary small talk, stood up obediently and followed her cat over to the old chest in the corner. Her mum, had after all, told her to trust her cat, when she gave her the neckless.

On top of the chest, sat three small dusty triangular bottles, each about four inches tall. Every bottle had a slightly different design, a cork stopper and a label. Maya studied each of them in turn. Did these strange bottles really contain magical potions?

Maya's head was spinning. Magic talking books, potion bottles, was she dreaming? No wonder her mum kept this place hidden away. Was her mother really a witch? Could Maya herself be a witchling? Whatever that was? She was now officially more puzzled, than the day her dad had stuck an additional red sticker, onto her Rubik's cube.

"These must be the potions then, eh Mischief?" Maya asked out loud.

On inspection, each bottle had a small cream coloured label, inscribed with a hand drawn picture. Maya picked up the first bottle, to examine it more closely. Her tongue circled her mouth in deep contemplation; like a freshly cut teenage toe nail, caught in the vortex of a draining bath.

On the label, was what looked like a roughly scribbled... toothbrush? Not what she had been expecting, at all. She replaced it and then inspected the second bottle. Maya frowned, obviously even more confused, than before. This bottle, had a picture of a scruffily drawn oval scrawled on it. Its shape was somehow familiar. Reminiscent of an elongated reptilian egg, but with strange hexagonal markings. The third label, showed what appeared to be a plant of some sort. A twig or seedling, with just a single leaf.

Mischief jumped up onto the chest. He circled the bottle with the toothbrush on the label, then sat down, behind it.

"This one Mischief?" Maya asked, breaking a nervous smile, for the first time.

Mischief purred his approval. So, with an apprehensive shaky hand, Maya obediently picked up the little bottle.

"What now?" Maya enquired uncertainly.

"Your first adventure in the magic realm, of course, silly girl!" the book replied, rather abruptly, making no effort not to sound patronising.

"Adventure? Magic realm? Really?" Maya asked anxiously, in a sudden tirade of verbal diarrhoea and self-doubt. "Where will I go?"

"Up to you little one," replied the book.

"Great help," Maya mouthed silently to herself.

"Oh, one last thing. When you're on the other side, beware of running water. No witch or witchling can pass over running water, that's very important," the book added.

"Why not?" Maya asked curiously.

"Your magic will not work over running water," wrote the book. "It drains your powers... if indeed, you have any?"

"Magic?" Maya gasped in disbelief. "I can't do magic!"

"We shall see little witchling. The gift, is strong in your family," replied the book.

Maya's mind was racing, her face now betraying, her stray and increasingly random thoughts. An involuntary smile spread across her face.

"What's so funny Maya?" her talking journal enquired, sounding rather bemused, by her reaction.

Maya blushed a little, then boasted with a rather silly grin:

"I can pass running water!"

"Really, little one? I'm impressed. That's strong magic indeed, for one so young!" the book replied, itself sounding reluctantly intrigued. "How?"

"I pass running water every day," giggled Maya. "Every time I pee!"

She'd always found that inappropriate toilet humour, was an excellent way to defuse anxiety and lighten the mood, in most situations. A trait she'd inherited from her dad. The only one, she hoped!

"Oh dear," sighed the book, as if talking directly to Mischief. "We're clearly going to have trouble with this one."

If Maya didn't know better, she could have sworn that her cat actually nodded his head, as if in agreement.

Maya's mind switched back now, to the task in hand. What an adventure. Could she really be about to cross over into a magical realm? She wasn't entirely sure what a realm, even was. Could she actually have magic powers, when she got there?

Maya looked down at the potion bottle in her hand. Did she have to drink it? What was in there? Bat's blood or eye of newt perhaps? Yuk, the very thought!

Maya braced herself and resolved to pop open the cork and have a sniff. Just one sniff. No way was she drinking anything out of these strange little bottles. Who knew how long it had been there, or what noxious liquid, these bottles might contain?

Tentatively, Maya eased open the stopper from the end of the potion bottle, then promptly juggled it in surprise, as out of the open-end, streamed ribbons of multi-coloured light. Each ribbon divided then sub-divided, again and again, illuminating the whole room with spiralling tendrils of bright light, which glowed and flowed, in every colour of the rainbow. Fern like structures of light poured and mixed into every corner of the room, then faded again, as quickly as they had come.

"Wh....? Whoa!" Maya couldn't finish her sentence, wrote the book.

Maya looked around the room with great expectation and excitement. Surveying every corner of the dim and dusty chamber, but all was as before. Nothing at all, had changed.

"Now what?" she eventually plucked up the courage to ask.

This time though, there was no response from her journal. Maya walked back towards the dressing table again and looked down at the book, which had just finished writing the words:

"Now what?" the silly girl asked, completely missing Mischief leaping through the magic portal, having turned her back at the crucial moment, just to walk over here and read back her own words.

Maya turned around quickly. Sure enough, Mischief was gone. She walked back over to the old chest, then turned again to face the full-length mirror. Now, something struck her. Something had changed. The reflection of the door in the full-length mirror was now moving. Faintly, but distinctly, it wobbled, as if liquefied. Maya turned on the spot once more. Was the door some sort of portal to this magical realm? But, as Maya turned to look straight at door, it looked normal and solid, just like a door should.

"Eh?" came the inevitable response.

Maya turned back once more, to face the mirror. The door's reflection was still shimmering.

"Eh?" Maya grunted in confusion.

"Really?" wrote the book.

Then finally, the penny dropped. Striking Maya painfully on the forehead. Bringing with it the realisation, that it was the mirror, not the door, that was moving. Although, what the penny had been doing, stuck to the ceiling like that, was never adequately explained, by the author.

Maya raised her hand hesitantly, to touch the dusty mirror. As her fingertips contacted the glass, its surface moved and rippled. Delicate concentric waves radiated outwards, as if in slow motion. The ripples strangely reminiscent of a recent event. When time had seemingly slowed, as she'd dropped her mum's toothbrush into the toilet. Something to which, she'd never confessed.

Maya pulled back her fingers in surprise. It had tingled slightly, but it wasn't an unpleasant sensation.

"Go on then, he's waiting!" the book insisted.

"He?" Maya enquired, but there was no response.

Maya dipped her fingers further into the glassy pool, then leaned in and looked around the back of the mirror, to check. At the back of the mirror, she could clearly see…, the back of a mirror. But no fingers! Very strange indeed, she thought to herself.

"Time to take the plunge," Maya whispered to herself. Then, with a final deep breath, to pluck up courage, she stepped slowly into the mirror.

Maya's head broke through to the other side, her face was tingling, but somehow, she felt safe enough. Maya surveyed the scene on the other side, anticipating a magical realm of fairies and unicorns and well, who knows what sort of creatures, which would surely be awaiting her arrival. However, in the second anti-climax in as many minutes. Maya stepped out of the other side of the mirror, tripped over its frame and crashed face first into the wall. Back in the same old dusty old room, that she'd started in. At first sight, nothing at all had changed. Except perhaps for the shape of her nose and the appearance of a new tell-tale greasy smudge, on the wall. The only other slight difference, was a puff of quickly dispersing white smoke.

Maya walked back around, to the other side of the mirror. Mischief was back again and was now waiting, rather impatiently, by a small door, directly behind the dressing table. She hadn't noticed this door before, but guessed it must have been there all along.

"How…, I mean what?" Maya stuttered, but the book didn't reply, not this time.

Instead, another voice replied.

"It's magic, you know…, all done with smoke and mirrors!" Mischief explained. "So, are you going to open this witch flap and let me out for a pee or what?"

"But, but, but… you're talking!" Maya gasped, trying desperately to gather her wits.

"Firstly, please don't address me as butt. I'm nobody's butt! Mischief, will do just fine!" snapped her cat indignantly. "I've not lived to be three hundred and six years old, just to listen to your cheek, little witchling. Secondly, of course I'm talking, how else am I meant to train you?"

"How old?" Maya gasped in disbelief.

"You heard! One of the perks of being a witch's cat… nine lives and all that!" Mischief responded.

"Welcome to the magic realm," announced Mischief.

Maya looked around once more.

"But nothing's different? We'll except for you, you're talking now," Maya complained.

"No, I've always talked. You're the one who's changed. Thanks to a little magic, even your rather inefficient human brain, can now understand me," her cat replied, rather dismissively.

"Oh," was all Maya had. She had so many questions, yet couldn't find the words, to ask any of them.

"Could today get any weirder?" Maya muttered to herself. Now apparently, she had magic and was going to be trained by her own cat. A cat, who apparently, can talk and claims to be nearly as old as Granny!

Maya was speechless. She simply stepped forward obediently and pushed open the little door, or "witch flap" as Mischief had referred to it.

Beyond the door, she could see a narrow, rather dimly lit corridor, leading to some stone steps. Mischief padded impatiently through the opening. Maya followed cautiously. Her eyes wide open, with a heady mixture of anticipation and disbelief.

Along the low ceiling hung a myriad of small silvery caterpillar shaped creatures, which lit up like fire flies, as they approached. They illuminated the way ahead, with a strange silvery light, then dimmed again, as soon as they'd passed. Mischief led the way down a tight stone spiral staircase and stopped at the bottom, waiting for Maya to open another witch flap for him. Maya pushed open the little door, entering into a cosy and brightly lit log cabin behind it.

"Welcome home," announced Mischief.

"Home?" came Maya's inevitable and rather bewildered response.

"Yes, home is where your cat is, and here I am!" Mischief explained proudly.

Maya looked around. Sunlight streamed in through old-fashioned four-pane windows and the open door. The cabin was furnished with well-worn, but none-the-less comfortable looking furniture, that her mum referred to as 'shabby-chic' and her dad just called 'shabby.'

There was an antique pine table in the centre, with a vase of fresh wild flowers and a jam jar full of assorted sticks. In the corner sat a very comfortable looking bed, which Maya just had to try out; bouncing her backside up and down, on top of the patchwork duvet with great delight.

There were lots of shelves, boxes and a sofa with scatter cushions. A log fire burned in a stone fireplace and over the mantel piece, sat a number of unlit, but used church candles. Strewn all around the room, were numerous open potion bottles of various colours, sizes and shapes. Maya realised, she still had hold of the bottle which she'd opened earlier, in her mother's secret room and she placed it instinctively, with the others. Had all these potion bottles been left here by her mum? Maya asked herself. Maya looked towards the open doorway. Mischief was now perched on a comfortable red cushion, on top of a wooden packing box, by the door.

Maya liked it here. No that wasn't it. She loved it. It felt cosy and welcoming. If she'd had to imagine a magical hideout, this would be it. Somehow strangely, Mischief was right, she already felt at home here. It was a log cabin, like she'd always dreamt of owning one day. It smelled of pine trees, wild flowers with faint traces of her mum's perfume. A bit like the loo back home (unless her dad had used it, of course).

Maya looked through the window. Familiar woodland was just visible through the dusty panes. She recognised the old overgrown railway line, that ran to the back of her house, but she had never seen this place before. Not on any of her frequent den building and pond dipping adventures, with her dad.

"Well little one, best feed the brushes now, they'll be getting hungry," announced Mischief, jumping down and leading the way through the front door.

"Grab yourself a training wand and follow me," Mischief instructed.

Maya looked around, rather bewildered by his request, focussing eventually on the jar of assorted sticks and twigs, which sat on the top of the table.

"Training wands?" Maya whispered to herself.

Maya picked out a rather bent looking pine coloured twig, about the length of a chop stick and tucked it into the inside pocket of her grey hoodie. Maya turned and followed her cat, feeling a strange mix of intrigue, excitement and complete bafflement at the unfolding events.

"Feed the brushes?" she asked curiously.

"Not going to fly far on an empty stomach, are they?" replied Mischief, in a rather dismissive manner, as he strutted around the corner. Maya shook her head, even more baffled by his response, before following the little cat outside. As she passed through the doorway, the heart shaped charm on Maya's neckless, glowed once more and as she turned around, the door and the log cabin faded in front of her eyes, and was gone.

"Your charm's a keystone. It's the key to your portal from this side too," Mischief explained, anticipating her next question. "So don't lose it!"

Maya clutched the little charm protectively in a clenched fist, in response.

Outside, Maya found herself in familiar woodland, backing onto a grassy meadow. It was surrounded by broadleaf trees and still buzzed with the sound of insects, despite the time of year. Birdsong filled the air.

Next to where the log cabin had been, were what looked like stables. There was however, something a bit strange about them. They were painted bright purple and blended tastefully into the background, in just the same way, as her Aunty Dot's holiday dresses don't.

Behind each of the doors, stood large...

"Toothbrushes?" Maya yelped with surprise, rubbing her eyes in disbelief.

No, she wasn't seeing things. Toothbrushes as tall as horses, stood behind each of the stable doors. Empty string nets hung from the roof trusses inside each one. Mischief promptly marched purposefully past each of the doors. As he passed, his nose twitched and the feed bags filled and swelled in turn, overflowing with bunches of verdant green leaves. Lunch for the brushes, Maya presumed. The unmistakeable scent of fresh mint hung in the air. The brushes started to munch appreciatively on the lush green herbs. Maya pinched herself, to check she wasn't dreaming.

A bright blue brush took a bite from a feed bag and ambled over to the stable door, as if inviting Maya over to pet it.

"He likes you," remarked Mischief.

"He?" replied Maya in disbelief.

"Blue for boys, dummy!" Mischief scowled back.

Maya frowned.

"Hey boy, do you like your bristles scratched?" she asked softly, approaching the brush with one hand outstretched.

"Watch yourself!" Mischief warned, "He's a wild one. Never been ridden. In fact, you're the first one to scratch him like that, without losing a finger or sometimes even a toe."

"Thanks for the warning, not!" Maya scolded, turning her attention back to the friendly brush. "What's your name boy?" she asked softly.

"Doesn't have a name. Never been ridden, never been named," Mischief commented, in a very disinterested and matter-of-fact manner.

"Poor thing," Maya whispered affectionately to the brush, whilst stroking him on the bristles. "I think, I'll call you Blue."

"How original!" scoffed Mischief, under his breath.

"Anyway, what do you mean ridden?" Maya enquired with a curious glance in Mischief's direction.

"Oh, please don't tell me you still believe in broomsticks?" Mischief gasped, with an air of superiority and exasperation, only usually mastered by cats and Maya's mum, when her dad's being told off for being silly again.

Maya didn't get a chance to speak. In what sounded like one breath, Mischief let loose a breathless and obviously well-rehearsed monologue...

"Ok, here's how it goes. Witches are mostly useless, completely useless without their cats, of course. Cats with sore butts are nearly useless too! Broomsticks are **not** comfortable and witches have bad breath and big mouths. Cats have nice fishy breath. These days no civilised cat will fly anywhere with their witch on nasty uncomfortable broomsticks. We only fly on something nice and flat, like a toothbrush, preferably with a comfortable cushion. Maybe, one day, we'll even train a witch to brush its teeth properly with fish paste too! So, giant toothbrushes. What else?"

"Oh," replied Maya, rather taken aback. "I see, I think?"

"One born every minute!" scoffed Mischief, obviously pleased with himself. "Your mother fell for that one too!"

"Eh?" mumbled Maya.

"Of course, they're not toothbrushes! Who except a gobby young witchling, would have a mouth big enough to fit a brush that size!" Mischief scoffed, then cleared his throat, as if readying himself to impart some great knowledge or self-proclaimed wisdom.

"Like all domesticated animals, witches' brooms have been bred for greater utility over the millennia. Wide beams for greater comfort. Front-facing short bristled brushwork for in-flight napping and to give you something to hold on to, for tight cornering. Built-in cloaking from non-magic eyes and most importantly... room for a nice comfortable cushion, for your cat on the back," explained Mischief, once again in a single breath.

"Oh," Maya responded, still trying to digest Mischief's explanation fully.

"They just happen to look a lot like toothbrushes now. Comes in handy too, if they're ever spotted," he continued.

"Really, why?" asked Maya, still looking rather puzzled.

"Would you believe your eyes if you saw a flying toothbrush?" Mischief replied, with a self-satisfied grin.

Maya nodded in acknowledgement. It made sense, well as much as anything made sense today. Then, there was a sudden glint in her eye. A lightbulb moment.

"Can I ride him?" Maya asked hopefully.

"I hope so," Mischief replied. "Every witchling needs a brush."

"Witchling?" Maya asked. "What exactly is a witchling?"

"A witch in training, little one," replied Mischief. "I sense you may have potential, but you're far from a witch yet. Clearly, you've never been cat trained!"

"Cat trained?" Maya repeated.

"Of course, how else do you think you'll find your wand?" Mischief replied.

"Wand?" Maya repeated. Mischief scowled. Maya was starting to sound more like a parrot, than a prospective witch.

"Well, you won't get very far with a training wand like that," replied the cat, gesturing towards the twig poking out of her inside pocket.

"Training wand?" Maya repeated again.

"Poly want a cracker?" Mischief enquired.

"Hoy!" Maya complained.

"Well, do you want to learn how to ride him or not?" Mischief enquired, sounding rather exasperated.

"Can I? Really?" Maya gasped. "How?"

"Focus your thoughts on your wand and call his name... then tell him what you want him to do. No words, just think it, instruct him, but not vocally. Feel it. Imagine it so. Use your mind's eye," Mischief instructed.

"Okay," Maya replied. She drew the stick or 'training wand' from her inside pocket. Then, closing her eyes, she focussed all her thoughts on Blue.

"Gently at first. Open the door to let him out, just think it. Then, stand back and allow him to come to you. Let him get used to your rather pungent teenage scent," Mischief coached, with a cheeky grin.

"Hey!" Maya complained once more.

"Then, if you have a way with the brushes and he doesn't attack. He might just, allow you to get close to him. Don't stare straight at him though, they spook easily. Then, if that goes well, after a couple of days, when you've won his trust. You could try hopping on board and see if you can manage a gentle hover," Mischief explained.

"Okay," Maya sighed, rather nervously, then announced:

"Come on boy!" as she slapped both her hands down onto her thighs, as if beckoning a dog to retrieve a ball.

"No!" cried Mischief, but it was too late.

With a loud crash, an over-enthusiastic brush smashed through the stable's door, knocking it clean off its hinges and headed straight for Maya. Blue shot between her legs and bounced up and down, like an over eager puppy. In one movement, he whisked Maya off her feet and shot forth, also collecting a very surprised looking Mischief, who slammed unceremoniously into Maya's back, as the brush lifted the pair of them up and into the air.

"Really!" Mischief complained bitterly. "Some witchlings might have thought to open the door first!" he scolded.

"Oops, sorry…, but how do you steer this thing?" Maya shouted with rising panic, hanging on desperately, with all the strength she could muster.

"Hmmm…, difficult one…, I'd say lean forwards for backwards, backwards for forwards, up for down, down for up…, or at a push…," Mischief paused, purely for effect and to convey his disapproval.

"At a push what?" screamed Maya, half in frustration, half in pure terror.

"At a push, turn around and face the way you're going, silly girl!" scolded her patronising cat.

"Oh," Maya blushed and shuffled around to face forwards, nearly dislodging her grumpy cat in the process.

"That is better!" Maya acknowledged, finally facing the way she was flying and grasping hold of the brush, firmly by the bristles. Mischief, negotiated his way nervously to the rear of Blue and, with a twitch of his nose, indignantly produced a plump red cushion, from out of thin air, on which to sit.

Now well up above the trees, Maya's pendant glowed once more and beneath them the stables too, disappeared from view. It wasn't long, before Maya and Blue were as one, in the air. Maya steering him by the bristles, turning this way and that. One minute, soaring upwards, to drag outstretched hands through low cloud and the next plunging down, to skim her feet across the tree tops. The brush responded to her every move and as their confidence and understanding grew, Blue even started to anticipate her next command.

"Great," complained Mischief. "That's all I need. A natural flyer!"

Maya and Blue soared and swooped with ease and style. Maya in particular, enjoyed the way she could turn her rather superior and patronising cat, into a wide-eyed ball of 'scaredy-fluff,' every time she looped the loop or instructed Blue to fly upside down.

Maya giggled and screamed with delight as they zig-zagged through the tallest trees, swooped over hills and plunged through valleys, playing chicken with oncoming trees.

"Best fun ever!" Maya shouted with obvious glee.

After a while though, Blue started to tire and pant heavily. The young witchling slowed, then brought her brush to a standstill. Hovering, to let her brush recover.

"Of all the irresponsible, pea-brained, dangerous and reckless witchlings, I've ever had the misfortune to train!" Mischief ranted.

Maya braced herself for a thorough dressing down. Now, it was her turn to feel like a big ball of 'scaredy-fluff.'

"That was by far," Mischief paused, as a smile broke out across his furry face. "The most fun I've ever had on a first flight!"

Maya giggled with relief. She felt exhilarated and elated. Adrenaline pulsed through her veins and common sense, had all but departed her.

"Watch this then!" cried Maya, climbing out of her seated position, now sporting a big silly smile. Mischief sensed an impending party-trick. Maya paused, balancing precariously, shifting her weight from one foot to another. Then, raising her arms out to each side, like an eagle, as she rose through a wobbly crouch and onto unstable feet. Now, sporting a big cheesy grin, she started edging slowly out to the end of her brush, arms still outstretched for balance. Maya swayed and tottered her way, right to the end of Blue, like a circus high wire act, but considerably less steady.

"Ta-dah!" she announced proudly, turning to face her feline audience.

Suddenly though, she felt cold. An icy chill filled the air. Maya shuddered. Her mum had often described that feeling as; "someone walking over your grave." This felt worse though. It was more like someone digging up your coffin, prizing it open and playing the xylophone up and down your ribs, using your own thigh bones as mallets. Maya was spooked!

"Watch out!" cried Mischief, but it was too late.

Distracted by Maya's antics, Blue had drifted through the air and crossed over the path of the fresh running waters of the River Doon. In that instant, Maya's magic drained from her and her brush, as quickly, as her dad's first beer on a Friday night.

Down, down, down, poor Maya and Mischief tumbled, falling after her stricken brush. Head over heels, squealing all the way, like a sunburned pig, which had just fallen onto a porcupine and bounced off into a stinging nettle patch.

"What do I do?" screamed Maya, in panic and desperation.

"Magic of course!" scoffed Mischief. "If you have any power left? A spell and quickly, or pray for a soft landing!"

"Something soft and quick, eh, …, er? Like, like… **Jelly!**" Maya shrieked.

"Really?" complained her incredulous cat.

Maya's panicked cry though, was half lost to the thunder of the air billowing past their ears, as they accelerated ever faster and faster, towards their impending doom.

Mischief screamed.

Maya screamed.

Mischief cringed and drew a pair of furry paws up to his face to cover his eyes.

Splat! Splat! Maya and Mischief hit the river at pace..., and the river turned a horrible sickening shade of blood red.

Blue too, had tumbled earthwards. Being lighter, he carried on the wind and clattered onto the grassy banks, landing heavily, like a lifeless wooden plank. Which he now was.

All fell silent.

Maya's body bobbed, face down, back to the surface of the now crimson river.

A river, which on closer inspection, now wobbled strangely and flowed, nowhere very quickly, at all. A river which had now apparently been transformed into thick red strawberry jelly!

Winded and still in shock, Maya raised her head and spat out a mouthful of jelly, then let loose.

"Yuk! Yuk-yuk-yukety-yuk-yuk!" she complained.

"Jelly?" cried Mischief, as he too bobbed to the surface, wiping the glutinous red slime disapprovingly from his whiskers.

Maya swam, as best she could, through the viscous slimy torrent, to collect her stranded cat. Then made her way to the bank, clearly winded and gasping for breath. Exhausted and bedraggled, they each dragged themselves out onto the river bank.

Tears of relief flowed now and Maya wiped her runny nose onto her arm. Leaving a long tell-tale snail trail of snot, up her hoodie sleeve, through the jelly.

"Hmm…, highly unusual, but effective none the less. Very few witchlings can still cast a spell like that, over running water. I might just make a witch out of you yet?" Mischief conceded, in what Maya took to be a back-handed compliment.

Maya's grin betrayed her satisfaction. She had powers in this magic realm. Powers, she could only have dreamt of. Not only could she fly on Blue, but she had just cast her first spell as a witchling. Now, she had hope too. Hope, that somewhere out there, in this magic realm, she could at last find her mother.

Half an hour later, they had finally scraped off most of the jelly. Maya's hair was matted and still caked to her scalp. Mischief's fur, now stood on end, like a black and white pom-pom. Maya's powers had slowly returned too, as they sat on the banks of this gelatinous river. She could tell this, from the way Blue had come to life once more and was now hovering impatiently, while Maya and Mischief preened themselves, to the soundtrack of:

"Yuk!" and "gross!" from Maya, as she pulled pieces of red jelly from her hair and nose and ears and…, well, almost everywhere. Mischief too, tutted every few seconds, as if to convey his disapproval and disgust at having to lick this gooey sweet slime, from his fur.

Finally, Maya stood up and made her way over to Blue. As if to signal their departure. Every step accompanied by a disconcerting squelch of jelly, but Maya was pre-occupied, excited…

"You do realise your pants are still full of jelly…," Mischief started to warn.

But it was too late. Maya swung her leg over Blue, to mount him and sat down heavily.

A moment passed.

"Double yuk!" Maya let out a grossed-out scream and announced:

"It's even gone up my..."

"Trouser leg!" Mischief interrupted quickly. "Time for home then! I think it's time for a change of clothing too, young witchling."

Maya couldn't hold back her giggles any longer.

Once Maya had returned the waters of the River Doon, to their more customary composition. Maya and Mischief flew home, to get Maya a bath and a change of clothes. On the way, Mischief suggested that she should get some rest and that they should rendezvous, later that night, back in her mum's secret room.

"You'll need to sneak out tonight, at about 11 o'clock, no later," Mischief instructed, but offered no further explanation, except to add a rather mysterious:

"You'll see, when we get there, little one." In response to her enquiring glances.

Maya made her excuses and went to bed early that evening, but she was much too excited to get any proper rest. Her mind was racing and 11 o'clock couldn't arrive quickly enough. Finally, as the hour approached, Maya dressed herself and crept out of her room. She tip-toed across the stairwell landing and opened the secret room door with her neckless charm. Shooshing every click and clunk from the outsized door, as it opened. Mischief was already inside. Sleeping on a comfortable red cushion in the corner.

Maya sat down in front of her book and opened it, using the heart shaped charm, as before.

"Hello little one, back for another adventure, I see," the book greeted her, its words writing themselves elegantly across its pages once more.

"Yes please!" Maya replied, eagerly.

"I hear you're quite the natural flier," her journal remarked.

Maya nodded, but looked slightly self-conscious, wrote the book.

"And your first spell too. Conjuring rivers of jelly, when you were just supposed to be out taking a simple brush flying lesson, apparently. Exactly, what part of staying clear of running water did you not understand?" the book scolded her gently.

"Ah, yes, sorry," Maya replied. Her cheeks, involuntarily blushing a bright beetroot red.

"Anyway, better get on with things and choose a potion... Mischief tells me tonight, could be a big night," her journal added.

Maya stood obediently and made her way over to the chest in the corner. She studied the potion bottles. There were three of them once more, including a new bottle, with what looked like a badly drawn fish on the label.

Mischief appeared, as if out of nowhere and jumped up, circled around this new bottle, then sat down expectantly behind it.

"This one?" Maya asked aloud, picking up the little bottle in her right hand.

Mischief jumped back down from the chest, as if to confirm his approval.

"One more thing, little one," called her journal. "Your portal, be careful in there now."

"Careful?" Maya looked puzzled.

"Yes, you have discovered your magical powers now. But, with your new powers, also come new temptations. Temptations to use these powers for your own gain. Your portal will reflect these... be sure that you follow only the right path, whenever you enter the magic realm," warned the book.

"Temptations? Why would it tempt me?" Maya enquired.

"Good question. Witches disagree on that one, but the general consensus is that it's some kind of safety feature, built in by the very first witches, who created the portals," explained the book.

"Safety feature?" Maya parroted back.

"Yes, in case you're ever tempted, to use your powers for greed or revenge," wrote the book.

"And if I was?" Maya asked curiously. She liked to pretend she had a darker side, sometimes.

"Not a good idea. Give in to temptation and follow the wrong path and your portal can trap you. Follow the wrong path and all that's good in you, can become lost in there," warned the book.

"Lost? Some safety feature!" Maya scoffed.

"It's meant to stop those who have given in to temptation, from using their powers for their own purposes," her journal explained. "Only those with good intentions, should ever be granted magic powers."

"Meant to?" Maya probed.

"Yes, well, that part works pretty well, but there's a problem," the book confirmed.

"Go on," Maya prompted, suspiciously.

"Well, we all have a dark side. Even good witches have stray thoughts and temptations. Within their portals, these can cause new paths to open up. Paths which lead them to confront their own inner-most desires and temptations.

It was designed to stop any who had strayed. Witches who were too weak to resist temptation. They would be trapped by their own dark thoughts and wishes. So, that way they'd be prevented from entering the magic realm. A fail-safe system, so that they could never abuse their magical gifts, not for their own selfish gain," explained the magical tome.

The book paused reflectively. Maya could feel a 'but' coming on.

"But?" Maya probed, once more.

"Well, we all have a dark side... life isn't black and white, good or evil. There are many shades of grey in between. Sometimes, even a good witch can be tempted to follow a darker path. Sometimes a good witch gets tempted too. In anger or in grief, they too can follow the wrong path," the book continued.

"And?" Maya prompted suspiciously.

"Unfortunately, when a good witch follows the wrong path, then they too will have to face temptation. Their dreams can be so real and powerful, backed by the magic of the portals, that many simply cannot resist them. Many weaker witches decide to stay in the dream world, one that's been created to tempt them. They choose to live out their dreams, rather than return and face reality. Good witches also become trapped."

Maya looked surprised.

"Surely they must realise and follow the right path eventually?" Maya asked curiously.

"Not that simple, I'm afraid," the book explained. "Often there's not enough time."

"Enough time? Enough time, before what happens?" Maya demanded.

"Well, if their witch's temptations lead them to a happy place, then there's often nothing in that reality for their darker side. It simply gets fed up and doesn't stick around for long."

"What?" Maya exclaimed, clearly bemused by her journal's explanation.

"A portal is a magical creation, which reflects your inner being and strange things can happen inside it. Sometimes a witch's personality actually splits... their dark side, well it simply ups and leaves," the book warned.

"Leaves?" cried Maya. "How can it just leave?"

"If there's nothing in that reality for your dark side. It leaves. It cleaves itself from its lighter side and continues on to the magic realm, without its other half," the book explained, rather remorsefully.

Maya frowned thoughtfully.

"But I thought you just said, that only those with pure intentions could make it through the portal?" Maya challenged, clearly still confused.

"Yes, yes I did," the book confirmed thoughtfully. "But their dark side's intentions are pure, I'm afraid. Pure evil!"

"Oh," was all Maya could manage.

"So, I'm afraid, the portals have unwittingly given rise to dark witches too," the book confessed rather sadly. "Worse still, many of their cats too, have followed them into dark ways!"

"And their good side? What happens to that?" Maya asked, with growing morbid fascination.

"Somehow without your darker side, you lose something; willpower, drive, passion. Whatever it is... we all need a little bit of darkness, don't we?" the book confessed, rather disconcertingly. "Without that part of you, it's as if your light side doesn't have the courage to leave. It simply gets stuck in the dream world inside the portal."

"And then?" Maya prompted, looking increasingly concerned.

"Then nothing, they're trapped forever, without purpose and reason and eventually that part of you just fades away, they say," her journal explained, rather mournfully.

"Yikes!" Maya summed it all up, rather eloquently.

"But I'm sure that won't happen to you, probably," the book added, not very reassuringly.

"Probably?" Maya repeated.

"Anyway, time you two were on your way. If you're going to be in time for the coven," instructed the book.

"Coven?" Maya probed. But this time, there was no answer. Question and answer time, was clearly over for tonight.

Maya braced herself, then popped open the cork on her chosen potion bottle. Fountains of multicoloured light spewed forth from its spout. Light filled every corner of the room, as before. Once again, the mirror started to shimmer, like an upright 'wibbly-wabbly-thingy.' Mischief led the way into the portal. All was as before. Glitter worms hung from the ceiling and illuminated the way.

Maya felt rather smug. No new dark paths here for me to follow, she thought. I won't be tempted like those other witches. Not me, I'm not greedy... I wouldn't wish for money or gold or kittens anyway... well maybe kittens, but what harm could that do?

Maya stopped. Two passageways now presented themselves. Eh? Which way? Gentle meows echoed through the corridor to her right. Maya turned that way instinctively, then Mischief brushed up against her leg and led her to the left. Maya shuddered as the penny dropped. She didn't feel quite so smug any longer and hurried after him.

Mischief pushed forcefully through the cat flap on the other side, letting it swing back into Maya's face, as if to rebuke her for her stray thoughts.

"Come on, we need to get a move on. I took the liberty of sending a carrier robin to Granny earlier," explained Mischief, marching straight through the warm, candle lit log cabin and out towards the stables.

"Sent a carrier robin?" Maya panted after him, trying to keep up.

"Tweeting, they call it these days, I believe. With a simple enchantment, birds make excellent messengers. Fast and very inconspicuous," Mischief explained.

"Granny, why Granny?" Maya grumbled, sounding utterly confused.

"Who else? Wise old bat, that one!" Mischief observed, rather disrespectfully.

"I needed to tell her that your mum's book was still open, but had stopped writing. She'll have called a special coven," Mischief explained.

Maya's heart missed a beat, at the very mention of her mother.

"A coven?" Maya gasped. "My mum's frozen journal. You **do** think she's trapped in a coven, don't you?"

"I don't know. Please, don't get your hopes up... it's a long shot," warned Mischief, but from the look in Maya's eyes, he could tell it was already too late.

"A million to one chance, but it's just possible, I suppose. It was a full moon two weeks ago, the night your mum disappeared. There's a coven held every full moon, but according to Granny, your mum didn't show up as normal," Mischief confirmed.

"And?" Maya prompted impatiently.

"Well, nobody saw her that night. But her frozen book, it got me thinking. The last thing you read from her book, it said that she climbed and fell."

"Fell where?" Maya pressed again.

"I don't know, but what if she fell, when looking for something in the Old Kirk. That's where they hold the Prestwick Coven. It's an old ruin, lots of crumbling stonework. What if some fell on her or she fell and hit her head?" Mischief suggested.

"Go on!" Maya prompted, her eyes wide with hope and excitement.

"She could have been knocked unconscious and gone unnoticed, hidden behind a coven stone, or inside the old Kirk itself, when the coven was convened. Then, once the coven was closed again, she could have been trapped inside it. It's the only thing I can think of, that makes any kind of sense," explained the cat.

Maya couldn't speak. She couldn't hear either. Her heart was pounding in her ears, like a rampaging rhino, cornered in a drum and tambourine store.

"Then what are we standing around here for?" Maya demanded impatiently, heading for the door, at pace.

Maya grabbed a hurried handful of mint, from a large wooden planter by the door, for Blue, as she headed for the stables. But Blue had already knocked the door off its hinges, by the time they were half way there. Flattening poor Mischief on his way to greet Maya and gorge himself on her minty treats.

Maya climbed onto her over-enthusiastic brush and thrust the remaining green herbs home in one movement. Blue sensed her urgency, and took to the air immediately, as Mischief ran frantically to catch up and jump on board. Soon, they were rising high into the night sky and heading for Prestwick Old Kirk.

It was a clear night, stars peppered the night sky and the chill night air stung at Maya's face, as they flew north. They made good progress. Seemingly invisible to the non-magic types, who scuttled about their business below and looked nothing at all like ants, even from this height. Mischief explained; that to see magic, you must have magic. So, they should pass overhead unobserved.

"That's why I couldn't see the cabin then?" Maya deduced proudly.

"Nope!" Mischief beamed.

"Oh!" Maya, responded rather disappointed. "Why then?"

"That's because you didn't have a keystone back then," Mischief explained.

"Keystone?" Maya prompted once more.

"Your charm, on the neckless your mum gave you. It's a keystone," Mischief explained. "A key to your portal, a key to the magic realm."

"Oh," Maya sat back corrected.

Prestwick lies only a few miles north of Maya's house, as the broom flies. So, the journey didn't take long, but it felt like an eternity to Maya. They stopped just once on the way, to avoid crossing running water. They crossed the River Ayr on foot, using the old cobbled footbridge, in the centre of town. They had no wish to repeat that morning's jelly misadventures tonight.

Finally, they descended over Prestwick town centre and the jumble of rooftops below, Maya could see a number of green clad figures, gathered outside the abandoned Old Kirk, which rises behind the dunes, near the golf course. Amongst them, she could easily pick out an untidy white mop of curly white hair, belonging to her granny. Granny was cloaked, head to foot in dark green robes, and stood amongst the tombstones, near to the ivy-covered gable ends of the ancient ruin. Maya reflected, that although a warm and friendly soul, to all she encountered, her granny could really be quite spooky sometimes.

The Abandoned Old Kirk at Prestwick

Granny looked very serious. She stood, broom in hand, chatting to an elegant old lady, also dressed in matching green robes.

"That's the High Priestess," Mischief explained, following Maya's gaze.

In her right hand, this old woman carried a gnarled dark wooden staff, with a bright green oval shaped crystal mounted on top. The jewel was held within a sturdy looking mount.

As they came in to land in the graveyard, Granny smiled over to Maya and gave her a reassuring wink. But Maya could tell she too was pre-occupied, and looked uncharacteristically nervous. Maya realised that on receiving Mischief's earlier 'tweet,' Granny must indeed, have come to the same conclusion, as Mischief had.

Maya's mind was racing. This coven thing, had it really been closed two weeks earlier, with her mother still inside? Whatever a coven was anyway? Could her mum really still be trapped in there? Was she alright? Two weeks without a cup of tea…, her mum struggled to go an hour between cups! And no chocolate either!

During their short flight, Mischief had explained, that only the High Priestess had the power to open the coven. Maya stared at this elegant old woman eagerly now. Granny whispered something into the High Priestess's ear. The old woman turned, looked over towards Maya, and met Maya's anxious gaze briefly. Then after a subtle nod of acknowledgement, she turned to face the old ruined church and raised her staff. Then she stepped forward, bringing the staff down heavily, onto what Maya strongly suspected was a toppled headstone. One, two, three times. The sound of each blow, echoed around the graveyard and brought a resounding hush, from the rest of the gathering.

Clearing her throat first, the High Priestess announced:

"I call upon all the coven and heirs!"

"Heirs?" whispered Maya, turning to Mischief.

"Witches in training. Like yourself; witchlings who want to join a coven," replied Mischief. "Goes back long before my time, I think your mum said they've been called that, since all the way back to the days of Peden. One day, when the heirs prove themselves, they may take their place in the coven, but until that day, they must wait, as you must now, here in the arena.

57

Mischief gestured with an outstretched paw, to the area around them. An area, which was now magically clearing itself of all noticeable obstacles, in front of their eyes. Maya watched bewildered, as tombstones flattened all around them in every direction.

"Peden?" Maya muttered to herself. She'd heard the name before somewhere, but just couldn't place it.

Bushes rustled and the rest of the coven slowly started to assemble from the shadows. All hooded in flowing green gowns.

"Aunty Dot!" gasped Maya. "Aunty Dot's a witch too?" she repeated, looking at Mischief, in disbelief.

Her mother's twin sister. Maya's rather shallow and gossip obsessed Aunty. Was there too. Sucking on a mint humbug. as usual. Maya smiled to herself. Granny frequently gave her second favourite daughter, bags of those sticky sweets. Whenever she was looking for some peace and quiet from Aunty Dot's endless gossiping.

"Again, what part of long line of witches did you not get?" scolded her cat.

Maya watched in wonderment, as larger tombstones started to tremble and move. Slowly, twelve large stones righted themselves, others pushed upwards, through the earth beneath. They formed themselves into a circle. Other smaller wooden rectangular objects, now also pushed up through the earth, to form pedestal seats in front of each of the larger stones. Maya realised, with some disgust, that these appeared to be the ends of long buried coffins.

She vowed, at that moment, that when she found her mum, which she would. She was definitely going to have words with her about her coven's choice of interior decor. No wonder witches got such a bad press in the past... this was seriously spooky!

Maya studied the scene closely. Soaking up every last detail. Scouring this coven, if that's what it was, for any sign of her mother.

"I don't see her!" Maya complained to her cat bitterly.

"Patience, little one. Wait for the shield to fall. A coven is not convened, until its shield's down," Mischief explained. "Then, if she's here, then we'll see her."

Maya bit her lip and clenched her buttocks in nervous anticipation. She watched intently. In the centre of the coven, a green crystalline orb glowed faintly. On top, sat a small empty silver dish. The witches assembled obediently, then in turn entered into the coven, in single file. Their brushes, now left hovering behind the coven stones. Each placed a small token or stone onto the silver receptacle and took their seats. Maya noted that as they did so, with a tiny bright flash, their tokens were transformed instantly into bright green crystals. With each crystal added, the orb below glowed more brightly, as if gathering their power.

Granny's old-fashioned broomstick stood out from the rest of the modern brushes. It was one of the original broomstick designs. Mischief had explained on the trip here, that the younger witches often teased her about it, but she insisted that it came in handy for sweeping the back path in her garden. And besides those new-fangled brushes, with short aerodynamic bristles at the front, might be faster and more comfortable, but they just looked plain wrong to her. "Flying toothbrushes," she called them. She wouldn't be caught dead on one.

The High Priestess entered the coven last. She raised her staff. Lightning then crackled between the stones and the central orb, lighting up the night sky, in a green and earie glow. A translucent luminous blanket, then fell over the entire coven, encompassing the Old Kirk behind it.

"The shield?" Maya asked excitedly.

"Yes," Mischief confirmed with a nod.

Despairingly, Maya scanned the coven for any sight of her mother. Over and over, she studied every head stone and upturned coffin, through the blur of increasingly desperate and tear stained eyes. But there was no sign. Her mum wasn't here.

"Sorry little one," Mischief consoled her. "I warned you it was a long shot."

The High Priestess looked around, as if hoping that another might appear, then after an apologetic glance towards Maya, reluctantly, she too took her seat. Maya's heart sunk further into her chest, then shrivelled and died.

"I really thought...," but Maya couldn't finish her sentence.

In silence and without any real expectation, Maya and Mischief circled around the coven, surveying it from every possible angle, but there was no sign of her mum. Not a single clue. They peered in and out of every window hole and door in the Old Kirk, but there was no sign of her there either. Nothing.

"Count the seats," Mischief whispered, as they completed their second lap.

"What?" Maya wasn't interested in seats, not at a time like this. She was sure, that Mischief was just trying to divert her from her rising despair and self-pity. She was right of course.

Reluctantly, Maya counted. One, two... eleven witches, together with the High Priestess, twelve, were now seated on each of the twelve seats, but one seat was still left spare. Her mum's seat, Maya presumed.

"Eh?" Maya grunted, as the discrepancy finally sunk in. She rubbed her eyes and started to count again. This time, she counted out loud, just to make sure.

"One, two, three …… twelve," seats were counted.

"One, two, three …… twelve," witches were counted.

But there was still one seat spare. This made less sense than algebra.

Maya counted the seats again, then once more with the aid of her fingers and big toes just to make sure. Same strange result each time; twelve seats and all twelve witches were now seated, however the seat beside the High Priestess, was still empty.

Mischief caught her confused expression.

"Weird, isn't it?" Mischief commented, but frustratingly, he just grinned and offered no explanation.

They sat watching the coven for another twenty minutes. Mischief tucked into a small red fish, produced from a pouch around his midriff, which Maya thought strangely reminiscent of the fish drawn on the potion bottle, he'd all but suggested she chose earlier.

"Red herring, my favourite," Mischief explained, as he gobbled it down hungrily. Maya could tell she'd been duped.

Maya stared forlornly at the coven. Occasionally, silently counting witches and seats on her fingers, much to her cat's obvious amusement. They could over-hear nothing of what was being said within the gathering. There was though, an unmistakable sadness and concern in the body language from within. Eventually and reluctantly the High Priestess gestured towards Maya and all eyes turned to look her way. Auntie Dot bowed her head sadly.

Maya suspected that they would want her to take her mother's place, but she didn't wait to hear the request. It was too soon and she hadn't given up hope yet. Not by a long way. She decided to leave. She would spare her Auntie Dot or Granny, the pain of asking her that question tonight.

Maya climbed back onboard Blue. Mischief followed and they spiralled up into the night sky. Tears streamed down Maya's face, as she flew back towards home and the disappointment of tonight's dead end, sank in. Maya directed Blue out over the sea, so as to avoid crossing rivers and their magic sapping fresh running waters. She wiped the tears from her face with her sleeve, leaving another long snail trail glistening up her arm in the moonlight.

Maya though was concentrating hard now, focused, trying to clear her mind of all negative thoughts. Turning again, she now headed Blue back inland, towards the lights of home. As she thought, her tongue licked the moisture from the light rain, as it fell upon her lips. Tongue waggling was an involuntary response for Maya, whenever she tried to engage her brain or whenever something was bothering her. Like now. Something was gnawing away at her subconscious. Something that Mischief had said earlier, when they were talking in the coven's arena. What was it, he'd said?

"That's it!" Maya announced excitedly. "Since Peden's day, you said! When you were explaining to me what heirs were."

Mischief hadn't explained who Peden was though, but Maya was sure she'd heard that name before, and recently too, but where?

Maya thought. Then she thought harder. Her tongue extending each time she focussed, and refocussed. Eventually her tongue had reached full extension. Her brain was on full power and finally she plucked the answer out of the air, like a toad capturing a particularly juicy moth for its supper.

"Mum, mum mentioned him too!" Maya announced. She'd heard her mum speak of Peden, the week before she'd disappeared!

"Whooo?" cried Mischief, sounding like a lonely owl, calling through the night, in search of a 'twit' from a prospective mate.

Maya didn't respond though. She was sure. Her mum had read her something about Peden, out of that little red book of hers. Maya had no idea what she'd said. As a fully paid-up member of the teenage fraternity, she'd been oblivious to whatever her mum had actually been saying. Faking interest and nodding and grunting occasionally, as she played games on her tablet. If only she'd listened. If only she'd paid a little attention. This could be important.

Then suddenly, it came to her as a blinding flash of light. Totally distracted and consumed by her own thoughts. She'd crashed headlong into a lamppost!

Maya woke with a sudden shudder, choking and spluttering on a cascade of cold water, as it splashed off her face. Mischief was standing over her smirking, pouring scorn and the contents of his chilled travel flask, over her head, to bring her around. She sat up suddenly, confused, soggy and bewildered. Maya wiped her face on her sleeve and shook her aching head. Mischief dribbled some more water over her head, just out of badness.

"Distracted, were we?" Mischief laughed. Unhelpfully stating the obvious, as Maya nursed a large bruised bump, which now emerged like a boil, from the centre of her throbbing forehead. She decided not to dignify his question with an answer and quickly changed the subject.

"What do you know about Peden?" Maya enquired sheepishly, still rubbing her forehead and grimacing with pain.

"Nothing much," her cat responded. "Well, to be more accurate, nothing much at all," he admitted. "Your mum once mentioned him. I think it was, when she was reading something out of that little red book. You know, the one she got from what's-her-face and became so obsessed with, recently."

Maya paused thoughtfully.

"What exactly did she say, it might be important?" Maya enquired thoughtfully.

Mischief paused and stroked his whiskers, as if impersonating Maya's mum's favourite detective, Hercules Porridge, as she often called him.

"It was over breakfast, I think. The day that your mum took you and your dad for that long walk along the River Ayr. You remember? You complained bitterly about it, at the time. Your face was lodged in that tablet thingy, as usual. Your dad was out of the room. Whenever he's not around, as you well know, that's when your mum often speaks to us about the more important issues in life. All she said was, something along the lines of... what was it again?" Mischief hesitated once more, straining every sinew of his mind, to recall her mother's words.

Thoughtfully, he continued:

"I think, she said something like; '*I didn't know they called them heirs... all the way back as far as Peden*'. Then she paused, smiled and said something quietly to herself like, '*Oh, now I get it, how clever*', I think that was it?"

"How clever what is?" Maya asked excitedly.

"I don't know. That idiot dad of yours came back into the room and interrupted her!" Mischief complained.

Maya thought back to that day herself. She could recall getting a new high score, on the great new game she'd downloaded onto her tablet and the name Peden did sound somehow familiar, but that was about all. It was the day before her birthday. The day before her mum had disappeared.

Maya's tongue appeared again, as if to assist her recollections. Memories floated back to her slowly, from earlier that day. She could picture her mum sitting in the conservatory, clutching that little red book. Maya recalled, her mum telling her that book had something to do with local history, but that was about it. She'd been given the book, by a girl called Evaline (the girl formerly referred to as what's-her-face by Mischief). Suddenly though, her mum had sat up with an excited look in her eye and insisted that they all went for a walk, along the banks of the River Ayr.

Maya recalled her mum blabbering on about the book enthusiastically, to anyone who wouldn't listen. Maya didn't listen, nearly as much as her dad. It was a drab an uninteresting little book, and had something to do with the history of Ayrshire and people from pre-historic times, back when Granny was still a girl. It had nothing at all to do with magic, vampires, werewolves or any other interesting mythical creatures. Maya thought it sounded really, really dull.

They had started their walk at Failford and headed south along the river bank. Even Maya had to admit it was lovely. The River Ayr carved its way through sandstone banks and ancient oak woodland. Thick woodland shaded the path beneath from the light November drizzle. It had been lovely, all except for the rain and the walking and the lack of internet, of course. They had stopped by a pebble beach, for a rather chilly picnic. All cuddling together under a travel blanket, which her mum had packed. Dad snoozed and Mum read from her boring little red book again, while Maya threw pebbles into the water, in an effort to concuss any passing trout.

Once Maya was satisfied, that all the fish had splitting headaches. They had made their way back the same way. Mum suggested that they should take a detour, doubling back along a muddy riverside track, so that dad could take lots of pictures of some sandstone steps carved into the cliffs, by some famous religious man. A sign dad read aloud, told of a preacher who used to address his congregation on the other side of the river. Mum was interested in it too. She said that this place was in her book, but Maya had feigned sore feet and wanted to head home. So, after allowing dad another dozen or so snaps of the sandstone steps, that went nowhere at all, they had turned for home.

Maya thought, on reflection, that her mum had seemed a bit distracted on the return journey. Normally, she focussed on criticising Dad's driving, but not that day. Her head was back in that book again. Even laughing out loud at one point and announcing, something like:

"Covenanters... how clever!", then thumbing her way through the book once more and scribbling in the margins.

Maya's heart missed a beat...

"The book, we need that book. She wrote something in it!" Maya yelped excitedly. "Mum wrote things in her boring little red book that day! The day before she vanished. It might be important!"

Mischief nodded his agreement and without another word, they both remounted Blue, (who now sported a rather impressive lamppost shaped indent, etched into the front edge of his brush). They made their way home hurriedly. Back to the woods behind Maya's house. Maya dismounted and led Blue impatiently into his stables using a freshly picked bouquet of mint, hastily plucked from a halved whisky barrel planter.

Maya walked cautiously towards where the cabin had been. Her neckless charm glowed and with that, the door to her cabin obligingly appeared, as if out of thin air. Maya marched on through the door and made her way straight through the cabin to the witch flap in the far wall. She pushed through the little door, carelessly letting it swing back into the path of Mischief, who followed closely, now slightly flat faced and grumpily, in her wake.

Maya stomped purposefully through the portal, leapt through the back of the mirror and, with hardly a word to her magical book, made her way downstairs and into the living room.

Nobody was there. Sat in the armchair, curled up and asleep. Nobody and No-one, were what Dad had christened next door's cat and the ginger and white moggy from three doors down. They seemed to spend most of their time in Maya's house. Mischief hissed and reluctantly Nobody opened an eye momentarily, then ignored him completely.

Maya picked up the little red book from beside her mum's favourite armchair.

It was entitled; 'The drawing down of the moon' and fell open at a page with a sketch of the sandstone steps that went nowhere. There was a short passage beneath the drawing.

"Look Mischief," Maya pointed, showing him the picture, then she read the caption aloud, very excitedly:

"Near Failford the covenanter Alexander Peden ... that's him*!"* Maya announced, her eyes wide as dinner plates.

"The covenanter Alexander Peden, preached to his congregation from a set of sandstone steps carved into the banks. His faithful congregation would gather on the banks on the other side, now known as Peden's cove. Legend has it, Peden fell to his death from the steps on a stormy night and it became known locally, as the covenanter's leap. His body was never found though. History does not back up this theory however, with him living on well beyond the year in which this event was alleged to have been witnessed. Rumours abound of foul play, look-alikes and avoidance of inheritance tax. All of which followed the preacher, who moved away in a great hurry after the incident."

That was all, nothing about witchcraft or arenas. Nothing that Maya felt, could help her to find her mum. Although, on closer inspection, the words covenanter and faithful had been underlined heavily in pencil. Also, in the margins, the title of the book had been scrawled, right next to the picture of the sandstone steps. 'The drawing down of the moon' was written in her mother's awful handwriting, followed by a large question mark and a silly doodle of a cat. That was all. Maya flicked through the pages with growing frustration, but there was nothing else.

Maya read the tedious little book, from cover to cover that night in bed, but she could find nothing else of any interest or relevance in it at all. By the end, she was bored rigid and more confused than ever. She still had no idea at all, why the book was even called, 'The drawing down of the moon.' The moon wasn't mentioned anywhere, she had even resorted to checking the page numbers, in case any had been lost or removed.

But no, the only mention of the moon, was in the book's title and her mum's scribbled writing in the margins. It was all very confusing. Was there a hidden code? She had to be missing something. Maya decided to sleep on it. On reflection however, it didn't make a very comfy pillow, so eventually she used her favourite cuddly toy cat Menorca instead.

Next morning brought with it, a little more clarity for Maya.

"Ok, let's start at the beginning," she suggested to Mischief at the breakfast table. "What is a covenanter anyway?"

Maya googled covenanter on her tablet... "A holy man, a Scottish term for a protestant preacher or devout believer. A common term once, back in ancient times, back before even her Granny was born," she paraphrased, for the benefit of her cat.

It didn't really help. What could all this have to do with her mum's disappearance?

After breakfast, Maya made her way up the stairs and opened the secret room door with her keystone neckless charm. Maya was preoccupied, churning over her thoughts on covenanters and irrelevant book titles, time and time again, to no avail. After opening her magical book and without even exchanging pleasantries. Maya broached the subject, with the book.

"What do you know about Peden?" Maya demanded.

"And good morning to you too," the book scolded.

"Oh, sorry, morning," Maya responded rather sheepishly.

"Not that much, to be honest. Not my subject really!" the book wrote. "Your Grandma calls him 'Pee'd' in, rather crudely."

"Grandma's a witch too?" Maya gasped.

"What part of long line of witches, didn't you understand, little one?" the book replied rather sarcastically. "Peden, hmm… not bringing back many recollections for me, but you could always try the locket guide."

"Locket guide, don't you mean a pocket guide?" Maya asked curiously, then frowned, as she read the books silent response.

'… don't you mean a pocket guide? The silly witchling replied, as if to question my undoubted magical expertise. She can get it from the top drawer herself. Pocket guide to witchcraft, really!'

Maya blushed and looked around. There was indeed a small drawer, that she'd only just noticed, on the right-hand side of the dresser. It slid open easily. Inside, sat a small silver oval locket, similar to the charms on her neckless. It was presented on a worn looking, red velvet pin cushion. It had a split ring for attachment to a neckless chain and a delicate swing clasp to keep it shut.

"Do I open it?" Maya asked hesitantly.

"Not in here you maniac!" came the rather abrupt and dismissive reply.

"Oh," Maya responded meekly. Clipping the tiny locket onto her neckless for safekeeping.

"Only in the magic realm and give it space. Don't say I didn't warn you!" cautioned the book.

Maya nodded, wrote the book.

Maya and Mischief made their way out to the cabin in the woods, in the customary manner; courtesy of a new potion bottle, with a hastily drawn locket on the label. It seemed the only appropriate choice, after all.

"Here?" Maya asked Mischief, removing the tiny locket.

"Not in here you lunatic!" chastised her cat, gesturing towards the door.

Obediently, although also rather bemused, Maya walked outside. She took off the locket tentatively and popped open the latch. The tiny locket burst open and a miniature book sprang out and leapt into the air, hovering about level with Maya's eyes. Tiny at first, it spun around in mid-air. Then, with the flutter of tiny pages, it opened. Its pages parted near the middle. An inverted double-page spread opened up, which on inspection, looked for the world, to be identical to the outer cover, except, now twice its original size. Again, the book spun and unfolded to reveal another outer cover, twice the size of the previous one. Again, and again, it spun around, unfolded and doubled in size. Maya stepped back and back again, as the locket book spun and doubled in size alarmingly, in just the way normal books don't.

With a final fluttering of a thousand pages, the mighty tome, now twice Maya's size, finally dropped to the ground with a resounding thump. Right on top of Maya's toes.

"Ouch!" cried Maya in alarm.

"Careful!" Mischief chastised her with a grin. "It's very old and valuable that is."

71

Maya hopped around, foot clasped between her hands and finally toppled, unbalanced and very undignified, heavily back onto her bum.

Slowly recovering some composure, Maya turned to her cat, who had clearly enjoyed her misfortune, a little too much, to ask:

"What do I do now?"

"Ask it something dummy," Mischief instructed, with an impatient sigh.

Maya had one burning question. She wanted to know what a magical text might have to say on the subject of Peden and the covenanters.

"Covenanters please," she commanded and the book flicked through its pages to about midway, to a page marked with a large capital L.

"L?" asked Maya, looking quizzically towards her cat.

"L for lots probably. It's in catalogical order. You'll soon get the hang of it," Mischief replied.

"Catalogical order?" Maya repeated. "Covenanters, filed under L for lots, really?"

"Yes. There must have been lots of them in the olden days, I guess?" Mischief responded, seemingly undeterred.

Maya rolled her eyes, then knelt down over the mighty locket book and read aloud:

"Covenanter, a protestant holy man or preacher. An office which was also often held incognito, in less enlightened and tolerant witch-toasting times, by the High Priest of the local coven or occasionally the High Priestess"

72

"Women were not always in charge, way back then, you know," Mischief interrupted. "Granny says that's why they called them the dark ages!"

Maya looked up horrified, at the revelation that once upon a time, men were in charge. Her mum wouldn't have liked that! Then, slowly regaining her composure, she continued:

"Covenanters would gather by day, respectable and in full view to preach. Whilst all the time secretly passing coded messages to the rest of the coven. Indeed, the very word covenanter comes from the traditional calling together of the coven, where the preachers would call upon all the 'coven and heirs' to meet at the next full moon."

"Coven and heirs, coven-ant-ers, how clever?" Maya whispered to herself, out loud.

Maya's heart, which had just jumped up into her throat, missed a beat. Her small intestine jumped up and dangled from her brainstem. It tugged furiously, to alert Maya to the possible significance of her own words, as she found herself repeating, the very words her mother had spoken on the day before she'd disappeared.

"It's a clue... it has to be," Maya spluttered, swallowing hard to rearrange her internal organs, back into a more conventional format.

Maya's tongue was out. Sticking out, not fallen out (for any readers, who were still slightly concerned by the random behaviour of Maya's body parts). Her brain was now fully engaged on the subject. Her heart thumping in her chest, like a chubby three-legged hamster in a loose-fitting running wheel. Excitement grew. Now, at last, Maya felt she was on her mother's trail.

"Calling down of the moon?" Maya now demanded of the locket book, with growing excitement. The book flicked forward to a

73

chapter on ancient rituals, filed conveniently under I. This time however, even Mischief just shrugged his shoulders.

 Maya started to read it aloud, once more:

"An ancient wiccan ritual. A few powerful witches were said to have performed the most dangerous of all incantations, known as the drawing down of the moon. Its true meaning long since lost through the passing eons. There are few records of these oldest of rituals, but one of the most ancient coven texts warns that even the greatest warlock or witch, cannot avoid the ravages of time, not unless the faithful harness the source of all magic power and touch the moon itself."

 "Touch the moon itself?" Maya repeated, clearly bemused.

She continued to read aloud;

"The most famous follower of this belief was known to his coven as Nedep. A powerful High Priest and ... what?"

Maya stopped reading, her mouth wide open, like a carnivorous venus flytrap, waiting for a plump insect for its supper.

"You're not going to believe this!" Maya laughed.

"I might?" Mischief replied curiously.

"No, no way!" Maya gasped.

"No way what?" Mischief enquired, still apparently unflustered by the whole story.

"Okay, I warned you," Maya cautioned and continued:

"...Nedep. A powerful High Priest and a wild dragon rider, believed that true faith could draw down the moon and allow it to be touched. To do so would bring that person great power, youth and

74

eternal life. Nedep, it's said, became obsessed by this quest for eternal life."

Maya looked up at Mischief, who simply stretched out a paw to clean, as if she'd said nothing unusual, and replied:

"So?"

Maya couldn't believe it:

"Dragons? Touching the moon? Eternal life? You're not telling me all this is real?"

"No. I'm not telling you anything. The locket book is," Mischief clarified unhelpfully. "Anyway, it's far too early in your training, to be getting into dragons. They'd toast a young witchling like you for breakfast and use your spindly leg bones as toothpicks."

Maya stared at him in disbelief, but Mischief didn't even look up from washing his outstretched leg. So, after forcing her own mouth closed again. Maya read on, pretending that she'd taken it all in her stride:

"Nedep had assembled a mighty coven. Legend has it, that he was the High Priest and in charge, the first and only time that the 'touching of the moon' spell was ever successfully performed."

"Again... what?" Maya broke off and demanded. But Mischief just moved onto his other paw and resumed his ablutions. Maya resolved to get to the end of this passage without further interruption. She could tell Mischief wasn't exactly bursting at the seams, to discuss these revelations. On she read, sure, well quite sure, that the moon hadn't literally been brought down to earth. Just a figure of speech, she reassured herself:

"As he reached out and touched the moon, Peden unlocked the power of the moon itself. The source of all magical power on earth.

He cast a mighty incantation, one of awesome and unrivalled power, to capture the moon's power in the form of a potion. But, for all his magical prowess and the strength of his coven. The power of the moon, was too much for even him. In that moment of greed, desiring eternal life, only for himself, Nedep was engulfed by his own spell. The magical power of the moon, locked the High Priest and his whole coven away in the potion bottle for all eternity. Nedep had his wish, eternal life, but what use is eternal life, if you're stuck in liquid form in a bottle?"

"Whoa!" was all Maya had. But now she noticed that there was a footnote at the end of the page, written in smaller print. She read this to aloud, as well:

"Seekers of the potion beware, for it is said that Nedep's potion is an elixir of eternal life. So powerful, that to even touch it, can stop time itself."

"Heavy!" Maya observed.

"Immortality," Mischief added, rather nonchalantly.

"What?" Maya was somewhat bemused by his sudden interruption.

"I, it's for immortality" Mischief suggested thoughtfully.

"I for idiot, more like," Maya replied. "What a doughball! Eternal life as a liquid, stuck in a bottle. Slushing around in there, all mixed up with witches, you hardly even know... brrrrr!"

Maya shuddered and laughed at the thought.

Mischief though suddenly looked more thoughtful, even taking a brief break from preening himself.

"It's all very interesting, but what on earth could all this have to do with my mum's disappearance?" asked Maya, still feeling thoroughly perplexed.

Mischief looked exasperated by her question.

"Seriously? What... a woman, of let's face facts, advancing years. Finding a clue to the whereabouts of the secret to eternal youth, on the day her daughter turns into a horrible teenager?" he ranted rather scathingly. "Face it... that's some serious anti-wrinkle cream in that bottle!"

Somewhere close by, a penny dropped, rolled around on its rim in ever decreasing circles, before toppling in Maya's direction.

"Oh," Maya replied sheepishly.

"But where?" asked Mischief. "If all the coven was consumed, its whereabouts would be lost too, wouldn't it?"

"That's all there is," Maya confirmed, despondently flicking over the page of the locket book.

"Hmm... what now?" Mischief enquired.

"We need to go back!" Maya announced with fresh resolve.

Mischief nodded in agreement, then added:

"Where?"

"Back to where we were, the day before my birthday. That walk by the River Ayr," Maya continued enthusiastically. "Mum saw something that day. I just know it. She was excited all the way home. Maybe she'd figured something out. You know, where the potion was hidden, or the location Nedep's coven perhaps?" Maya's eyes glistened and she beamed with excitement and fresh hope.

The Covenanter's leap

Maya gazed down at the mighty locket book.

"How do I close this thing?" enquired Maya, clearly keen to be on her way.

"Mischief simply clapped his paws together three times, whereupon the mighty tome sprang up, into the air, and started to spin and fold in on itself. Time after time it folded and spun around in mid-air, halving in size every time, until it had returned to its original size. Whereupon, it dropped to the ground, hardly visible in the long grass.

Maya gathered it up quickly. She placed the tiny book back into the locket and carefully attached it to her neckless once more. Next, she made her way around to the stables, just as the door flew off its hinges and Blue shot out to greet her. He bounced up and down, like an over-eager puppy at the sound of 'walkies.' Maya really had no idea, why she even bothered shutting the door behind him at night.

Soon enough, Maya and Mischief were sat in their customary positions on-board Blue. Then, with a pointless kick from Maya's heels, as if she were riding a pony, they set off on their way. Soaring up, over the tree tops, out over the fields and roads until they came to the River Ayr. They levelled off and banked at speed, following the meandering banks of the river, heading towards the sandstone steps to nowhere. Nobody spoke during the journey, but they couldn't hear him. He was back at home, asleep on the sofa. Besides Maya and Mischief were both deep in thought. Mulling over the earlier revelations, about Nedep and his potion for eternal life.

There was something else bothering Maya too. Again, her subconscious was clawing away at her on the subject of Nedep. Demanding that she engaged both her tongue and brain, once more on the subject. Obediently, out came her soggy thinking appendage, circling her plus size teenage mouth, in seemingly random bursts, like a cat chasing a catnip toy on a stick.

Finally, as they approached the site of the sandstone steps to nowhere, Maya's tongue retreated into her mouth courtesy of a sour tasting midge, but its work was done.

"How are you at anagrams?" she asked smugly, unsuccessfully trying to hide a self-satisfied grin.

"Go on then," Mischief replied, sensing the smugness in her voice.

"Peden the respected preacher by day, or written backwards … Nedep the High Priest and mighty warlock by night?

"P-E-D-E-N, N-E-D-E-P, clever girl," Mischief conceded, rather reluctantly.

"They were one and the same person, don't you think?" Maya suggested.

Maya took Mischief's silence, as confirmation of her theory.

They landed at the base of the red sandstone steps, where Peden had preached to his congregation on the other bank. Encouragingly, it was known as: 'The Covenanter's leap,' according to a small white sign, next to the safety barrier, which barred the way. Each step had been carved out by hand. Hewn from the solid sandstone bedrock through which the river cut. Around thirty well-worn steps raised into the air, then simply stopped, high above the river below, as if there had been a rock slide, many years before.

The Covenanters Leap at Peden's Cove on the River Ayr

Maya knew there was something here. There had to be.

"Now what?" Maya asked. Suddenly realising that she'd not really thought this part through.

"Use your training wand?" Mischief suggested.

"Oh, yes. Okay," Maya replied uncertainly. Pulling the slender stick out from inside her jacket.

Maya closed her eyes and raised the wand above her head, then commanded:

"Show me, show me the coven."

Maya spoke hesitantly, without any real conviction. Her wand glowed faintly, as if reflecting her lack of self-belief. Maya recalled the Prestwick Coven and how Mischief had divulged; that only the High Priestess, had the power to open their coven. How could a novice witchling like her, ever hope to discover Nedep's hidden lair? Equipped as she was, with a simple training wand. A coven which had managed to elude detection, down through the countless eons, that had passed since Nedep's day.

Suddenly though, the sun poked out from behind the clouds and a shaft of sunlight, lit up the steps in front of them. Illuminating each one in turn, as the shadows lifted. Maya held her breath expectantly, surveying the scene in front of her, with eager anticipation. Had something changed? Had it worked? Had she really revealed the entrance to some ancient lost coven?

Now, as she stared, it struck her. She was sure beyond any shadow of a doubt, that nothing at all had happened. Nothing had changed. Just the movement of clouds past the sun.

Maya slumped, then gathered her resolve and tried once again.

"Reveal any magic!" she cried, this time with more conviction.

Maya's wand glowed once more, brighter this time. At that moment Mischief too started to glow. Her spell revealing the startling revelation that a witch's cat, much to his obvious displeasure, indeed possessed some magic powers. But that was the extent of the illuminations and revelations. If there was something else here. Its magic was clearly well beyond Maya's meagre magical abilities to discover.

Maya was all out of ideas. As moments turned into minutes, they scoured the river banks and sandstone steps in search of clues and inspiration. Disappointment turned to disillusionment and despair.

"We're missing something," Maya complained, her frustration clearly building.

Mischief thought for a minute, then asked:

"What else was it that your mother had underlined, in the that book of hers again?"

"Faithful, wasn't it?" asked Mischief again, answering his own question, before Maya had a chance to respond. "You said, your mum had underlined the word faithful, right?"

"Yes, but I thought that just referred to Peden the preacher, or even his congregation?" Maya replied.

"Possibly, but what if it's code, or even another anagram?" Mischief suggested.

Maya engaged her brain on the subject:

"If hat ful ..., a hill fut..., ah tuffle..., hmm."

After a few more minutes of silent and ultimately uninspired letter jumbling. Neither of them could come up with anything sensible. Faithful, was not an anagram for much at all, they agreed. So, maybe it was some sort of code then, they speculated. Maya started to let her mind and tongue loose on the subject at hand, in a seemingly random verbal tirade...

"Faithful... people of faith... preachers or followers... the coven... but where? Nedep or Peden's coven..."

On and on Maya rambled. Minutes passed. Minutes that rapidly started to feel more like hours, to her poor cat. Finally, Mischief covered his ears with his paws, as if in pain. He could listen to no more.

Maya though was undeterred:

"The covenanters... the covenanter's leap... leap... coven-and-heirs leap... a leap... that's it!" Maya announced suddenly.

82

"What's what? What could you possibly get from that?" demanded her bemused cat.

"Faith, a leap, it's a leap of faith! That's the way to the coven... the coven and heirs, they had to take a leap of faith!" Maya insisted. "The covenanter's leap."

"Hmm... sounds plausible, I suppose," Mischief conceded reluctantly. He was starting to suspect, that Maya might be brighter than he'd given her credit for. Something, he could never bring himself to admit, of course.

"Remember, in Mum's book? Peden was seen falling from the steps... the covenanter's leap, but he didn't die. He moved away soon afterwards. Maybe he was seen entering a coven?" Maya suggested.

Mischief looked intrigued by the possibility.

"No wonder he left in a hurry. In those days, you didn't stick around to be accused of witchcraft!" Mischief agreed.

Mischief looked thoughtful.

"A coven... your mum. If she entered the coven. You know, if she found Nedep's lost coven and got trapped inside, her story would stop," Mischief confirmed, he too was clearly getting excited.

Maya nodded eagerly. She'd thought of little else since reading about Nedep's downfall, but hearing Mischief say it out loud, now made the possibility, suddenly much more tangible.

"What exactly did her book say?" Mischief asked impatiently.

The words were now etched into Maya's memory. She had read them over and over again, searching repeatedly for clues, in vain.

Maya recited her mother's journal, word for word:

"She knew exactly what she had to do, no time to waste, it was midnight and she climbed by the light of the full moon. She knew in her heart though, that her magic would not help her now, not where she was headed, but she had to try. She stepped out slowly and carefully, summoning every ounce of her courage. Her mind was made up now, this was it, it had to be here. The stone crumbled beneath her feet as she stepped out and fell..."

There was a pause as Maya and Mischief both turned, in perfect synchronicity, to stare at the top step of the sandstone staircase.

"A leap of faith," announced Maya.

"And if you're wrong?" Mischief asked.

"A leap of death?" replied Maya, apprehensively.

There were two obvious and equally likely solutions, that now confronted Maya. Either her mum had walked, to the top of these steps, in the belief that she had discovered the leap of faith. The entrance to Nedep's coven. A coven, that held the potion for eternal youth. Or she had stepped out, in a leap of faith and plummeted to her death, on the rocks below. Her broken body swept away, by the river that ran beneath. Its running fresh waters concealing her magic from her journal, which still remains open, to this day.

Maya was silent for once.

"You're thinking, what I think, you think, I think you're thinking. Aren't you?" clarified Mischief, with all of his customary simplicity.

Maya nodded, without really taking in a word. Then, nervously stepped out onto the bottom step, of the sandstone steps to nowhere. She knew she had to try. Nervously, Maya took a few more tentative steps, up the sandstone staircase.

"You're also probably thinking that, if this truly is a leap of faith, then you can't use any magic to save yourself, even if you're wrong," announced Mischief.

Maya stopped in her tracks.

"As you climb, you'll be stepping out over running water, where your magic powers won't work. But I'm sure you realise that?" he added.

"No!" Maya cried, in sudden despair.

She hadn't been thinking that at all. Quite the opposite in fact. She had been running over levitation spells in her head. Maya did so hate it, when that know-it-all cat of hers, was right.

Regardless, Maya continued to make her way slowly up the steps, her heart thumping in her chest, like a runaway tortoise, which had chosen to hibernate in a cement mixer.

Every step a terrifying and exhilarating mixture of dread and excitement, at the prospect, that maybe, just maybe, this might finally be the moment that she was to be reunited with her mother. One way or the other.

Nervous sweat broke out across her brow, like soggy pimples on a teenage troll.

Maya reached the top step, swallowed deeply, then...

"Stop!" cried the little cat. "Just a thought. If you're going to take a leap of faith, in the hope that you can, what was it, 'touch the moon' and enter the coven? Shouldn't you wait for the moon to actually appear first?"

Maya suddenly felt quite sick. Nauseous at the prospect of her sudden demise, due to such a basic mis-calculation. He was right of course. Peden's followers had returned to the steps at midnight.

Her mum's book too, spoke of her making her way by the light of a full moon. Touching the moon, she had to admit, was likely best done, when there was actually a moon there to be touched. If there was an entrance to a coven here, she had better return at mid-night.

"Good point. I was wondering when you were going to spot that one, my faithful furry feline accomplice?" Maya lied unconvincingly.

It was the longest day ever. Maya dared not return home or seek out Aunty Dot, with the news. She knew, that she would surely try to talk her out of it, or even insist that she should take her place. So, there they stayed, waiting for nightfall. Maya throwing pebbles into the river and Mischief swatting midges. They talked it through, time and time again, but it all still made sense.

Maya told herself it was a 50:50 call. A gamble worth taking for her mother, but nagging away in the back of both of their minds, was the unspoken fear that haunted them. The nagging ache in their hearts, that if her mum had survived, then why had she not emerged from this hidden coven.

It had been too long. Best case, she was trapped in there, conjuring chardonnay, trashy novels and chocolate. Awaiting her rescue. Caught in a trap. A trap which Maya was about to walk straight into herself. Worst case, well, it did no good to dwell on that, she told herself.

As the light faded, Maya built a fire. She chose an already charred piece of turf, they both strongly suspected, that her mother had used some two weeks earlier. Maya collected fallen twigs and tried to light it, the old-fashioned way. Soon however, she discovered that her outdoor skills were somewhat lacking and, as Mischief was keen to point out. Using her training wand to conjure sausages and a box of matches, with which to light the fire, wasn't really getting back to basics. Soon enough though, they were both cheered by the warmth of the fire and set about toasting the sausages, over the open flames. Unfortunately, the fire also served as an attack beacon for every midge, within a five-mile radius.

Night fell and stars gradually started to peak between the broken cloud, in the sky above them. As the cloud cover lifted, the moon rose over the far bank, illuminating the bottom step of the sandstone steps to nowhere. As the hours passed, the moonlight made its way carefully up each of the steps, illuminating them in turn, one at a time, until at five minutes to midnight, finally it crept onto the top step. This could be no coincidence.

Slowly, Maya made her way onto the bottom step. Each step thereafter, was taken more tentatively. Maya was nervous. Her mind was racing and her heart bounced off her ribs, as if desperately trying to escape from its bony prison. Self-doubt grew, with each hesitant step she took towards the top. Eventually, Maya came to the final moonlit step and jelly legs wobbled their way precariously onto it.

Maya looked up. The moon was huge, beautiful. Much larger than she'd ever seen before. Magnified by the swollen lens of her now tear-soaked eyes, she felt as if she could actually reach out and touch it. Raw courage carried her inevitably towards the point of no-return.

Maya leaned forward, and as she did so, she stretched out her hand. With this, a shaft of moonlight ran up her arm and touched her outstretched finger. Illuminating it suddenly with a dazzling flash, as her hand pointed towards the moon. Maya reached out. The moon appeared even closer now... much closer. Maya could nearly touch it. She knew she could. Maya felt, no, she believed, that she could actually step out and touch the moon.

She was sure, she believed it now... she had faith. Her love for her mother, had led her to this point. Maya stepped out in a leap of faith, to touch the moon, the stone crumbled beneath her feet and she fell...

Nedep's potion

Maya fell into a moonlit chamber, magically suspended above the rocky frothing waters of the River Ayr, which ran beneath it. Though invisible from outside, from within, it was blindingly bright, gleaming with reflected silvery moonlight. Gradually, Maya's eyes adjusted to the light. Maya could now make out twelve large silver pillars, which rose some twenty witches' hats into the air, around a central plinth, then to one side, a shadow, an outline...

"Mum!" cried Maya, springing headlong towards the collapsed figure, who lay on the floor in front of her. It was her mother alright. There was no mistaking that mop of hair and poor fashion sense!

As Maya's hand reached out, to grab her mum's ankle, it passed straight through her, as if she wasn't there at all. Again, Maya grasped for her mother, this time moving up to her shoulders. Once again, her hands passed right through her mum's body. It was as if she was a ghost. An apparition or a hologram, trapped outside reality, suspended between this world and the next.

"Mum, Mum.... **Mum**!" Maya cried in anguish. But there was no response. Maya gazed in horror and amazement at her mother. She lay peacefully enough. She didn't look dead. But neither was she alive!

Maya slumped back onto her bum. Shaking with nervous energy and frustration. She stared at her mother, lying in front of her, face down on the floor of this strange coven. One arm outstretched beyond her, grasping tightly onto something. Maya studied her mother's hand. It held a small unremarkable triangular green potion bottle.

"Nedep's potion?" Maya gasped out loud.

Maya thought about grabbing the little bottle. Maybe Nedep's elixir could revive her mother, but she saw sense quickly. That's exactly what her mum must have done. The footnote in small print in the locket book. It had warned her about this. Its cautioning words now echoed in her mind, like a ghost from the past:

"Seekers of the potion beware, for it is said that Nedep's potion is an elixir of eternal life. So powerful, that to even touch it, can stop time itself."

Maya knew that she'd be no use to her mother, not if she too were to join her. She had no time for tears either. There had to be a way to revive her mother. There had to be something here, a clue and she was determined to find it.

Maya started to look around, she had to make sense of this somehow. This was obviously a coven of some kind, Nedep's coven and a very fine one too. That explained why her mother's story had stopped. Twelve magnificent silvery crystalline pillars, rose from a floor of pure white sand. No old tombstones with coffins for seats here, Maya thought to herself.

In front of each of the twelve crystal pillars, sat twelve marbled pedestals and right in the centre of the coven, was a clear crystal orb. Thirteen green blue crystals sat on a silver jewelled tray, which perched on top of this central orb. Maya gulped, realising, that with all the crystals still in place, the legend must be true. The entire coven must have been consumed in a cataclysmic magical misfire, which had engulfed them all, where they sat.

Maya started to talk to her mum, she wasn't at all sure that her mum could hear her, but what harm could it do? She told her mum what they'd been up to, since she'd disappeared. Then scolded her severely, for not disclosing this magical double-life earlier and in particular for being reckless enough to get herself trapped in here, all for a stupid jar of super strength anti-wrinkle cream, as Mischief

90

had called it. Maya wrapped up the lecture, by telling her mum about the mis-adventures of Nedep, although she was sure that her mum had already deduced most of that, for herself.

"And look Mum. All the crystals are still here. All those poor witches, slushing about in that tiny bottle with Nedep… a man, for all eternity. Yuk, can you imagine? All that power… the power of a full coven and even then, they couldn't…," Maya couldn't finish her sentence. Out popped her tongue. It returned swiftly to home base, with what she was sure, was a marvellous flash of inspiration.

"Of course, how stupid of me!" Maya chastised herself, out loud. She looked down at the crystals and beamed.

"All that power!" she whispered excitedly. "The crystals Mum… the full power of a whole coven, if I could…"

Maya reached impatiently into her jacket and produced her training wand.

"Please work, please, please, please," Maya pleaded.

Maya took a deep breath, raised her training wand above her head and focussed her thoughts on the little stick. She grasped it firmly in her hand and braced herself. Maya closed her eyes and concentrated. First on the training wand in her hand. Then, when she had that. She searched out the crystals, using her mind's eye. Maya visualised them, connected her wand to them in her mind and readied herself, to cast the spell.

Maya felt it build. She sensed the power. Unlike anything she'd ever felt before. She tingled from head to foot, as if someone had just dropped an electric eel into her bath. Her wand glowed, the keystone charm in her neckless glowed, the crystals on the orb glowed, as Maya commanded:

"Awaken!"

Magical power crackled from the tip of her wand. Lightning flashed between the coven stones and to and from the crystals on the orb. At that moment, a mighty magical blast shot forth to where her mother lay.

Maya had focused everything she had into that incantation. Every ounce of her strength, every drop of her energy and willpower. She had harnessed the power of Nedep's coven too. Power well beyond any she could ever have imagined wielding herself. It was extraordinary, exhilarating and terrifying, all at the same time.

Maya could smell burning now, as her over-loaded training wand burst into flames and crumbled to ash, in her hand. Yet for all its great power, as she opened her eyes, Maya watched in horror and disbelief, as the magical beam passed straight through her mother and simply dissipated through the coven walls.

Maya tried and tried again, without any real hope or belief. Without her wand, she couldn't muster nearly as much power. It was exhausting too, with each successive attempt, becoming weaker and less potent than the last. Maya drained herself and all her remaining magical power in the process. Tears of frustration flowed now, as Maya sank to her knees. Emotionally and physically spent, she curled up on the floor next to her mum and cried herself off into an uneasy sleep.

Morning arrived, as it often does, early the next day. Announcing itself, with the rising of a large orange ball over the horizon (a much less common event for those readers from Scotland). Maya awoke with a start. The morning sun, not moonlight, now shone through the coven walls and illuminated Nedep's mighty coven.

All was as she had left it, the night before. Her mum still lay motionless and semi-translucent on the floor beside her. The coven, if anything was more impressive by the bright morning light.

The coven's silver pillars glistening with an iridescent sheen, she hadn't really appreciated the previous night.

Maya rose slowly to her feet. Turning to face the way she'd entered the coven. A small flash of sunlight caught her eye. It sent a narrow sunbeam across the coven, as if reflected by a small mirror or a metallic item of some kind. Maya bent down, next to her mum's sleeping body and retrieved the small object. It was a tiny tarnished brass hour glass. It might be an ancient egg timer, but for its diminutive size. Perhaps for quails' eggs? Or might it have been used for a board game Maya speculated?

On closer inspection, it wasn't even working properly. The top chamber was only half empty, but no sand flowed into the lower glass. Maya turned it the other way around, but the hour glass and its sands stayed in the same position, as only the brass setting rotated around the inner glass.

Maya's curiosity was peaked, "What's the use in an egg timer, that you can't turn over?" she asked herself out loud.

The sand inside was loose, but whatever she tried, Maya could not get it to flow. Maya turned it over once again and in so doing, she noticed an inscription on the base. It looked strangely new, as if cut into the brass, just the day before. The writing was tiny, but in the strong sunlight, her keen teenage eyes could just make out the inscription, which she read aloud to her mum.

"Only the power of the living wand or a pure coven can restart the sands of time."

Maya's tongue was out now, stalking an explanation in the morning light, like a gecko on the desert dunes, hunting fire ants. The bug, or rather the thought that she was tracking, when it finally arrived, was so juicy; that she briefly juggled, the now suddenly very precious, little hourglass. Maya steadied herself and clasped it safely, cupped between two sweaty palms. Maya whispered aloud to her mum:

"The sands of time."

Maya realised, that in her hands, she now held the sands of her own mother's time on earth. The sands had stopped and with them, so too had her mum. Stuck like this, she would indeed sleep for an eternity, as the locket book had warned. She might not be dead, but she was trapped for now, outside of time itself.

But hope too had returned. The tiny inscription gave her something to cling onto. No, two things, on reflection. Either the power of a living wand or a pure coven could restart the sands of her mother's time once again.

Maya permitted herself a smile. How hard could it be? She had two clear options; to locate a living wand (whatever that was) or just persuade a few 'pure' witches to help her?

It did, on the face of it, all still feel rather elaborate. It was only a simple egg timer, after all. All she had to do was to restart the sands. Could it really be that difficult?

Instinctively, Maya shook the tiny object in her hand. With rising horror, Maya watched as her mother's holographic-like appearance faded almost completely, then slowly, agonisingly slowly, reappeared, piece by piece, limb by limb.

"Oops, sorry Mum!" Maya apologised rather meekly.

Next, Maya tried all her magical powers to restart the sands, held within the tiny hourglass, but this had no effect either. Time and time again, she commanded the sands to flow. She had no wand, but supposed she could still focus her mind's eye on the task in hand. But it was no use. The sands stayed still. Even when Maya once again harnessed the power of all the coven stones, it was still no use.

Maya was determined though. She'd find a way. The inscription said that either the power of a living wand or the power of a pure coven could restart the sands of her mother's time. So, whatever they were, she'd track them down and release her mum. This wasn't fair. Not fair at all.

Morning had also brought with it some additional clarity for Maya. Somewhere, from the muddle of her haunted dreams. She'd realised what her mum had really been up to that fateful day. Why she'd felt compelled to search out Nedep's coven and his potion, on the first available full moon.

It was Granny's book, now on its final page, that had led her mother here. That's why she'd been so upset, when she read about Granny's trip, to the house where she was born. Her mum had realised that Granny's book was coming to the end of its story. It was on its last page. Only Nedep's potion could save her now. It was a truly noble cause, not the petty pilfering of super-strength wrinkle cream, that Mischief had suggested. Maya resolved she'd find a way. Nothing would stand in her way now.

"Nothing!" Maya declared, out loud to her mum.

Maya knew it was time for her to leave though. Time to track down this living wand or a pure coven. Whatever they were? She removed one of her training shoes and then a rather sweaty sock, in which to wrap the precious sands of her mother's time, before stuffing it into her safest pocket.

Maya bent down, to kiss her partially visible, not-quite-a-ghost mum, on or around her cheek. Then, she made her way back through the wibbly-wobbly area in the coven wall. Through which she'd deduced, she must have entered, the night before.

Maya stepped confidently out from Nedep's coven, her foot only just landing on the edge of the top sandstone step. She wobbled for a few nerve-jangling seconds. Teetering on the edge of oblivion, before regaining her balance. Mischief was curled up and still asleep, on a comfortable red cushion, at the bottom of the steps. Exactly where she'd left him the night before.

"What do you know about pure covens and living wands Mischief?" Maya demanded impatiently, as she reached the bottom step and her cat opened a curious eye.

"And good morning to you too," Mischief replied.

"Sorry, but it's important. Mum, she's in there, but not really, like a ghost, but not a ghost, she's alive, well sort of... she's see-through, transparent. I can't touch her!" Maya babbled.

"Slowly, little one. Take a deep breath and tell me what's happened. Slowly, from the minute you stepped off the top step and neglected to tell me you were okay," Mischief instructed.

"Oh, oops... sorry," Maya apologised, rather sheepishly. Calming herself down after a few deep breaths, Maya started to explain, exactly what she'd found in Nedep's coven. Every last detail. Mischief was unusually attentive. Maya could tell he was worried.

"I tried and tried, again and again, to wake her, but even with the power of all those coven crystals, I just didn't have the strength," Maya repeated sadly.

"I'm not surprised. This is powerful magic we're dealing with here. Way beyond our capabilities little one," Mischief consoled. "I'm surprised you didn't fry that little training wand of yours in the process."

"Ah, about that...," Maya started, but she could tell Mischief was deep in thought.

"Okay, a living wand. That's a real long shot. Not been one of those in a thousand years, by all accounts," Mischief muttered, as if talking to himself, rather than Maya.

"A thousand years!" Maya complained bitterly.

"I'm afraid so," Mischief confirmed.

"What is a living wand anyway?" Maya asked curiously.

"Well, legend tells of a sapling wand, possessed of awesome power. The offspring, they say, of mother nature herself. Mother nature, who will present herself as an ancient magical tree, only once every millennium. Mother nature, however will not reveal herself to anyone. None, but the purest of heart and one who doesn't covet the power of the living wand for themselves, can ever find and wield its magic. You can imagine, just how few takers there are for that one!" Mischief scoffed.

Maya's heart sunk deep into her chest.

"What about pure covens then?" Maya asked anxiously.

"I think you best talk to Granny about them," Mischief replied rather evasively. "And, I think she'd appreciate an update on her favourite daughter too."

Maya nodded. She knew Mischief was right. They climbed onto Blue and set off for Granny's, to pick her brains and let her make them breakfast... Maya could almost taste the homemade pancakes.

Granny was relieved, at first anyway, to hear that her mum had been found, but then distracted and thoughtful. Maya could tell, that the old woman, was deeply worried by her story.

"An incantation so powerful that it consumed a whole coven, a powerful coven too, much more powerful than ours. I don't like it.

A spell that's frozen your mum out of time itself. That's well beyond any magic I know of. Nedep was a dragon rider, as I recall. And a bit of a dish in his day too!" she explained, raising an eyebrow and smiling in a way, that always made Maya feel a bit uncomfortable.

"He was a great dragon rider and a mighty warlock into the bargain. He had bonded with a wild dragon, very rare indeed, which he rode bare-back. A magnificent beast... and so was the dragon!" Granny recalled, with a mischievous grin.

Maya smirked and shook her head, then took out her sock, containing the sands of her mother's time, to show Granny the inscription.

"Pure covens Granny, what do you know of them?"

"Pure witches are dragon riders. Snobs though, if you ask me. They do however, have the most powerful coven in all the land. If anyone has the power to release your mum, then they do, I suppose," Granny replied thoughtfully. But Maya could tell from the look in her eye, that the old woman was troubled.

"I'd better call the search parties off then," Granny announced, suddenly changing the subject.

"Search parties?" Maya enquired.

"Of course, think we've been sat on our backsides waiting for your mother to walk through the door?" Granny scoffed. "Age has some advantages you know. I have friends in almost every coven up and down the land. They've been scouring the magical realm, day and night, looking for any trace of your mum."

"Wow," Maya was impressed.

"And the misfits too!" Granny announced proudly. "They've been brilliant!"

"Misfits?" Maya was intrigued.

"Misfits... lots of my friends are misfits. Your Aunty Dot too. You know, witches who's magic misfires sometimes. Witches or magical creatures, that some say don't merit a place in a coven," Granny explained rather sadly.

Maya looked horrified. That wasn't fair at all.

"What do you mean their magic misfires?" Maya asked curiously.

Mischief answered:

"Magic doesn't come easily to all witchlings... some find it more difficult than others. Some have challenges, like magical dyslexia or Tourette's. Witchlings who can't control their magic properly. Many witches don't want to be around a witch, whose magic isn't under control. It gets pretty hazardous around all witchlings, when they're training. But those who find it more difficult, are often shunned or worse."

"That's terrible!" Maya objected. She really didn't like what she was hearing. "So, they're not allowed to join the covens?"

"Not very often, our coven is one of the few more enlightened ones that allows misfits in its ranks," Granny replied. "But most covens, still don't let them join at all. It's a shame. Yet, they've still helped to look for your Mum. There out there now. She was always kind to them too. They don't forget that!"

Maya felt angry and rather humbled. She vowed that one day she'd repay their loyalty and kindness, but for now, her mum had to be the priority.

Something else was bothering Maya too and she knew that she couldn't hide anything from Granny.

"What is it Maya, something else eating away at you dear? A question you really don't want to ask me perhaps?" the old woman probed.

Maya smiled. Granny could always see right through her.

"My mum, she's not as shallow as...," Maya started.

"Her sister?" Granny completed her sentence.

"Yes, but more than that. It's not like her to take such a risk, just because of my birthday and getting older. Not just because of the appearance of a couple more laughter lines. I don't think that's why she...," Maya stuttered, she was really struggling with this.

"My book?" Granny interrupted.

Maya nodded sadly.

"Mum was reading it, the day before she disappeared. Something upset her. Something made her take a terrible risk," Maya stuttered.

Granny moved closer, hugged her and explained:

"It's on its last page now, I believe, but that's ok. At my age you don't go on many new adventures in the magic realm and besides," she grinned. "I tell my journal to write in very, very small print. I still have some unfinished business you know."

Maya smiled and sobbed a little, then laughed uneasily, "A cunning old bat," my dad calls you, for once, I think he's actually right about something."

Granny scowled disapprovingly. A reflex, whenever Maya's dad was mentioned or in fact, whenever he opened his mouth.

Maya sensed that her granny had spoken enough, on this rather delicate subject. She looked down at the precious egg timer, still clasped in her hand, and decided to return to the question of her mother's rescue.

"So, pure witches, Granny. Tell me about them," Maya prompted gently.

"That would be the Deeds. Not the friendliest or the most helpful of covens. Snobs, if you ask me. No, it's worse than snobbery," Granny scowled.

"Snobs?" Maya pressed.

"They think their better than the rest of us. On account of being dragon riders," Granny explained. "Every last one of them rides a dragon. They say it's in their blood. True or pure witches, they call themselves. Legends say, that only a pure coven, can unlock the secret of eternal life or some such nonsense. Hence the pure coven you seek. Lot of rubbish if you ask me, but they're not a coven to be taken lightly. Especially not their High Priestess. She's a right piece of work, that one!"

"Will they help me?" Maya asked anxiously.

Granny looked her in the eyes, hesitated, then cleaved Maya's heart in two with her blunt response:

"No."

Spell

"No? What do you mean, no?" Maya demanded, outraged by Granny's answer.

"Sorry, my dear, but the Deeds don't do favours for anyone. They're notoriously war-like and exclusive. They help no-one but themselves. Not, unless there's something in it for themselves," Granny explained.

"They look down on all other witches," Mischief interrupted. "Unless...?"

"Unless what?" Maya demanded, clearly incensed by what she was hearing.

"Unless you show up on the back of a dragon, I suppose," Mischief conceded, looking rather worried.

"Okay... where do I get one then?" Maya demanded.

"**You** don't!" Mischief scolded. "The Deeds ride the only domesticated dragons I've ever heard of... and nobody, I mean nobody, tangles with a wild one!

"But if the Deeds ride them. They must have tamed them at some point!" Maya insisted.

"Nope!" Mischief replied unhelpfully.

"Nope?" Maya pressed.

"Nope... they bond with them from the moment they hatch out the egg, apparently. Only way to tame a dragon," Mischief insisted.

"Ok then, how do I get my hands on a dragon's egg then?" Maya insisted.

"Oh, that's easy... just walk up to the first enormous fire-breathing, wild witch-munching dragon you meet. Say excuse me and ask it, if rather than scoffing you for lunch, it would kindly give you one of its eggs. An egg, which by-the-way, it's nurtured for the last hundred years. That almost always works," Mischief scoffed sarcastically.

"Witch munching?" Maya gulped.

"Yep!" Mischief confirmed.

"So, it's hopeless then?" Maya whimpered.

"Oh no, I didn't say that," Mischief replied, with a twinkle in his eye. "There is another way."

"What other way?" Maya challenged.

"Well, you could always compel a dragon to do your bidding," Mischief divulged, rather pensively.

"Go on," Maya encouraged him.

"Fire your wand in a dragon's breath, then you earn the right to command the dragon, for a while anyway," Mischief explained.

"A while?" Maya probed suspiciously.

"Well, at least until it feels hungry again," Mischief smirked. "But commanding a dragon, might just buy you enough credibility in their eyes, for you to be granted an audience with the Deeds,"

Granny smiled and nodded reassuringly towards her. Maya took that as all the confirmation she was going to get, that it was worth a shot.

"Find me a dragon then!" Maya demanded enthusiastically.

"No, not yet. You'll need a proper wand first?" Mischief suggested.

"Oh, yes. Okay, find me a wand then!" Maya demanded, slightly less enthusiastically.

"Okay then. I'm really not sure about dragons, but I think you're ready for your first real wand," Mischief conceded.

"Where do I get one?" Maya asked impatiently.

"That's not how it works, little one. You must tell me," Mischief replied.

Maya looked with pleading eyes towards Granny.

"He's right, I'm afraid," the old lady confirmed.

"What?" Maya was perplexed. "I'm new to this, how should I know where to find a wand."

"Ah, good question," Mischief responded. "Because this isn't just any wand. This is your wand. So, only you can find it, and therefore, only you know where it is."

"But I don't know where it is?" Maya pleaded.

"Hmm, that could be a problem then. It can take years," Mischief replied.

"Years! I don't have years!" Maya protested, clearly outraged.

"Do you at least know where it isn't then?" Mischief teased. "That might narrow the field a bit."

Maya glared daggers at him.

Mischief let her stew for another few seconds, then reluctantly, in response to Granny's withering glare, decided to put Maya out of her misery.

"You alone must choose your wand. To do so, you must follow your mother's advice. It will lead you to your wand," Mischief explained.

Maya looked puzzled at first, then smiled to herself and muttered:

"Follow your heart," under her breath. As she did so, she felt for the heart shaped charm, on her neckless.

"Where would my heart take me, if I was looking for a wand?" she asked herself out loud, as she closed her eyes to concentrate.

Maya rubbed the delicate charm, between her thumb and forefinger.

"Follow your heart," she whispered again. Visualising her mum's face, through her mind's eye.

Maya smiled gently, as a memory came. A special place for all her family. A place where she'd played with her mum and dad often. Her cousins, grandparents, friends and aunts too. There was one day in particular, when she was younger, much younger. It was a warm day. Mum was smiling and content. Even Dad was behaving himself for once. She was no older than three or four years old. So, naturally, hide and seek was still the best game in the world.

Maya hid amongst the numerous tangled trunks of an impressive redwood tree, the 'peekaboo tree,' as it was then known. It grew by an old stone archway set in a fern covered grotto. She held her breath, not daring to breathe, in case it should give her away. Then, when her pray came into view, she sprang out to surprise her papa. Who obligingly fell to the ground and rolled around, as if dying of fright.

Culzean Castle walled garden, arch and spreading redwood 'peekaboo tree.'

"You've killed him, you little monster!" her mum had joked, grabbing her by the shoulders and whisking her off her feet, giggling through the air, before landing her on her back. Down came her mothers' lips, planting a loud tickly soggy wet raspberry on Maya's exposed tummy.

"I'll turn you into a frog, you little menace!" her mum had threatened. "This is where I got my wand and I'm not afraid to use it!" she'd announced, picking up a red wood twig and pretending to zap Maya into slimy amphibian form.

A memory, now made all the more pertinent, by recent magical revelations.

Mischief looked up, as Maya smiled and drifted further off into her memory. Between her fingers, the neckless charm glowed gently and Mischief and Granny exchanged knowing looks.

Maya knew the place. The place she'd find her wand.

"Where are we going then, little one?" Mischief asked gently, as Maya re-opened her eyes.

"Culzean castle... there's a walled garden there. That's where I'll find my wand too Mum," Maya replied, with tears welling in her eyes.

Culzean wasn't that far away, not as the broom flies and they would soon be on their way. But bellies were empty and that was no way to start another adventure. Granny conjured up a breakfast, the old-fashioned way. Pancakes and ice-cream for Maya, some fresh mint for Blue. Mischief tucked into some of Granny's leftover sausages, from the night before. Maya had tried to conjured him a platter of scarlet coloured fish, but without a wand, it didn't look right at all, and Mischief didn't touch it. On reflection, Maya knew it didn't really matter, it was just going to be another red herring anyway.

Maya, said her farewells to Granny in the back garden, where Blue was now waiting for her. Patiently munching his way through what remained of Granny's herb garden. Parting hugs complete, Blue carried them up into the skies. Maya directed him west, across the beach and onwards, out to sea, to avoid the perils of crossing the rivers which lay inland. Then, they tracked the coastline south, past Greenan Castle, the cliffs known as the Heads of Ayr and the picture postcard fishing village of Dunure. Eventually, as they flew over the sands of Croy beach, the impressive outline of Culzean Castle, loomed over the cliff tops on the horizon.

Culzean castle, Ayrshire

Blue soared high above the cliffs, then circled around the magnificent sandstone castle, before following a tree-lined path, which Maya knew led to the walled garden. Maya brought them in to land on a wide lawn, next to a greenhouse, sited within the impressive garden walls.

"A word of warning little one," Mischief announced, as they dismounted. "Your wand. It has to be the right one for you. Only you will know."

Maya nodded.

"But be wary. Don't be tempted by imposters," Mischief warned. "Dark forces are often drawn to young witchlings, especially as they seek out their wands... there's quite a black-market trade going in wands and magic spells these days. Some may try to trick you into verbal magical contracts, often for something much more valuable."

"Dark forces?" Maya probed, sporting a rather worried expression.

"Yes, keep your wits about you, little one, tricky things goblins," Mischief warned.

Maya just laughed. She wasn't falling for that one. There are no such things, she reassured herself. She wasn't going to be taken in, not by another of Mischief's wind-ups. Not today.

Maya knew Culzean well. She'd been a member of the young naturalists' club here, when she was younger and her family still visited often. Maya smiled to herself. Every time they took poor Grandma to Culzean, she would have to stop, caught short, and pee in the bushes. Her dad always delighted in announcing proudly to everyone in earshot, in a loud happy voice:

"Look everyone, a 'young' naturist!" Well, at least it made him chuckle anyway.

"This way," Maya announced confidently, marching Mischief on past the greenhouse. A structure that had always confused Maya, being constructed from glass and painted white wood.

"Why some idiot ever decided to call it a greenhouse, is beyond me. There's nothing green about it!" she complained.

Mischief just groaned and shook his head in exasperation.

Maya had played here often when she was younger, but now that she was a witchling in training, she wondered if things would be any different. She wandered around the gardens, with Mischief reluctantly trudging some way behind her. Cats, and Mischief especially, Maya concluded, really didn't do walkies.

Maya loved this place. It brought back many fond memories. As a small child, she could still recall playing peek-a-boo with her Papa, amongst the multiple trunks of the spreading redwood tree. Playing hide 'n' seek with her cousin Ollie too. Hours of fun, watching poor Ollie run in circles, from her hidden vantage point, high up in the old hollow fir tree. Dad would often pick her up and hide her inside it. Sometimes, he would even remember to come back and try to find her again.

They wandered around the walled garden for what felt like hours. Mainly because it was. Several times, they walked through the greenhouse, in and out of the old wooden cabin, with the moss-covered roof and on through the orchard. Looking for a wand, a magical twig or at least, a tempting looking stick. But nothing called out to Maya. No wands sought her out. No special looking sticks or twigs presented themselves as candidates for her magical wand. She found nothing special or unusual here, within the high walls of the garden, and Maya knew in her heart, that her wand, had to be special.

"Are you sure about this place, little one?" Mischief asked eventually. Maya didn't reply.

She too, was beginning to suspect that this might not be right place after all, and it was starting to get late.

As they passed the impressive multi-trunked redwood tree for the third time, Maya felt a sudden disturbing and unwelcome chill. A shadow fell momentarily over the dark rocky grotto. She shivered, more in fear than with cold, but the shadow lifted again quickly.

Wings beat suddenly through the air above them. Then a loud "Caw!" broke the silence, as a large black raven-like bird, flew off over the high red brick walls of the walled garden.

There, in the shadows of the grotto ahead, Maya now noticed a small crooked figure, with a peculiarly oversized head. It hobbled clumsily. Its face still hidden, obscured by the shadows. It had apparently, just started laying out, what looked like a second-hand stall.

"Watch out, it's a gobhoblin!" Mischief announced.

Maya was flabbergasted. Could it really be?

"Don't you mean a hobgoblin? Maya enquired.

"No, over-sized head, huge mouth and a nasty limp. No, that's definitely a gobhoblin!" Mischief confirmed. "Nasty things goblins! And that face... yuk, like a pug with a toothache, eating a toffee with a gravel centre!"

Maya laughed. She really wasn't sure if there was such a thing or whether this was just another one of Mischief's bad jokes, at the expense of this poor creature. But from its silhouette, it did appear to have a very big 'gob' indeed and also a pronounced hobble. So, a gobhoblin it was, Maya decided.

As they approached, Maya could now read the signs displayed on its stall, which read:

'Wand twigs for sale'... 'Nearly new witches' boots and britches' and 'Spell books.' There was even a sign offering to exchange, 'New witch's cats for old!'

"This looks interesting!" Maya teased, grinning broadly in Mischief's direction. Mischief turned away and raised his nose and tail into the air, in obvious disgust.

As the crooked figure turned around and stepped into the light, Maya realised that it was indeed, some sort of goblin. There was no mistaking this creature. It was straight out of a bad fantasy novel. A concept, that readers should be all too familiar with.

A grotesque cliché, with outsized features; nose and ears to match its enormous mouth. It was ugly... no really ugly! It looked as if it had:

"Fallen face first out the ugly tree and hit every branch on the way down!" as her dad used to say, whenever describing any of Mum's friends or work colleagues.

Maya's illustration of a Gobhoblin, age 8. "It looks like Daddy!"

Suddenly, the poor creature was pushed rather roughly out of the way, by a very handsome looking young gentleman, with neatly combed blonde hair. He was tall, but not that much older than Maya. He was all smiles and pearly white teeth and a dead-ringer for Maya's latest crush, out of the movies.

"Here's the eye candy. Careful now, don't trust him!" warned Mischief in a sideways whisper.

"Wand twig Miss? Nice plump ginger witch's cat, in exchange for your old scruffy black and white one?" grinned the handsome salesman, as they approached.

Mischief hissed his disapproval.

Maya couldn't hold back a smile, at her cat's expense.

Maya walked closer, to inspect the goods for sale, trying hard not to gaze longingly into the sapphire blue eyes, of this very attentive young gentleman. She could already feel herself starting to blush.

"Like a nice redwood twig Miss? Or a twig taken from that magic peek-a-boo tree, behind you?" the handsome salesman suggested. Then abruptly, he shoved the crooked little figure once more, as if to suggest, that it should demonstrate the wands. The gobhoblin dusted itself down obediently, then gestured. Pointing a dirty spindly finger and grubby fingernail towards a selection of twigs, which Maya presumed to be wands, laid out in front of them.

"Hmm…, we are looking for a wand, I suppose?" Maya replied uncertainly, though she really didn't much care for the treatment this young man was dishing out to the poor gobhoblin.

"Redwood, like your mum's Miss? Or dark, snot wood like her sister's?" the salesman enquired shiftily.

"Hm…. how much?" asked Maya.

Mischief stared daggers into her back.

"One spell Miss, that's all, for the redwood. But this one, finest snot wood, it is. It's worth a lot more Miss. But for a pretty face like yours. I is willing to give you a bargain. For you, it will cost you just one spell and the promise of the bottom of your shoe Miss, so I can repair her boots, see," the handsome salesman offered, whilst gesturing towards the gobhoblin's grotesque and painfully deformed bare feet. Which Maya now noted were covered in cold sores and blisters.

"My boots?" Maya asked, quite bemused by the young man's request.

"Just the base of them Miss. You can keep the rest. Magical sweat, you see. Not to be too indelicate Miss, but witchling sweat. Only

113

thing that'll soothe a poor gobhoblin's aching feet," the salesman replied, with all the sincerity of a tiger shark, on his first day supervising children's swimming lessons, at the local pool.

"But I would waddle like a duck, if I had no … sole… on… my… shoe," Maya stuttered, gathering her thoughts and looking increasingly suspicious. Mischief's warnings about dark forces ringing in her ears.

"I'll take an I.O.U. If you'll just sign here, Miss," the handsome salesman suggested, holding out a feather quill pen and turning a piece of parchment, covered in small print towards her. "Don't want you hobbling about, not like the lovely Samantha here."

"Samantha?" scoffed Mischief, under his breath.

Maya looked down briefly at the parchment, then back up into the eyes of the dreamy looking assistant.

"Those eyes," she accidentally whispered aloud and swooned visibly. Blushing, once more, Maya reached out her hand, as if to take the feather pen. The salesman smouldered, his best smoulder, in response. At the last second though, Maya pulled back her hand, pointed her index finger and shook it back and forth, as if to chastise the young man.

"No thank you," Maya scolded. "I don't think I want my wand twig to be **taken** away from any tree. Besides, that's not how you spell sole, as in the sole of a shoe anyway! I don't think I'll be trading away my **soul** today either, thank you very much!"

Then in a much gentler tone, Maya addressed the gobhoblin directly:

"But your feet do look cold and sore Samantha. And your feet, they do look to be about my size. So, you may have my boots."

Maya eased them off and handed them to the gobhoblin, who looked shocked and rather humbled, by this young stranger's generosity.

Maya marched on through the archway, trying hard not to grimace with pain, as she stepped gingerly on the sharp gravel path beneath her feet. She really hadn't thought this through, but Maya couldn't admit that now. Not in front of Mischief.

"I'm impressed, little one. You kept your wits about you. That took courage too," acknowledged Mischief, walking at heel for the very first time.

"You certainly told him. But why give the gobhoblin your boots?" Mischief asked.

"She needed them. Didn't you see her feet?" Maya replied.

"No, I looked the other way," Mischief replied.

"You must never look away, not when someone's in need. No matter what they look like, or how much easier it is," Maya replied, in a very matter of fact way.

Mischief felt humbled, ashamed, but above all, proud of his new friend. This little girl's a bit special, he thought to himself. Especially given her rather dodgy parenting.

Suddenly, Maya stopped in her tracks. Now transfixed and frozen to the spot, deep in thought. The tip of her tongue was racing around her lips, as if panicked, like a plump goldfish with a nosebleed, dropped into a tank of hungry piranhas.

"That wasn't here before!" she announced, squinting suspiciously at the magnificent oak tree, which now blocked their path.

Mischief had to agree. They'd not seen this tree before. Not on any of their numerous laps around the walled garden today. And, as a rule, trees generally stay pretty much where they're planted.

Maya was certain. If a tree like this had been here before, she'd never have tired of climbing through its tangled branches. She couldn't have forgotten this tree.

It was clearly ancient, twisted and bent out of shape. Its bark, deep and furrowed as a rhino's armpit. Its leaves though, still fresh and a vibrant green, though all around, the other trees had long since shed their leaves. Under the spreading boughs of this impressive gnarled giant, grew a carpet of out-of-season wild flowers and a single sapling, with just one new leaf.

Maya studied the little seedling closely. She somehow felt inexplicably drawn to this little sapling. It held her gaze. Maya couldn't express why, but something deep inside her connected with it. Somehow, she knew in her heart, that their fates were now entwined.

Maya, finally broke her gaze and looked up at the ancient oak. She cleared her throat, crossed her fingers and started to mutter to herself, nervously under her breath:

"Please, let me be right about this, please or the cat will never let me live it down, please, please, please."

Maya smiled nervously and addressed the tree politely:

"Hello?" she asked uncertainly.

There was silence. Maya could feel herself blushing. Silence, accompanied by yet more silence, was then served up with an excruciating large slice of extra quiet suspense, as a garnish on the side. Then, just as she was beginning to give up all hope, more silence arrived, as if to confirm her embarrassment still further.

116

Mischief was going to have a field day. She'd not live this down, not in a hurry.

Finally, as Maya's shame built to a silent deafening crescendo, a loud crack suddenly shattered the peace. Then a squeaky wooden creaking noise followed, as what looked at first like a narrow crevice, broke through the thick bark of the tree's trunk, about half-way up.

This widening crack, spread slowly across the full width of the ancient tree's trunk, then eventually opened wide, as if to yawn. It resembled something very old, creaky and wooden, slowly arising from its slumbers. A crooked smile, now appeared through the bark, on the trunk of this aged and crooked tree. Kindly, almost human features, now materialised from its thick bark. A bulbous bur for a nose and two oval knots, formed into eyes. Which blinked twice, with accompanying clicks, like made by a pair of delicate wooden castanets.

"He calls to you, doesn't he, my dear?" the tree replied, in a gentle old-lady voice.

"Mmm," Maya squeaked in acknowledgement.

"We've been waiting a long time for someone like you," the face in the bark responded.

"Like me?" Maya asked, rather puzzled.

"Your kindness to the gobhoblin. You did not judge her by her features, nor condemn her for her part in her master's trickery. You saw only that she was in need, and you did not turn away. It speaks of one who is indeed, pure of heart," replied the spirit in the ancient tree.

Mischief's furry jaw dropped in disbelief, hit the gravel path beneath and slapped him firmly across his whiskers, on the way back up.

"My sapling, why do you wish her help?" asked the tree.

"My mother, she's trapped... powerful magic has frozen her out of time, in Nedep's coven. There's an inscription. It says, she needs a pure coven or a living wand to free her, is...?" Maya couldn't finish her sentence. Her heart was in her mouth.

"A worthy cause, my dear. You may take her with my blessing. She has already bonded with you. I feel it, and I see more than a hint of destiny in your eyes," the tree responded reassuringly.

With those words, a slender bough dropped down, like an outstretched arm, as if gesturing towards the little sampling. Then the tree spirit yawned and closed its eyes once more.

"Thank you," Maya whispered gently.

Maya smiled, bent down and held out her hand, towards the little sapling. It began to wiggle and wriggle back and forth, as the earth crumbled around its base. Slender roots shook off the soil and wound themselves, one by one, around Maya's wrist. The delicate roots coiled around and tightened, as the sapling moved up, onto Maya's outstretched hand. Then, the little sapling cuddled up safe and secure, into the palm of her hand.

Maya knew she had her wand now. It had called to her. A living wand, no less. She beamed from ear to ear. Could this little sapling really be the key to releasing her mum from her timeless prison?

Mischief looked up at Maya, astonished and bemused.

 "You're going to be impossible now, aren't you?" he groaned.

"Yip!" Maya confirmed happily.

118

"What will you call her?" he added. "Please not another Wandy or Twiggy McTwigface?"

Maya paused, she stared down at the little magic sapling with a broad grin on her face, then asked it gently:

"If you're going to be my wand, I think I like 'Spell', do you?"

The little sapling's roots gripped her wrist tighter, as if to say, "Yes."

"Blue," she called and her brush flew down obediently to pick them up. "Thank you," Maya whispered softly to the ancient tree, "I'll look after her. I promise."

The tree's bark hinted at the faint trace of a smile, whereupon its wooden face faded, as if to sleep for another thousand years.

Maya beckoned her brush closer and climbed tentatively on board, carefully protecting her new found friend, cradled in her arms. Mischief too jumped on board behind her, still clearly dumbfounded and apparently for once, actually lost for words.

They rose up into the air and headed off homewards, back to the log cabin in the woods. Maya kept the little wand seedling warm, covered by her sleeve all the way back. She rode very carefully for once. She had a very precious cargo now. It was beginning to get colder and the light was fading, but Maya felt warm inside. She was already picturing the next full moon and a daring midnight rescue mission for her mum. She couldn't wait.

Back in the log cabin, Maya found a pretty little flowerpot and placed it on the bedside table. She filled it with soil from the herb garden outside and watered it. Mischief had stayed outside for a while, observing the local birdlife hungrily, but now followed her in and curled up on a comfortable red cushion in the corner to sleep. Spell moved gently from Maya's outstretched wrist and onto the pot, then snuggled her roots into the warm moist soil. Maya smiled to herself, as she slipped through the witch flap and back into the portal beyond.

Today had been a good adventure, she thought to herself, as she ascended the stairs back to the secret room. Stepping carefully through the mirror, Maya turned to greet the magic journal. It was already open and spoke first.

"You are full of surprises, little one!" the book wrote.

"I know, a living wand chose me! I don't believe it," Maya answered excitedly.

"I heard," the book responded, lifting its cover, as if to point to Mischief, apparently now sleeping, cuddled up on a comfortable red cushion in the corner. "You have the makings of slightly above average witch, Mischief tells me. But look after that wand of yours, its's special. Very special indeed!"

Maya frowned over towards Mischief:

"Average, eh? And how exactly, did you get here so quickly?" Maya asked her cat. Then, without waiting for a response, excitedly, she turned back to the book and asked:

"Do you think Spell could really help me to release my mum?"

"Definitely... perhaps," responded the mighty tome.

"Definitely... perhaps?" Maya parroted back anxiously.

"Once it's a little older and properly fired, of course," replied the book.

"Fired?" Maya asked, looking a bit concerned.

"To realise her full potential, she must be fired in a dragon's breath," the book explained. "All wands need fired, but a special wand like that, she needs fired in a dragon's breath. Besides, a certain cat tells me you may have aspirations of dragon riding one day."

"Dragon's breath?" Maya gasped, panic rising within her. "Mischief did say something about that before, but I was sure he was kidding. You are both kidding, right?" Maya pressed, now sporting a brow, furrowed deep enough for planting potatoes.

"I'm sorry, little one. You seem to have mistaken me for a portal guardian with a sense of humour," the journal wrote.

"Oh!" Maya winced. "Will it be dangerous?" she asked apprehensively.

"Oh yes," the book replied, in a matter-of-fact tone, "but, if you're prepared..."

"Prepared for what?" Maya interrupted.

"To track down dragons, of course," snapped the book, clearly not taking to Maya's habit of interrupting its explanations.

"I can't track dragons!" Maya complained indignantly.

"Yes, Mischief mentioned that might be a problem. So, while you were busy planting your new wand, in a pretty flowerpot. He was outside tweeting Granny with a messenger robin," announced the book.

"Granny?" Maya complained. "She's ancient... you can't send her out chasing dragons!"

"No, little one. Mischief requested that Granny ask Evaline, if she would be happy to show you the ropes tomorrow," wrote the book. "She's an excellent tracker, you know. So, if there are still any wild dragons out there, she's your best bet at tracking one down.

"Oh...," Maya sighed, with obvious relief. She was still buzzing with excitement though. Eagerly, Maya pressed the book once more:

"So, then, when Spell's been fired. Then I'll be able to release my mum, right?"

"Probably... I said, if you survive the dragons and when Spell is a little bit older too," cautioned her journal.

"Survive! What do you mean, **if** I survive? And older! How much older?" Maya demanded, her anxiety missing second and third and jumping straight into top gear.

"Two, maybe three?" the book replied.

"Hours? Days? Not weeks, surely not weeks?" Maya demanded anxiously.

"Hmm... no, I was thinking more in terms of years, little one. "Sorry," the book finally apologised, as Maya crumpled to the floor in despair.

A dragon's fire

Next morning, Maya was in a bit less of a hurry to get to the magic realm. Although, she desperately wanted to see Spell and Blue again, all the book's talk the evening before, of 'surviving dragons' and 'firing her wand' in a dragon's breath, had been running through her head all night. If it wasn't for one of Mischief's midnight combined cuddle-and-drool episodes, to take her mind off it, she might not have slept at all.

She'd tossed and turned all night long. To say that she had mixed emotions, about yesterday's adventure, didn't really do it justice. Her head was spinning. Elation at finding her first real wand, and a living wand at that. Fear, at the thought of tracking down a wild dragon. But most of all, crushing disappointment, at her book's assessment of the timescale it might take to develop Spell's powers, sufficiently to release her mum. Maya couldn't wait that long to wake her mother. She longed for the days, when all she worried about was French homework.

Maya was up bright and early, well before mid-day. Dad was already outside 'mauling the lawn' as her mum often called it. Inevitably, he'd do 'half-a-job,' leaving it unedged, patches missed and looking much worse than when he'd started. So, the coast was clear for now.

Maya made her way upstairs and unlocked the secret room with her neckless charm. Closing it behind her, she made her way over to the dressing table and sat down to open her journal. Maya broke a nervous smile, as Mischief jumped up onto the dressing table to meow hello, before dropping back down onto the floor once more.

"Where did you come from cat? I'd swear sometimes you can walk through walls," Maya laughed rather nervously. She placed the heart-shaped charm into the recess on the book's metal cross-straps, which sprang open, with a satisfying clunk. The magical book creaked open and began to write....

"Are you ready?" the magical tome enquired.

"Maya nodded," wrote the book.

"Packed a lunch and werewolf repellent?" her journal asked, obviously sensing her nervousness.

"Werewolf repellent!" Maya squeaked, in a high-pitched panicked voice, sounding like a dolphin, talking through helium, sucked from a party balloon.

"Sorry, couldn't resist it. Only kidding, besides the dragons ate the last of those bad boys years ago!" the book added, in a particularly uncomforting manner.

Maya laughed nervously and patted her lunch box.

"Best Café Ginger sandwiches," Maya boasted.

Maya walked over to the chest, accompanied by her faithful cat. Three small potion bottles sat on top of it, as usual. Mischief jumped up and circled the end bottle, before perching behind it. It had what appeared to be a curiously long thin egg shape, patterned with hexagons, drawn on its label.

"This one Mischief, why not?" Maya asked, whilst picking up the bottle and taking it over to stand in front of the full-length mirror. Staring into her own dusty reflection, Maya took a deep breath, clenched her buttocks for courage, bit down on her bottom lip and slowly opened the bottle.

Tentatively, Maya withdrew the cork stopper. Vibrant fountains of colour erupted from the little bottle and the room filled with every colour of the rainbow. As the room slowly returned to normal,

Maya tested the mirror nervously with her forefinger. It rippled like the surface of a magical upright 'wibbly-wobbly thingy' to her touch. Maya stepped forward into the mirror, then re-appeared from its back, accompanied by a tiny puff of white smoke. Mischief followed close on her heels, then led the way through the witch flap and down the narrow passageway without a word, as if he'd seen it all a thousand times before.

Maya pushed through the witch flap, at the other side of the portal, and entered into the cabin in the woods. Mischief was already there. Nestled down on a comfortable red cushion, in front of the log fire.

Maya smiled, as she walked over to the table, bent down and held out her hand, towards her sapling wand's overnight pot. She spoke gently:

"Good morning, Spell. Are you ready for an adventure today?"

Spell shook the soil off her roots, in response, and climbed carefully onto Maya's outstretched hand. Then wrapped her roots around Maya's wrist, squeezing it gently, as if to say, "Hello." Maya beamed down at the little sapling with affection, then followed Mischief out through the door and into the dappled shade of the abandoned railway line. The log cabin disappearing from view behind her.

Blue knocked his stable door off its hinges and whinnied with delight, as Maya walked towards the stables. She stroked his bristles and slipped him a peppermint. with a hole in it (somehow for a mint-munching brush, it seemed more appropriate than a sugar cube, for a treat). Maya led Blue out into the clearing, with a handful of freshly picked mint leaves, which she'd plucked from a nearby planter. Then, they all jumped onboard Blue. Mischief pulled a fluffy red cushion, from out of thin air and they took to the skies.

Right on cue, another brush appeared over the horizon and headed towards them. This was Evaline, Mischief explained. "Granny says she's an excellent tracker, she'll soon be on the trail of those pufflings." But didn't bother to explain what a puffling was.

"She's a powerful witch, not much older than you, but half feral, if you ask me," Mischief continued. "Spends more time hunting in the woods and playing in the fresh air, than she does on her mobile phone or tablet!"

Maya winced in shock and disbelief.

Evaline nodded, by way of a greeting. Maya could tell instantly, that she wasn't one for small talk. She was a formidable looking figure, for one so young. Slender, with long flowing auburn hair and Maya judged, probably about as tall as she was. She was dressed from head to foot, in what looked like animal skins, with a wooden bow swung over her one shoulder. There was an edge to this girl, an intensity in her eyes. Matted hair, dirty calloused hands, and muddy leather handmade boots, all spoke of the rugged and rather wild character, that Mischief had described.

"Dragons, is it?" Evaline opened the conversation.

"Pufflings," Mischief clarified in response. "She has a wand to fire."

"Really, aspiring dragon rider, are we?" Evaline smiled. "Brave."

"Am I?" Maya asked, turning back towards Mischief for reassurance.

Mischief nodded.

"That's right," Maya confirmed hesitantly. "He tells me you're a tracker?" Maya asked.

"Girl's gotta eat!" Evaline smiled, kicking her heels in and heading off inland.

126

"Eat… what in the name of Granny's cat, does she have to track down to eat?" Maya demanded, kicking her heels together, like she was riding a pony.

Mischief didn't reply. He was readying himself for Maya's next question. He didn't have long to wait.

"What did she mean… dragon rider?" Maya finally asked, whilst banking left to follow on Evaline's heels, as she headed them towards an impressive looking viaduct, that cut through the valley ahead.

"Plan B," Mischief replied, rather cryptically.

"What's plan B?" Maya probed suspiciously.

"It comes after plan A of course. I'll tell you later. For now, can we just focus on firing your wand and not hitting that… aaaah!" cried Mischief, as Maya banked left once more and then sharp right. Maya followed Evaline closely, as she zig-zagged through the arches of the mighty viaduct, just for fun.

Evaline wasn't wasting any time. Skimming over tree tops, ducking under low branches, even looping the loop for no reason other than to torment poor Mischief. Maya matched her every manoeuvre; turn for turn, loop for loop and swoop for swoop.

Maya was starting to enjoy herself. She strongly suspected, that she might have found a kindred spirit, in this Evaline girl… although probably with the exception of her taste in clothes and especially when it came to mealtimes.

They flew over a small village called Dalrymple, then on more purposefully for a while, following the road for a couple of miles, until they came to a fork. The fork seemed irrelevant, there was after all no matching knife or spoon, so they ignored the stray cutlery and carried on to where the road split two ways instead.

They flew south for a while. Maya couldn't help but notice a strange green glow coming from a pendant hung around Evaline's neck.

"What's that?" Maya asked curiously.

"Mum gave me that. Its glows, whenever I head south. Sort of a flying compass. I think," Evaline replied, producing a delicate green spherical pendant, hung from a chain around her neck.

"My mum gave me this too," Maya explained, showing off her neckless. But Maya didn't get the impression that Evaline was the sort who cared much for jewellery, nail painting or even brushing her own hair, for that matter.

Suddenly, Evaline veered downwards, entering a meandering river valley, which ran beneath. Maya recognised this place. Dad had brought her here often. Its treacherous steep paths were the perfect place to take his elderly mother for a tumble... "where there's a will!" he'd announce, letting her lead the way down the steeper sections.

It was near a place called Hollybush, on the banks of the River Doon. It was very picturesque, nestled in broadleaf woods and situated in a deep river valley, beneath a large country house. The shallow River Doon babbled over pebbles, then narrowed causing white water to cascade between roughly arranged lines of larger boulders. These had been set into the flow, to create fishing pools for the anglers, who often frequented this place. Upstream the dappled sunlight reflected off the surface, sparkling watery diamonds glinted in all directions and small winged insects swarmed just above the water's surface, playing Russian roulette with the fish, who's shadows circled in the pools beneath.

Evaline guided her brush along the narrow riverside path, crossing reed beds and brushing past numerous prickly ancient holly trees.

Finally, she slowed, bending forwards and leaning over the front of her brush, as if searching for tracks in the mud. Finally, she came to a stop, deciding to land next to a footbridge, which crossed over to a small island in the river.

"Are we there yet?" asked Mischief, finally opening his eyes, and waiting for his stomach to come in to land.

"I think so," Maya replied, hoping for some confirmation from Evaline.

Evaline though was silent and looked intense. She had already dismounted and was bent over, to inspect the dirt more closely. There were numerous jumbled animal tracks running in all directions.

"Anything?" Maya whispered instinctively, as Evaline crouched in front of them and slowly slid a bow from over her shoulder.

Evaline, still crouched, moved silently a few meters along the muddy path, before bending down to pick some fresh...

"Yuk!" gasped Maya, as Evaline pressed the dropping between thumb and forefinger, before bringing it up under her nose for a sniff, and finally pressing it to the tip of her tongue.

"Yikes!" Maya whispered. Aghast at this feral witch's behaviour.

"Five minutes... less perhaps," Evaline turned and whispered. Now, drawing her now rather disturbingly tanned forefinger to her lips to shoosh Maya's protestations. A single arrow slipped silently from the quiver, which hung over Evaline's left shoulder.

Evaline's head turned suddenly. Like she was a wild animal picking up on a scent, a noise... something. Maya couldn't tell what.

Silently, Evaline threaded her bow and raised it to her shoulder, drawing back its string to her eye in one movement. She turned slowly from the waist up, until her arrow was aimed straight at Maya's head.

"Wha...?" Maya didn't have time to respond. She froze to the spot and waited for her life to flash before her eyes, sure that she was about to meet her fate.

Woosh... Evaline unleashed the arrow, which shot over Maya's left shoulder. The draft tickling her cheek as it passed.

"Wha...?" Maya stammered in shock and outrage.

"Shot!" cried Mischief, apparently highly appreciative of Evaline's narrow miss.

Maya couldn't believe it. She turned and stared in horror. First at Evaline, who was now sporting a satisfied grin. Then, in disbelief, back towards Mischief, who was staring into the woods behind her. Maya followed his gaze. There, directly behind her and pinned to the trunk of a holly tree, hung a large hare, pierced through the heart by Evaline's arrow.

"Lunch," Evaline announced, with a proud grin, marching past Maya, to retrieve her prize.

Maya had packed her favourite Café Ginger prawn sandwiches, with all the healthy salad removed and replaced by salt and vinegar crisps and a family sized packet of marshmallows. Next to this feral warrior, she felt quite inadequate, all of a sudden. But equally as certain, that she'd not be sharing!

Maya turned the other way, as Evaline produced a knife and swiftly prepared her 'lunch'.

"So why exactly are we here?" Maya asked, turning to address her furry sidekick, so as to avoid watching Evaline's gruesome meal preparations.

"Because of the witch's wheel," Mischief replied.

"The what?" Maya, was really none the wiser, for his reply.

"The witch's wheel. This way, I'll explain on the way," Mischief replied, leading them off down the muddy path.

"Evaline, followed. A newly fashioned, furry and blood-stained pouch, now dangling from one end of her bow, which was slung once more, across her back.

"Quick witchstory lesson," announced Mischief. "Long ago in these parts, if you were accused of witchcraft. They strapped you to a granite stone, a wiccan table of old, and rolled it down that embankment on your left. If you landed face up... and survived, the logic was, you were a witch. Only magic, they reasoned, could have stopped it from tipping over, onto the heavier witch carrying side... so they burned you alive."

"A bit harsh!" Maya winced.

"If, on the other hand, it landed the other way, witch down... you were innocent. Well squished and very dead, but innocent."

"Oh, very fair!" Maya observed. "Anyway, what's that got to do with dragons?"

"Okay, dragons are magical creatures, right?" Mischief proposed.

"I suppose so, I've never seen one," Maya acknowledged.

"That's because you didn't have magic before, remember without magic, you can't see magic. So, even if one flew bye, you wouldn't have seen it," Mischief explained. "But there is a downside to being magical."

"Apart from the witch's wheel?" Maya interrupted.

131

"How do you think wild dragons top up their magic?" Mischief asked, with a particularly morbid smile. It could mean only one thing.

"No!"

"Yes."

"No!"

"Yes."

"No!"

"Yes… witch munchers, the lot of them!" Mischief finally confirmed.

"So, what are **we** doing here?" Maya demanded, looking around rather anxiously.

"Pufflings!" announced Mischief.

"Pufflings?" Maya pressed.

"If you're going to have any chance of firing that wand, without being eaten, we need pufflings," Mischief replied.

"Baby dragons," Evaline chipped in, sensing Maya's continued confusion.

"After a wheel toss or ten. With all those magical witch bits lying around; arms, legs, fingers and heads, scattered all the way up the hill… it was always a happy hunting ground for hungry young pufflings," Mischief explained, delighting in the look of horror on Maya's face.

"And the pufflings still come here, nowadays?" asked Maya. "Even though there's no witch wheeling?"

"Who told you they'd stopped?" Evaline asked, looking puzzled and walking straight past Maya, who was now transfixed and frozen to the spot with fear.

"She's kidding right?" Maya pleaded.

"Well, they don't get out much around here," Mischief apologised. "Rather old-fashioned in their beliefs and customs, the locals of Hollybush.

Maya heard herself swallow, but decided, on balance, it was probably all a wind-up.

"Here it is!" Mischief announced, as the path along the riverbank petered out.

"What?" Maya replied, looking around.

"The Holy Bush!" Mischief responded, pointing a paw towards an old ewe tree.

"That's not a holly tree?" Maya complained.

"No, who said anything about a holly tree," Mischief scoffed. "This is the Holy Bush."

With that Evaline pulled back the bough of a large ewe tree, to reveal a hand carved, not very round granite table. Maya stared at the stone and in particular, at the rather nasty looking brown stains pooled on top and dripping down its sides.

"Holy Cow!" Maya announced.

"No, Holy Bush. I told you," Mischief corrected.

"That's the witch wheel, isn't it?" Maya asked, rather sheepishly. "And those stains?"

"Yup!" Mischief confirmed, with a little bit too much morbid enthusiasm.

Maya suddenly felt quite sick. Was it all true?

Evaline however, was not so squeamish. She was already inspecting the dirt, once more.

"Anything?" Mischief asked.

Evaline shook her head, looking rather deflated.

"What do dragon footprints look like anyway?" asked Maya curiously.

Evaline chuckled, then looked her deep in the eye:

"It's said... they look exactly like, the last thing you'll ever see... alive!"

"Yi...!" but Maya had lost her, "Yikes!" with fright. She was now seriously spooked by this place.

"However, as a tracker, you're looking for tiny semi-webbed, crocodilian scaled tracks, three front facing digitals, with carpal padding and non-retractable talons, four if they're polydactyl. One rear facing proximal claw, highly pronounced," Evaline announced.

Maya just gazed back open mouthed.

"Oh, and digitigrades too.... they carry most of their weight on the front of their foot, on the pads, especially for combat or take-off," Evaline clarified, picking up on Maya's blank expression.

"Okay, Evaline seems to have a reasonable handle on the basics of dragon tracking. I propose, she leads for a while," Mischief suggested, adopting the safe middle position, between the girls, as they set off in search of pufflings.

They tracked silently through the woods by the river. Well, Evaline and Mischief moved silently. Maya stood on every brittle twig or patch of dry rustly leaves. She dislodged loose stones and stumbled clumsily over tree roots, whenever they presented themselves. Each time, much to Evaline's obvious disgust and growing irritation. They followed a muddy path through the woods. There were lots of interesting animal footprints. Evaline was soon in her element...

"Deer, fox, weasel, rabbit...," Evaline announced, in a whisper as she picked up on nearly invisible tracks leading off through the undergrowth. No pufflings though, not a trace.

After an hour or so, Mischief decided to take over and show Evaline, exactly how it should be done. Much to her obvious displeasure.

Her commentary however, soon resumed. Delighting in announcing, all of the trails that Mischief was now missing. Mischief chose to ignore her.

"Weasel, red deer, roe deer, more deer and then eventually, as Mischief continued, not to take the hint, came; "Oh dear!"

"What?" Maya asked excitedly.

"This one's a 'crabbit' pussy cat!" she snorted with laughter, as she 'accidentally' trod on Mischief's tail for, some long overdue revenge.

Evaline turned to Maya smirking, as a hissing black and white furball shot up the nearest tree.

"Payback time!" she whispered, under her breath.

Maya snorted with laughter.

After a couple more hours of hard tracking, following the banks of the river and up and down the steep hillside, they stopped.

135

"Where are the pufflings?" Maya asked out loud, her frustration growing. Evaline just shrugged her shoulders. They circled back downhill towards the little island, near to where they had first landed. Evaline led them to a small footbridge, decorated with pebbles, set into its concrete foundations. Pulling back some of the branches, by the side of the bridge, Maya uncovered a sign. 'Pirates Island,' it read.

Maya was getting weary and looking forward to taking the weight off her feet. They crossed the footbridge to the island beyond. There was a small clearing and a picnic table on the other side, but there was still no sign of any pufflings.

"Good place for lunch?" suggested Mischief, handkerchief tied around his neck and licking his lips, as a can of red herring opened itself in his outstretched paw. Maya sat down to feast on her sandwiches and offered Evaline first choice. Maya didn't mind going hungry, if it meant she could discourage Evaline from tucking in to her own 'packed lunch.'

"What are those?" enquired Evaline curiously.

"Sandwiches... stupid girl!" scoffed the cat, still sore at her earlier 'crabbit pussycat' jibe and 'accidental' tail stomp.

"No, those..., over there!" Evaline insisted, pointing to the base of a large 'monkey puzzle' tree. Getting to their feet slowly, the little group made their way over towards a collection of tiny muddy footprints. As they approached, they could see a trail of tiny crocodile-like footprints meandering towards and then disappearing into the undergrowth. Every so often, the bushes smouldered and hot orange and black embers floated on the breeze, as if freshly scorched.

"Baby dragons?" Maya speculated.

"Pufflings," corrected Mischief.

"Caw, caw, caw!" came a loud call, from high up in the branches of the impressive 'monkey puzzle' tree.

As if in response, an unwelcome chill filled the air. A huge dark winged shadow descended from the skies above and enveloped the small island.

"Down!" Evaline whispered, grabbing Maya down onto her haunches then pulling a fir tree branch firmly down over their heads for cover. They huddled together, motionless and terrified. Maya's eyes closed tight in fear. Mischief cuddled in too, shivering with fright. Above their heads, they heard a 'whooshing' noise, accompanied by a chill downdraft, that froze them to their very cores.

After a moment or two of complete silence, Maya opened her eyes. Mischief too, started to dust himself down. Shivering with cold and still shaken, the little group emerged from their hiding place. Freshly laid frost glistened and hung from every branch and leaf.

"What was that?" asked Maya, shaking and wide-eyed, as a bush baby after a double espresso.

"Close, too close!" Mischief replied shakily. "That blooming bird nearly gave us away!"

"Wild dragon. Big one!" Evaline confirmed.

"Best get that wand of yours fired soon. You'll need a proper wand, if that thing finds us!" Mischief warned, looking deep into Maya's terrified eyes.

"They've gone!" Evaline gasped.

Maya turned, following Evaline's gaze, towards the base of the monkey puzzle tree. The footprints had vanished, as if the down draft from the mighty beast's wings, had scoured all traces of its offspring from the earth. The embers were out too, the trail of tiny footprints had been erased. The trail had, quite literally, gone cold.

Evaline then explained in great detail, how certain types of wild dragons, will often conceal, the tracks their young leave. Only during their first and most vulnerable weeks. "Frosting," she called it. Maya felt frosted alright. Chilled to her very core.

The puffling search continued, though without any further success. They scoured the little island, but found no further trace of the pufflings' trail.

Hour after hour, the girls squelched through the mud looking for more dragon prints. Evaline found a fox and a badger print, even a three-legged newt, which she said was called Tiny, but no trace of a dragon.

"How do you know its name's Tiny?" asked Mischief curiously, falling straight into Evaline's trap.

"Because he's, **my newt**!" Evaline and Maya laughed back in unison. Dad often used that one, but as all teenagers know. It's only funny when someone your own age tells it.

Mischief just groaned.

The members of the 'dragon trackers gang,' as they were now calling themselves, eventually sat down wearily, right back where they had started, several hours before. Maya took a marshmallow from her bag.

"What's that?" asked Evaline.

"Marshmallows... little sugary clouds of...," Maya stopped mid-sentence, as she passed one thoughtfully to Evaline.

"Hmm...," Maya's tongue was out, testing the air. Seeking out inspiration on the breeze. She was on to something.

"That's it!" she announced suddenly, her tongue starting to flicker in and out of her mouth, like a greedy kitten with a saucer of cream.

"What's what?" asked Evaline.

"The clouds!" announced Maya, "We've been looking in the wrong place! Dragons fly, of course!"

"What do dragonflies have to do with anything?" asked Mischief.

"No, dragons fly, not dragonflies! We need to look in the clouds!" Maya corrected him, suddenly gazing skyward.

"Your head's obviously already there," Mischief muttered under his breath.

"Blue," Maya called impatiently, choosing to ignore his jibe.

Blue was close-by. With an enthusiastic 'swoosh,' Maya's brush came in to land. Evaline too summoned her own brush, with a barely audible whistle. There was no further objection, to this sudden change of plan though. They were all getting tired and frustrated and a change of tack, seemed in order. Soon enough, they were all in the air, soaring high above, what a large white sign, now informed them was the Hollybush estate.

"There!" cried Evaline, pointing excitedly, to a cloud with a faint hole in the middle. A hole made by something in flight, Evaline explained. Then another... and another... and another. She really was an excellent tracker, even in the air.

They followed the trail through the clouds, like a tongue following a trail of giant polo mints.... except the clouds were not minty and the brushes weren't very tongue-like. Still, the author stuck stubbornly with this dodgy visual simile. They were soon many miles away from where their search had begun. Eventually, they found themselves heading out over the sea. After a few miles, the trail led them to an offshore island. Maya recognised its rugged outline. It was Arran. In the distance, low clouds enveloped an impressive mountain summit. Maya was familiar with that too. She'd often refused to climb it with her dad. When it came to unnecessary physical exercise, she was quite sure, that she was in fact, half cat.

"Goatfell!" Maya announced.

"Off what?" Evaline joked.

"Goatfell, the mountain," explained Maya. "It's the big one."

As they cleared the low cloud, Arran's picturesque coastline also came fully into view.

It was beautiful, the sun was starting to set. Maya lapped up the view. Marmalade skies, turned blood orange with a hint of blueberry jam, as the sun dipped behind sugar-topped mountains. Now, viewed from the marshmallow clouds, it was even more spectacular. Somehow the view, was making Maya feel hungry again.

The last in the long line of fluffy polo mint clouds, hovered low above the impressive Glenashdale Falls, on the south end of the island. Blue swooped down over the giants' graves (a bunch of silly old stones, Maya's dad calls such 'hysterical arty-facts'). They landed on the visitor's viewing platform; a large wooden structure overlooking the imposing waterfall.

The view of the falls was spectacular, as water cascaded over the cliff and crashed onto the rocks beneath, raising clouds of mist high up into the air. But nobody was looking at the scenery. They were looking for dragons, or pufflings or footprints. Looking for something, anything.

After a couple of minutes, Evaline was the first to speak:

"The trail's gone cold again, hasn't it?" she sighed.

"Maybe not," Mischief corrected her, rather smugly. "The more observant trackers amongst us, would surely have noticed a tell-tale sign. There, see. A furball!"

"What?" asked Evaline, sounding rather confused.

"Isn't it obvious, well to any talented animal tracker?" Mischief replied, turning up the volume on his usual air of superiority and sarcasm.

"What?" Evaline whined, at the infuriating cat.

"For those of a you with a limited vocabulary and observational skills," Mischief pronounced, in his most superior and arrogant tone yet. Then, after another pause for effect, he began to explain:

"Down there, fur-ball, on rocks, behind the falls. Don't you see it?"

The girls' eyes strained and followed Mischief's outstretched paw. Sure enough, a disgusting looking ball of fur and fish-bones, clung to the side of a rock, just visible through the mist and cascading water.

"So?" Maya prompted him.

"So," Mischief continued. "Everyone knows that cats are sensible creatures. Cats hate water. So therefore, any cat near a waterfall, must be a witch's cat. No cat would choose to be here, not unless they were on witch-sitting duty."

Mischief paused for reluctant nods of approval from his audience, who had decided to go with him on this, so far.

"Everyone knows that dragons eat witches. Also, that cats, being highly sensitive creatures, as we all know, tend to bring up fur-balls,

141

when watching their witch being munched alive by dragons!" Mischief announced in his best matter-of-fact way. "So, therefore, logically speaking, the dragon's lair is behind the falls, directly above the furball. Obvious really?"

"What?" squeaked Evaline.

"What?" squawked Maya.

"What's wrong?" objected Mischief, rather defensively.

"Rewind pussy cat!" screeched Maya, "Dragons eat witches. I thought you were kidding?"

"Of course not, why else did we bring a dragon slayer?" Mischief replied and gestured towards Evaline.

"What?" squeaked Evaline.

"What?" Maya squealed.

"What?" replied Mischief, rather defensively.

"Nobody said anything about dragon slaying!" Evaline scolded, glaring at Mischief, with daggers in her eyes.

"Oops, really? I'm always forgetting that bit," Mischief replied, looking back with large ashamed: please-love-me-because-I'm-so-cute-and–furry eyes.

There then followed a prolonged moody silence. One that all women, of whatever age, master instinctively. A look that no man or suddenly very unpopular male pussy-cat, can ever tolerate for more than a few seconds, before averting their eyes.

"Let's check it out anyway," Maya conceded eventually. "We're here now, what have we got to lose?"

"A furball?" Mischief muttered under his breath.

"Not helping pussy cat, really not helping!" scolded Maya, now shaking visibly with fear.

"But your magic, you can't cross running water remember," Mischief interrupted, changing the subject quickly.

Maya's tongue was out again though, foraging around her lips, sniffing out inspiration, like a pig on a truffle hunt, she was on to something.

"Not crossing…, just going out to the middle and coming back the same way," Maya corrected nervously.

"A technicality…, but yes, clever girl, it just might work?" Mischief conceded.

Maya edged Blue tentatively into the air and then cautiously and very slowly, out over the edge towards the waterfall. Evaline followed equally as warily.

"Or we might all die horribly, smashed to pieces on the rocks beneath, before the dragons eat us anyway," added the cat.

"Tell him to stop!" Evaline shouted.

Maya led them out towards the waterfall and Blue hovered in the spray, facing the impressive cascade, not quite half way across.

"Hold on!" Maya cried.

"You're not thinking, what I think, you're thinking?" Mischief enquired. Suddenly, he was the one who was worried.

"Unfortunately, I think, I am!" declared Maya.

Suddenly, with a dig of Maya's heels, Blue lurched forward and they crashed through the waterfall. They were soaked. Evaline followed, emerging drenched and bedraggled, through the foaming deluge.

143

Mischief hissed. Now resembling a half-drowned water rat, he shivered in equal measures with shock and cold. He was not impressed!

"Cats don't do water! You know cats don't do water! I'm quite sure that the dragons fly around the waterfall, not through it!" Mischief added, in a very disgruntled tone.

"Oops, 'm I bad?" replied Maya, managing a nervous, but well satisfied grin. He had deserved that one, even if it came at the cost of a good soaking for herself and Evaline, it had been well worth it.

As their eyes adjusted to the dim light and spray behind the falls, they could just make out a rocky ledge and what appeared to be the entrance to a cave. A dim red light flickered from deep inside.

"Yuk…. what's that smell?" asked Evaline, covering her nose with her hand.

"Dragon's breath," Maya replied, "I'd recognise it anywhere. Dad tells Mum she has it, first thing in the morning after a curry and a chardonnay or two."

"Your mum has wine and curry for breakfast?" Evaline gasped. "Mine too!"

Maya didn't bother to correct her. She was too preoccupied with the red glow, coming from within the cave. Was she really foolhardy enough, to risk taking them into a witch munching wild dragon's lair? But Maya also knew, that if she was ever going to have the power to release her mum, she needed to fire her wand properly. And for that she needed dragons.

Maya edged Blue forward, then landed them on the slippery rocky ledge. Evaline followed. They all dismounted, very slowly, taking great care with every step. A fall here, they all knew, would be lethal. Blue was spooked. Mischief was spooked. Even Evaline looked spooked. Maya tried to reassure her brush, with a nervous pat on the bristles, but her hands were shaking too. She was just as spooked as everyone else.

"Come on in, don't be shy!" boomed a friendly voice from inside the cave, "We've been expecting you."

"Expecting us?" Maya whispered, turning anxiously to face Evaline; "How?"

"Come on in, don't be afraid little witchlings," boomed the voice again.

"Should we?" Maya asked nervously.

"No dragon's fire out here," replied Mischief.

"Good point," Maya conceded reluctantly.

Slowly, the nervous party edged its way along the ledge and into the cave. Inside, huddled around a fire, stood a very impressive looking huge red dragon. Its head adorned with long rapier sharp horns, fangs not out of place in a Jurassic Park movie, yellow piercing eyes and its wings, folded by its side. For all his fearsome features, his manner seemed friendly enough.

Behind him and curled around a roaring fire was a smaller green dragon, she looked as if she might be a lady dragon; judging by her long lashes and proximity to what looked like a giant tartan handbag. She appeared to be protecting a nest, containing two tiny sleeping hatchlings and a clutch of curious looking bronze-coloured eggs with hexagonal markings.

"Pufflings," whispered Mischief.

Somehow, the eggs looked strangely familiar to Maya. Now she understood.

"Like on the potion bottle," she whispered back to Mischief, nodding towards the strangely patterned eggs.

"Come in, sit by the fire…, dry yourselves. You all look cold and wet," the huge red dragon spoke gently, in a kind and reassuring tone.

Were these really the fearsome witch-munching monsters, she'd been warned of? Maya asked herself.

"How did you know we were coming?" asked Evaline.

"With this nose. I'm afraid we picked up your smell quarter of an hour ago," replied the mighty red dragon, gently tapping his impressive talons to the end of his long snout. "Not to be indelicate, but your cat really needed that wash!" the dragon chuckled with a slightly toothy grin.

"Cheek!" hissed Mischief.

"Don't be afraid," the green dragon reassured them. "We lit you a fire. We thought you might need that little wand twig of yours fired?"

"Why yes, but …., but, don't you …, I mean, do you, em …?" Maya stammered, not knowing how to ask the question.

"Eat witches?" the large red dragon interrupted, with another reassuring chuckle. "No, these days our diet has changed somewhat. Do you witches still eat frogs and snails?"

"You don't, do you?" gasped Maya, turning to stare accusingly, long and hard into Evaline's eyes.

"No!" Evaline rebuffed her sharply, sounding rather offended. "Not unless the hunt fails."

Maya just glared. Surely, she was kidding?

146

"Come on in, sit by the fire, warm yourselves and tell us your story," said the green dragon, gesturing them towards the fire with her wing. "As you can imagine, we don't get many guests around here."

The girls smiled and started to relax. The fire was welcoming and the dragons did, for now at least, appear to be friendly.

"So, if you don't eat frogs and snails, then what do young witchlings eat these days?" enquired the large red dragon, in a joking manner.

"We love these," Maya replied, grabbing a handful of marshmallows from her bag. She reached inside her jacket pocket for Spell, who clasped her roots around Maya's wrist, to hold on tight.

Evaline gasped, as Maya pulled out the fragile looking living wand.

"May I?" Maya asked Spell. "If you're going to be fired here, then we might as well have them toasted."

Toasted marshmallows, after all, are nearly as good as pancakes. Maya gently threading a couple of marshmallows onto the end of Spell. As she skewered the last one, she winked towards Mischief.

"Nice enough now, but when toasted over a dragon's fire…, delicious!" she added.

"So, what are you dragons eating these days, then?" Evaline asked, awkwardly trying to making polite conversation.

The impressive red dragon stood again, stretched and yawned sleepily before replying;

"Well, my dear," he started, circling around in front of the cave entrance. "These days we don't get many witchlings…, so we have to make do with their cats too. More roughage you understand.

147

Good for the bowels and the bones are excellent for our pufflings' scale development apparently."

There was a loud "slap!" followed in close succession by two more, as Maya's jaw bounced off the dirt floor. Followed closely in turn by Mischief's and Evaline's.

"Sorry, really I am, but the rest of the pufflings are about to hatch and their mother, well, she hasn't eaten for nearly an hour," the red buck dragon apologised insincerely, grinning broadly and looking over towards a small pair of smouldering witchling boots on the other side of the cave.

With those words, the fearsome red dragon started to draw a deep breath.

"Run!" shouted Maya, pushing Evaline to the side of the cave and raising Spell defensively. But it was too late.

"No!" shouted Mischief, as flames leapt from the red dragon's nostrils and mouth engulfing Maya in a ball of fire. The flames roared on and on and on. Evaline, for all her courage, froze helplessly to the spot.

Maya was gone.

Mischief turned his head to look away, as smoke and a sickly-sweet toasting smell, filled the cave. The dragon's flames carried on and on mercilessly and the ball of flame grew larger and larger, as if the dragon had decided to roast poor Maya's body in front of them. It was too horrible. Evaline was frozen to the spot with fear and in shock. She knew that she would be next. Tears welled in her eyes as she watched, transfixed and helpless, unable even to turn away.

The fireball grew still larger and stated to glow with a silvery white, then multi-coloured light. Brighter and brighter the ball of fire and light grew and slowly, very slowly the wall of flame started to recede back towards the mighty red dragon.

There emerging from the centre of the flames, standing proud and defiant, holding Spell aloft, was Maya. Spell had been fired in a wild dragon's breath. Maya had a proper wand now, not just a magical sapling, not any more. Spell, now a true living wand, glowed silver and bright, except for three rather over baked, sweet-smelling and blackened marshmallows. Spell's powerful magic pushing the dragon's flames back, inch by inch. Flames billowed around Maya, as if deflected by a mushroom shaped magical forcefield. Maya with her long blonde hair, looking rather bedraggled and singed, was still very much alive. A picture of concentration and determination, willing back the flames.

Eventually, the fearsome buck dragon took a breath and the wall of fire suddenly receded backwards, towards it. As the flame reached the end of the dragon's snout, there was a loud pop and momentarily, fire filled the whole room. Then the flames were gone. The dragon's flame was out. The ensuing pressure wave, saw Mischief, Evaline and the green mother dragon, all blown backwards against the cave walls.

Splat! Splat! Two enormous globs of dragon's ear wax shot out from the large red dragon's ears and splattered, firstly one way, off the wall, then half a second later, it hit. Evaline full on!

"Yuk! Double yuk!" screamed Evaline. There she stood, motionless, face blackened, hair swept straight upright, waxed into position and smouldering. She was covered, head to foot in thick yellow dragon's ear wax and soot.

"Yuk, yuk-yukety-yuk- yuk!" Evaline protested once more.

"Oh dear," gasped Maya.

"She's a candle!" sniggered Mischief.

Maya tried hard not to laugh, but the cheeky cat did have a point. Poor Evaline, did look very much like a very well melted and rather sooty church candle, smouldering in the gloomy light of the cave. Her long auburn hair, now waxed into a vertical wick, by the blast.

Both dragons were now cowering back against the walls fearfully.

"They're afraid of you now Maya. Are you going to finish them off?" enquired Mischief.

"No! Why would I do that?" Maya scolded him.

"Just the way it is," Mischief explained. "Dragons eat witchlings for their magic, but more especially, so they don't grow up to be witches. That's because witches turn dragons to stone. So, in turn, they don't eat more witchlings. Dragons don't even like the taste that much, apparently," he added. "That's why they toast their witches so thoroughly."

The red buck dragon nodded timidly in agreement, still cowering against the wall.

"That's just silly!" Maya snapped, "And gross!"

At that moment, a crack came from the dragon's nest, directly in front of them. One of the bronze-coloured eggs had cracked and was now wobbling back and forth.

"It's hatching!" Maya gasped.

They watched in amazement, as the top of the shell slowly lifted off, in a perfect hexagonal. First a claw, then a little purple nose emerged. Two oval yellow eyes opened wide. Maya bent down, as the miniature purple puffling shook the shell off its head and slowly unravelled a tiny pair of perfect, nearly transparent, gossamer wings. Maya held out her wand, pointing it towards the little puffling. The smaller green dragon looked away, fearing the worst. She couldn't bring herself to watch now.

"Go on then," Maya encouraged gently. The tiny puffling shuffled forwards, towards Spell and started to sniff the toasted treats on the end of Maya's wand. A curious red forked tongue appeared and started to lick, gently at first. Soon, the tiny puffling, began to nibble hungrily on one of the toasted marshmallows. In next to no time, it had finished off the whole thing and let out a rather delicate satisfied burp, accompanied by a miniscule puff of white smoke. Its perfect forked tongue, then slurped every last morsel from its sticky, scale-covered lips.

Maya was now smiling so broadly, that the back of her head was in serious danger of unzipping and tumbling off, down her back. Now, with a flick of her wrist and Spell. Maya sent the remaining two marshmallows into the air, where they hovered, as if carried on a magic breeze, which of course they were. One flew in the direction of each of the adult dragons.

Tentatively, the huge red dragon, followed by the smaller green one, nibbled on the strange new food, then gulped it down. There was a short pause and a loud slurping noise, as the red dragon licked its, now rather blackened, lips.

"Not bad, not bad at all!" he declared appreciatively.

Maya had realised, that she didn't exactly know where marshmallows came from, but that didn't matter. She had a plan. Maya raised Spell once more and demanded;

"Marshmallow trees please!"

From that day on, marshmallows grew on trees. Well, they did in this dragons' cave anyway. Marshmallow bushes of all varieties (both white and pink) sprouted from the walls and every corner of the dank cavern. Maya was rightfully rather proud of her impromptu interior decoration.

"No more eating witchlings or their cats, agreed!" Maya demanded, pointing Spell at the big buck dragon.

"Agreed," the dragon conceded, cowering rather meekly.

"Thank you for sparing us," the green dragon spoke gratefully. "Our hatchling, will you name him?"

Maya looked down at the little dragon, with a broad cheesy grin. Its big yellow eyes looked up at her affectionately and he blinked three times.

"Go on then," said Mischief. "Name him and he'll be bonded with you for life."

"Bond with a dragon and you may ride him, when he's a bit bigger of course," a very waxy Evaline added.

"Wow! My very own dragon," Maya gasped. "I can't believe it. If you like it, I think I'll call you Blink?"

The tiny puffling looked up approvingly and rubbed up against her shin. Maya picked him up and gave him a cuddle, before returning him gently to the mother dragon.

"Can I visit? Soon please?" Maya asked.

"I think he would like that," the green dragon replied, with a smile, nudging the little puffling back into the nest and curling her tail around her clutch of eggs and pufflings, to keep them warm.

"Can we go home now?" asked Evaline rather sheepishly, still smouldering in the corner… "I think this wax has begun to set!"

Maya tried not to laugh.

Mischief didn't.

All the way back to Evaline's tent, on the outskirts of Fullerton Woods, it was one candle gag after another…

"Evaline, can you shine a light on something for me? Evaline, please stop smouldering! I thought we were going to be snuffed out back there. Take your jacket off Evaline, you must be melting!" Mischief teased her relentlessly.

"Mischief, stop that!" Maya scolded. "Can't you see you're getting on her wick!" Maya just couldn't help herself.

Evaline was very quiet and as intense as ever, hardly responding to the constant jibes. She was starving and looking forward to roasting her earlier kill over an open fire for her dinner, much to Maya's disgust.

"She's hungry and 'set' in her ways, you might say?" Mischief observed, with one last parting shot.

"Poor Evaline," smirked Maya, as she watched her new friend waddling through the front flap of her animal skin tent. "Do you think she'll be able to chip her way out of all that wax?"

"No need, she'll probably just melt down in front of her fire. She should be out in a couple of days," scoffed Mischief. "Time we were getting you home too... it's a big day tomorrow."

With that, Blue took off again and they flew home, across the sea, through the fading light. Guided by the faint orange glow from Ayr's streetlights in the distance.

"Strange though, don't you think?" Mischief started.

"What?" Maya asked curiously.

"Almost as if those dragons were expecting us," Mischief explained.

"They were, thanks to your rather pungent aroma," Maya teased.

"Yes, funny that. Yet we were flying into the wind, all the way there!" Mischief responded. "That's some sense of smell, even for a dragon! Don't you think?"

"Oh!" Maya replied thoughtfully. She wasn't at all sure what to make of that. Had they been set up? On reflection, how did the dragons know that they were there to get her wand flamed? Maya couldn't help but think that something or someone had given them away too, just as they were closing in on the pufflings. No, Maya told herself, she was just being paranoid. Although, as her dad used to tell her, it's not really paranoia, if they are all out to get you!

Soon enough, they were back safe in the log cabin, on the old abandoned railway line. Blue was fed and bedded down for the night in his stable and Mischief snuggled down onto his comfortable red cushion to sleep. Maya walked over to Spell's overnight pot, to let the little wand uncoil her roots and bed down for the night.

"Thanks Spell, you were awesome today," she said, as the young sapling bedded down for the night. Slowly, Spell bent over in her pot, as if to take a bow.

Maya opened the witch flap and with one final satisfied glance back at her sleepy companions, she slipped into the portal. She followed the light of the glitter worms up the stairs, but suspected that this grin of hers would have illuminated the way back, without their help.

Back in her mum's secret room again, Maya stepped back through the mirror and sat down in front of the grumpy old book, exhausted but happy. Somehow, Mischief had beaten her back and was circling another comfortable red cushion in the corner of the room. Maya shook her head in disbelief and snorted loudly, instead of the intended chuckle.

"I swear you can walk through walls cat!" she sighed.

"Well done," the book spoke slowly, its words writing across the page, as it did so. "Mischief told me, that you showed real courage and compassion today. Perhaps you do have the makings of a fine young witch."

Maya grinned proudly.

"But why, oh why did you take on fully grown dragons? Nobody, in their right mind, takes on a fully grown dragon!" the book chastised her.

Maya looked puzzled.

The book appeared to sense her confusion, replying:

"Surely, Mischief told you? Every other witchling I've ever met, simply fired their wands in a bonfire."

"Mischief reckoned we needed a dragon's fire, you know for a living wand," Maya explained.

"Hardly necessary, if you ask me. But rekindling the embers on a pufflings' trail or dragon's kill or even simply gathering the ashes from their cave, when they clean it out every morning, it's usually pretty straightforward," wrote the book.

"What?" Maya gasped, glaring at the guilty furball, curled up in the corner of the room, snuggled into his comfortable red cushion for cover. One paw, now clasped over his head, pretending to be sound asleep.

"Oops," Mischief muttered to himself.

Quickly, as if to save her cat's blushes, the book changed the subject.

"You've done well today, little one. Very well. Your wand is strong now. Perhaps stronger than any I have ever met before. But still, I fear you may not yet possess the skills you'll need, to release your mother from her sleep," warned the book.

Maya slumped at its words, but she had suspected as much, from the book's earlier warnings.

"You need practice. So, I have a special challenge in mind for you tomorrow. If I'm right, maybe, just maybe… hmm, I wonder?" the book pondered out loud.

Maya was about to ask what, but the book spoke again, bringing their discussion to an abrupt stop, before she got a chance.

"Get some rest, little one. We can talk about it in the morning. If you're still feeling up for a challenge?" the book asked, whilst closing its covers for the night.

Transformation spells

Morning broke and used its jagged edges to chased the moon over the horizon. Maya recognised the tell-tale signs. An orange fiery ball rose up into the sky and it wasn't dark any longer. Sunday morning, no school. It was only a couple of weeks until Christmas, but it didn't feel much like Christmas, not without her mum. Dad hadn't even put up a single decoration. Let alone a tree.

Maya though, was full of excitement. She knew, she was making progress. More than that, she had fired her own living wand in a wild dragon's breath. Maya had felt Spell's power running through her, when she'd confronted the wild dragon. It was awesome. Now she truly believed, that Spell, someday soon, would have enough power to release her mum. The wait, however was agonising. How she wanted her mum back for Christmas. No, Maya needed her mum back for Christmas.

Maya was soon bounding up the stairs. Intrigued to find out what this mysterious challenge, that the book had suggested the previous day, was all about.

As she entered the room, her eyes were immediately drawn to the chest in the corner. She could clearly see, that there were three potion bottles on top of it, as usual. Today though, something was different. Today they all had badly drawn animals scrawled onto the labels. On each of the bottles, were pictures of what looked like an eagle, a wolf and... Maya gasped with excitement... a snow leopard. She loved snow leopards.

Apparently:

"They're.... soooo fluffy!" Maya exclaimed, hardly able to contain her excitement.

Eagerly Maya made her way over to the book and placed the heart shaped charm into the recess on the lock, where the book's metal straps joined. It sprung open as usual and her journal greeted her.

"Morning, little one. Up bright and early for another adventure, are we?" the book wrote.

"Yes please!" Maya confirmed enthusiastically.

"Well then, let's see how special you really are then, little witchling, shall we?" suggested the book.

"Special?" enquired Maya, with a slightly quizzical expression.

"It's been a thousand years since anyone laid their hands on a living wand like Spell. A wand gifted from the witches' mother tree, Mother Nature herself. Let alone fired it in a fully grown wild dragon's flame. So, let's see if you are indeed a very special young witchling or just very, very lucky as your cat Mischief assures me."

Maya scanned the room. Picking out her cat, still lying curled up on top of his comfortable red cushion, for a special withering look.

"Let's see if you can perform a transformation spell," the book continued to write. "If and it's a very big **if** indeed. If you can, and **if** you really are, a true child of nature, then you'll transform and become, really become, one of these magnificent beasts. If you really are as special, as we hope you are. Then, perhaps you can help these creatures, in their time of need."

"Wow! I'd love that," gasped Maya eagerly.

"Snow leopard, snow leopard... please, please, please," she chanted impatiently under her breath, as Mischief, now apparently wide awake, jumped up onto the chest and started to circle the potion bottles.

Mischief paused, first behind the bottle with the eagle on the label and then lingered intentionally, behind the bottle with the wolf, as if to tease her. Eventually, and rather grudgingly, he sat behind the potion bottle with the snow leopard on its label.

"Yes, yes, yes!" Maya called out, with mounting excitement.

Maya picked up the little bottle and sat down in front of the book, still grinning with anticipation.

"What do I do now?" she asked eagerly.

"Not sure. I've never seen it myself, but the ancient texts say, that as you pop the cork, you must connect with the magic realm. If you can make that connection from this side, then as you step through the portal, you will become the creature to which you have made the link."

Maya nodded, although not entirely sure that she had really understood. Then, rather impatiently, she popped open the stopper and light poured out from the bottle and filled the room, like a million coloured fire flies, reflected in a glitter ball.

As the lights faded again, Maya approached the mirror, her eyes now focussed on her own rippling reflection ahead of her. She looked for a reflection. A vision, a clue to the beast with which she was sure she could connect. She stepped through the mirror, but there was no animal reflected to her, let alone a magnificent snow leopard. She saw only her own reflection.

Maya's heart pounded in her chest, like a giant wombat playing the digeridoo. In that instant there was a miraculous transformation... from an eager young witchling, full of self-belief and anticipation. To a very disappointed young girl, who now stood at the back of a mirror, looking at her own nose smudge on the wallpaper. A smudge caused by her own clumsy collision with the wall, just a few days before.

159

Maya walked back around the mirror. She was certainly not a snow leopard. It hadn't worked. Nobody spoke (but as he was still outside, scratching and meowing to get in, no-one heard him). Once Nobody was finished, and eventually after what felt like an age, the book broke the silence:

"Oh well, too much to hope for, I suppose."

"No, no, it can't be!" Maya complained. "I can do this, I know I can do this..., if only I had Spell."

"Spell is magical, she cannot pass into this realm, I'm afraid little one," the book spoke softly, sensing Maya's deep disappointment.

Maya's tongue was out though, she was thinking hard. "Her face now contorted itself into strange inexplicable shapes, like a goblin licking an ice-cream through a letter box," wrote the book.

"Hey, I read that!" Maya objected. "If only I could see her, I know she could help me, I feel it!" Maya insisted, turning again, approaching and staring deep into the mirror once more.

Deeper and deeper, she stared into the mirror, as it rippled in front of her. Eyes fixed forward, not blinking. Little by little her reflection started to mist and swirl... then... could it be? Yes... maybe..., she could just make it out. The unmistakeable pattern of the wallpaper, complete with nose smudge, on the wall beyond!

But this time, Maya was not deterred, she thought her way around the back of the mirror, looked left. Stopped suddenly in shock, thought my goodness; my bum looks big in these jeans, then continued to think herself on towards the witch flap?

She willed it open and in her mind's eye, she walked down the passageway; thinking on the glitter worms for light, as she went. Then Maya stopped, she'd forgotten something, or rather someone. She envisioned Mischief, by her side and soon enough, reassuring footsteps padded along behind her.

Maya was looking forward to this. She wanted to prove herself. To show that doubting book, that she could do it. That she had the ability and power. She resolved to find Spell and prove her journal wrong.

This was new though, walking through her own mind's eye, in her portal to the magical realm yes, but suddenly she sensed another presence. Maybe someone or something else was here too? Maya shuddered, had her thoughts betrayed her? Too late, she realised that she'd been tempted. Tempted by her own magical power. Her motives for this transformation, were as much about proving her own magical prowess, as helping the poor creature she would become. Glitter worms lit up the passageway ahead, but new passages started to appear off in the distance.

These were darker and glowed red, as if lit by a myriad of tiny red eyes. She watched, as one twisted, like a viper, one way, then the other, as if searching for something or someone. Off to her right-hand side, Maya could make out another new passageway. This one was dark too, it grew closer, much closer and as it opened, an icy chill ran up her spine. She felt her nerves jangling, like the sensation of dragging a metal fork over an unglazed pottery plate. Maya shuddered. She wasn't alone. She had an awful thought. Was this her dark side? Or worse? What if a dark witch was looking to get their hands on Spell? Had her stray thoughts betrayed her living wand too? Maya had to protect Spell.

Panic was taking over. In her mind's eye, she had already started to run. She could hear something behind her, but these were not Mischief's footsteps. A noise like the beating of distant wings, closing in on her from behind. She felt a chilling sensation, like cold breath down the back her neck.

"Caw!" came a chilling and familiar cry from behind her.

Maya burst through the witch flap and into the light, slamming the undersized door behind her. She was in her log cabin. Surely, she was safe here? Maya always felt safe in this place, whatever that thing was, it couldn't follow her in here, could it?

The chill faded from her bones, but she reasoned, that if she lingered long between realms in her portal, it might find her again. Maya scanned the room, there was Spell, she was safe, just where Maya had left her. Maya's mind's eye trained on the little sapling. Maya was still shaking, but focussed and even more determined than ever. She wanted this now, for the poor creature in need. The snow leopard. If that thing, whatever it was, had showed up to frighten her off, or even to get its hands or perhaps claws on Spell. That however, just meant, Maya wanted it all the more.

Her mind's eye focussed fully on Spell now, Maya held up her real hand towards the mirror and called out;

"Help me Spell?"

The little wand began to glow silver in the mirror, she grew brighter and brighter.

"Snow leopard!" Maya announced, with new found self-confidence and authority in her voice. Another fountain of colours burst forth, this time through the portal, emerging from the mirror itself. Engulfing Maya and Mischief in all the colours of the rainbow. They swirled around her head, as Maya, followed by her faithful side-kick, stepped forwards into the mirror. As she entered the portal, Maya was sure she could see, not her own reflection this time, but a pair of black and white furry ears and some very long whiskers indeed!

Maya opened her eyes slowly. This was different. She wasn't in the secret room any more, nor was she behind the mirror. Neither was she in the portal or the cabin in the woods, or anywhere else that she recognised. As her eyes adjusted to the dim light, she realised that she was in some sort of a cave. A cave carved out of snow and ice. It was cold, very cold. Cuddled in beside her, was a tiny snow leopard's cub. Probably the cutest thing on the planet, bar nothing! The cub rolled over onto its back, rocking back and forth, trying to scratch an itch.

"Grr…, if you have to show off, next time, could you pick something without flees?" moaned the cub. It sounded rather grumpy and very familiar.

"Grr…, oh…, Mischief, is that you?" Maya leopard growled curiously, whilst examining her new over-sized furry front paws. "Just look at those claws!"

"Anywhere you go, it seems, your faithful witch's cat is destined to follow you!" came Mischief cub's grudging, yet somehow comforting response.

Maya leopard chuckled, with a deep throaty growl. Looking down at her furry paws once again, she could see that Spell had joined her here too. The little saplings roots, were clasped securely around Maya leopard's front forepaw. Maya leopard smiled, displaying a rather intimidating set of over-sized canine teeth.

"Thanks," she growled down softly. Spell's roots tightened around her forepaw, in acknowledgement.

"I wonder where we are? And why we're here?" Maya leopard asked, hauling herself uneasily onto her paws.

"Grouch!" Maya leopard cried, feeling a sudden sharp and crippling pain. Looking underneath herself, she could see that her back paw was bent over and hung limply beneath her.

"I think it's broken," Maya leopard winced, casting a worried look towards her faithful cub.

Two furry ears twitched as one, tracking around on the top of her head, like miniature woolly radar dishes. They pointed in perfect unison, towards the cave entrance. Distant barking noises carried in on a cool stiff breeze. Tentatively, Maya leopard hobbled over to the snow lined entrance to the cave, on three paws and peered out cautiously. Snow was falling lightly and a chill wind blew. A panorama of impressive mountains and endless blue skies, unfolded in front of her as she edged forward. She was high up, on a mountainside, well above the snow line. Deep snow carpeted the ground and cloaked occasional stunted high-altitude pines. Down in the valley below, a small mountain village was just visible, beneath thin wispy trails of chimney smoke.

Then, ears and eyes as one, Maya leopard focussed straight ahead. One, two, then three men in furs. Guns slung over their shoulders, with dogs straining on the leash, emerged from the woods immediately below. They were not that far from the entrance to the cave. Maya leopard froze instinctively and stared through sapphire eyes. To her great relief, they were not headed this way. She watched for a minute, motionless, as if frozen to the spot. It was a frozen spot too, even in this thick fur coat, that wind was bitingly cold. Especially cold, where there was little fur!

Note to self, Maya leopard mused. In future, in cold winds, keep your furry tail firmly down over your bum!

The dogs were still searching for a scent, but now they were well past the entrance to the cave and heading in the opposite direction. Maya leopard had just begun to breathe again, when a deeper chill cloaked the mountainside. A familiar unwelcome shudder ran up her spine, as if Death himself was playing the xylophone, up and down her back bone, using her own ribs as mallets.

"Caw, caw, caw!" suddenly broke the silence, as a large jet-black, raven-like bird swooped down, seemingly out of nowhere. It landed behind Maya leopard on top of an accumulation of snow, piled high above the entrance to her lair. Its eyes focussed intensely on Spell.

"Caw, caw, caw!" came another deafening squawk from the bird. Its wings outstretched and flapping wildly. Its cold dark eyes, now alternating their focus between Spell and the hunters.

Maya turned her head to look back down the hill. The men had stopped and all of them had now turned to look her way. A tall blonde bearded man at the front, raised his arm and pointed straight at her. Behind him a second hunter slipped a gun from over his shoulder.

"Caw, caw, caw!" came another mocking cry, as the bird swooped down, as if to grab Spell from Maya leopard's forepaw. Maya leopard's reactions were too fast though, pulling her front paw away, just in time. In a flutter of wings and feathers, the bird rose up and over Maya leopard's head and into the air. With one final distant mocking cry:

"Caw!" it was gone. But the damage was done.

Maya leopard backed into the cave, awkwardly on all threes.

"Hunters!" Maya leopard announced, panic welling up inside her.

"What?" was all the little cub could muster, in response.

"Grr…, I can't run and you're too small," Maya leopard thought out loud. "This must be why I'm here? To save the snow leopard and her cub," she whispered to herself. It made sense to her now.

165

The mounting yelps of hunting dogs, barking outside was now echoing alarmingly, around the tiny cave.

"Good idea!" Mischief cub agreed. "So, can we get straight on with the saving part... now please?"

"We have to stand and fight!" Maya leopard announced defiantly, raising Spell on her right forepaw, towards the narrow entrance.

Mischief cub looked strangely uncomfortable, as he began to speak:

"Gr... ah, possibly I should have mentioned this earlier, but..., er, em..., that is to say. You can't!"

"What?" Maya leopard growled in frustration and disbelief, baring a large pair of canine teeth at her cub with menace.

"Can't use your magic to fight or hurt non-magic types..., er, not unless you want to go over to the dark side?" he continued.

"Now..., really..., now you tell me... grrrreat!" Maya leopard snarled.

"Oops!" replied the little cub, cowering further into the corner. The snarling and yapping of the dogs approaching the entrance to the cave, was now reverberating alarmingly around the frozen walls of their icy prison.

"Do something!" cried Mischief cub in desperation.

"What?" Maya leopard growled back.

The lead dog strained on its leash, rearing up on its hind legs and dragging a hunter behind it. It entered the cave. The hunter's other arm held his shotgun. Two fingers now poised and ready on its trigger.

"Ice-cream!" Maya commanded in panic.

Spell glowed, and in an instant, all was black. All except for a faint lingering silver glow from the end of the little sapling. Gradually, the strange silver light brightened and filled the small area at the back of the cave. Between the cowering leopards and the hunters and their slobbering hounds, now stood a wall... a wall of solid ice-cream. It hid them completely from all prying eyes and covered their scent, from some very confused hunting dogs.

Ice-cream, vanilla of course, a perfect match for the icy cave walls, but equally as important; it was Maya's favourite. They waited in silence, for the muffled noise of the hunters and their bewildered beasts, to subside. Then when all was quiet, the cub spoke first.

"Ice-cream, really?" Mischief cub whispered, half relieved, half astonished.

"Mum always says, when all seems lost..., there's always ice-cream!" came a very relieved whisper in response. "And she's always with me, whenever I really need her."

"She is a witch of rare wisdom indeed, your mum," agreed Mischief cub, a smile breaking out across his furry face. "Especially when it comes to ice-cream. What now?"

Maya leopard held Spell to her injured hind paw. Spell and Maya leopard's paw began to glow as one, lit by a silvery magical light. After a few seconds, slowly and very tentatively at first, Maya leopard put some weight onto her injured paw and smiled at Mischief approvingly.

"And for my next trick, she announced, proudly pulling a spoon magically from the end of her seedling wand:

"I'm going to make all that ice-cream disappear!"

Spoons, as it turned out, are not much use in furry paws, but long snow leopards' tongues, more than made up for it.

167

An hour later, bellies full, and several ice-cream related brain-freezes later, Maya leopard and Mischief cub, broke through the ice-cream wall to freedom. The barking from the dogs had long since vanished into the distance, but Maya knew it wasn't safe to stay here anymore. Their den had been discovered and the hunters would be back.

"We have to find a new lair, before night fall," Maya leopard warned, leading Mischief cub, his belly nearly the same size as he was, cautiously out of the snow cave entrance.

It was cold..., no, very cold, as they trudged through the deep snow. They walked for miles past frozen lakes, frozen mountain streams and penguins set into solid ice. Three polar bears huddled together around a mobile phone, ordering pizza and extra electric blankets. Ok, slightly over the top, none of that, but you get the idea, even a snow leopard gets...... ccccold!

Making matters worse, her tail, a fifth limb, over which Maya leopard seemingly had little control, had been held high and proud for most of the journey. By the time they had found a suitable hole, under an old tree, in which to shelter. Jack Frost had not so much been nibbling at her butt, as had tucked into a five-course meal and made a complete pig of himself!

"Grr, my bum hurts!" Maya leopard announced loudly, with heart felt self-pity, reminiscent of a mild case of man flu.

It was at this low point, that Maya learned another very important lesson. As a witchling, sporting a powerful wand, you must be especially careful, what you wish for.

"I'm so cold, I wish I could just light a fire under my butt!" she shivered. A worried look of realisation quickly creeping across her furry face, in response to Mischief cub's horrified gaze.

Spell glowed.

"Groooowwwwwch!" Maya leopard growled, butt ablaze, her agonised howls of pain, enough to set off a small avalanche, in the slopes above them.

Just as well really, as luck would have it, an avalanche was exactly what was called for. Both to put the fire out and cool her smouldering butt down, at the same time.

As the pungent smell of smouldering snow leopard butt diminished, Maya leopard and Mischief cub cuddled together in the tree hollow and fell asleep. Sore butt yes, but contented, really contented. Knowing that the little snow leopard cub and her mother would now be safe. It was worth it. This Maya had realised, was the reason she was here. The reason mother nature herself, had granted her the living wand. She vowed right there and then, to use her gifts wisely and not to waste them, especially not on setting fire to herself any more.

Maya leopard dreamt of returning home to her cabin in the woods and could see herself open the witch flap, climb the stairs and return to the secret room. Sure enough, she awoke to find herself stepping back through the mirror once again. She was back in her mum's secret room, as if it had all been a dream, as if nothing had changed. But she knew, in her heart, that it had all been real. It had to have been real, after all, her bum still really, really hurt!

"Well done little one. I'm impressed, really impressed," the book wrote, almost humbly.

"I'm sore, really sore!" replied Maya painfully.

The book chuckled unsympathetically. "Maybe some ice-cream might help?" it enquired, chuckling again, as it closed for the night.

Maya locked the door behind her as usual and made her way slowly downstairs, her knees held together to minimise unnecessary buttock friction.

"That you, little one?" her dad called. "Where have you been? Never mind. Special treat tonight, ice- cream for tea!"

"No, not tonight, please Dad," Maya replied turning distinctly green at the thought.

Maya visited the cave on Arran every day, without fail. She was amazed by how fast pufflings grew. Who knew? Marshmallows turned out to be the new dragon super-food. Even better, Blink was growing up to be a complete Maya sook. Bouncing up and down, flapping his wings and snorting excited sparks, from both nostrils, whenever she visited. Maya loved her visits and they played and frolicked together, on the beaches around Arran for hours at a time.

Blink could fly within a week and soon flew circles around Blue and Maya in the air. Within another week, he was the size of a Shetland pony, but many times more powerful. He had magic too, bonded to Maya, Blink could hear her thoughts, well simple commands anyway. Okay, one. Maya could think of him and blink three times. Sure enough, no matter how far off, he would soon appear. Well, when he was in the mood and wasn't eating, sleeping or chasing moths, butterflies or eagles.

As Maya scratched his back on the beach, one morning. She tickled the purple scaley beast behind the ear. Instinctively Blink crouched down on the sand and stretched out his wings.

"He wants you to ride him," Mischief explained, unable to disguise his smile.

"This is awesome!" Maya cried, as Blink jumped into the air, with Maya clinging to his neck, for dear life. Powerful wings beat down, launching them further into the sky. Three more beats and they were now up hundreds of feet. Blink was amazing, they moved as one. In each other's heads from the first minute; barrel rolling through the sky, skimming across the water, dipping wing tips and Maya's witch's boots into the millpond of Brodick harbour and looping the loop above Goatfell, just for the fun of it. It would have been the best time of her life, except it just wasn't. For every moment of elation and joy, there were two of guilt and despair, at the thought of her mum, still trapped in Nedep's coven.

The next full moon was due. It was Christmas Eve and Maya knew exactly what she wanted for her Christmas. It certainly wasn't in any of the badly wrapped brown paper bags her dad had suddenly panic bought and shoved under a lop-sided plastic tree with three bobbles, in the lounge. Mum had apparently put the decorations somewhere safe. That meant no mortal man, much less her dad, could ever find them.

Maya, now with new found optimism, following her successful transformation spell, would return to Nedep's coven tonight. Then, following another leap of faith, finally release her mother from her slumbers. Unlocking the sands of time with her living wand, as the fresh-looking inscription, cut into the base of the tiny brass egg timer, had foretold.

She was sure she could do it. Although both Mischief and her book had advised caution. Not to get her hopes up, suggesting that next Christmas or even, the one after that, might be more realistic. Time for her and her wand to develop their powers, they'd cautioned. But Maya was having none of it.

So it was, after yawning dramatically and making her excuses to her dad, she trudged wearily upstairs, for an 'early' night. Instead, Maya sneaked into the secret room. She made her way through the portal, with Mischief at heel and picked up Spell. Outside her log cabin, Blue had knocked his stable door off its hinges once more and greeted her enthusiastically.

Soon they were on their way. Soaring into the night sky on Blue, with Mischief perched on a comfortable red cushion, in his customary position behind Maya. They followed the banks of the River Ayr and headed for the sandstone steps to nowhere. Maya

172

couldn't wait to see her dad's face, when she showed up, with the best Christmas present ever.

Soon enough, Maya found herself at the base of the sandstone steps to nowhere. Maya didn't have long to wait, the moonlight already illuminated most of the sandstone steps, when they arrived. After just a few minutes, moonlight crept on the top step to signal the stroke of midnight. Maya started her ascent. Slowly, Maya made her way onto the bottom step. With each step her anxiety grew. Maya's heart and imagination were racing. Self-doubt growing with each tentative step towards the top. Finally, Maya came to the final moonlit step and elastic legs wobbled their way precariously onto it.

Maya looked up. The moon was huge, beautiful. She knew that if she reached out now, she could touch it. Raw courage and determination carried her inevitably towards the point of no-return.

Maya leaned forward, and as she did so, she stretched out her hand. With this, a shaft of moonlight ran up her arm and touched her outstretched finger. Lighting it up suddenly, in a dazzling flash, as she pointed towards the moon. Maya reached out, the moon was even closer now... much closer, she could nearly touch it, she knew she could, she could actually step out and touch the moon.

She was sure... she had faith. Her mother was waiting inside. Maya stepped out, in a leap of faith, to touch the moon and fell once more into Nedep's coven.

It was just as impressive as she'd remembered. Twelve large silver pillars, which rose some twenty witches' hats into the air around a central plinth, where sat a clear crystal orb, topped with the coven's keystones.

"Hello Mum," Maya greeted her not quite a ghost mum. She reached inside her own top pocket and retrieved the now rather pungent sock, in which she'd kept the sands of her mother's time safe. Perhaps on reflection, she should have re-wrapped the little hour-glass in a clean sock, Maya thought to herself.

Maya glanced at the freshly cut inscription on the base, reading it aloud to her mum:

"Only the power of the living wand or a pure coven can restart the sands of time."

Maya placed the little brass egg timer on the floor, next to her not quite a ghost mum, then raised Spell above her head. She glanced again, over towards the coven crystals, in the centre of the coven. She would need their help too.

"Okay Mum, brace yourself. I give you the power of the living wand!" Maya announced. She closed her eyes, focussed her mind's eye on Spell and then onto the crystals.

Maya sensed the power surging through her. It was exhilarating, frightening, awesome. Unlike anything she'd ever felt before. Spell glowed, the keystone charm in her neckless glowed, the crystals on the orb glowed, as Maya commanded:

"Awaken!"

Magical power crackled from the tip of her wand. Lightning flashed between the coven stones, which lit up and shone brightly, as-if energised for the first time in hundreds of years. Bolts criss-crossed between the pillars and to and from the crystals in the orb and finally, a mighty magical blast shot forth to where her mother lay.

Maya had focused everything she had into that incantation. Every ounce of her strength, every drop of her energy and willpower.

Maya opened her eyes and...

Plan B

Infuriatingly, the author chose not to put his few remaining readers out of their misery. Not just yet.

Instead, Mischief watched, as a figure silhouetted black against the full moon, made its way from the hidden coven and onto the top step. Then, taking slow unsteady steps, as if wobbly on their feet, after emerging from a long sleep, or untold trauma, tentatively the figure descended the sandstone steps, one at a time.

Mischief looked up into the all too familiar face. Tears of despair ran down Maya's face, as she slumped, exhausted and broken to the ground. There were no words. How could there be? Maya curled up into a ball and Mischief cuddled down next to her for comfort.

An hour passed, before Maya found her words again.

"So, what did you get me for Christmas then cat?" Maya asked half-heartedly.

"Not what you'd been hoping for obviously, but I do have something," Mischief replied softly,

"Mm... what?" Maya asked, half-heartedly.

"Plan B," Mischief divulged.

Maya sat bolt upright.

"What's plan B?" Maya demanded.

"Remember, when Granny warned you that she didn't think that the pure coven, The Deeds, would help you?" Mischief asked.

"How could I forget?" came Maya's scathing reply.

"Well, they will now," Mischief revealed.

"What? Why?" Maya was bemused.

"The puffling. He's bonded to you... like Evaline said, back in the cave. When you bond with a dragon, you can ride him," Mischief replied.

"Yes, I know, but how does that help?" Maya was still playing catch up.

"A pure coven. A coven composed purely of dragon riders," Mischief explained.

"So, you think they'd help me now that I have a dragon?" Maya asked hopefully.

"If you joined them. Yes, they'd help," Mischief encouraged.

"Maya hugged him a little too tightly, then thrust him away, again a little too quickly.

"You're sure?" Maya asked anxiously again. "What if they don't like me?"

"Like you, little one," the rather shaken cat replied. "They ride domesticated dragons. You've bonded with a wild dragon and carry a living wand. No, they won't just like you. They're snobs... they'll love you!"

"I need to know more, where are they? How do I find them? How do I get them to help me? So many questions," Maya continued impatiently.

"Granny," replied Mischief. "Granny, she'll know a lot more about them. And I think, she would appreciate an update too," Mischief responded.

Maya nodded her approval.

They flew off to Granny's house without delay, as fast as Blue could carry them. It seemed a shame to wake her so early on Christmas morning. So, they did.

Soon enough they were sat around the breakfast table, being waited on, hand and foot by the old woman. Piles of freshly made pancakes appeared, as if by magic. Which being a proper granny, of course, she didn't use.

"Some things taste better, made the traditional way," she explained.

Priorities tastily out of the way, Maya brought Granny up to date. It's not often her Granny was lost for words, but as Spell crawled down Maya's wrist to say hello. The old woman was rendered speechless.

"Is...,?" Granny started.

"Yip!" Maya replied, beaming with pride. "And I've got a dragon too... a wild one! He's called Blink."

"Wild... not wild, wild?" Granny gasped.

"Wild as a wild thing!" Maya replied, again beaming from ear to ear.

Granny listened, fascinated, as Maya brought her up to speed on her new friends Spell and Blink. But her tone changed, when it came to relaying the crushing disappointment of last nights failed attempt to rouse her mum.

"I'm so sorry Granny, I tried as hard as...," Maya started.

"Shoosh! Don't you dare!" Granny stopped her. "You've done brilliantly. Your mum will be so proud of you, when we eventually figure this out!"

Maya's eyes glistened and she nodded.

"Now, about this pure coven, the Deeds," Granny changed the subject. "You would have to join them, for sure. They're not the sort of people to go out of their way to help others, especially outsiders. Dragon riders they are. Not much time for the likes of me, an old 'broomy' as they'd call me, I'm afraid. But you and your dragon and especially that living wand of yours. I'm surprised they haven't come looking for you already."

"Do they all have dragons?" Maya enquired.

"Oh yes, but not like Blink. Spoilt girls most of them, bought domesticated dragons, 'pedigree flamers' they call them," Granny explained. "Not really a match for a wild dragon like yours of course, but still plenty powerful. Formidable creatures, and faithful and obedient, once bonded to their witch or witchling. More than a match for a simple witch like me. And they know it too, they have little or no time for their 'inferiors,' as most of them believe us to be."

Maya looked worried.

"I suppose that's why we were all so surprised, when young Evaline left to join the Deeds, lovely girl. If a bit rough around the edges," Granny continued.

"A bit rough? You can say that again!" Maya interrupted.

"You've met then," Granny smirked. "She didn't seem the type at all, good heart. You can tell, but she was gifted a dragon and had passed their initiation too, so good luck to her. Maybe she can change their ways from the inside.

"The Deeds?" asked Maya curiously.

"Oh yes, sorry. That's what they call themselves. Very proud of their bloodlines and heritage that lot. Descended from dragon riders and destined, they believe, to be the finders of the living wand, or so they claim. They believe that they are the chosen ones and that they are pure indeed, the 'Deeds' for short," Granny explained rather scathingly.

"They don't sound very nice, but maybe, if I talked to them and showed them Spell, then they might agree to help Mum?" Maya asked hopefully.

"Maybe, why don't I tweet young Evaline. She could tell you more," Granny suggested.

Maya agreed. She was looking forward to seeing Evaline again. Granny went out into the back garden, bewitched a small robin and sent it on its way, with a hastily scribbled message for Evaline, held securely in its beak.

Less than an hour later the bird returned. A small scroll of official looking parchment, now strapped to its leg and sealed with green wax.

"My, they are keen to meet you Maya," Granny grinned. "That looks like an official Deeds' invitation, if I'm not very much mistaken," Granny added with a smile.

Maya grabbed the little bird off the windowsill and removed the message. Maya released the robin, then unrolled the parchment and read it aloud:

"Your request for an audience with the coven of Deeds has been granted. At midnight an escort shall call and take you blindfold to the arena, where you may state your business."

Granny looked apprehensive.

"Be careful Maya," the old lady warned. "I don't trust them; not sure I would tell them about your mum or Nedep's potion yet. That potion she's holding would be very valuable to them. If their coven is indeed powerful enough to release your mother from this spell. In comparison to eternal youth, the fate of an ordinary witch, like your mum, means nothing to them."

The old woman paused for thought, then continued her advice:

"If you join their coven, then as one of them, they would be duty bound to help you. As the mother of a Deed, your mother too would also be considered pure, a Deed as well. They'll look after their own."

Maya reflected on how Granny really was, as her dad had often joked, "a cunning old bat!"

The new heir

Christmas was a subdued affair without Mum. The whole family crowded round to Granny's and waited to be fed. Leaving the old woman to, 'do her magic in the kitchen.' Maya now understood much better, how the old woman managed on such occasions and kept a lookout whenever non-magical types (i.e., the men) approached the kitchen in search of cold beer. Maya also better understood her Aunty Dot's terrible cooking. Her magical misfires abounded in the kitchen, included 'helping' Granny with a rhubarb and mince crumble, complete with her own version of custard; Aunty Dot's own magical recipe for crème froglaise!

After a rather deflated family dinner, they had returned home. Dad had tried his best to cheer her up, trying to keep her entertained with made-up stories and bad 'dad' jokes. It wasn't really his fault, that he was hopeless at it. Maya tried to make the most of things, but it was hard. Eventually, they both found solace in endless repeats on the television and Maya left him snoring in front of the TV. Under cover of darkness Maya tucked two pillows under her duvet and took Blue and Mischief back to Granny's house.

Granny presented her with copious home-made sponges and cakes, in an attempt to make her already swollen Christmas belly even more uncomfortable. She warned, that Maya might have to spend some time with the Deeds, in order to gain their trust, and that she'd send Aunty Dot around in the morning to slip one of Granny's memory potions into her dad's morning coffee. It would keep him from worrying.

As night fell, Maya blinked three times and summoned her faithful purple dragon. He must have been close-by, as only a few minutes passed, before the sound of beating wings broke the silence of the still night air. Blink hovered briefly above her, then descended rather clumsily onto Granny's lawn, his tail colliding with the new shed, as he landed. Maya smiled and stroked her little dragon's snout, who rumbled with pleasure and glowed purple in the night, in response to her touch. After a good old tummy rub, Maya rolled over and scratched her oversized puffling's belly too. Blink bedded down on a pile of old wood (previously known as granny's new garden shed), now strewn out behind the house.

At midnight the Deeds' dragon escort arrived. Two elegantly presented witches, with long flowing turquoise robes, adorned in intricate gold stitching, in the shape of dragons breathing fire. They rode on the back of huge dragons, magnificent beasts, one dark green, one black as the night sky, with heads covered in horns and long snouts from which dripped fire and dragon snot in equal proportions. They too landed on the back lawn. They dwarfed Blink, who snarled at them aggressively, seemingly undeterred by the mis-match in size.

The youngest auburn-haired witch dismounted and approached. Maya recognised her immediately. Big smile, matted hair and beneath her elegant Deeds' robes an unmistakeable home-made animal skin hunting outfit. She bowed and smiled towards Granny, who reciprocated graciously.

"Evaline, nice to see you again," Granny greeted her.

"Behaving yourself for a change Betty, are we?" Evaline replied, beaming broadly.

"Certainly not," Granny responded.

Evaline now turned towards Maya, still sporting a friendly smile.

"The location of the Coven of Deeds is a closely guarded secret," Evaline announced, in an official tone, as if meant for the other dragon rider to overhear.

183

Evaline handed Maya a turquoise silk blindfold, winked and whispered:

"It's ok to peek. I did. I won't let on."

Maya smiled. She liked Evaline, she was straight talking, if a bit fearsome, but instinctively Maya felt that she was someone she could trust.

Maya gave Granny a great big hug goodbye, then climbed aboard Blink for the journey. Mischief too, jumped onboard the little dragon, summoning a comfortable red cushion for the trip and Evaline presented him too with a blindfold. They took off into the night sky, escorted on either side, by splendid 'pedigree flamers.' Each sporting gold embroidered ebony saddles and black dragon skin reins. Their robes caught the breeze and rose elegantly above them, like silken bat wings, as they flew. Maya rode bareback in torn jeans and a hoodie. She was now suffering from a severe case of fashion envy. Blue flew behind, in close formation, feeling a bit left out and sorry for himself.

They flew for just fifteen minutes. Maya, peeking out from beneath her blindfold, the whole way. She recognised where they were going instantly. It was known locally as Cambusdoon, a beautiful patch of woodland and meadow overlooking the River Doon. It wasn't that far from her home at all and she was often marched around its muddy paths by her parents, as an excuse to get her off her tablet. They circled around and landed on the top of the hill, next to an old ruined stone archway. The remnants of an impressive mansion house, once used as a boarding school. Another huge black dragon, with an even more ornately decorated gold embroidered saddle, was perched on top of the arch. It had no rider. The stone beneath it crumbled to dust, at the touch of its talons.

Evaline dismounted her dragon and approached Maya's dragon. She reached up and removed Maya's blindfold, with a smile and another wink, before offering her hand to help Maya down from Blink's back. Maya accepted and pretended to be surprised by the view. She looked out over the hillside towards the River Doon below. Beyond the river, far in the distance, she could just make out the sea and the silhouette of Greenan Castle against the moonlit sky.

The ruined stone arch at Cambusdoon Park

A dark figure in long turquoise robes, wearing an ornate golden jewelled tiara, stepped out from beneath the stone archway. In one hand she carried a simple wooden staff, with a bright turquoise crystal set into the tip. This was the High Priestess, Maya presumed. Evaline and the other witch bowed in front of her and Maya followed their lead. With the smallest nod of acknowledgment, the High Priestess walked past them, heading towards the edge of the hill. She stopped above a large flat stone, embedded in the ground, then raised the staff above her head and pointed it up, towards the moon.

185

"She'll raise a special coven tonight, just to hear your request," explained Evaline.

"Stay here in the arena. I'll request that you're granted the status of an heir. I take it that is why you're here, right?" Evaline confirmed.

"Y... yes, right," stuttered Maya, rather taken off guard. She hadn't expected things to go so quickly.

"I call upon the coven and heirs," the High Priestess cried, before bringing her staff down heavily three times, onto the stone beneath.

The earth shook beneath them with enormous power. Twelve huge pillars of glimmering turquoise crystal, pushed their way effortlessly up through the turf. On the horizon, the unmistakeable silhouettes of ten dragons and their riders soared into view. Smaller pedestals of blue-green marble, now pushed their way up in front of each of the larger pillars and glimmered in the moonlight. Maya was awestruck, she had never seen such a magnificent display.

"Twelve seats for thirteen witches," Maya muttered under her breath.

Evaline overheard her, and smirked as she moved forward.

"It still gets me too," she whispered.

Maya just smiled.

Mischief smirked.

"Still not figured it out?" he added rather patronisingly. "Every good witch knows, you only need twelve seats, if you're going to seat a coven of thirteen. So, until the High Priestess takes up her seat, there is always a space left for one more."

186

Maya and Evaline exchanged blank looks.

One by one, the witches arrived. Each mounted proudly on the backs of their respective dragons. The dragons' wings beating down powerfully together to slow their descent, creating a breeze strong enough to carry Maya's hair from her shoulders. Then, almost in unison, they dismounted. It was an awesome sight. The dragons themselves were impressive, but so many. So well trained and immaculately presented. Maya was transfixed, enchanted by the scene unfolding in front of her. Her jaw dropped and she watched open-mouthed in wonderment. The Deeds witches were all dressed in matching flowing turquoise robes with gold embroidery. In gold lettering the word, 'Deeds' was emblazoned on each of their dragon's ebony saddles. Maya couldn't help wishing that she was one of them. She was, for want of a better word, bewitched by the spectacle.

Evaline, left Maya now and joined the ranks of the assembling Deeds. As the witches entered the coven, each of them raised their hood, up over their head. Before taking their seats, each witch stooped and dropped, what looked like a pebble, onto a small golden tray, which sat atop a stone orb, in the centre of the coven. Then in turn, each of the thirteen dragons flapped up and landed on one of the impressive crystal pillars.

Finally, the High Priestess entered the coven, dropping the thirteenth pebble onto the central stone orb. There was a blinding flash of blue light, as both the orb and stones were transformed into translucent turquoise crystals, which matched the outer pillars. The crystals and pillars glowed and pulsed with a dazzling blue light. Lightning crackled between the pillars, and to and from the crystal orb, in the centre.

"The crystal's ball," Mischief explained.

"For looking into the future and telling fortunes?" Maya asked.

187

"No, silly girl, how can you look into the future? It hasn't been written yet," responded the exasperated cat, very dismissively.

Then, rather more helpfully, Mischief explained that the coven stone or crystal's ball, is what focusses the power of all the witches in a coven. But that this was no ordinary coven. He had never seen magical power like it before.

Maya's eyes were drawn back to the coven. The High Priestess now pointed to Evaline, whose distinctive straight but matted auburn hair, Maya could still recognise, as it poked out untidily from beneath her hood.

Evaline stood and addressed the coven for about a minute, gesturing occasionally in Maya's direction. When she sat down, there appeared, from the gesticulations of a number of the witches, to be quite a heated debate going on inside. Although Maya and Mischief, couldn't hear a thing. After a couple more minutes, the High Priestess raised her staff, as if to bring the discussion to an end, then pointed it towards Evaline. Evaline nodded and the staff moved around the circle. The next witch nodded too, but after that came two shakes of the head.

"They're voting now," Mischief explained, but Maya was already counting the votes. This was serious. If she didn't get enough votes, she'd have no chance to save her mum.

"Six for and five against," Maya replied as the staff moved around again to the final witch... another shake.

"No, a tie.... what happens now?" Maya pleaded anxiously.

"The High Priestess must decide," replied Mischief, for the first-time, anguish now evident in his voice too.

The High Priestess was shaking her head.

"No, no, they can't… I haven't even spoken to them. They don't know me or even about my mum," Maya whimpered, with tears welling in her eyes. Evaline stood and spoke once more, gesturing frantically, then pointing to Blink and then at Maya. She clasped her wrist, as if she might be talking about Spell, then slowly, sadly she took her seat again.

Once more, the High Priestess shook her head, but this time seemingly more in resignation, then finally she nodded. Evaline clenched her fist, looked over to Maya, smiled and nodded.

She was in.

The coven adjourned and the High Priestess and Evaline returned to speak to Maya. Maya shuddered, as the ashen faced woman approached, there was something about her that spooked Maya. She was cold, emotionless, not ugly, but somehow Maya felt that one word or look from this old lady, could suck all the joy out from whomever she addressed. Mischief cowered courageously behind Maya's legs. The High Priestess spoke now, in a cold monotonous and official voice:

"You have been nominated for a seat in the Coven of Deeds and the coven has ratified your challenge. You may now call yourself an heir. Evaline has nominated you and pleaded your case, amidst much concern. She will therefore be the one to train you, in the three challenges you must now face."

Maya shuddered, catching a final icy glance from the High Priestess. The High Priestess glared at Evaline. Obediently, Evaline bowed and Maya followed suit, before the old lady withdrew.

"Thank you," Maya squeaked, rather meekly. It wasn't really enough, but what else could she say.

Evaline smiled at first, then looked much more serious and intense.

"It's going to be hard. They'll make it especially tough for you," Evaline warned. "Although you have bonded with a wild dragon and bring with you a living wand, which by the way I am just giddy to see in action again. Many of the older ones are set against you, they're afraid of you, I think. They say, that as you are not born of a pure Deed blood-line, that you have no place here. But Spell and Blink, they speak of your credentials. You have more right to be here than any of us, but you must be wary. Trust no-one. They will make it hard for you. Trip you up, whenever they can, by fair means or foul."

A test of wits

Evaline escorted Maya to the challenger's tent. It was a leather wrapped, tee-pee style of dwelling. It was modest, but cosy. There was no bed, but there were plenty of animal skins laid out on the floor, for her to sleep on. There was a small wood burning stove, a few old-fashioned pots and pans (which she presumed must be strictly for decoration, with Maya's cooking ability) and a small wooden table, upon which sat a large chunk of cheese and a loaf of crusty brown bread to eat. Strange green things lay on top of the table, that Maya presumed were vegetables. She had heard of these... from the days before pizza and chicken nuggets.

There was plenty of rainwater for drinking, which collected in a water butt outside the tent, and planters with bunches of fresh mint for her brush Blue to munch on. Blink bedded down on a flat pile of rocks outside, which he flamed until they glowed red hot, then circled around, snuggling down into a comfortable sleeping position, like a giant purple asbestos cat.

Maya conjured five small marshmallow trees for blink to nibble on during the night, (it was important that he got his five-a-day after all). She deliberately chose to ignore the bloodstained sack, left for him by the Deeds. She had no idea what was in there. Best case, she presumed, it was part of some poor unfortunate forest animal. Worst case, well she knew only too well what Blink's parents used to munch on. It really didn't bear thinking about. No Maya decided, a balanced diet of marshmallows would be just fine for her dragon tonight. Balanced, in that the number of pink and white one's on each tree always matched... Maya's O.C.D. was laid bare.

The tent was warm and comfortable and Maya was tired, but sleep still did not come easily. Her head was spinning from the events of that night. Not to mention worrying about her mum. In the early

191

hours of the morning, exhaustion finally won the battle and at last Maya managed to drift off, for a few hours of haunted and restless sleep.

Morning broke, much like an egg. Emerging from its shell of darkness, at the crack of dawn. A large yellow yolk appeared over the hills in the east and heated gently as it rose into the sky. Maya was weary and her training got off to a shaky start. She found it hard to concentrate properly, but Evaline was great. She was fun, and on exactly the same, rather crazy wavelength, as Maya herself. Evaline was practical too, straight down to business and no messing about. Well, no, not really, lots of messing around actually, and they became friends quickly.

Training began quite formally, with a short lecture from Evaline. Maya stood to attention and saluted her new friend sarcastically. From that day on, Evaline would be known to Maya as sergeant and Evaline would in turn, refer to Maya as private.

"Listen-up private, we have just twenty-seven days ahead of the next full moon, to lick you into shape, so pay attention!" barked Evaline, trying to sound as official as she could.

"Yes sergeant!" Maya shouted back obediently.

"First test, a test of wits, not just intelligence mind, but cunning and logic. It's about 'deductive reasoning,' whatever that is, and most of all... in your case private, I suspect pure dumb luck. So, basically you're doomed!" Evaline announced in military style, with a broad grin.

"I can't train cunning and intelligence. You'll either have the wits when it comes to it, or not, but I will give you some good advice, so listen well," she continued.

Evaline scanned around, to make sure she wasn't being overheard. Her tone had changed now, she spoke slowly and deliberately. She

192

was deadly serious, and to prove it, she mustered up as many big words as she could:

"You have many adversaries here. There are many who were opposed to your challenge and they will endeavour to thwart you, using fair means or foul. Some fear your powers and especially your living wand. They hide behind the pretext, that you are not of pure Deed blood. So, trust no-one! That's lesson 1. Got it private?"

"Yes sergeant, lesson 1, trust no-one!" Maya bellowed back obediently.

Maya didn't like to mention the fact, that she had no idea what a 'pretext' or a 'thwart' was, but she supposed that a thwart, might be something that would grow on the end of the nose, of one of the older witches.

Eveline cast her eyes to either side once more, then leaned in towards Maya. She looked rather furtive and whispered:

"I can't cheat, so I didn't tell you this, Okay?"

Maya nodded in acknowledgement.

"The first test. It's more of a gentle warm up," Evaline explained. "The High Priestess usually uses a rotating table and you have to find your own wand... take your time, always remember lesson 1 though. It's really quite simple in some ways... it shouldn't **WEIGH** on your mind too much," then Evaline winked at Maya and unleashed a broad grin.

Then casually, as if it were an afterthought, she added:

"You sit the first test tonight."

"Tonight?" Maya squawked.

"No point in wasting time and training you, not if you fall at the first hurdle, is there private?" Eveline explained.

Maya shrugged her shoulders, it was logical enough, she supposed, but she hadn't slept well last night and her brain was already feeling fuzzy. A test of wits tonight, was not something she was looking forward to, not one bit.

"Second test, magical ability. Once again private, I can teach you nothing. As custodian of a living wand, your powers are already much greater than my own. Possibly even a match for those of the High Priestess herself, I expect. But remember, Spell is young and her powers are still but nothing, not compared to the power of the whole Deed's coven. So, the coven will test you, and test you to your limit. Do not underestimate this test private!" Evaline warned, looking very serious indeed.

"And the final test Sergeant?" Maya asked, with growing discomfort, half expecting to hear how Evaline was going to wriggle out of helping her at all.

"That's why I'm here!" Evaline grinned, "Dragon combat. I'm pretty good at it, even if I do say so myself. You did notice that there were no spaces left in the coven yesterday, didn't you?"

Maya nodded. Though she hadn't really attached any significance to it.

"To take your place in our coven, private, you must retire one of the lowest ranking witches. The High Priestess will choose who. You must take on whomever the High Priestess believes is no longer strong enough, to sit amongst us. Another good reason to remember lesson 1 private!" Evaline announced.

"Lesson 1, trust no-one sergeant," Maya barked back obligingly, with a smile.

Dragon combat training started immediately. It was all about multi-tasking, Evaline explained. Probably why there were no warlocks in the coven, Maya deduced for herself.

First, Evaline showed her how to use her wand to form a shield. A mushroom shaped magical force field, capable of deflecting oncoming stun spells. Spell did this with ease and she could tell that Evaline was impressed at the strength of the shield that Maya could conjure.

Stun spells were next.

"Elaborate magical words, whose meanings had been lost down through the eons of time," Evaline explained, then...

"Stun!" Evaline hollered, knocking Maya a bruising twenty witches' hats across the arena, dazing her in the process.

"Sorry, but you needed to know what it feels like," Evaline apologised, with a grin that betrayed exactly just how much she had enjoyed casting the spell.

Maya dusted herself down and gave Evaline one of her best withering stares.

"You need to recover quickly and keep your wits about you, should one get through," Evaline explained, as Maya got to her feet slowly, wobbling on unsteady legs, like a new-born giraffe. Maya stooped in order to pick up her wits from the arena floor, before turning to face her opponent once more.

Maya practiced the stun spell over and over again. That was straightforward enough, but the real art was to coordinate her stun and shield spells. That was tricky. Evaline showed her how it was done; dropping her shield momentarily, she cast the spell, then raised her shield again quickly, so as to avoid a hit from her opponent. It was all about timing and it wasn't easy, not easy at all.

Evaline suggested, she should first practice with low impact stun spells. It was a good call. Maya's first stun bolt rebounded off her own shield, knocking her painfully backwards, across the arena floor once more.

"Ouch!" cried Maya. "That really stung!"

Evaline just laughed.

When Maya finally got that bit right, she forgot to raise her shield again and Evaline took great pleasure in highlighting her error, courtesy of a painful incoming blast, from her swiftly drawn wand.

After a couple of hours, Evaline could sense that Maya was gaining in confidence, but also, that she was starting to tire.

"That's enough for today, get some rest and put your thinking head on," Evaline suggested, suddenly bringing the day's training to an abrupt conclusion.

Evaline looked Maya in the eye once again and reminded her:

"Always remember private, lesson 1 and don't let it **WEIGH** on your mind. Oh yes, and if I were you, I would make a bit of an entrance tonight. Many in the coven doubt you, still more fear your powers. You can use that to your advantage. If your challenger already fears you, when it comes to dragon combat, the battle is half won."

Maya gave Evaline an appreciative smile and attempted a mis-timed fist pump, nearly clipping Evaline on the chin, for her troubles.

That evening, as the moon rose above the trees surrounding the arena, the coven assembled around the old stone arch. There was much excitement and expectant mumbling amongst the Deeds, as they gathered. The High Priestess took centre stage, dressed in her fine robes and carrying the jewelled coven staff. She stood directly in front of the old stone arch, facing the others.

Maya had dressed in some old turquoise robes, which she'd borrowed from Evaline. They were elegant enough, she supposed, but without any of the Deed's ornate gold embroidery.

Following Evaline's suggestion, Maya had decided, that she would make a big entrance tonight. She had a plan and had practiced it time and time again with her dragon, well downstream of the Deed's camp and away from prying eyes. With a bit of dramatic flair, a simple cloaking spell would suffice.

Maya raised Spell above her head, then slowly, she and Blink vanished from sight. Spell was then placed into her inside pocket ready for the performance to begin. Silent as an owl in flight, the invisible dragon took to the air and climbed high above the arena. On Maya's signal, a kick in the flank, the little dragon glided down in a steep dive, silent and unseen, gathering speed. They levelled off and sped across the arena, coming from the direction of the moon, but below it to avoid casting any tell-tale silhouette.

Just fifty witches' hats short of the arch, in response to her second signal, Blink reared up suddenly and spread his wings, instantly eclipsing the moon. Blink bowed his head forward and let forth a huge fireball, which laid down a long red carpet of flame in front of them. Blink's momentum brought them in to land and Maya walked down her dragon's neck, stepping elegantly without breaking stride onto the grass in front of the arch, de-cloaking as the flame subsided. To the onlooking coven, judging by the hush and the odd muted gasp, it was perfect.

It had appeared, as if Maya had just blocked out the moon and had been brought forth in a fireball, born from a wild dragon. Not one of their tame domesticated 'pedigree flamers,' she told herself. Maya held her hand aloft and Spell climbed obediently from her inside pocket and up into to her more accustomed position on Maya's wrist; just to emphasise her status, as the bearer of a living wand.

There was a stunned silence, only finally broken by one of the older witches breaking wind.

"When you're quite finished showing off," the High Priestess rebuked Maya, in a deep scathing voice.

Her comments would have put Maya firmly back in her place, were it not for a big thumbs-up, she spied from under Evaline's robes.

"This is not yet about your magical abilities," the High Priestess chastised her once more, but Maya could tell from the half smile, that she too, had appreciated Maya's talent for the dramatic.

The High Priestess pointed her staff towards the ruined stone archway. Then, she swung it to one side and tapped the heavy wooden staff three times onto one of its sandstone blocks.

Dark green smoke billowed forth, obscuring the view through the archway completely. Gradually, as the smoke cleared it revealed a small room, with hand carved stone walls on three sides. In the middle of the room, stood a small round wooden table with three legs. Two identical black boxes, shimmering in the moonlight, sat on top of it. They were each covered in tiles or scales of some description and both had an identical silver loop on top. Witches' crooks hung from cast iron hooks by the door.

The High Priestess produced a third box from somewhere under her robes.

"Each box is covered with dragon scales, so no magic power can see its contents. This is not a test of your magic powers, young witch. You must use your wits alone. I will referee and my decision is final!" the old lady warned.

The High Priestess looked Maya in the eye.

"Do not undertake this lightly, for as an heir to the Coven of Deeds, if you choose to take on these challenges, you must be prepared to risk everything."

Maya nodded her agreement. She was trying to look confident, but nervous sweat now pricked her brow, like soggy acne on a teenage troll, betraying her welling insecurity.

"Ok, let all in the coven know, that the challenge of the turning table has been accepted. Your wand please," the High Priestess demanded.

Reluctantly, Maya unravelled Spell's roots from around her wrist and placed her wand into the box, which the High Priestess now held in the palm of her hand. The High Priestess closed the box, turned, entered the room and bowed down. Placing the box, slowly and very carefully, on top of the table, exactly equidistant from the other boxes. With one swift movement of her hand, the table was spun and the High Priestess withdrew from the room. The old woman turned now, to address Maya once more. Maya shivered instinctively at her gaze.

"The room is sealed. No-one may enter and only one box may be removed from the room. Once outside, only one box may be opened. Choose well, use your wits. Choose incorrectly and you will forfeit your wand and your challenge for a place in our coven will be void," announced the High Priestess.

"Oh," Maya replied involuntarily, sending a worried glance in Evaline's direction. Evaline, shrugged her shoulders and grimaced, as if to confirm that she'd never heard this demand, to forfeit a wand, before today either.

199

Maya hadn't realised that the stakes would be so high. But she couldn't back down now. The fate of her mum and now her wand Spell, depended on her.

Maya was perplexed, this didn't seem like much of a test of her wits though. Was this first test really, no more than a simple game of chance? The table spun around and around, so fast that the boxes were just a blur. Which-ever box she chose. It would just be a matter of chance, wouldn't it?

Mesmerised by the spinning boxes, Evaline's advice and warnings ran through her head, once more....

*"Take your time. Lesson 1, trust no-one and don't let it **WEIGH** on your mind,"* Maya recalled. "It's a test of wit, not just logic."

"Lesson1, trust no-one?" she mumbled to herself, but Maya didn't even understand, who it was, that she shouldn't trust.

There was nobody in the room, not to trust! Neither was there anything which she could touch, let alone weigh. She wasn't even allowed in. As the table started to slow, it began to wobble. A wobble that became more pronounced, as the turning table came to a halt. Eventually it came to a stop, then settled back a quarter turn and came to rest.

"Choose wisely," commanded the High Priestess.

Maya's mind was racing, but the boxes were all the same. Had she missed something? Had the box with Spell inside been different in some way?

Maya took a deep breath, she needed to think this through. Evaline's advice;

"Trust no-one," what did that mean here?

Did that refer to the High Priestess herself? Had the High Priestess used slight-of-hand to trick her? Maya was sure, she hadn't. She couldn't have. She had been watching closely, very closely. She felt instinctively, that she was missing something though. She had no idea which box to choose. This might indeed, come down to pure dumb luck, just as Evaline had joked earlier.

Maya composed herself, closed her eyes and tried to connect with Spell, but it was as the High Priestess had warned her. The dragon scales, did indeed shield the box from her mind's eye and no magic could penetrate these boxes. Without Spell, she had little power of her own anyway. Nor would Spell move without Maya's command. She cursed herself. If she'd just had warning or had her wits about her earlier, she could have asked her wand to do a jig or simply kick the lid off, whenever the boxes stopped. But it was too late now.

Maya could feel thirteen pairs of eyes burning into the back of her head, waiting and expecting. Her heart pounded in her chest, beating faster than that of an over-weight hamster's, let loose in a cattery, just before lunchtime. She picked up a witches' crook, but it was just for show. She needed to stall for time. They were all looking on now, willing her to fail. Maya could feel it.

Evaline's other piece of advice came back to her, just in the nick of time:

"Take your time."

Maya stopped, composed herself again and resolved that she would. This was just too important, after all.

Maya shuffled anxiously from one side of the doorway to the other, glaring at the boxes, looking for a blemish, a mark, a hair, a sign. Anything that could distinguish one box from the other, but there was nothing. They were all identical and equidistant from each other.

She closed her eyes. Time and time again, Maya rewound the scene and went over what she had just witnessed, in her head. The High Priestess had closed the box, that was the only difference she could think of. There was no difference between any of the boxes.

"Trust no-one," Eveline had warned her, but what did that mean? That she couldn't even trust the referee? Or not even Evaline herself? Maya's mind was spinning with questions, but no answers were forthcoming. And what was the 'weighing' clue all about?

Ok, she took a deep breath, what was it her dad told her? Hmm, if you've got a big problem... something about when he eats elephants. One fork-full at a time, that's it... sort of, but he doesn't even eat elephants! They needed to talk, Maya liked elephants, but not for lunch!

Somehow though, her rather confused musings had helped.

"Who do I trust?" Maya asked herself. Ok, she decided one thing, she trusted Evaline. Why else would she have vouched for her to the coven or given her any advice at all. Let alone train her in dragon combat. She didn't trust that High Priestess though. She was seriously creepy.

Maya thought back to the problem at hand. The only difference that Maya could think of, was that the High Priestess had touched the box with Spell in it. If lesson 1 really applied here, then it was the High Priestess, that she shouldn't trust. And if she can't trust the referee, what chance did she have?

Eyes still shut tight, tongue out, Maya at last started to focus her thoughts properly. Suddenly, out of the muddy waters of confusion, her tongue stopped trawling for inspiration around her lips and returned home from its fishing trip. Maya had landed a single minnow of possible hope... fingerprints!

That was it, fingerprints... there should be fingerprints left on the shiny scales on top of the box, that the High Priestess had touched. The one with Spell inside. Maya opened her eyes and gazed at the top of each box in turn, then back to the High Priestess.

Maya's heart dropped into her witches' britches. She hadn't been quite as observant as she thought. The old woman was wearing gloves, fine black silk gloves. Unlikely to leave a mark, a fibre or any clue whatsoever.

Maya closed her eyes once more and her tongue was back on the case again. She could visualise the boxes spinning, wobbling and coming to a stop.

No, ... no they hadn't. They had spun, wobbled, stopped and moved back, just a little, before coming to a stop. Did that mean anything?

Maya's tongue returned again, this time landing a larger catch.

Of course, now she understood. Thank you Evaline, she thought to herself. It was kind of obvious, when she thought on it. The table must be on a slope. A very slight slope and as it slowed, it started to wobble, with the slightly uneven weight of the boxes. The box with Spell in it, was full and so slightly heavier. It weighed more, so it would settle to the bottom, to the lowest point. That was it! She was sure now and the box on the left, it had settled back to the far corner, as the table had stopped.

Maya bent down level with the table top, she couldn't make out much of a slope, but from her new vantage point, she could just see that there was a coin under two of the three legs of the table. The table was lower at the left and towards the back, where the only leg that had no coin placed under it was. Logically therefore, that had to be the position of the box that weighed the most. Hence why it had settled back there.

Maya knew the answer now, and allowed herself the slightest hint of a smile.

Maya raised the witches crook, picked up the box from the left-hand side, using the silver loop on top and pulled the little black box from the table top, slowly towards herself. Out of the corner of her eye, she could see the first signs of a smile creep across the High Priestess's face.

Maya froze.

Lesson 1, trust no-one, Evaline had said it repeatedly. Did that just mean that someone had tampered with the table by putting coins under the legs. Trust no-one, rang in her ears once more, but she didn't know who her enemy was yet, not for sure.

Oh no, another one of dad's little anecdotes came to mind. Her mind flashed back, to just a couple of months ago. They had been playing chess and he was grinning like a good poker player doesn't.

"What are you up to?" she had asked him suspiciously, deciding not to play yet.

"Ah, as a great tactician once said. "To know what your enemy is up to, you must first put yourself in their shoes."

The great tactician, was of course himself, but she had won the game by asking herself simply: what she would do, if she was in his position. It had, much to his disgust, led her straight to the trap he had laid for her.

Maya thought on this now. She didn't know who had put the coins under the table legs. However, on reflection, it did tell her two things. Firstly, whoever had set this up, had access to the room before the trial started and secondly, they had coins on them. So, if I was in their position, how would I have set a trap for myself?

Maya and her tongue pondered hard on the subject, before she spoke again.

"Logically this is the box, but this was not a test of logic. Evaline has warned me that this is a test of my wit. I still have my wits about me and I smell a rat here. Maya paused again, then addressed the High Priestess:

"I can take only one box out of the room, right?"

"Yes, only one," confirmed the High Priestess.

"And I may open only one box when outside the room?" Maya asked again.

"Yes, that is so," the High Priestess replied, without showing any sign of emotion.

"Then…, oops!" Maya cried unconvincingly, dropping the box 'accidentally' to the floor, just inside the room. The box hit the ground and the lid opened allowing two large gold coins to spill out onto the floor.

There was a lot of murmuring and the odd gasp from the onlooking coven, as if this was not the normal outcome. Evaline in particular looked shocked.

Maya looked up at the High Priestess. Still, she showed no emotion. Not a flicker.

Maya turned back towards the table. Another box had now settled to the same low point on the table, from where she had just removed the first box. Now, Maya lifted this box.

"So, logically this box is now the heaviest box and therefore, it must be the one with my wand in it?" Maya announced, again turning to face the High Priestess. Once more, there was not so much as a twitch from the old woman.

"Oops!" Maya repeated. Again, the box bounced off the ground, but this time, a single gold coin rolled out and onto the floor. Maya glared at the old woman. The High Priestess met her eyes without so much as a blink. Maya shuddered and turned away once more.

Maya raised the crook once more and picked up the only remaining box. Carefully, she brought it outside the room. She looked the High Priestess in the eye, as if something was still bothering her. Whoever, had set the trap wanted her to fail the test and forfeit her wand, that part made sense. But how could they be sure that she wouldn't pick the correct box by pure dumb luck? Had Evaline set her up after all? With all that talk, that hinted of a weighed down box or had Evaline given her the vital clue?

Maya wasn't sure. In fact, the only thing she was sure of now, was that she didn't trust the High Priestess. Not one whisker of a witch's cat.

"I don't think I was meant to do that, was I?" Maya enquired.

"You were told the rules and you remain within the rules challenger," answered the High Priestess, showing not so much as a glimmer of emotion.

But something had been bothering Maya. Something else about the rules themselves. She repeated them now out loud, as well as she could remember;

"Only one box may be removed from the room and once outside, only one box may be opened, if I recall correctly?" Maya asked, still not sure herself, where she was going with this.

"That is correct," the High Priestess confirmed.

Again, Maya's head was spinning, matching the rhythmic motion of her oral thinking appendage, as it circled her lips once more.

"Only one box may be taken from the room, I get that, but why add once outside, only one box may be opened?" Maya asked rhetorically.

Maya stared deep into the cold eyes of the High Priestess. Who stared back again, with not so much as a blink.

"It makes no sense. Not unless..., unless there is more than one box outside the room, of course? And if that's the case..., lesson 1 would definitely apply," Maya answered herself. She looked the High Priestess in the eye once more.

There was no reaction from the High Priestess, nothing.

"I don't think you even put the box with Spell inside it into the room at all?" Maya accused softly, waiting for some reaction. Any reaction, but still there was none. This was a lady, not to play poker with, Maya resolved.

Maya continued undeterred with her train of thought;

"Spell went into the box and you took the box into the room, but as you reached out and placed it onto the table. You bent over, with your back turned to us. There was no need for that bend though. Not unless you were hiding something. Not unless a fourth box was being removed from inside your cloak, a box to replace the box with my wand in it. You left nothing to chance at all, did you?" Maya announced.

For the first time, the High Priestess did not meet her eyes. There was perspiration on her brow, not much, but enough to signal to Maya, that she was indeed onto something.

"I choose to open the fourth box. The one still hidden in your cloak," Maya announced.

"And that is your answer, for all who are gathered here to witness?"

"Em… yes, I suppose so!" Maya confirmed hesitantly, her earlier certainty evaporating into an all-engulfing fog of self-doubt.

"Be it known that the challenger has …

(There was a long and unnecessary pause, longer than in most reality TV shows, when someone's about to be kicked out. Which most sane people, and also most readers of poorly composed fiction, find entirely unnecessary and highly, highly irritating!)

… passed the first test and has shown a wit worthy of the Coven of Deeds," announced the High Priestess.

With that, and to gasps of disbelief from the assembled coven, the High Priestess removed a fourth box from beneath her cloak and passed it to Maya. Maya sighed and passed wind rather noisily, in relief.

Blushing slightly, Maya opened the box to reveal her wand. Spell stretched out her roots and crawled back onto Maya's outstretched hand and from there began to wrap herself around her wrist.

"You have indeed successfully 'turned the table' on us," the High Priestess announced. "Although, had you simply followed the clue in the name of the test and turned the table over with the crook provided, we might all have got to bed a lot sooner!"

"The turning table," Maya sighed.

"It would no doubt have led you to much the same conclusion, but in a fraction of the time. I enjoyed your approach though, but often the simplest solution is the best, my dear," the High Priestess added.

Maya reflected, that after all the deception and trickery at the hands of the High Priestess, it was Maya herself, that ended up being publicly rebuked. This High Priestess, was definitely not a lady to be underestimated.

As the coven dissipated for the evening, Evaline came over sporting a big grin, which spread from one ear to the other and gave Maya a great big hug to congratulate her. Maya thanked her discretely for the clues.

"I couldn't just tell you, and to be honest, I'd never seen it done like that before. Very tricky! It was always just the heaviest box before, not even I thought of knocking over the table either," Evaline joked, less than modestly.

"It was for your own good though. Good training. You will need to have your wits about you, to pass the next two tests. They are much tougher and much more dangerous, but for now, it's a great big pat on the back from me. The hard work starts tomorrow private!" Evaline laughed, slapping Maya heavily across the back.

A test of magic

After the test of wits and a full day's training with Evaline, Maya was drained. For the first time in ages, she slept soundly.

Dragon combat training, resumed early the next morning, after a 'nutritious' breakfast of pickled onions, cherry tomatoes and chocolate muffins.

Maya, as well as conjuring up, what she felt was an excellent breakfast, could now manifest an effective magical shield and a more than passable stun bolt. However, her timing was still an issue; whenever Maya dropped her shield too early, Evaline would delight in punishing her with a quick stun bolt, catching her off guard with a painful blast, while her defences were still down.

Drop her shield too slowly and her own stun bolt would fire into her shield, before bouncing straight back at her. And that really hurt too. They ran around the arena all morning, working on Maya's timing. Although sometimes it felt more like she was practicing the art of flying backwards and landing painfully. As they broke for lunch, Maya was yet to land a single stun bolt on Evaline.

The afternoon was much the same, but to be fair to herself, Maya noted that the frequency of her painful humiliations was at least reducing. As she got better, she even started to enjoy it. It was also more than just timing, point and shoot. Evaline showed Maya how, by angling your magical shield, incoming bolts, which normally knocked you backwards, could be deflected. They would glance off your shield, hardly unbalancing you at all. This, Evaline told her, would be the key to staying on-board her dragon, should she ever graduate from ground-based training, that is.

The other, more risky option, was to meet the bolt head on. With all your weight and forward momentum behind your shield, it was possible to bounce the incoming bolt, straight back to where it had come from.

Maya was much improved, though completely exhausted by the end of the afternoon. Yet, she still hadn't so much as knocked Evaline out of her stride.

Three days later though, things had changed. Maya could almost match Evaline's shield timing and bolt delivery. Although Evaline was still more nimble. Maya's shield and bolt-strength were growing and she was actually holding back Spell's power, so as not to hurt her friend. Encouraged as she was by this, she was yet to land a telling bolt on Evaline. Just the odd glancing blow and they hadn't even taken to the air yet.

Maya had moved on from stun spells though. Fire bolts were Evaline's weapon of choice, it turned out. Tumbling molten magical balls of fire, that really packed a punch. Playing with fire turned out, unsurprisingly to be much more dangerous, but also much more fun and Maya presumed that her eyebrows would grow back in, some day.

Several days of dragon training had passed, without even a mention of dragons from Evaline. At breakfast Maya, now feeling more confident, broached the subject of when they might actually be getting around to:

"... some dragon combat training, you know, with actual dragons?"

"Progress test today, then maybe, we'll see if you're ready, private," Evaline replied, beaming with anticipation. Maya was pleased, but apprehensive. Evaline appeared to be looking forward to this a little too much, for her liking.

They walked out together, but neither one spoke. Once out in the arena, Evaline turned towards Maya and looked her straight in the eye. This time there were no jokes.

"If you stop holding back that wand of yours... I'll stop holding back too!" she announced coldly.

Maya was stunned. She had no idea that Evaline knew she was holding Spell back and much less idea that Evaline herself, was holding back too. Maya acknowledged her opponents offer, with a nod.

They faced each other across the arena. Maya was ready now. Spell's shield now more powerful than ever before. They bowed respectfully to each other.

"Lesson1!" cried Evaline, shooting a stun bolt into the dust at Maya's feet. A cloud of dust flew up under her shield, blinding Maya momentarily. Evaline cartwheeled across the arena and bounced up into the air above her, delivering a bolt from height and at close range. Maya only just managed to parry it with her shield, whilst peering through bloodshot eyes. The blast though, had knocked her unceremoniously onto her bum.

Evaline was on the move once more, two bolts in quick succession as soon as she landed. Maya parried these more successfully and regained her feet again. As Evaline spun and moved again, Maya unleashed her most powerful bolt yet, but Evaline's shield was well angled and it glanced off. It was now Evaline's turn to look shocked. That was a perfect parry, yet still she found herself knocked back and onto her hind quarters with some force. Spell could pack quite a punch.

There was a look now on Evaline's face, that Maya had never seen before. She didn't like the look of it much. Like a vengeful cart-wheeling ninja, Evaline bounced across the arena. Evaline's reflexes allowed her to avoid Maya's next two bolts completely, before unleashing three bolts herself, in quick succession. Maya had never seen her opponent unleash stun bolts that quickly before, it was like a magical machine gun. Maya picked herself back off her backside once more and dropped her shield.

It drew another bolt from Evaline. Maya stood her ground this time; braced herself and at the last moment raised the most powerful shield she could muster, bouncing Evaline's bolt straight back at her with twice the original power. Now it was Evaline's turn to be taken by surprise and her shield was poorly angled, as the bolt hit. A hit so powerful that Evaline's shield dissolved and she was thrown back twenty witches' hats across the arena. Maya lowered her shield and ran to see if her friend was okay. Maya offered her a hand up. Evaline grabbed it, shook her head and smiled.

"Dragons it is then, you're ready for dragons now," she wheezed, clearly still winded by the blast.

Once they were rested, dragon training could begin.

Maya closed her eyes and with three blinks summoned her dragon from his perch up in the oak trees that surrounded the arena. Blink leapt into the air and flapped his wings twice, before gliding in to land next to her. He rumbled from deep inside to greet her and Maya patted him affectionately on the flank.

Evaline summoned her dragon with a loud wolf whistle. As it flew in, Maya's jaw dropped. This was not the dragon Evaline had flown on to collect her from Granny's. This was no 'pedigree flamer' like the others, this was a wild dragon, like blink. Half the size of the big flamers, which the other witches rode on, but still a good head above Blink, as they stood facing each other and exchanging snarling fiery threats.

"You ride a wild dragon too?" Maya gasped.

"Oh yes, mother helped me raise it from an egg. Those pedigree flamers are good for show, well behaved at covens and on other

213

ceremonial duties and they do have a lot of magic power. But they're no match for the fierce heart of a wild dragon. And in the arena, these guys will fly rings around any flamer in the coven. It's like riding a tiger through a cattery of pampered Persian pussy cats!" Evaline explained.

Maya laughed nervously.

"Ok, let's see what you've got… follow me, if you can?" challenged Evaline.

Maya smiled, hardly able to disguise her pleasure at the prospect. Although, the thought of being unseated from her dragon in mid-flight, weighed heavily on her mind.

They took to the skies at speed, looped the loop at a reckless pace, then headed for the forest that lined the arena. Maya was sure that she could match any manoeuvre that Evaline could muster. After all, Mischief had often told her, that she was a natural flyer, when she was riding on her brush. Blink was agile too, smaller and faster than Evaline's dragon; he responded quickly to her every touch and command. She was going to enjoy this!

After just thirty minutes, Maya reflected on just how wrong she had been. Evaline helped, once more, to untangle Maya's bruised and battered body from the top of an old oak tree. Her latest collision had been almost a pleasure, when compared to the discomfort of the prickly pine and monkey-puzzle trees, that she'd previously ploughed into.

Over lunch, outside the challenger's tent, Evaline tended to Maya's cuts and bruises, whilst Maya probed her about how she had ever learned to fly like that.

"My mother taught me. You know, how to hunt the old-fashioned way. In the forest with a bow and poison arrow," Evaline explained, with quite some enthusiasm.

That explains the bloodstained sack for Blink's dinner the other night, Maya thought to herself. A cold shudder running up her spine.

"Stalking and hunting down wild deer and boar through the woods, racing and dodging between the trees, was hazardous and demanding, but great training for a dragon rider," Evaline continued. "Mind you, one nick from the end of a poison arrow, out there in the woods, that could be the end of you."

"Really, and your mum still let you?" Maya was intrigued. "My mum didn't let me walk to school alone until last year, let alone hunt wild boar with deadly weapons!"

"Mine neither… that school run's much more dangerous, all those 4 by 4s and frantic mums and grannies attempting reverse parking!" Evaline joked and shuddered at the thought.

"My mother prepared me well though, I always knew how to make the antidote, just in case. Wolfslair, a rare berry only found around here in the shadow of that rocky outcrop, up there. See on the other bank of the river," Evaline explained, whilst raising her right arm to point it out.

Maya followed Evaline's outstretched arm and nodded as she picked out the rocks and cliff face, to which, she was sure, Evaline had just pointed.

"No magic has ever worked on that poison, only a potion made from wolfslair berries and common meadow wart can cure the toxins from our arrows and the smell isn't bad for keeping midges at bay into the bargain," Evaline continued with a smile.

Rather unexpectedly, Evaline grabbed Maya's hand. She glanced around rather nervously, then whispered:

"You'd do well to remember that. You know, just in case."

215

"Just in case what?" Maya asked, but just then, one of the Deeds rounded the tent and Maya got the distinct impression, that the conversation was over.

That afternoon's dragon flying lesson continued in the same vein.... left, right, up, down, branch... ouch! Right, left, left, down, right, ... no, the other right, tree... ouch!

By about 4 o'clock in the afternoon, Evaline called it a day.

"It's a day!" she announced.

"What is?" Maya asked.

"Twenty-four hours silly!" Evaline joked. "Besides, I think you've knocked down enough firewood for a fine bonfire this evening!"

Since Mischief had elected to sit out the hazardous training rituals, in favour of napping on his comfortable red cushion. Evaline had taken it upon herself to put Maya in her place every so often.

Maya giggled.

"Anyway, big day tomorrow private!" Evaline added.

"What's tomorrow?" Maya asked eagerly, hoping that at last, they might actually get around to some dragon combat for real.

"Tomorrow's another day private. I do wish you would keep up!" Evaline scolded with a smile.

But tomorrow wasn't to be just another day, as Evaline explained later, over yet more stale bread and cheese. Tomorrow, as it turned out, was the day selected by the High Priestess for her second test. A test of Maya's magical ability.

Maya was expected to meet the coven, as the sun rose over the arena, by the old stone arch. Maya wasn't surprised. In fact, she now expected that these tests would come, whenever the coven felt she was most tired or vulnerable. The first test had been set on her first day and after a sleepless night. What better time to test her wits? Tomorrow morning, Maya would still be exhausted and battered from her dragon combat training. That's when, they would test her again and tonight she already knew, would be another late one. Maya had decided that for herself.

"I hope you'll be making another big entrance tomorrow?" Evaline prompted, with an expectant grin, as they parted company.

"You'll see," Maya replied. She wasn't giving anything away, but Evaline could tell from Maya's grin, that she was up to something.

This time, Maya had decided that her entrance would be no modest party piece. No parlour-trick. The inspiration had come to her earlier that week. She had flown on her brush towards the River Doon. Evaline had warned her to steer clear of the water and Maya had recounted her favourite witch's joke:

"I know how to pass running water you know," she'd boasted.

"Really," Evaline sounded impressed.

"Every time I pee!" Maya giggled.

She never got tired of that one, but it had given her an idea. An idea, which she'd explained to Mischief later that evening, as they sat around the wood burner in her tent.

"All witches lose their powers over running water, right?" Maya confirmed.

Mischief nodded reluctantly, fearing a reworking of that same lame old joke.

"But with a powerful living wand like Spell. I've noticed that I still have some magical ability left, whenever I stray out over the waters," Maya confessed.

217

"Up until you reach the midpoint, yes, then they're all gone," Mischief corrected her.

"No, that's what I'm telling you," Maya continued. "Even beyond the mid-point. Not much, not at first. Spell's powers are growing and she's recently spouted a new bud. I wonder if she'll flower soon, or just grow another leaf?" Maya added unhelpfully, straying completely off the subject.

Mischief frowned, prompting her to get on with it.

"After dark," Maya continued. "I've, well, I've been practicing with Blue and Spell. I've had a good soaking every night this week, but every time I tried it, I got out a little further.

"I just thought you'd started bathing?" Mischief interrupted.

"Ha ha!" Maya responded, with her best sarcastic teenage sneer. "I've been getting further every time. That is, until last night."

"What happened last night?" Mischief asked.

"I made it all the way across without getting wet," Maya confirmed sheepishly, as if admitting to a great and shameful secret.

"Really?" the cats eyes shone wide in surprise, reflecting in the dim light, as if set in tarmac and illuminated by an oncoming truck.

"Well, when I say that I didn't get wet? That's not quite true," Maya confessed.

"Oh no... you didn't?" chuckled Mischief.

Maya nodded and blushed with embarrassment.

"You have to concentrate hard and clear your mind of everything. It takes a lot out of you and I had forgotten to go earlier and...," Maya finally realised, that less information on this particular subject, might perhaps be her best option.

218

Mischief dissolved into laughter. It was infectious and Maya also lost control too, so much so, that she nearly wet herself for a second time.

That night Maya practised again, but this time Mischief had a few additional suggestions.

"If you really want to engage in these parlour tricks, to impress your new friends, I may have an idea," he'd suggested.

Far away from the arena, some way downstream on the banks of the River Doon, Maya and her cat practiced with Spell, all evening.

"Fire bolts Spell, your mightiest… lay her a carpet of fire on the far bank," suggested Mischief. Maya closed her eyes, raised Spell and made it so.

The first two fell short, fizzing out across the water, trailing steam and bubbles behind them, then exploding with an unexpectedly high-pitched pop. On the third attempt however, her range was true. The far bank lit up with flames, much like a dragon's bed.

"Well done, but one more thing. You only have the power to cast such a spell before you cross the river's mid-flow. We need to disguise it or perhaps to delay it somehow?"

"What if it were to take a detour?" Maya asked with a glint in her eye.

Mischief raised a furry eyebrow and suggested:

"Maybe a little magical black shrouding smoke, just for effect?"

Maya was now looking forward to this, as they plotted the show to come, late into the night.

Wolfslair

An orange diamond of light pierced the night sky and cast a long shaft of sunlight from the top of the hills, that lay to the east. It stretched down the hillside, finally illuminating the waters of the River Doon below. That was their cue and Maya climbed on board Blue and took to the air, flanked by Blink. The coven was gathered on the other side of the river, atop the hill, waiting by the old stone arch. Thirteen witches in full ceremonial gowns, eagerly awaited her entrance.

Maya set out over the Doon, mounted on Blue. Blink accompanied them and rose into the air on Maya's right flank. Their shapes still shrouded from sight, by the dark shadow cast by the steep embankment on the far side of the river. Now, nearing the midpoint, Maya raised Spell above her head and steadied herself with a final deep breath. Maya unleashed a firebolt, shrouded completely from sight, by a cloud of dark billowing smoke. It set off unseen into the dim light of the dawn, on a long and deliberately elliptical course.

Maya clapped her hands. It was the signal for Blink to light up the night sky with his purple glow and to unleash a fireball all of his own. Now, sitting proudly astride her broom and illuminated for all to see, by the purple glow from her wild dragon, Maya emerged through the heart of the oncoming fireball, with Spell held aloft just as they reached the midpoint of the river Doon. She felt her magic draining from her quickly now, but Maya kept her course, kept her concentration, kept her faith in Spell and Blue and in their magical bond. She knew they could do it.

Behind Maya, the roar of the hidden firebolt thundered in her ears, as it burned through its blackened shroud and zipped under Blue and beneath the belly of the little dragon flying alongside. It passed far too close for comfort, almost shooting Blue out of the air, but their wobbles went unnoticed. The firebolt roared beneath Maya's feet and on towards the far bank where it exploded right on cue. As they neared the far bank, it had laid down an impressive carpet of fire ahead of them.

Maya landed Blue safely onto the far bank and dismounted, with nearly half a witches' hat to spare. Desperately trying not to grin from ear to ear, she walked slowly down the red carpet of flames and embers which stretched out, in front of her.

No witch should be able to cross running water. Not without plummeting into the waters beneath, much less apparently cast a powerful firebolt spell from beyond the mid-flow of the river. A place, where no such magical powers should exist. Maya was rightfully pleased with herself.

A moment of such awesome gobsmacking originality, power and magical talent, only really spoiled by cat whistles and cries of: "Go girl!" coming from a scruffy black and white cat, sitting on a comfortable red cushion.

"That should put the fear of spinach for tea into whoever it is they choose to challenge me in the arena," she boasted quietly to Mischief, as he joined her side.

The High Priestess was the first to speak:

"I see from the vulgarity of your entrance that, yet again, you wish to be tested at the highest level possible. Then, so be it."

Maya's bubble was burst, well and truly. She was going to object, but Mischief said first, what she was already thinking.

"Lesson 1?" the cat whispered up to her.

Had Evaline duped her? Had her friend tricked her into setting herself up for even more difficult challenges, under the pretext of frightening her future challenger? A challenger Maya realised now, if things went wrong today, that she might never face.

No, Maya shrugged off the notion. She trusted Evaline, she was a true friend. She would trust Evaline with her life.

"The second test, magical ability... our traditional test would not be a true test for you. Not for a witch of your considerable powers, or so it would appear," the High Priestess pronounced, raising a curious eyebrow. "For a witch with a living wand, the coven will only accept the highest level of incantation," she continued.

Maya cast a worried glance, down towards her cat.

"A transformation spell of our choosing," the High Priestess demanded. There were audible gasps from the coven behind.

"We have all heard tales of how you saved an injured snow leopard and its cub from hunters, through transformation into its form. Maya glared at Evaline. Who blushed, as if to confirm her guilt, in just the same way her Aunty Dot doesn't, after blabbing a story relayed in complete confidence.

"Blabbermouth," Mischief whispered accusingly under his breath.

"If true, your powers are a match, even for my own," the High Priestess conceded.

Maya nodded to acknowledge, that the story was indeed true.

The High Priestess showed no emotion and continued:

"Very well, a fawn is injured in the forest, somewhere on the far bank. Predators are closing in on it. Your test, is to become the fawn and save it from the destiny which now surely awaits it. Fail and you too will suffer its fate and your wand, your challenge and your badly trained dragon, will also be forfeit."

Blink grumbled disapprovingly, as Maya stepped forward to accept the challenge. She now had a lump in her throat, that went all the way down to her witch's britches. She knew that she had no choice. This was for her mum. She couldn't fail.

Maya had never tried a transformation spell from within the magic realm before. She was worried. Previously, she had only accomplished it through the mirrored gateway in the secret room, but she supposed the process to be similar.

She closed her eyes and grasped Spell tightly. Spell's roots grasped back, but her grip was much weaker than normal. With sudden horror, Maya realised that the little wand was already exhausted. Her powers almost completely spent, by all her needless magical antics. Crossing the river had taken nearly everything that the little wand had.

Desperately trying to look undeterred, Maya focused her thoughts and closed her eyes. In her mind's eye, she set off in search of the fawn. She thought her way to the other bank. It was hazy at first, then shapes emerged, through a clearing fog. She started searching through the forest, rounding oak after ash, after whatever that funny looking bush was. She was looking for tracks, trying to feel the presence of the poor injured animal. Trying to sense it and to connect with it.

Spell though was tired, far too tired, Maya realised. Her mind's eye view was already fogging over. Tantalisingly, a white tail appeared in the distance, then was gone. She couldn't make a connection, not like this. Not at this distance, not with Spell exhausted this way.

Maya opened her eyes again.

"I need to get closer. Come on Blink," Maya called, then paused. "No sorry, I have to take Blue now, we're not yet good enough in the trees together, little dragon," Maya explained apologetically, as the young dragon's head dropped in disappointment.

Maya wasted no magical energy this time. She gestured for Mischief to join her and flew her brush up the river bank. They dismounted and crossed the old disused railway bridge, a few hundred witches' hats upstream.

On the other side, the search began once more. The old-fashioned way. On foot. Maya was soon in the woodland, eyes focused on the ground ahead of her. There were animal tracks, lots of them. Paw prints; from what looked like very large dogs and the tracks of cloven-footed animals, which Maya presumed were deer. The tracks ran in all directions. How could she possibly pick out one trail from this? It was hopeless.

Despair started to creep in and reluctantly, Maya had to concede, that she wasn't quite the tracker, that she'd hoped she was. There might not be much time either. If the predators that the High Priestess had warned of, were indeed closing in on the injured fawn.

She needed help, a tracker. Mischief though, would have to do.

"A fawn, an injured fawn. Can that nose of yours help?" Maya asked hopefully.

"I'll try," Mischief replied, betraying no great confidence in his own tracking skills, after having been put to shame, by Evaline a few weeks earlier, on the trail of the pufflings.

Good fortune, for once appeared to be on their side, as Mischief soon picked out a small cloven print, a print with a spot of blood next to it. Mischief, encouraged by this flush of early success, pointed the way with his snout, like a bloodhound. Maya, realising that few deer walked backwards through the woods, then took over and led the way in the opposite direction.

They were soon on the trail, well a trail anyway. Scrambling along the river bank, pushing their way through shrubs and nettles and jumping over ditches.

Maya was like a bloodhound, except she had no shaggy tail, only two legs and no furry coat. She did however have a wet nose and that seemed to do the trick. Small cloven hoof prints led the way. Mischief pointed out their uneven depth, the fawn was limping badly. There was blood on the ground too, spots every few witches' hats. Then different tracks joined the trail. Maya looked towards Mischief, deeply worried.

"Puppies?" Maya asked hopefully, having already guessed what her cat was about to say. "Very, very large puppies maybe?"

"Wolves!" Mischief's words stopped Maya in her own tracks, "Six of them."

Maya was usually a fan of a good six pack, especially belonging to a certain actor out of one of those Twilight vampire movies, she liked so much, but this time she looked spooked.

"We need to get ahead of them," Maya announced with new-found urgency.

Mischief nodded his agreement and they both squeezed onto Blue. Once on board, they took off, flying low above the tree tops. It was a risk. They couldn't follow the fawns tracks like this. But their gamble was rewarded. It was as if Maya now had x-ray vision, picking out the wolf pack below, one by one through the leafy canopy. Ahead, quite some distance off, Mischief's keen eyes picked out a flash of white rump, exiting the river.

"There it is, the fawn!" Mischief cried.

Either instinctively, to cover its tracks and scent, or in a misguided attempt to cross the river, the fawn had entered the water and had then been swept downstream. It had been washed up, exhausted, further down river on a sandy beach on the same bank. They flew on and landed close-by. The unfortunate creature was cold and injured. A broken arrow protruded from its right flank.

"Poor thing," whispered Maya.

"I can save it, with a transformation. I know I can, but I need to get closer. Spell is still weak. I need to touch her," Maya explained.

Maya approach slowly, as the fearful fawn backed away on unsteady legs. Maya held out her hand. Spell clung to her wrist and started to glow gently. The fawn was nervous at first, then stopped, as Maya's mind's eye made contact. The fawn seemed to understand. It lay down and closed its eyes, exhausted and seemingly close to death.

Maya moved towards the little fawn and stroked it gently on the neck, before placing her hand on its forehead. It was calm now. And soon, Maya was too. Maya focussed on the fawn, she could hear it breathe, sense its heartbeat. It was racing. Maya's own pulse too was raised, in response. Faster and faster, until it matched that of the injured beast. They beat as one now, synchronised, together. As Spell glowed with all the energy she could muster. They were now one. Maya was the fawn.

"Meeeh!" Maya fawn bleated (that's ouch, for those of you who don't speak fawn). They were in agony, but there was more here. She was weak, so very weak now. Spell too, hung limp and almost lifeless, loosely wrapped around Maya's front leg. With the last of her magic power and what felt like the last of Maya's energy reserves, she healed the wound. Spell glowed dimly and the arrow head slipped slowly outwards. The flesh slowly healing behind it.

Maya fawn felt little relief though, her head was still spinning and all her magic was spent.

Mischief picked up the arrow. Maya watched through woozy eyes, but she already knew what he was about to say...

"A poison arrow!" he gasped in horror.

Maya realised now, too late, that it had been a trap all along. She had fallen right into it. Of course, the arrow had been poisoned. An arrow shot by a Deed witch, riding on the back of a wild dragon she presumed. Lesson 1 rang in Maya's ears... trust nobody. Evaline had betrayed her.

Evaline was the one who had manipulated her all along. Misleading her in the first test of wits. Having her waste her magical strength on parlour tricks, tricks that only earned her harder initiation tests and exhausted her powers. Even before that, she had let Maya risk her life, to fire her wand in a wild dragon's fire, all the while withholding that she had her own dragon, back in the Coven of Deeds. And now, just for good measure, she had fired the poisoned arrow. The arrow which had just delivered the toxin now circulating through Maya fawn's body. How could she have been taken in so easily?

Despairingly, she looked up at Mischief. A true friend. Maya suddenly had so much to say, so much to explain. But now, she had neither the energy nor the ability, being a fawn, to communicate at all. And the poison was strong, her head swam in the intoxicating venom from the arrow. A deadly poison shot from the bow of a 'friend', whom she had trusted. A 'friend' who had betrayed her. That betrayal, it hurt as much as any wound from a poison arrow could. A Deed poison that...

Wait a minute! Maya fawn's tongue returned to home base with a sudden recollection. A poison that Evaline had been at some pains

227

to explain to her, exactly how to make the antidote for… "Just in case."

Maya's head was spinning. Not just from the poison. If she could just summon some magic power. She could break the bond, but if she left now, the fawn would surely die. It wasn't an option, for Maya was the fawn now. Bonded with the frightened animal, she could not leave half of herself to die. To do so, would also forfeit the challenge and any chance, she had, of ever joining the Deeds and releasing her mother.

But, if Evaline had trapped her, why would she have told Maya about the antidote? It made no sense, not unless, in spite of how it all looked now, she was still her friend? As uncomfortable as she was with it, Evaline was now her only hope. Stumbling to her feet, Maya fawn started to draw with her hooves on the sandy beach, in the highest stakes game of picture charades, she had ever played.

Mischief guessed out loud, perplexed by the woozy artwork.

"Dog, dog's head, dog's head… soup, no, not soup… drink, cave, lay, eggs, chickens, ogre, no troll, magic… no, yes, magic soup, no… close, potion… yes potion." The pantomime and Mischief's wild panicked guesswork went on for minutes, until finally he had it…

"Dog's head and chicken soup served to a troll in a cave!" announced Mischief finally, proudly sitting down, job done.

Mischief sat back and thought, while Maya rested. Slowly, clarity returned to the little cat's muddled brain:

"Not dog, wolf?"

Maya fawn nodded.

"Not cave… from the number of chickens and eggs, I'd say layer or lair?" Mischief conjectured.

228

Maya fawn nodded again.

"Not soup, he had already established that, it's a potion she needs, not a school dinner!" he scolded himself aloud, in frustration.

"Some sort of wolfslair potion I'd guess, if your life depended on it. Which it does," Mischief announced, proudly stroking his whiskers, as he did whenever he thought he sounded remotely like that detective on the television, who Maya always referred to as Hercules Porridge.

Exhausted Maya fawn lay back down to rest.

"But, if that was the case, why didn't you just write it down in the sand in the first place?" Mischief asked, with a patronising grin in Maya fawn's direction.

Maya fawn felt too tired and disoriented to be embarrassed. Just as well this wasn't the test of wits though. Maya fawn feared that she would have failed already. With her front hoof, Maya fawn now wrote shakily in the sand, *meadow wart and wolfslair berries.*

"I don't know anything about plants!" Mischief objected.

Aunty Dot does, Maya fawn hooved into the ground.

Mischief sighed reluctantly. He didn't relish the thought of explaining what was going on, to Maya's mother's rather shallow twin sister. But plants were one of the few topics, if you exclude mindless gossip, that Dot could claim to be knowledgeable about. Mischief didn't do much magic these days, but this was an emergency, so with a twitch of his nose and every ounce of magical energy he could muster, he summoned Aunty Dot.

Uninvited summons, are, as a rule, generally frowned upon in the witching community. With good reason.

Timing is just a matter of luck. Fortunately, Aunty Dot had just finished on the toilet. Dot was just pulling her trousers up, as she was summoned. She had a very surprised look on her face indeed.

A shocked Aunty Dot, somehow felt compelled to explain her appearance, "A moment earlier and I was having a..."

"Enough information!" Mischief interrupted, just in the nick of time. "Maya fawn needs your help; wolfslair and meadow wart, think you can help?"

"Ok. Hi Maya fawn, like the new look!" Dot replied. "Think so, I'd know it if I see it. I sometimes use it as a little pick-me-up for the postman. And he does! If, you know what I mean?

Mischief just clasped an exasperated paw to his forehead.

"Think you can make it?" Mischief asked Maya fawn, helping her onto all fours once more.

Maya fawn led the way on shaky legs, like a new-born giraffe taking its first tentative steps. She headed slowly up the bank, towards the rocky outcrop, the one that Evaline had pointed out to her, the other day. Mischief took up a position at the back of the group, watching out for any sign of the wolf pack. The wolves had last been seen searching the bank, near to where the fawn had jumped into the water, but he knew it wouldn't be long, before they would pick up its scent again.

Aunty Dot was on form, thanks to the charms of her new postie, and Granny's dubious guidebook on; "How to possess the man of your choice." She was currently up to speed on the basics of simple botanically based potions. Dot soon clasped a large clump of what she hoped was meadow wart, in her right hand.

Maya fawn was exhausted though, the poison was really taking its toll now. They moved more slowly with each leaden step she took, but, after one last undignified shove on the bum from her Aunty Dot, Maya fawn made it up onto a ledge, below a rocky outcrop. This, she was sure, was the place that Evaline had been at such pains to point out to her.

Maya fawn fell to the ground, she was spent. In front of her, a cave burrowed its way deep into the river bank. The rocky outcrop was covered in ferns and the rocks glistened in the dappled sunlight, as they dripped with water falling from the sheer rock face above. Maya fawn looked again towards the cave. Near to its entrance, she noticed a small green bush laden with red berries.

Maya fawn let out a sigh of relief. She had made it. She had begun to doubt Evaline, she really had, but her friend had come up trumps this time.

Her relief was short lived though.

"Don't see any wolfslair here?" Aunty Dot announced, sounding puzzled and looking around. "It has distinctive purple flowers and broad leaves, little blue berries too. Grows in dry arid conditions... you really don't come across it very often in Scotland you know."

Maya fawn stared in horror at the red berried bush with its small leaves, then down at the ground below. The mud beneath her feet was covered with scratch marks and paw prints leading to the cave beyond. She had led them to the wolf's lair alright, straight into Evaline's trap!

There was no hope now and Maya fawn blinked three times, closed her eyes and drifted off into unconsciousness. Maya's final thoughts were that at least she would die, with her friends by her side. That was how she wanted it.

"Wolf prints!" Dot shouted in sudden alarm.

"Lesson 1!" sighed Mischief. "Evaline's tricked us again, the cave. That's the wolf's lair!"

"And they're coming home too!" Aunty Dot added, spotting a pair of sapphire eyes, piercing through the undergrowth.

They were trapped. There was no way to escape. The far side of the escarpment dropped over a sheer impenetrable cliff and the wolf pack was closing in from the direction, from which they had just clambered up onto the ledge. There was no way up either, it was a sheer rock face, they couldn't climb any further.

"Any ideas?" asked Mischief, cowering and retreating slowly from the oncoming pack. The wolves advanced slowly, deliberately, they edged forward, backs arched with sabre-like canine teeth bared, growling and drooling in anticipation.

"Got any gossip?" asked Dot.

"What?" Mischief demanded incredulously.

"I like gossip and if we're all going to be eaten, I'd like one last piece of scandal please!" Dot snivelled.

"Really?" Mischief gasped.

The first wolf, an enormous white beast, stepped out onto the rocky escarpment, followed closely by another. Mischief and Aunty Dot stepped backwards, huddling instinctively around Maya fawn, forming a protective circle of two. Mischief's fur, now puffed up like a hamster, which had chewed through the TV's power cable, now cowered and 'bravely' covered Aunty Dot's rear. No mean feat, according to Maya's dad.

Deep growling and slobbering noises filled the air, as a third and fourth wolf snarled up the banking to join with their leader, the large white alpha male.

"Do something!" Mischief pleaded. His own magic exhausted by summoning Dot to the 'rescue.' Aunty Dot was not exactly renowned as a talented witch. In fact, quite the opposite, she was a misfit, but this was her moment to shine and lives depended on it. A pressure that her own unique blend of magical Tourette's and dyslexia could well have done without.

Dot raised her wand and cast her spell:

"Stunofication! Oh bother, no, smoky bacon! Sorry, fire flies or something like that!" With that, her wand glowed briefly, before summoning two limp and uncooked rashers of streaky bacon and a couple of very confused insects, in place of the intended stun and firebolts.

The smell of the smoky meat tit bits, only serving to hunger the advancing carnivores further.

"Tumble drier!" was the next stray random thought to enter her panicked and jumbled mind.

"Jodhpurs!" was next.

"Boy's knickers!" being her final random offering.

At least, the appearance of a large white tumble drier took out one of the wolves as it fell to earth; landing on a big black wolf at the back, just as it was joining the others from the woods. As for the rest of her spells though, to be honest, they were just pants!

The alpha male crouched down, snarling and displaying a set of fangs, which would not be out of place, in any horror movie. His hind quarters shuffled, readying himself to pounce. Dot was in his sights. His eyes focused in like lasers on her neck. He crouched, pupils fixed and dilated. He would make the first kill.

Above them, the noise of beating wings. Followed closely by a powerful fireball. The acrid smell of burning wolf butt and fur filled the air. The sound of yelping and whimpering wolf rang out across the escarpment, as the alpha male turned, his proud tail now blackened, singed and tattered. He fled. Once the alpha had retreated, it was closely followed by the rest of the pack, as another wall of flame, billowed from above.

Lots of girly tears, hugging and slobbering followed and when Mischief was quite finished, Dot joined in too.

"Blink, you saved our bacon!" announced Dot, waving the two slices of raw bacon proudly from the end of her wand.

"Clever girl," Mischief muttered under his breath. Casting his eyes down to Maya fawn. Now realising, that Maya's last conscious action, had been to blink three times and summon her trusty dragon.

Celebrations were short lived, though. Aunty Dot bent down to check if Maya fawn was still breathing. She was, but it was laboured. She didn't have long.

"We need a potion, an anti-dote and a powerful one and quickly or she'll die," Mischief declared nervously.

"I'm her Aunty Dot... does that help?" came the unwelcome response.

"Think... Mischief think!" Mischief scolded himself.

Maya fawn groaned. A last flicker of life perhaps, Mischief thought. But the fawn's tongue was out, still twitching, then receded suddenly.

Mischief had seen this before.

"Maya! Maya! Stay with us... what is it?" Mischief demanded.

A single hoof raised off the dirt floor and stretched out towards the bush covered in red berries.

Mischief's heart sank again:

"But that's not wolfs..."

Mischief didn't finish the sentence.

"Quick the berries, grab a handful and crush them with that herb your holding!" Mischief ordered with great urgency.

"But that's not wolfslair!" Dot objected.

"Yes, but sometimes plants are known by different names. You know, depending on where they grow," Mischief explained. But he was met only by a baffled look.

"Look, if you were a witch here. You know, if you flew with the Deed's over Cambusdoon. You might very well know these berries as wolfslair berries too. Berries from the wolf's lair... no?" Mischief tried again to explain.

"You think?" Dot didn't look convinced, but grabbed a handful of the berries and started to squeeze them anyway.

"Maybe Evaline told Maya the truth?" Mischief continued. "I think that's what Maya's trying to tell us!"

Dot, mixed in some of meadow wart herb and bent over Maya fawn. Ready to squeeze the gooey mixture into the little fawns open mouth. Dot turned to face Mischief and looked him straight in the eyes:

"What do you think? Can we trust this Evaline or not?"

Mischief didn't respond at first. He looked worried and hesitant.

"We'll only get one shot at this. Maya will die shortly, unless we do something!" Dot prompted him again.

Mischief thought hard, then lied:

"I'd trust her with my life!"

All Mischief could really think of was lesson 1 though. Right now, he wouldn't trust Evaline to hold his ice-cream, but she was now Maya's only chance. However slim the chance and somewhat ashamed by his earlier cowardice. He vowed that the consequences of this decision, would be his alone to bear.

Dot nodded.

Mischief nodded.

Dot squeezed and gooey drops of viscous green liquid dropped into the fawn's open gape.

Maya fawn's tongue retreated and the fawn took a shallow laboured breath, as if it might be its last. Nothing happened… twice, then…

Maya fawn sat up abruptly, choked violently then spluttered and wheezed. Suddenly, her eyes opened wide, as if in utter panic. Her once bright eyes dimmed visibly and rolled to the back of her head, as she fell backwards, lifeless. Maya fawn was rigid and motionless. It was as if she had just swallowed a cyanide cocktail.

"She's dead!" screamed Dot.

"No, no, no…," muttered Mischief.

Mischief just stared, his heart split in two. He knew that this was his fault. He would never forgive himself. They must have been poison berries and Maya had paid the ultimate price for his stupidity and Evaline's treachery.

Unseen, a large black bird watched on, through black beady satisfied eyes, from the shadows of the cave.

Blink roared in grief. His purple glow dimmed to charcoal black. The earth shook beneath them, as the little dragon shot a fireball into the sky above, as if to signal the passing of a great witch and his friend, into the witches' afterlife. Above the clouds darkened, the wind gathered and howled. Rain fell and thunder clapped all around.

"Caw, caw, caw!" came the piercing gloating cry of a raven like bird, as it swooped down towards Maya fawn's body. Talons raised and targeted on Spell.

Mischief's reflexes were faster though, batting the foul creature off course, with a lightening flash of his paw. His claws tearing a flutter of black feathers from its wings.

The bird stayed airborne though and made for the cover of the trees.

Aunty Dot moved forward sobbing. She removed her jacket, then bent down to place it respectfully over Maya fawn's lifeless body.

Rain filled the puddles, which now accumulated on the ledge in front of the wolf's lair.

Mischief stared down at Maya fawn's poisoned body, unable to reconcile his part in her demise.

"Caw, caw, caw!" the bird called once more, as if mocking, then it rose, into the darkening sky and was gone.

Startled by the familiar and chilling call of the departing bird, Maya fawn opened one eye, then looked up, as if to say;

"What's up with you miserable lot? Who died?"

It had worked. Aunty Dot had indeed lived up to her name and produced the anti-dote.

Lots of girly tears, hugging and slobbering followed and when Mischief was quite finished, Dot and Maya fawn joined in too.

They stayed for a few hours, sheltering in the wolf's lair, out of the pouring rain. As the day cooled to night, they warmed themselves on a fire, lit by a very attentive purple dragon. Then toasting rashers of bacon courtesy of Aunty Dot's magical misfire.

As Maya fawn rested, she reflected on the day's events. She had been saved by the unquestioning devotion and courage of her friends and family. And as for Evaline, she wasn't sure. Maya knew that without that antidote, she'd now be dead, but without the poison on the arrow in the first place, hmm... did lesson 1 now apply to Evaline too?

As Maya's strength returned, she broke her bond with the fawn and it returned to the forest.

Maya insisted that Aunty Dot return home too, to keep an eye on Granny.

"After all, she really can't be trusted alone with that new handsome postie, can she?" Maya joked.

Maya knew, that she had to return to the Coven of Deeds. For much as she hated it, and lesson 1 kept ringing in her ears, she still needed their help to save her mother. Now, with only one challenge remaining, she was closer and more determined than ever.

It was nearly mid-night when Maya came in to land in the arena. She passed two pedigree flamers and their riders heading out, in the direction of the wolf's lair. They had a large wooden crate slung underneath them, as if sent to collect something.

Their riders exchanged confused glances, at the sight of Maya's approach, shrugging their shoulders, before circling back to where they had just taken off from. Maya landed near to the ruined stone arch. Out in the arena, stood the lone figure of Evaline, soaked by the rain, holding vigil by a smoky log fire. Shivering with the cold, as if she'd been waiting there all day and night.

By the time Maya landed though, many of the Deeds witches had appeared from all over. There was quite a commotion. All the witches wanted to talk to her and to hear her story. They were all there, all except for the High Priestess.

Out of sight, a cold pair of beady black eyes glared from a tree branch above the old stone arch, then took off into the night sky without so much as a "Caw!"

There was an air of disbelief amongst the Deeds. Maya felt more like a celebrity, as she pushed through the coven, to get to Evaline.

"Thank you, you know, for the anti-dote. I did it!" she whispered, as she swung Evaline around in a crushing embrace.

Evaline smiled rather nervously.

Mischief though watched on, through cold suspicious eyes. He would never trust Evaline again. He swore it.

When all the commotion had died down, Maya and Evaline made their way back to Maya's tent. They passed the wooden crate lying on the ground, now detached from the dragons, which had been carrying it earlier.

"What's that for?" Maya asked suspiciously. But she had already deduced the answer, before it came.

"Sorry, but it's for your body, I'm afraid," came the chillingly honest answer.

"Should I ask why they've left it out?" Maya enquired solemnly.

"No!" Evaline replied bluntly.

A shiver ran up and down Maya's spine, like Jack frost was playing the xylophone on her backbone, using a pair of icicles.

Dragon combat training

There were precious few training days left, before the next full moon and the day of the final challenge. The first couple were spent on dragon riding skills.

Manoeuvring around trees at speed, sudden starts, stops and most of all on balance. Evaline instructed Maya on how to shift her weight quickly and effectively, to help her dragon's manoeuvres and turns. This, was made all the more difficult, because of Evaline's insistence, that they should do it with one hand tied behind their backs. Apparently, to mimic the effects of carrying their magic shields.

"The shield arm," Evaline explained, "is only to be used to move your shield. Never to aid your balance. Do that and you will drop your guard with every twist and turn that your dragon makes. You'd be like a sitting turnip to your opponent, private!"

"A sitting turnip? Don't you mean, a sitting duck, sergeant?" Maya protested.

"No, I've never seen a duck sit still, they flee for their lives whenever I'm hunting them, from the back of my dragon?" Evaline grinned.

Maya shrugged her shoulders, she had to concede the point.

"But turnips, on the other hand, usually remain relatively motionless!" Evaline explained, sporting a broad sarcastic grin.

Once Maya had mastered the art of not crashing into every tree in her path. Chasing live prey animals through the forest was on the menu (not literally), thanks to a very obliging young fawn and her family, which they came across in the woods. After two full days,

Maya finally got within, what Evaline described as, "a good bow's length," of the stealthy young fawn.

"Ok, then, I think you're ready," Evaline finally conceded.

The next morning Maya was nervous, there were only three days left to prepare for dragon combat in the arena, before the next full moon. And she was still to put all these new found skills together. It was frustrating, but she trusted Evaline's judgement.

In an unguarded moment, Evaline had let slip that her training and wild dragon, made Maya more than a match for most of the witches in the coven:

"Except for the coven champion, her apprentice, her apprentice's apprentice, the High Priestess herself and her daughter, of course," Evaline added.

Maya was almost 50% sure, she was joking.

She trusted Evaline, but Maya also knew her well enough by now, to know that Evaline was hiding something. She was holding something back and whenever Maya asked; how she briefly came to be part of the Prestwick Coven. Evaline would change the subject or suddenly remember somewhere else, that she needed to be.

Finally, the big day had come. Evaline had finally agreed that Maya was ready for the arena. Mischief watched from the side lines, as did many of the Deed's witches. There was great excitement in their ranks. Evaline in the combat arena, Maya soon realised, was something of a spectacle.

Maya took to the arena on the back of her dragon. Her magical shield raised. At last, she was face to face with Evaline and her wild dragon. Evaline hovered on her mount, some twenty witches' hats above the arena floor.

"What now?" Maya asked, as they faced each other.

"Whatever comes naturally to you… you have all the skills. Now, let's see if you can put them together," Evaline replied with an expectant grin. She looked as if she too had been looking forward to this moment, for quite some time.

Evaline bowed. Maya bowed.

Smack! A stun bolt knocked Maya clean off her dragon and into the dirt.

"Lesson 1, do we really have to start back at lesson 1, private?" scolded Evaline.

That one hurt! It hurt Maya physically yes, but much more, it hurt her pride. Mischief clasped his paw to his forehead in exasperation and a murmur and mocking chuckles rumbled through the assembled audience of Deeds.

Maya vowed that she would never take her eyes off an opponent again and lower her guard. Dusting herself down, she remounted Blink and hovered facing her foe, once more. Evaline moved to her left and unleashed a bolt. Maya followed its path closely and deflected the bolt with ease. She lowered her own shield to fire back at Evaline who… who wasn't there anymore. Maya scanned left and right.

Smack!

Maya was on her back again! Evaline was hovering directly above her and grinning down.

"Don't watch the bolt, feel the bolt, anticipate the bolt! Never take your eye off an opponent, never! And just for good measure private, flying for most of us, is a three-dimensional sport!" barked Evaline, sporting an even bigger grin than before.

Maya was beginning to hate that she liked this girl so much. She spat out another mouthful of dust and mounted up once more.

That was the punishing pattern of the day... smack, after smack, after smack. Maya took hit after hit and landed on her back. Evaline laughed and barked down at her:

"Private!" Followed, each time, by an explanation of what she had done wrong. It was hard work and painful at times, but Maya was getting better each time and even started to enjoy herself. She was learning with every bout. Maya was almost disappointed when Evaline called an end to the days training, as the light started to fade.

Mischief had watched every bout without saying a word, it wasn't like him at all. That night Mischief was silent over tea as well. Maya knew something was on his mind.

"Ok then, out with it. What's wrong pussy-cat?" she demanded. She knew, he hated being called that.

Mischief looked up and straight into her eyes.

"I thought you wanted to get your mother back?" he whispered eventually.

It was a question that floored Maya. More than any stun bolt Evaline had unleashed that day.

"Wh..., wh... ?" Maya stuttered.

She hadn't even managed to ask the question, when the answer came pouring out of the little cat, with venom:

"So, when did you decide to take up your new career as a punchbag then?" Mischief challenged her. "All I saw today was; left, right, smack, down on your bum. Right, left, smack, down on your bum! Up, down, smack, down on your bum again!"

244

"It's difficult!" Maya objected.

"It's very difficult to win, if you don't even try to outsmart your opponent!" he continued with his tirade.

"What?" Maya was flabbergasted by his attack.

"When you play chess, do you wait for your opponent to attack and defend whatever game it is, that they want to play?"

Mischief paused for effect, while he hoped it was sinking in.

"Do great generals set out to battle, with no plan of attack, waiting to see what their opponents would to do first?"

"N... no ... I..," Maya really had no defence.

"Do they hold back their strongest soldiers, for fear they might upset their enemies?" Mischief's barrage continued.

Maya thought for a moment. He was right. So intent, was she on learning, on correcting her own mistakes. She had been completely focused on not losing or not losing quickly and being humiliated. She had lost sight of the task in hand. She had to practice winning. She had more powerful magic and a stronger shield than Evaline, but she hadn't used them. To defeat her opponent, she needed to attack. No more holding back and she needed a game plan. She did hate it when Mischief was right. She knew, he'd never let her forget it.

Maya nodded, then conceded:

"Okay, I'm listening."

Mischief, who she soon referred to, as her little furry general, was now in command:

"Lesson 1, always remember lesson 1, trust no-one. Evaline is right about that!

Lesson 2, Use all your strengths –

Use your strongest bolts and shield, make her feel your power! Make her fear you!

Lesson 3, Never let her get behind you –

If she gets behind you, you're a gonner! Blink is smaller and faster than her dragon. Blink can turn faster and corner quicker. If she's on your tail, bank hard and turn out quickly the other way, twice should do it, then use that lead to loop over or under her. Sight her back before you fire.

Lesson 4 Know your opponent –

When she fires first, she almost always heads up, then fires. Her next move is down. After that she goes right, then it's left the next time. She repeats herself. If she parries your shot, she goes right first, then she heads up with the next move she makes. Visualise it, see it in your head. Anticipate where she's going to be and fire your bolt, before she gets there.

Lesson 5 Plan your attack-

Get the first shot off, if you can, but know your next moves in advance, are you going high or low, fast or slow. Mix it up and never, never repeat yourself!

Lesson 6 Stop having fun and smiling at your opponent!"

Maya blushed shamefully.

Once Mischief's tirade had subsided (somewhere around lesson 37). They talked late on into the night. With pieces of left-over stale bread and cheese, they played out attack and defence scenarios in front of the fire, until Maya (the girl formerly represented by a lump of stale cheddar) fell into a deep sleep. A slumber filled full of dreams of dragon combat, tactics and flying cheese.

Next morning, on the way to the arena, Maya asked the obvious question:

"Ok, so how is it, that you're so good at all this?"

"I was watching yesterday. Studying every move and..." Mischief hesitated.

"And what?" Maya pursued a fuller explanation.

"Ok then," Mischief conceded. "My old coven did something similar. Though, we used brooms and lightening-bolts. You know, long before all this being a witch's cat and gateway guardian malarkey happened to me."

Maya was intrigued:

"Go on then?" she implored him.

"Of course, it is a far more noble and skilful art than dragon combat. For duels undertaken riding aboard a brush or old-fashioned broom, demand real skill. Unlike dragons, whose skins are impervious to fire bolts and lightening, a brush will readily burst into flames and drop you from the sky to a fiery grave. In brush duels, there are no second chances!" Mischief explained with notable pride in his voice.

"Were you any good?" Maya asked, having already guessed the answer, from his smug tone and the expert lectures, from the night before.

"Of course not! I wasn't just good. I was undefeated!" Mischief declared proudly, with his chest puffed out like a peacock's!

Maya laughed.

"A pity though," he continued. "They banned combat like that about a hundred years ago. A real shame, and over a technicality too."

"What technicality?" Maya asked suspiciously.

"Technically speaking, there were quite a lot of fatalities and well... you know?" Mischief sounded a little sheepish.

"No, I don't know!" Maya insisted.

"Technically, there was no one left, willing to fight me," her cat confided.

Maya tried hard not to laugh, but couldn't hold it in. She snorted in a most undignified manner, before bursting into a fit of inappropriate giggles.

Day 2 of dragon combat training started off much the same way as day 1. The sun rose. Also, Maya and Evaline were laughing and joking all the way through breakfast, but the moment they set foot in the arena, for the first time, Maya's game face was on.

Maya made the first move forward and unleashed a bolt twice as powerful as anything she had thrown the day before. As they had rehearsed, Evaline evaded vertically down, parried the first bolt, but was obviously shaken by its force.

Evaline fired back and true to form, she flew her dragon to the right. Maya however, was already on the move and safe to lower her shield and fire. As Evaline moved towards her new position, Maya had already released her next bolt, anticipating her opponents move. More powerful again, it struck Evaline full on, collapsing her shield on impact.

Smack! Evaline was on her back.

Evaline didn't look happy, not happy at all and remounted her dragon without a word or making any kind of eye contact.

The next bout started, with Evaline firing first and twice in quick succession. Maya though was already on the move. She flew vertically and unleashed her own double bolt at Evaline, who parried the first and moved down… straight into the path of the second fire bolt.

Smack! Evaline was on her back again, bewildered and disoriented by its power.

Again, and again, and again… Smack! Smack! Smack! Evaline hit the deck, scowling in disbelief and frustration. A small crowd had started to gather. Evaline on the receiving end, was apparently not something, that any of them were accustomed to seeing.

Maya didn't get it all her own way though, Evaline was smart and she had allies too. Two other witches had been observing the bouts closely. They started to coach her. Passing advice and messages after every encounter and gesticulated in frustration each time that Evaline was on the receiving end. They too were learning Maya's tactics. Anticipating what she would do next. Evaline had started mixing up her own routine too, she was much less predictable, often doing exactly the opposite from what Maya expected her to.

Another spectator had joined them too. Hidden from sight amongst the high branches of an old oak tree, a large black bird watched over the final morning bouts, with cold disapproving beady eyes.

Much to Maya's frustration, Mischief stayed silent. He gave Maya no more help. Evaline's whole demeaner had changed too. She was serious and intense now. There were no more smiles, no laughter, no fun and strangely, no return to the arena after lunch.

A message was delivered to Maya in the arena by a small thrush, saying that the High Priestess had sent Evaline on an important errand and that Maya had now completed her training.

"Good!" Mischief announced.

"What's good about it?" Maya demanded. She was worried that Evaline was upset or hurt and that she still wasn't ready for the test to follow.

"She was learning too much about you, your moves and your tactics. They all were," explained the cat.

"So?" Maya pleaded, not wishing to acknowledge, that the little cat was starting to make sense again.

Mischief glared and started his rebuke:

"So? They know how you think, how you move? And you don't even know who your opponent will be. Anyway, you're ready. What you need most now, is a day of rest."

He was right. Maya was tired, very tired and so was Blink. Late nights, a heavy training schedule and restless sleep, had all taken their toll. She was exhausted and her head was now so full of tactics, that she completely forgot to be nervous about the next day's challenge and slept soundly for the first time in days.

Maya snored until 2 o'clock in the afternoon the next day. Blink slept in too. He snored even more loudly, puffing white smoke through his nostrils, as he dreamt of marshmallows and oncoming trees.

After a hearty brunch of chicken nuggets, chocolate, tomatoes and pickled onions. Maya walked around Cambusdoon and down to the river with Mischief. There was no sign of Evaline though. Maya spent the remaining afternoon with Mischief and Blink, relaxing

250

and talking fresh tactics once more. As the sun set in the west and the full moon rose through the gathering clouds, inevitably her self-doubt and nerves had started to kick in.

Dragon combat

Just before midnight, Maya mounted onto the back of her trusty purple dragon and patted him on the neck. Mischief perched behind her as usual, on a comfortable red cushion. In response to a gentle kick from her heels, Blink flew them the short hop to the arena. Maya had resolved that there would be no energy sapping stunts tonight, no fireballs, no crossing running water. Although she couldn't help but think, with these nerves, passing running water was a real possibility!

As they landed in the arena, not far from the stone arch, the coven was rising in magnificent and awe-inspiring crystalline splendour. Just as it had done, on her first night. A full harvest moon hovered over the turquoise pillars. The coven filed in, one by one, to drop their stones onto the small golden tray, which sat upon the crystal's ball. The Deeds took their seats within the coven and each of their dragons took their places, perched on top of the pillars behind them. Finally, the High Priestess took her seat and as the coven shield dropped. The coven was closed. Maya stood, as an heir in the arena, to await the High Priestess's decision, as to whom she must face in combat.

Magical lightning sparked between the pillars and to and from the crystal's ball, in the centre of the coven. It glowed brighter and brighter, as it focussed the power of the Deeds' witches and tapped into the strength of their dragons. Maya could feel the power. It excited and scared her, in equal measure.

The High Priestess rose and pointed her staff towards the crystal's ball. Blinding magical lightening crackled between the crystal orb on the end of her staff and the crystal's ball.

The High Priestess retracted the staff, although the connection to the crystal in her staff still remained, and a blinding light now shone from it too. Next, she pointed the staff towards the hooded figure directly opposite her, who rose and crossed the coven. The hooded figure bowed respectfully, then quickly plucked the jewel from the outstretched staff and concealed it furtively beneath her cloak.

"Eh?" Mischief mumbled to himself.

The coven shield was lowered and the High Priestess and the hooded figure now made their way out from the inner sanctum of the coven. The hooded figure turned the other way, but the High Priestess walked straight towards Maya. The rest of the Deeds remained seated within the coven.

"That's curious?" observed Mischief, but there was no time to discuss whatever "that" might be. "Good luck, little one, I must leave you now. Here take this, as we discussed last night... just in case."

With that, Mischief passed her a small jar, which Maya received gratefully and quickly tucked into her inside pocket, out of sight.

"Remember lesson 1 and don't let them catch you off guard," he added, dismounting from Blink's back, still clutching his comfortable red cushion.

Maya's heart skipped a beat and she clasped Spell for reassurance. The High Priestess approached and addressed her directly, her eyes piercing and cold:

"The coven has convened and accepted your challenge. Should you choose to proceed, know this. There are no vacant places in the coven and you must prove yourself in dragon combat to claim your seat. This is a binding magical contract and there can be only one winner."

"I accept," Maya replied, trying to sound confident.

"A dragon duel, it is then, challenger." The High Priestess bellowed. "I have decreed that you shall fight our champion."

Maya could feel her eyes open wide in horror, like two fresh eggs, cracked into a frying pan. Her heart sunk. She had not expected this. Why would the High Priestess risk her own champion? It didn't make any sense. Why risk displacing her champion and not one of the older and, let's face it, more frail members of the coven. Why? Why... not unless she was sure that Maya stood no real chance of defeating their champion?

A dragon and rider flew into the night sky, silhouetted against the moon and hovered in the air above the arena.

"Our champion awaits you," the High Priestess announced, with a cold heartless smile.

Maya turned nervously to face her opponent, raising her magical shield well in advance.

"Lesson 1," she mumbled to herself, she would not be caught off guard, not now. This was for her mum. She was completely focused now, more powerful than she had ever been. Armed with Spell and well-rehearsed in Mischief's new tricks and tactics. She was sure that she could match this dragon and its rider, champion or no champion.

The High Priestess launched a slow burning fireball into the air, with a loud woosh, to light the arena and counted slowly down from 13,12,11,10,9,8,7...

Her opponent reached up to lower her hood... 6,5,4... the hood dropped and...

254

"To the death!" cried Evaline, launching her first bolt on the count of 2.

"Mortify!" Evaline sent the **death** spell firebolt and soared diagonally upwards towards Maya in a move, more aggressive than she had ever imagined possible.

That first bolt was nearly enough, though Maya just deflected it, she was knocked sideways and wobbled perilously close to being dismounted. Maya's concentration was broken.

This was a fight to the death!

A fight with Evaline. Nobody had said anything about a fight to the death! Maya teetered on the edge of oblivion, knocked half off her dragon, her shield and mind completely unfocused by what had just happened.

"Mortify!" came a second cry from above.

Instinctively, Maya kicked her heels hard into her dragon's flanks, just evading a second killer fire bolt, delivered with venom from her 'friend' Evaline above.

"Stick to the plan!" cried Mischief from below. "You can beat her. You know you can!"

Maya finally got her focus back and banked Blink sharply in an anti-clockwise direction. She faced her opponent now, with a look that sent shivers up Mischief's spine. Spell and her shield now glowed red with fury.

"That's new!" Mischief observed.

Now, it was Maya who unleashed a fire bolt with all of her power. She kept her shield down and moved forwards diagonally. Maya then unleashed another powerful bolt, aimed well down and to the left. The opposite direction from which, she knew Evaline could be expected to fly.

Dodging the first bolt, Evaline turned quickly and flew straight towards the second oncoming stun bolt. Evaline swerved just in time, but it was still more than a glancing blow. She rode it, but only just. Evaline was hurt, Maya could see it in her face. Her shield was nearly down. Evaline knew that she was no match for the power of Maya's living wand. Not with the fury Maya had now put into that last bolt. Stun or not, they would still do her serious damage.

"Game on!" Evaline laughed, as she plucked the coven staff crystal, still glowing with blinding light, from inside her cloak and placed it into a golden setting, mounted on the front of her saddle.

The light and energy from the coven doubled and doubled again. It flowed from every member of the coven, who had remained seated, channelling their power through the crystal's ball which now connected with the jewel mounted on Evaline's saddle.

Evaline's shield now glowed turquoise, fortified with the power of the whole Coven of Deeds. A power much greater than even Maya and her living wand could muster.

"Mortify, mortify, mortify!" cried Evaline, without lowering her shield. A spread of 3 killer firebolts pierced her shield whilst still raised and bore down on Maya.

Blink moved before the order came, Maya's full magical power went to her shield as she half parried the closest death bolt. She dug in her heels with all her might. The bolt exploded on her shield as her dragon dived, only narrowly avoiding the other two. That bolt had landed with a ferocity unlike anything she had ever felt before.

Maya stayed on..., but only just. Maya was groggy now, most of her strength already spent. She knew she couldn't take another bolt like that. She needed time to recover.

Mischief had suggested a plan. A plan of last resort, in case things went wrong, but never in her wildest dreams, did she think she would be playing that card so early. And now she would have to think on her feet. Maya shot upwards and kept on going, further and further she climbed, up into the clouds. She needed time to think, time to recover her strength. Evaline laughed, shrugged her shoulders, as if now playing to her home crowd, below in the coven, and followed slowly from some distance behind.

Maya soared high towards the cover of the low clouds, heading ever so slightly southwards towards the River Doon. Beneath, in the reflected glow from the coven, she could just make out the shadows of a dozen or so figures, moving stealthily through the long grass in the direction of the coven.

"Mortify!" A death firebolt shot forth from Evaline, but Maya steered Blink around it with ease. Evaline needed to get closer than that, if she was going to land one of her killer bolts. A game of cat and mouse ensued. Maya dodging Evaline's killer firebolts and hiding behind the clouds. Returning fire when she dared. Evaline tried to close the gap, but Maya kept her distance. Flying out over the Doon, whenever Evaline got too close or flew to intercept her.

It was just as Maya had discussed with Mischief, the night before. Evaline feared to follow Maya out over running water. Her parlour tricks ahead of the magical challenge, might yet pay off for her. It went on for some time; a game of chess with neither player willing to over commit. The occasional firebolt was exchanged, but not from any range that threatened the other's reflexes. It gave Maya time to recover. Time to think.

The dragons though, were tiring and under thickening clouds the visibility was steadily deteriorating. This was the cue for new tactics. Maya gained height once more, flew into the thicker cloud and manoeuvred, whilst she was still out of sight. Blink hovered trying to regain his breath. Maya was patient, she waited and waited, then as the sky darkened further, the moment was right.

Maya dived Blink steeply and at great speed. Approaching Evaline unseen initially, from above and behind. Maya fired, landing glancing bolts twice from closer in, but now with the power of all the Deeds in Evaline's shield, they had little effect. Evaline gave chase, but pulled up short of the river, unwilling to get closer to the running water.

"This is your plan?" Evaline taunted.

Maya didn't respond.

"Stick to the plan," Mischief's parting words echoed in her head, and this was their plan. They knew Evaline was cunning and that might be her undoing? A darker cloud drifted in overhead. More cover for another run.

Maya had decided. This would be her final run. One way or the other.

Evaline, however was expecting her tactics this time. She had noticed a flash from Maya's wand, just before that last attack. Maya had manoeuvred behind her, before launching her attack. But Maya's firing from behind, had reflected on the metal mount on Evaline's saddle and this would be, all the warning she needed.

Evaline would keep her back turned, lure Maya in close, turn and raise her shield when she saw the flash. Then, at that moment, unleash a barrage of 3 killer firebolts through her shield to mortify her foe from close range. Maya would have no time to respond. Evaline grinned to herself in anticipation. Her counter trap was set.

Evaline caught a glimpse of Maya's dragon, as it rose through the dark thundercloud, trying to outflank her and take up a position above and behind her once more. Evaline smiled to herself, but took no evasive action. She simply hovered and watched for the reflection, that she was sure, would now seal Maya's fate.

There was an eerie silence. The clouds darkened still further and the breeze stiffened, as thunder clouds gathered and engulphed the pair of them. Eveline waited, her eyes focused forwards on the reflective metal mounting on her saddle.

A bright flash came soon enough and Evaline spun around with lightening reflexes. Shield now held high towards the flash.

"Mortify, mortify, mortify!" A spread of three killer bolts shot at close range penetrated her raised shield, homing in with deadly accuracy, centred on the source of the flash.

This was however, no stun bolt that Maya had released, as she attacked from above. It was instead, the contents of the jar, which Mischief had passed to her earlier. A jar of glitter worms, concealed under her cloak and released above her head, as Maya sped towards her foe, plunging beneath Evaline at the last moment. A hundred miniature lightening conductors spread out and ignited the thunder cloud in a blinding and disorientating electrical discharge, seen from miles around.

Even with her shield raised high, this might have been enough to knock Evaline from her dragon in itself, but that had never been Maya's plan. Now, beneath her blinded opponent and with Evaline's shield held up high in defence. Maya unleashed a powerful stun bolt at close range, from below. Not focused on her unguarded foe, but centred on the Deed's coven crystal. A crystal which now flew into the air. Molten metal sprayed out from the melted setting on Evaline's burning saddle, as the crystal plummeted towards the earth, like a falling star through the night sky.

The damage though, was not restricted, at such close range. A reign was torn from Evaline's clenched hand and with it blood from a couple of badly torn fingers. Her dragon too was winded and disoriented, its wings beating out of time as it tumbled and fell from the night sky. Neither did Evaline appreciate the impact of the stun bolt to her hind quarters. Unseated from her now flaming saddle, she spiralled downwards, bum smoking and only just able to hold on to one reign, with her remaining undamaged hand.

Evaline corkscrewed helplessly downwards, smoking like one of the Red Baron's victims, straight out of a black and white war movie. Evaline hit the dirt, landing heavily, face down in the mud of the arena floor. Her dazed dragon's wings instinctively spread out over Evaline, to protect its mistress, where she lay.

Maya followed her opponent down to the arena floor, resisting the temptation to finish her off, with a close-range blast. Curiosity was gnawing away at her now. Maya took the opportunity to loop down, in a long arc, low over the figures she'd seen moving through the long grass earlier. Maya gasped in horror, as she realised who they were.

This was not the Prestwick Coven, as she'd half expected. No Granny and her Aunty Dot were there, but as for the others, they were a ragtag collection of strange creatures and witches young and old. Even a rather familiar looking gobhoblin, with a fine new pair of boots. Maya realised with rising concern, just who they were. These were the misfits. Granny had brought her friends on some sort of misguided away trip, deep into the Deed's territory. Granny held the coven staff (an old walking stick) and they'd formed a crude circle, a misfit's coven, around an old wooden ball, a base from one of Granny's lamps if Maya wasn't mistaken. Maya could hardly believe her eyes.

Granny, it would seem, had suspected that there would be foul play, but it was just as well that Maya had won. What could they ever hope to achieve against the power of the Deeds? Maya thought to herself. They would last about as long as a bacon sandwich at a vegan party, when the lights were switched off.

Maya landed, dismounted Blink, giving him a well-earned pat on the flank. Then, she turned and approached the High Priestess, who awaited her, standing next to the ruined stone archway. Still quite breathless, but trying to sound very official and witchy, Maya panted:

"I have prevailed and claim my seat in the Coven of Deeds. There is no need for more bloodshed today."

Under her breath though, Maya mumbled, "Lesson1," and pointedly, kept her shield up and facing the old woman.

The High Priestess just smiled. She had never smiled like that before. Maya didn't like it, not one bit. This lady made her feel uneasy at the best of times. She didn't have long to wait though, to understand why she was grinning.

"Mortify!" came a cry from behind her. Maya spun on the spot, her shield covered the bolt, just in time, but it was a direct hit. It was too powerful for Maya at this range and her shield folded completely. Maya was thrown a full twenty witches' hats across the arena floor.

From under the wings of her dragon, blooded and staggering, but now clutching the muddy yet unmistakeable glowing crystal from the Deed's coven staff, in her one remaining good hand, stepped Evaline. Her shield was raised and her wand held high above her head, in the blooded fingers of her left hand. Her wand and shield again restored to full power, full Deed's Coven power.

Maya was stunned, winded and unable to get to her feet. She simply shook her head in disbelief.

"The better witch has won," gloated the High Priestess coldly.

Evaline moved towards her slowly.

"Finish it Evaline, my dear!" insisted the High Priestess.

Maya bowed her head. She knew it was over. She had lost. Maya knew that her time with the Deed's had changed her though. She too had become a warrior. At least now, as she prepared herself to die, she had some consolation. She had given it her all. Her opponent, who in spite of her injuries, still had the wit and determination to follow the falling gemstone, as it fell from the sky, was indeed a worthy victor. Death at Evaline's hands, brought her no dishonour.

Evaline walked slowly towards her fallen 'friend.'

"Kill her!" demanded the High Priestess, with venom.

Maya bowed her head and closed her eyes. Mercifully, it wasn't long before the unmistakeable sound of:

"Mortify!" rang out across the arena.

A killer bolt let loose with the power of a full coven behind it. Found its target full on. A direct hit, which blasted its target into ashes and dust, with an almighty explosion, so powerful that it felled everyone in the arena and the Coven of Deeds.

Motherly Love

Granny (a.k.a. that cunning old bat), had fired upon the Deed's crystal ball with all the power, that the makeshift Misfit's coven could muster. Her firebolt exploding the Deed's crystal ball into a million fragments.

"Now it's a fair fight. Finish it, Maya!" Granny shouted.

But Maya had already moved and fired. Evaline, dazed by the blast, was caught completely off-guard. The power of the Deed's coven was gone. Evaline's shield, now no match for a direct hit from Maya and Spell. It buckled and Evaline flew through the air. Her wand torn from her hand and shattered, into a thousand splinters, by the force of the blast.

Maya's shield was raised again now. She rose purposefully to her feet. Her living wand drawn and eyes fixed on Evaline. Maya marched over and stood menacingly above her disarmed opponent.

Betrayal and wrath were etched into Maya's furious gaze. Once again, her shield shone red with rage. Maya leered down with uncharacteristically murderous eyes at her 'friend.' A 'friend' who had just betrayed her and tried to take her life. Maya raised her wand.

Evaline looked with pleading eyes towards the High Priestess, who stood cold and emotionless, at the head of the arena. The High Priestess simply shook her head, with an air of utter disappointment.

"Yield!" Maya demanded.

"I yield," panted Evaline.

"It's over," Maya announced, then lowered her wand and turned exhausted, to face the High Priestess.

"No, it's not over!" insisted the High Priestess, her remarks now addressed directly to Maya.

"It's a binding magical contract and it's to the death. Now finish her!" the old woman demanded.

"**Mother?**" cried Evaline in despair.

There was a stunned silence.

"Mother?" Maya repeated, "You're... you're, her mother?" Maya gasped. She was horrified. Maya shook her head slowly, in utter disbelief.

There was no response from the old woman. No denial. No acknowledgement. Nothing.

"And you want me to kill her?" Maya pressed the point, once more. She couldn't believe this. "You're actually asking me to kill your own daughter, in front of your eyes?"

Maya stared at the High Priestess's cold emotionless face, then cast her gaze back down towards Evaline.

Evaline was destroyed. Not just defeated and resigned to death. Her heart had been ripped out. She had been betrayed by her own mother. It was a look that Maya would never forget, not for all the rest of her days. A look of total betrayal and despair, as if her very soul had just been cleaved in two.

"You accepted the challenge! You knew that you must replace her, if you were going to take her place in our coven, didn't you? We have a binding magical contract and you must kill her, now!" insisted the High Priestess once again.

Maya just shook her head in bewilderment:

"How can you ask that of me? I thought she was my friend... and you, you're her mother!"

There was no reaction from the High Priestess. The silence was deafening, agonising...

Maya eventually felt compelled to fill the silence:

"Nobody saw fit to tell me. I didn't know that this was a fight to the death! Not until your daughter here, tried to 'mortify' me. You tricked me. You both tricked me, but how could you select your own daughter, for a fight to the death? How could you do that, knowing she might die?

The High Priestess just laughed. She actually laughed. Now, looking Evaline in the eyes for the first time, the old woman finally replied:

"Lesson 1, I'm afraid Evaline. You were the most likely to defeat her. The best choice for the job. And, if you had done your job properly, she would be dead and that living wand of hers, would now be mine. With that power, the Deeds would be unstoppable. It's our destiny!"

Maya just glared in disbelief:

"All this for my wand? Your own daughter's life, really? And now what? Now that I've won?" Maya asked, to spare Evaline the indignity.

The High Priestess addressed her reply to Evaline once more, in a cold calculating voice:

"Unlikely as that was, especially after all your excellent preparations Evaline, it would make no difference. It still does not change the outcome. Maya has prevailed and with you, well, out of the way shall we say. She, will now take your place, by my side in the coven.

As her High Priestess, as a dark witch, after her first kill. I will command her and she will be powerless to resist my will. Either way, you see. I will command the power of the living wand. A win-win, you might say?"

Maya was speechless. The High Priestess almost sounded pleased with herself. She was actually proud of this plan. A plan which now involved the death of her own flesh and blood, in front of her own eyes. Maya's eyes were once again drawn, to the wooden crate left out in the arena, waiting to be filled.

The High Priestess turned to face Maya again:

"I did try my best to avoid it several times, but you gave me little choice."

Maya's tongue was out, gathering the pieces of a very unpleasant jigsaw. All its pieces, now laid out in front of her, fully for the first time. Shaking her head, Maya started to assemble them verbally:

"Every test was fixed. The rotating table... a trick to win my living wand. You got Evaline to set me up. She planted the idea that I should WEIGH up the solutions and choose the heaviest box. The wrong box."

"Very good," the High Priestess replied.

Maya paused for thought, then continued:

"The test of magical ability too. You had Evaline hunt the fawn with a poison arrow, didn't you? She poisoned me?" Maya continued, glaring down at her 'so-called' friend.

There a nod of confirmation from the old woman.

"Poor Evaline, such loyalty and look how you repay her!" Maya cast her eyes once again down to Evaline, still sobbing at her feet. Her anger now replaced by pity. "There's still good in her. I know it. She has been my friend, or was that all a lie too, Evaline?"

Evaline shook her head, but she could not meet Maya's eyes.

The High Priestess laughed again:

"Good in her? No, I think not. Only in so far, as she is an obedient daughter," scoffed the old woman. "No, she befriended you. She won your trust and she lied to you. She poisoned you and just for good measure, she was the one who sent you to the wolf's lair to be eaten alive."

The High Priestess actually laughed before continuing:

"That was her idea alone. A nice touch. I was so proud of her, at the time."

The High Priestess paused, just long enough to enjoy the sight of Maya's jaw dropping, hitting the ground and slapping her across the face, on its way up.

Still with a cold calculating voice, the High Priestess continued her explanation:

"Time and time again, she's tricked you. She plotted your downfall from the beginning and just now, in the arena, she tricked you again and tried to kill you. It is your rite, as well as your duty, to take your revenge now. Your duty as a witch, to complete our binding contract!"

Evaline's sobs grew ever louder.

"So, kill her! Now!" the High Priestess pressed her case impatiently, with fresh venom in her voice.

Stunned silence echoed around the arena.

Maya could feel the rage rising within her, with every word that the High Priestess uttered. Fury at the treachery and duplicity of her so-called 'friend'. Fleetingly, she was actually tempted to take her revenge. It would almost be an act of mercy, for poor Evaline now. But such an act was not within Maya's soul.

Maya knew in her heart, that for all her pain. It was, but a fraction of the pain and utter betrayal, that Evaline now suffered at the hands of her own mother. Maya's rage turned to pity, as she replied:

"No, I don't believe she's evil! You tricked her too. You manipulated her all along. Your own daughter. Just as you're doing to me now!"

Maya stood defiant.

"Not evil, really?" laughed the High Priestess. "Evil by name, evil by nature, this one! I made her that way."

"What?" Maya was clearly confused.

Mischief had moved to her side. He spelled it out for her, "Evaline Deed, she even named her, Evil indeed!"

Maya's jaw dropped again.

Granny interjected:

"Just like her mother, eh Cruellen? Cruellen Deed or Cruel indeed! Monsters your bloodline, and named as such, all the way back, since the days of Nedep himself."

268

Maya shook her head in disbelief once more.

"Kill her now! Take your rightful place in our coven," insisted the High Priestess, once more.

Maya had heard enough, in disgust she turned her back to leave.

"Without our power, our pure coven. You'll never awaken your mother!" Cruellen mocked.

Maya stopped dead in her tracks.

"What?" Maya mouthed.

Maya turned again, to face the High Priestess. Her tongue was out again, marching around her lips rhythmically, like it was beating time in a military band.

"I didn't tell you anything about my mother," Maya spoke softly, thoughtfully, screwing up her eyes to scrutinise the old lady.

"Evaline told me. See, she betrayed your trust too!" the High Priestess hissed in response.

"No, no she didn't. Lesson 1, remember. I didn't tell her about my mother. I didn't tell any of you!" Maya replied, now sounding somewhat distant.

Maya turned once again towards Evaline. The fog of rage finally clearing from her mind. Slowly, she shook her head from side to side, in disbelief.

"You set this all up from the very start, didn't you? she whispered accusingly, now directing herself to Evaline.

"I knew you were hiding something. Time after time, whenever I asked, you refused to tell me, why it was, you'd joined the Prestwick coven. You changed the subject or made excuses and

269

left, whenever I mentioned it. It was all a set-up, right from the very beginning, wasn't it?" Maya probed.

Evaline nodded, snorting back tears of despair.

Maya paused again, for breath. Her head was spinning:

"You... you set my mum up as well? First you befriended her, then you sprung your trap!"

Maya paused, as the pieces started to fall into place, then gasped:

"You passed her the little red book, didn't you? As her friend, Mum must have confided to you, that Granny's book was on its last page."

Again, Evaline nodded, but she couldn't meet Maya's eyes.

Evaline's deception, was now all too horribly clear to Maya:

"You tempted her with tales of a family secret. One passed down through the generations. Tales of a powerful potion. A potion which you knew, could save her mother. As descendants of Nedep, you all knew about his coven, about touching the moon. The promise of eternal life. It was all planned from the very start. You set a trap for my mum. To get her to retrieve Nedep's potion!"

"Very perceptive young witchling," interrupted the High Priestess.

Maya ignored her and continued:

"But that wasn't all, was it? You could have sacrificed any of your minions to retrieve that potion. No, that wouldn't do..., because like Nedep himself, you didn't have the power to break the spell and claim his potion. You needed the power of a living wand. The only great magical power that Nedep himself, did not command. The reason he failed, or so you thought. You needed the power of a living wand and you'd stop at nothing to get it. So... so you needed me!"

Evaline's sobs grew louder and she nodded once more.

Maya felt her wand hand raise itself in anger, fury pulsing through her veins once more. She shook with rage. It was all becoming horribly clear now. Evaline had betrayed both her and her mother. Some friend, but now, as she looked down at Evaline, Maya lowered her wand again. She couldn't help but pity her.

"My mum was just the bait then?" Maya whispered accusingly. "You befriended her, just before her hapless daughter came of age to enter the magic realm. A silly, innocent little girl, who you could manipulate to do your bidding. An unsuspecting fool, who you could set off to follow a breadcrumb trail, to find a living wand for you. Didn't you?" Maya asked softly, now turning accusingly, to face the real mastermind behind this elaborate deception.

Maya glared at the High Priestess. It all made sense now.

"Bravo!" the High Priestess applauded.

Maya's tongue and brain, had switched into overdrive:

"The fresh inscription on the brass egg timer. Freshly cut by you! You've played me for a fool, right from the start. You used that little hour glass, to set me off on a trail, for the one thing you really wanted, but could never find yourself. That inscription sent me off to seek out a living wand, to save my mum. Only an innocent, still pure of heart, as yet uncorrupted by the temptations of magic, could find it. You knew that only someone, who sought a living wand, but not for their own gain, could ever be offered it. Eventually, that inscription led me here too, to seek out the help of a 'pure' coven. Here, where you knew exactly how to part me from Spell!"

Maya gazed at Mischief in disbelief:

"And like a fool, I brought it to them. Just like they'd planned. All they had to do then, was take it from me!"

"It was Evaline's plan. So, take your revenge," insisted Cruellen.

"No, I don't believe you. She's not that cruel. She did it out of duty, love even. Love for her own mother, and look how you repay her!"

Maya now looked down towards Evaline.

"There **is** good in you, Evaline, I know it. You were my friend. I know you were. You told me about the antidote. That wasn't part of your mother's plan, was it?" Maya asked defiantly.

"You did what?" barked the High Priestess, rage written large across her face.

"You chose to save me. You didn't choose to fight me. She chose that!" Maya affirmed.

Evaline just nodded. Her heart torn to pieces. She couldn't speak.

Again, it was Maya who broke the silence, now looking back towards the High Priestess:

"You see, I know there's good in her. Whatever name you gave her. All those things she did, she did them for you. I too, would do almost anything for my mother, but I will not kill for her. Not for anyone. Not your daughter. Not my friend. This is wrong!"

Maya shook her head again. She understood how and why, but she could never understand Evaline's mother. A mind so warped by greed, that it was willing to sacrifice her own daughter for power and eternal life. What could have driven her to this?

"Why mother, why choose me to fight her?" Evaline's anguished cry pulled at Maya's heart strings, like a crow feasting on fresh carrion.

The High Priestess chose not answer.

But Maya had already deduced the answer to that question too. Though she realised, this would bring only further suffering to poor Evaline.

Maya shook her head in disgust. She spoke more softly now, but her loathing for the High Priestess, was clear for all to hear:

"Sorry Evaline, but I believe, we're back to lesson 1 again. Your own mother had you to do all this. So, that if it all went wrong, as it has done now, the trail all pointed to you."

Evaline raised her bloodshot eyes in horror:

"What?"

Maya gulped back her own welling tears and laid bare Cruellen's darkest secret:

"So, if it did all go wrong. I would hate you. Enough to kill you and take your place. And I'm sorry to say, that I've been tempted, on more than one occasion today, to do just that."

"Kill me? Why did she want you to kill me? Her own daughter, not one of the others?" Evaline sobbed. She was devastated.

Maya too was sobbing now, but she felt compelled to answer for the silent old woman:

"She knew that you were the only one here, who was enough like me. The only one who still had a heart, a soul and could truly be my friend. Nothing hurts like betrayal, especially betrayal by your friends. Except that is, betrayal by your own mother, I suppose."

It was all falling horribly into place now, Maya sneered with disgust and wiped away her own tears, as she continued to unravel the plot out loud:

"Only your betrayal, a friend's betrayal, she reasoned, could provoke me enough to kill. So, if you didn't kill me first, then she wanted me to kill you. To kill a friend and lose my soul. To turn me to the dark side. Only then, could she be sure of controlling me in her evil coven. Me and with me, the power of my living wand."

The High Priestess just shrugged her shoulders, as if to confirm it was true.

Maya looked away disgusted, then addressed poor Evaline once again.

"She set you up from the start too... what was it, that she called it; a win-win? Either way she'd get her hands on a living wand and Nedep's potion!" Maya hissed. "It was all planned from the beginning, right down to the very last detail."

"Very perceptive young witch, very perceptive indeed. We would have made a great team you know, you and I," replied the High Priestess.

"No, I could never do your bidding!" Maya insisted.

Mischief chipped in too now:

"You were the bird. Above pirate's island, when we were on the puffling's trail and at the snow leopard's cave too! Only the High Priestess of the mightiest coven in the land, would have the power for such a transformation. You've had your beady eyes on us every step of the way!"

"Very good, little cat," the High Priestess replied, in a patronising tone. "Had you just got yourselves toasted by the dragons or shot by one of those obliging hunters, I could have collected the wand and saved us all, a whole lot of trouble."

"In the wolf's lair too. You were there to gloat and tried to steal the wand from Maya fawn's body, didn't you?" Mischief observed.

"I do like wolves, ruthless hunters, but messy eaters. I couldn't risk them damaging the wand," explained the High Priestess.

"All very clever. Horrible, unforgiveable, but cunning, I suppose. All except for one thing…," Maya suggested.

"What?" sneered the High Priestess. "Don't presume for a minute that you know my mind, little girl. You could never even imagine the path that brought me here!"

"It wouldn't have worked anyway," Maya answered.

"Of course, it would. With all the power of that wand. I'd have all the power of the Deed's pure coven too, more than Nedep ever had!" the High Priestess insisted.

"No, neither you or Nedep could ever claim that prize, the potion for eternal life. It wasn't Spell and more magical power you needed. Only the power of a 'pure coven' could ever unlock the potion, Granny told me that's true, but you're not a pure coven. Pure evil, maybe!" Maya insisted.

It was the High Priestess's turn to look shocked.

"Rubbish!" she spat back with rage. "You understand nothing!"

"It wasn't my wand, not more magical power, that you needed. You needed their strength. They have the key," Maya pointed to Granny and the rest of the Misfit coven. "They are the pure ones, pure of heart, something you can never be. I understand now, only they can ever hope to awaken my mother."

275

"Baloney!" cried the High Priestess.

"Oh yes," Maya replied defiantly. "They have risked their lives for me and for my mum, for love and friendship. Not for greed, not for the power of a living wand or Nedep's potion of eternal youth. This coven of yours is not pure, it's pure evil, and I want no part of it."

With that Maya turned and walked to join her misfit friends.

As Maya turned to walk away. The High Priestess bent down and thrust her own wand into Evaline's trembling hand.

"Nonsense, don't listen to her Evaline," Cruellen insisted. "If she's too weak to kill you. Then you must kill her! There's still time. The contract is still in place!"

Evaline rose slowly to her feet, her hand grasping her mother's wand firmly, as she raised it into the air. She turned, now to face Maya's exposed back. Mischief called out a warning:

"Maya!"

But it was too late. Maya's shield was down. She was defenceless.

Evaline smiled and brought down her mother's wand for the final act. Evaline dropped the wand suddenly across her knee, snapping it in two:

"No mother, I won't! I will never obey you again!" Evaline threw the broken pieces to the ground.

"Get yourself a new wand, a new coven and a new daughter while you're at it. Goodbye mother!" and with that, Evaline followed her friend from the arena.

"You don't know what you've done, the pair of you!" called Cruellen defiantly. "Mark my words, this is not the end! I did this for you, for all of you. **He** will come... and when that day comes,

you will be the ones who come grovelling to me for help. You'll
see!"

A new coven

In the weeks and months that followed, Maya and Evaline went their separate ways. Evaline left the Deeds and re-joined the Prestwick Coven. The girls needed time apart, before they could ever hope to become friends, once more. Somehow though, Maya knew that they would. Mischief however, would never trust Evaline again. Too much muddy water had flowed under that particular bridge, for him.

Maya had a different plan anyway. She would not join the Prestwick Coven. She would make her own.

It took a week to construct. Assembled lovingly from already fallen tree trunks, which were sawed and trimmed by hand. Maya insisted it had to be just right and everyone chipped in willingly. All Granny's misfit friends helped with the construction, even a gobhoblin named Samantha, proudly sporting a pair of Maya's old boots. Day after day they cut, shaped and smoothed the wooden trunks for the coven posts and seats. Each was lovingly sanded down and erected in a large circle. Twelve impressive natural pillars and matching stools standing proud and in full view, on the hillside overlooking a wild flower meadow.

Maya's Coven, Afton Woods near Ayr Hospital

Maya was gathering a new coven, one in which all would be welcome. Whether they were magical misfits, witches, gobhoblins, green, purple or any shade in between. Able bodied or those with different gifts, from lands near or far, no matter what their beliefs, all would be welcome, so long as their hearts were true.

Word spread fast through the witching community and they came, with only one goal in mind; friendship and to help others in need. Their first task though was clear, to help Maya get her mum and their friend, back.

Maya resolved, that there were other things which had to change too. No more spooky or fancy magical, awe-inspiring elite covens would be conjured here. Nor would it be raised in secrecy and under the cover of darkness. This coven would be a simple wooden structure, clearly visible for all to see. A coven, not hidden away, like all the others had been, down through the ages. Twelve simple wooden pillars and twelve wooden seats. Much to Maya's disappointment, she knew there could be no flowing robes, no dragons or fancy saddles, no crystals set in precious metals. It really was such a shame!

It was built on a hillside, facing east to catch the moon's rays as it rose. Maya knew just the place. The hillside where her Papa had last gazed out upon, from his hospital bed. He'd squeezed her hand gently, smiled at her and looked out of the window through the eyes of a child, in wonder, one last time, before he passed.

Maya felt at one with nature here, the wild flower meadow below buzzed with insects and was surrounded by broadleaf trees, who's leaves rustled soothingly in the breeze. Every time Maya returned to this place, she would remember her Papa with great fondness.

After weeks of blisters, it was complete. Just in time for the full moon. Construction finished early in the morning and Maya spent the rest of that day gathering together her coven, a pure coven...

pure of heart, that was. Each was to bring with them a small object, a token of who they were or what was precious to them.

The sun set in the west, piercing through dark purple stripes of cloud, stretched out low above the horizon. Each silhouetted against a blood orange sky. Shapes in the clouds reminded Maya of a marmalade tiger, crouching behind the island of Arran and ready to pounce. Then, as the moon rose high into the starlit night sky, they started to assemble. Gathering in the meadow, below the new coven. Many more came, than the thirteen required for any normal coven.

Samantha, the gobhoblin was the first to enter. She placed a newly germinated seed on top of the crystal's ball. Perhaps as a token of a new beginning. The coven's 'crystal' ball was nothing fancy. An up-cycled wooden lamp base from Granny's hallway, topped with a plain black steel tray. As Samantha dropped her token onto the tray, it transformed into a small blue green crystal. Maya had left out paint and brushes. Samantha painted a light blue stripe onto the crystal's ball, then proudly took her seat.

Granny's old wooden lamp stand had been placed in the centre of the coven, together with as many coloured paints and brushes, as Maya could lay her hands on. As each member entered the coven and placed their own token on top. They picked up a paint-bush and painted a different coloured stripe onto the ball, to celebrate their diversity.

So, it went on, eleven more pure souls entered, painted their chosen colour and placed an object onto the crystal's ball; a small unicorn, an emotional octopus, an elephant (a very small one), a picture of mum, dad, granny, a photo of a horse and several cats followed. Whether intimate, painful or frivolous, all were welcome and none were judged.

Mischief and Aunty Dot watched from the side-lines. Blink had perched on one of the wooden pillars. He enjoyed being the focus of attention. Many of the misfits had never seen a dragon before.

Once twelve were seated, Maya entered the coven and placed the tiny hour glass onto the ground beside the crystal's ball, within which, the sands of her mother's time stood still. Maya painted a stripe onto the crystal's ball, then picked up her ornate High Priestess staff (a stick she'd picked up in the woods on the way there).

Outside the coven many still gathered and some exchanged hurt looks, that they were still left on the outside. Were they really only to be observers or just heirs in this new coven too? Still to be shunned as magical misfits, now even by their own friends? But Maya did not take her seat yet. She turned and gestured for them to enter too. Maya raised Spell above her head, where it glowed brightly in the night sky.

Mischief spotted, 'that look' on Maya's face instantly and started to explain to Aunty Dot:

"Every good witch knows, you only need twelve seats, if you're going to seat a full coven. So, until the High Priestess takes up her seat, then there is always space left for one more."

"Oh, yes," Aunty Dot acknowledged, clearly still totally confused. But as more and more of the misfits entered and each sat in turn upon the one remaining empty seat, which always magically presented itself for the High Priestess to sit, soon even Dot got the idea.

Every misfit would get a seat tonight.

"Will that make it more powerful? You know, strong enough to undo the spell and release my sister?" Aunty Dot asked Mischief.

Mischief looked worried. He shook his head thoughtfully.

"I hope so, but honestly, I fear not. A new coven, with only a single dragon and very few of them with any reliable magic. A lovely gesture, her mother would be very proud of her, but I just don't see how it can work," the little cat confessed sadly.

And so, it went on. One by one, the misfits and magical outcasts entered, painted a stripe on the orb and placed their token upon the crystal's ball. Until all who came, were seated. Even Mischief, with the special allowance of a comfortable red cushion, took his place.

More tokens of every description were added. There was a gasp of disbelief, as one of the outcasts dropped in her mobile phone. Something no young aspiring witch, could ever do without... surely?

Maya looked around expectantly, as if she was waiting for just one more.

Obligingly, one more arrived. Just in time. A head of white curls bobbed over the horizon. Granny puffed her way up the hill. She joined, as the others had, but instead of a token, she placed her crystal from the Prestwick Coven onto the crystal's ball. For one night only, she would join this "new-fangled" coven, as she called it, rather disapprovingly. Maya nodded her approval and whispered to Mischief, under her breath:

"Cunning old bat!"

Granny glared at her disapprovingly (ears like a bat too, apparently!). Then Granny took her seat. With that, Maya sat on the remaining seat, to close the coven.

The crystal's ball glowed and sparked with magical power, a power that was truly pure of heart. It lit up the night sky, well enough to read a paper by anyway, but Maya knew this was nothing compared to the power of the Deeds. In the centre the crystals shone and energy pulsed into the sands of time which flowed... nowhere, in exactly the same way, that sand doesn't.

Mischief looked anxiously at Maya:

"It's not working!"

Maya looked worried. She glanced despairingly towards Granny.

"Wait, have patience girl," Granny responded softly.

For the 'cunning old bat' had been busy sending messages all that afternoon, using all manner of garden birds. Calling in favours, from the considerable number of other 'cunning old bats,' who she had helped in her time. Each of whom, now sat in a new coven, having placed their own crystals onto another coven's crystal's ball, just as Granny had done. So, on the stroke of mid-night, as the final guest, 'cunning old bat' took Granny's seat in the Prestwick Coven, the chain was completed.

Bolts of magical power shot from one coven's crystal's ball to another. Each coven's power seeking out their missing crystals, joining the covens together, into a magical spider's web that stretched the length and breadth of the entire country. Well, not really that far. Granny had, after all, upset quite a few covens too, during her wilder days.

The air crackled with static electricity and magical power. There was power here, great power, but also pure intentions. To help Maya and her mum. More and more magical power arrived in the coven. It focused onto the crystal's ball, which now concentrated a beam of 'pure' magical energy onto the little hourglass. A magical timepiece which now, started to levitate and spin gently into the air. As more and more power surged into the sands of time, grain by grain, painfully slowly at first, they started to flow once more.

283

It took every last ounce of magical energy from everyone in the chain of covens, but it worked. The power of the newly formed magical world-wide witching web, was like nothing ever seen before. Maya grinned. She knew that her mum could return now. She was sure, it had worked.

Maya gathered up the tiny hour glass in her hands and watched the sands flow, through tears of joy welling up in her eyes. She turned and smiled to her Aunty Dot, who tried to smile. Then rather disgustingly, pulled a half-eaten mint humbug out her mouth, into a used wrapper, so she could smile and gossip properly.

"I'll keep that safe for you dear. I've seen how you fly that brush of yours!" Aunty Dot suggested. Taking the precious sands of time from Maya, for safekeeping.

There was great celebration, as word spread of their success. Misfits and outcasts jumped and danced for joy. Magical flares lit up the night sky and the horizon glowed in all directions, as coven after coven, followed suit. Spreading the good news, like the beacon fires of old, lit on hilltops, to warn of approaching Viking invaders.

In all the confusion of the celebrations that followed, only Mischief noticed the empty seat. For, with a contented smile on her face and every last ounce of her energy expended, Granny had slipped away. Her book, a long time now on its last page, had finally closed.

Mischief gave the girls time to celebrate, but when it came time to leave, the little cat took them gently to one side, to deliver the unwelcome news.

It rained all the way home. Aunty Dot accompanied Maya back to her cabin in the woods, to await the arrival of her mum.

To add to the bittersweet misery of their success. Maya's mum did not come flying home, as fast as her broom could carry her, as they had all expected. Minutes turned into hours, sitting in near silence. Soon eager anticipation, turned to worry and dismay. Still there was no sign of her. Something was wrong. So, eventually, they mounted their brushes and headed for the covenanter's leap and Nedep's coven, once more.

The moon was still high, illuminating the final sandstone step, as they approached. Maya led the way impatiently up the steps, then paused, to gather her courage and let Aunty Dot pant her way up the steps, behind her. Mischief also made his way wearily up the staircase to nowhere, muttering:

"Cats don't do stairs or water," under his breath, as he stared apprehensively, at the river below.

Maya was the first to take the leap of faith. Holding out her arm, a shaft of light shot down from the moon to touch her outstretched fingers. As she touched the moon, she took a step forward. A leap of faith. Maya fell and disappeared.

Mischief was next. His claws drawn and digging into the sandy coven floor on landing.

Aunty Dot followed shortly after, courtesy of a blindfold and a couple of margaritas, swigged from a flask, drawn hastily from her over-sized handbag.

Inside Aunty Dot found Maya. She was stooped and weeping over her mother's still motionless body.

"I can't wake her, I can't!" Maya wailed in frustration. "It's not like before. She's solid again, well sometimes… she keeps fading in and out. I tried Spell too… nothing. I think we've lost her!"

"No dear, it's okay, I think she just needs the antidote," Dot replied, with uncharacteristic calm and composure.

Maya was anything but calm though, she was frantic:

"What, after all we've just been through, we still need to find an antidote?"

"Well, no dear, I wouldn't say that exactly," Dot replied. "You see we're twins, identical twins. I was made for this moment. I am her other half you see."

"You mean, like when dad calls you spare parts?" Maya snorted, like an undiplomatic pig, through her tear-soaked snout.

"No, not exactly and I shall be having words with your father when we get home!" Dot corrected her sharply, looking slightly annoyed.

Now, Dot bent down to kiss her sister, gently on the cheek.

"I am her other half, you see," Dot explained. "I complete her. Somehow the 'cunning old bat' has always known, I guess. I am, as my very name suggests... the Aunty Dot!"

And with that final awful pun, dreadful enough to awaken even the undead, from a timeless slumber, Maya's mum finally returned to solid form.

"See!" Dot announced proudly.

Then faded once more.

"Oh," Dot added. "I really thought that would work!"

"What, a peck on the cheek?" Mischief replied scornfully. "The power of a pure coven and all the combined power of every coven in the land including Maya's living wand couldn't wake her, and you thought a peck on the cheek and an awful pun would work?"

Even Dot blushed:

"Well maybe?"

Mischief turned to apologise on Dot's behalf, but stopped. Maya's tongue was out. He knew the signs only too well, by now.

"On to something?" Mischief probed.

Maya didn't answer at first, then asked:

"We all saw the sands restart, back in the coven, right?"

"Yes... and...?" confirmed Mischief.

"So, what if it did work?" Maya mused. Her tongue still performing oral gymnastics, her wobbly logic, now balancing awkwardly on the end of a very narrow balance beam.

"Then she'd be awake, and solid," Mischief responded, clearly unsure, where Maya was going with this.

"But she is, well sometimes. She's fading in and out, as if trying to return, but something's stopping her?" Maya thought out loud.

"What could be holding her back?" Mischief probed, but Maya had already turned to face her Aunty Dot.

"Dot, when you collected the sands, to keep them safe. Where exactly did you put them?" Maya asked rather suspiciously.

"In here." Dot replied proudly, raising her mighty handbag. "Where I keep all my stuff safe!"

"You stuffed the sands of my mum's life into your handbag with all that other junk!" Maya rebuked her sternly.

"It's quite safe," Dot reassured her, starting to rummage around inside. She rummaged and rummaged, then rummaged some more. Then, bending down, one piece at a time, the contents were emptied onto the ground.

A brush, another brush, hankies, new and used, sweet wrappers, a bag of mint humbugs, another bag of mint humbugs, a drinking flask, gloves, more hankies, more mint humbugs, keys, her phone, more gloves, more mint humbugs, her purse...

Mischief clasped a paw to his forehead in despair.

On and on, Dot produced a collection of 'useful' artifacts, until the pile was twice the size of her handbag, then...

"Ah, here it is!" Dot announced. Proudly producing the precious time glass, held within its delicate brass mount.

There were gasps of disbelief as Dot placed the precious, and now very sticky object, with the rest of her junk. There, stuck fast to the side of the tiny hourglass, was a half-sucked sticky mint humbug, now slipped free of its wrapper. The hour glass within twitched, as if trying to free itself, and as it did so Maya's mum appeared more solid, then faded again once more, as the glass and sands inside stopped again. Stuck fast by the unwanted presence of a very sticky fluff encrusted, half-sucked mint humbug.

The silence was deafening. Maya just glared in disbelief.

"Oh, I wondered where that got to!" Dot remarked, plucking the rather fluffy and gooey mint humbug from the side of the hour glass and popping it into her mouth.

As she did so, the hourglass mechanism, was once again free to rotate. Obligingly, this time Maya's mother slowly materialised fully. Then, as everyone held their breath, she stayed solid. With a loud yawn and stretch, Maya's mum finally awoke groggily to announce:

"You wouldn't believe what I was just dreaming about... dragon fights, covens and wolf's lairs. Giant humbugs too, they were the worst! What a dream. Honestly Maya, you've no idea what I've

288

been through my dear, really you don't. How did you get here anyway? Has anyone brought me a cup of tea?"

Maya hugged the life out of her mum, again and again, while her Aunty Dot proudly explained; how she knew all along that her 'antidote' would work, if they just gave it time.

Mischief just glared and retorted:

"Humbug!"

Maya sat back, grinning from ear to ear, finally releasing her mum from a vice-like squeeze. Then, suddenly smacked her mother on the arm, to the beat of her own words:

"Don't-you-ever-do-that-again!"

"What?" Mum protested innocently.

"Open a bottle without reading the small print," explained Mischief.

"This little bottle?" Mum replied, holding up the small potion bottle in her hand. "I was thinking. What harm could it really do, you know, if we just gave Granny a little sip?"

Aunty Dot and Maya exchanged glances. Tears pooled in their eyes, before Maya broke the silence.

"It's too late Mum," she sobbed gently. "Mischief says she slipped away, earlier tonight."

Maya's mother froze at the words, then she slowly placed the little bottle back down on the pedestal, from where it had come. She had no words. She was too late. The girls just hugged and things got soggy.

On the way back home, they filled Maya's mum in on all that had really happened since her disappearance; how they had tracked her down. Found Blink and Spell. Evaline and Cruellen's elaborate plan for them to find and deliver the living wand, the Coven of Deeds, the three tests and how Granny had saved the day and made the ultimate sacrifice. Inevitably, it sparked another bout of girly weeping and when Mischief was finished, the girls started too.

It didn't seem fair that Granny hadn't been able to say goodbye, or see Maya's mum returned home safely. The rain was in their faces the whole way home, but it never seemed to wash away the tears.

They flew back to Granny's house first, having decided to pack Aunty Dot an overnight bag and to feed her fat ginger cat a leg of cow, for supper.

The house was dark and quiet, as they entered. It felt cold and damp now. No warming fire or welcoming hug. A pair of empty slippers sat in front of Granny's seat. Mum started to sob again quietly, as they made their way through the house. Every object seamed to jog a childhood memory. The front room was silent too. Only the ticking of the clock and a gentle snore.

Snore?

"Granny!" cried Maya.

"What?" cried Mum.

"What?" cried Dot.

"What?" cried Granny, waking with a start, jumping half out of her wrinkles.

"What's all the fuss about? Can't an old lady like me slip away unnoticed to go to the toilet, without a search party anymore?" Granny protested.

Maya ran in for a hug.

Aunty Dot glared at Mischief.

"What? All I said was that she'd slipped away!" Mischief replied defensively.

"And that her book had closed!" Aunty Dot screeched.

"It did," replied Granny. "I came straight home and left the magic realm, no use in wasting space in your book, not if you don't have to. There's no knowing when one of my daughters might get herself into trouble again!" Granny laughed.

Maya just shook her head.

Besides Maya, as I told you before, with my current font size, my book has got a few more years in it yet, I expect!"

As girly tears and runny noses flowed in equal measure, Mischief summed it up best, muttering under his fishy breath:

"Cunning old bat!"

"This is not the end!"

That, on the face of it, was the end of the story. However, judging by the title of this paragraph and the number of additional chapters, a handful of more switched-on readers, began to suspect that there might be a lot more to this particular story, than anyone, but Cruellen, had ever suspected.

Shortly after Maya's mum had been released from her time prison. Granny took it upon herself to seal Nedep's coven. So that, no-one else would be tempted by his potion and end up frozen out of time. She left, sporting a pair of dragon scale gloves and returned later the same day, with noticeably fewer wrinkles and a definite spring in her step. So much so, that for some reason, her journal took it upon itself to add several more pages.

Over the months that followed and through the many other adventures that Maya and Mischief shared together, in the magic realm. It was Cruellen, who still tormented Maya's dreams. What on earth, could ever have driven Cruellen to betray and even sacrifice her own daughter? Was it simply just greed and a lust for power?

Most of all, Maya was tormented by Cruellen's unrepentant parting shot:

"Mark my words, this is not the end! I did this for you, for all of you. **He** will come… and when that day comes, you will be the ones who come grovelling to me for help. You'll see!"

What did she mean:

"I did it for you," and who on earth was **he**?

The answer, when it came, was more devastating, than anyone, but Cruellen, could ever have foreseen.

Part II - They came from the north

They came from the north. They attacked without warning or provocation. They showed no mercy. For witches everywhere, there was to be no escape.

Night after night they returned. Dark shadows approached through the night sky. Silent as any owl in flight. Deadly and unseen.

Then that sound; a spine-chilling, piercing cry like no other. A noise which reverberated and shook you to the core. Like the last petrified screams of the dead, being dragged by demons, through the gates of hell itself. An unearthly cry, that announced their fury. The black fire. A weapon like no other. Smouldering balls of black and purple flame, erupted from these shadows in the night sky, engulfing all whom they touched.

It started on 'Auld Hallows Eve, Halloween, The Day of the Dead,' whatever you choose to call it. Once a day of celebration and fun, for all witchkind. Not now, not anymore. This was now a day of reckoning for all witches, witchcraft and perhaps even for magic itself.

A winged fury had descended upon the magic realm. Coven after coven was attacked and devoured, by these deadly foes and their all- consuming black fire. Black and violet flames, which leapt from one witch to the next. Spreading from coven stone to witch's broom, devouring their magic. Feasting on their magical powers, leaving all witches powerless and their wands and brooms charred and burnt to cinders. Covens burned on through the night, consumed by a strange black flame. Icy cold to the touch, it burned with an unearthly purple glow, until all the magic was gone.

One by one, night after night, coven by coven and witch after witch. Nowhere was safe. The few who escaped, the lucky few, headed south in fear. Powerless to resist, they just fled.

Black shadows, death dragons they called them, now ruled the skies. Pitch black, save for the bloody scars they inflicted on each other, as they squabbled and fought amongst themselves. No magic could touch them, no spell had any effect. Not except to alert the beasts to the presence of the unfortunate witch, who had cast it.

No witch was safe. They sensed magic. Like bloodhounds on the wing, they tasted its presence, like a scent carried on the breeze. Then, relentlessly and mercilessly, they tracked each futile spell, back to the witch who cast it and consumed them with their fiery breath.

There was more going on here, these were not just random attacks. The beasts were organised, they were following a plan, working together, making their way further south, every night.

This wasn't just a war on witches, it was the systematic extermination of magic itself.

The first attack

The Prestwick Coven was the first to be hit. Its courageous witches tried to resist, but they were powerless against this new foe. Some fled on their brushes, only to be tracked down by these deadly winged assassins, who shot them from the skies, seemingly just for fun.

Most of the coven gathered in the centre of the Old Kirk. They huddled together, focussed all their powers into a mighty magical shield, and stood defiantly against the onslaught. A shield, which crackled with the combined magical power of the whole coven. Only to prove completely ineffective, against the power of the black fire, which engulfed them all, in a single fireball.

The Prestwick Coven was lost, its witches rendered unconscious or dazed. They staggered away on foot, disoriented and powerless. The once impressive, albeit rather spooky Prestwick Coven, now set ablaze. Their coven's crystal ball, which harnessed their collective powers, now burned with the black flames. The coven pillars, or tombstones, to the casual observer, cracked and toppled. The coven seats; ends of long buried coffins, which pushed up through the earth, now ablaze with black and violet flames. Black acrid smoke hung in the air above. A single green distress flare shot skywards, then their magic fell silent.

Maya's mum had escaped with her life, but only just. Her wand burnt to cinders, her magic gone. She'd stood defiantly, back-to-back with Evaline, their newest recruit. Their wands drawn, in a final desperate stand against the death dragons, but even they, were powerless against this foe.

Maya's mother had cast her last spell. It homed in on the shadows above and found its target. It passed straight through the beast, without so much as a blink from those piercing red eyes. Then in response, the lead dragon let loose its fiery breath. A black fireball, billowing smoke and ash, tracked back down the path of her spell, like a heat-seeking missile. It found its target. As the black flames engulfed her, her powers were gone.

Only Evaline had escaped, with her powers still intact. Only then, thanks to the very timely intervention from her own dragon. It plunged through the black smoke and flames to her rescue. It swooped down at the last moment and wrapped its wings around her, just as the fireball engulfed her together with Maya's mum. It seemed, that only dragon scales, offered any protection from the black fire. Cocooned in her dragon's wings, Evaline had escaped the fate that befell the rest of her coven.

As the flames subsided, Evaline's dragon unfurled its wings once more and she sprang into action. Evaline mounted her dragon and took to the air. She was surrounded, hopelessly outnumbered and outgunned. She was a dragon rider at heart. There and then, she swore to herself. If she was going to die tonight, she would meet her death with courage and on the wing.

First, she steered her dragon upwards, in a relentless and steep ascent. Then, as she soared above her assailants for the first time, she made for the cover of the low cloud and the plumes of rising smoke ahead of her. She circled around, getting her bearings, then dived through the night sky, using the light of the full moon behind her, to disguise her descent. A strategy her own mother had once taught her, in the days before she'd turned fully to the dark side.

Now, Evaline would meet her foes head on. Tonight, she vowed, she would die a good death. A death, her dragon riding ancestors would be proud of. As she dived towards the swarming dragons, her pendant necklace glowed, brighter than it had ever done before. A family heir loom, passed down from her mother, which she always wore on a gold chain around her neck. It shone now, like a beacon in the night sky, as if out of respect, for the passing of a courageous warrior.

Evaline raised her wand, high above her head and unleashed her most powerful spell. A death spell firebolt tracked down the lead dragon. It found its target, a direct hit, but passed straight through the beast. It didn't even flinch. Evaline too, was powerless against them.

But there was to be no final glorious battle. No fireballs greeted her attack. Much to Evaline's surprise and bewilderment, the death dragons simply parted in front of her, as she approached. She passed straight through them, without even a single fireball being unleashed in retaliation.

Was this just out of respect, for one of their own kind, her dragon? Why had she been spared? Perhaps, simply so that she could tell the tale and spread fear amongst the whole witching community. She didn't know. All she knew was, that it just didn't feel right. Why had she been spared the fate, afforded to so many of her friends tonight?

Evaline fled south towards Ayr. She checked her flanks anxiously, but none of the dragons gave chase. Instead, as Evaline looked over her shoulder, they gathered and circled over the wreckage of the what had once been her coven. Evaline's new home.

Evaline turned on her dragon and hovered for a while to watch them. The battle was over and the victorious death dragons now circled the coven, cutting off the escape of the few remaining powerless witches, who staggered and stumbled around the smouldering remnants of all that remained.

A dark shadow appeared on the horizon. Another death dragon, now loomed into sight. Much larger than the rest and on its back, a

298

dark shadow, a rider. The death dragons dropped from the sky in response and formed a perimeter around the coven. Evaline hovered silently in the night sky, helpless to intervene, tears in her eyes, dreading what might be about to unfold.

The dragon rider approached. This dragon was huge, much bigger than any she had ever seen before. It bore ancient wounds, but no fresh scars. Evaline knew that this was the dominant buck. The alpha male, that none of the others had dared to challenge. On its back, a rider, hooded and cloaked, all in black. This dragon too, now descended and came in to land amongst the ruins of her coven. The ring of death dragons parted respectfully, each bowing their head, as they let the mighty beast through. Evaline watched transfixed, as the shadowy figure dismounted. As it did so, the rider revealed a skeletal hand, carrying a staff of some kind. A staff topped by a long, curved metal blade; a scythe.

"The Reaper!" Evaline gasped in horror.

Evaline shivered, as he approached the first of the witches, who had been corralled together by the death dragons. With dismay, Evaline recognised this witch. She knew her well. It was Maya's mum. Though clearly dazed and disoriented, she stood upright, proud and defiant.

The cloaked figure stopped in front of her. He tapped the bottom of his scythe to the ground. Maya's mum, now crumpled to her knees, before him. Her head forcibly bowed. Evaline could barely watch, as the Reaper raised the mighty blade into the sky, as if to strike her down. Evaline had never felt so helpless.

Was this the end for Maya's mother?

"Anne," Evaline whimpered. The sight of her good friend at the mercy of this fiend, was more than she could bear.

Anne's arm now raised up slowly towards him, quivering as if she was trying to resist, but she could not prevent it. Maya's mother's hand twisted over suddenly, painfully. Her palm now facing upwards towards the Reaper.

Now, from under his cloak, he drew his other skeletal hand. It reached forward, as a cold chuckle carried on the wind. The Reaper simply tapped a single bony finger onto the palm of her outstretched hand.

Anne collapsed at his icy touch. It was death's touch and Evaline knew in that moment, that her friend was gone.

"No!" Evaline cried despairingly. How, oh how could she tell Maya? Tears welled in her eyes.

Evaline could hardly watch, as witch after witch, the whole coven was paraded in front of the Reaper. Friend after friend, met the same cruel fate. The Reaper made his way slowly and mercilessly through them all. There was fear in their eyes, like nothing Evaline had ever seen before. Hazel and Aunty Dot were next. Shona, Rose and then Mhairi followed. The younger girls and coven heirs, were not spared his cruel touch and sadistically, he kept them to last.

Evaline watched transfixed in terror, powerless, completely helpless, but at least she was still alive. She was cool headed enough not to rush in. There was no use in her blazing in there, just to give them her life too. She would have to warn the other covens, raise the alarm. But how could she tell Maya? That was the bit she feared the most. How, oh how, was she going to tell Maya?

With the executions over, the Reaper remounted his dragon and with a couple of powerful beats, from its tattered wings, the mighty beast took off, as if to head back north.

Suddenly though, the Reaper stopped his mighty beast, pulling back fiercely on its reins. In response, the fearsome dragon stopped

300

its ascent and hovered in mid-air. Then, slowly the Reaper turned, and stared straight towards Evaline. Evaline felt an icy chill pierce her heart, it cut right through her. It shook her to the core and rendered her motionless with fear. She was discovered. Her pendant glowed again brightly, as if to confirm her detection.

Evaline wanted to look away, but somehow, he held her gaze. In that brief moment Evaline felt a strange and frightening connection to this cruel shadow. Was this her time too?

His gaze lasted only a couple of seconds, but they felt like the longest hours of her life. She felt hollow inside, she sensed pure evil. Evil yes, she'd met that before, but there was something else here too. Something that she couldn't quite place. Then he turned away, kicked in his heels, and the Reaper, mounted on his immense buck dragon, flew back north. The death dragons too, now launched into the night sky, as a squabbling and unruly rabble. They followed their master into the night, forming a rough V-formation behind him.

As the last dragon cleared the horizon, Evaline returned. She flew through acrid smoke, back towards the smouldering remains of her once proud coven. Her dragon was spooked, bucking its head back and forth, frightened and confused. Evaline herself was spooked and her dragon sensed it. Black smoke rose into the sky and choked them, as they approached the charred remains of the coven. Tombstones smouldered and the bodies of her friends lay motionless on the ground, gathering ash, as it settled from the still night air.

Evaline landed her dragon. She patted the uneasy beast on the neck as she dismounted, in a half-hearted gesture to reassure it.

Evaline crouched down next to Anne's body. Anne lay face down in the dust, one arm outstretched towards her home, as if reaching out with her final gasp, for her beloved daughter Maya. The other lay by her side, holding her sister's hand. Twins, who had entered this world together, just minutes apart, had now departed it the same way. It seemed fitting at one level, but none of this felt right. It was horrible.

It was eerily quiet, smoke from the burning coffin seats filled the air and only the gentle crackling sound, from the remaining dying embers of the black fire were still audible. Evaline stood again, surveying the scene, helpless and bewildered, as to what she should do next. She simply stood and looked around in despair.

"Hhh...," an exhausted sigh broke the silence. A survivor?

Evaline's head turned back to Anne, who's outstretched fingers now clawed at the dusty floor of the coven. She was still alive!

Evaline crouched down beside her and gently cradled her head onto her lap. Anne's eyes opened wide, as if in sudden shock and fear. No, this wasn't fear, this was utter horror. A terror beyond anything that Evaline had ever witnessed before. Anne shook uncontrollably now, her eyes darting back and forth wildly, unable to focus. Then, as if coming to her senses, slowly she raised up her hand in front of her eyes and let out a harrowing scream.

Evaline grabbed Anne's hand and turned it towards her. Burned into the flesh of her palm, cutting straight across her lifeline. It read simply:

26.11, 14:05

"What?" Evaline asked her friend, but there was no response.

There was something else strange. Evaline stared at Anne's palm. Beyond the new mark, burned deep into her hand, her palm was smooth, no other marks or wrinkles. Now her lifeline simply stopped. It just ended. Completely erased from her flesh.

Evaline was perplexed, but she recognised the date somehow. It was coming back to her now. Was that Maya's birthday? Yes, but why?

Maya's mum stared back, Evaline could feel her friend shaking uncontrollably. She opened her mouth slowly and whispered with a final breath, before slipping back into unconsciousness:

"When his torture ends. That's when... I'll die!"

Cousin Emma

Maya was visiting the Coven of Deeds. She'd been having a great time, since the arrival of her big cousin Emma. Emma's whole family was on holiday at the family caravan. So naturally, Emma had to escape somehow.

She'd explained to Maya many times how:

"A week in that 'tin can' with her mum, dad and in particular her annoying big brother Ross and more especially his feet, was more than she could take."

Emma had a friend in the Coven of Deeds too. Well, a girl, who's cousin's friend had once mentioned her on Facebook, but she had taken the opportunity to visit Maya, when she was close-by anyway.

They had spent the day together. In the morning, they'd flown to Culzean Castle, but right now they were relaxing in Cambusdoon Park. 'Hanging out' near to the ruined stone arch, that marks the site where the Coven of Deeds rises every full moon. Maya had really enjoyed spending time with her cousin. Emma lives in Wales, so they didn't get the chance very often. Maya had even managed to ditch Mischief, for the day. He'd reckoned that there might be far too much girly chat for his liking, so had simply curled up to sleep on his comfortable red cushion. Maya was picking up lots of useful hints, about how to be a proper teenage witch too.

Emma, like her mother, Aunty Helen was rather an obvious witch, even to the casual observer. Nobody could miss it..., well, not nobody. Emma's dad, Maya's uncle Kenny and Emma's brother were utterly clueless! Not to mention, the fact that they had no idea whatsoever, of their own family's long witching heritage.

Emma was funny. Maya had come close to wetting herself with laughter, at her tales of how she tormented her mum and dad. Emma recounted, how the entrance to her magic room, was hidden in her bedroom cupboard. As a result, she could nip in and out, whenever she wanted. Whenever she slipped into the magic realm however, she always nipped back into her bedroom first and left behind a series of lookalike trolls to torment her parents. Each enchanted as her double, they would punish her mum and dad mercilessly. Emma had collected a whole wardrobe of trolls to choose from.

There was 'Sleepy Emma,' who stayed under the covers all day, refusing to get out of bed, let alone leave her room. She was a favourite all summer long, especially when the sun was out.

There was 'Grumpy Emma troll,' who she'd enchanted to disagree with whatever her dad said instantly. It would then glare at him, with an air of total disdain and listen to no reason.

Then there was; 'The Switch'... a troll who feigned interest initially in whatever her parents were wittering on about, then crushed them with a monosyllabic teenage:

"Meh!"

The 'Meh troll,' who didn't feign any interest in anything and had only one inevitable response, to every question posed.

The 'Dressing up troll'... who constantly tried to leave the house at night, in progressively skimpier and more revealing outfits and had perfected the combined hair-flick and giggle manoeuvre, whenever boys were present. That troll was particularly effective at tormenting her dad.

The 'Revision Troll'... who stayed in her room all day, but made endless beeping noises, like she was constantly on her phone or tablet, the minute the bedroom door was closed.

305

There were others too, that Maya couldn't wait to try out herself including the 'Phone zombie', the 'Tablet android', the 'Make-up and nails airhead troll', the "I fancy a tattoo or piercing troll' and finally the 'Goth troll'. All guaranteed to drive mums and especially dads to despair. So many to choose from. Maya couldn't wait.

"It's almost made bringing up my parents a rewarding experience," Emma explained proudly.

Maya had brought along her dragon Blink to meet Emma. Unsurprisingly, Emma loved him.

"He's just a big softy," she giggled, as he nuzzled into her shoulder, wiping dragon drool all down the sleeve of Emma's favourite top. Being from Wales, she had a soft spot for the 'winged beasties' as she called them, in her best, yet not very convincing Scottish accent. Blink always enjoyed himself here too. Not only did Emma make a fuss of him today, but there were lots of other dragon riders and a particularly cute looking female water dragon called Flame, who Maya strongly suspected, may have caught his eye.

Dragon riding was a tradition in the Coven of Deeds, from way back, even before the days when Evaline's mother ruled them, as their tyrannical High Priestess. Now though, since her banishment, they had turned to much more peaceful ways and Maya and Evaline had both become frequent visitors.

There was of course, another very important reason that Maya enjoyed meeting up with Emma. His name was Bandit. Bandit was Emma's horse. Well, that's still what her dad believed anyway. She had won numerous show-jumping medals on him, over the years.

"Dad says he just flies over the jumps," Emma giggled, at his expense. That really wasn't much of a surprise, not given his true nature, in the magic realm.

Emma, was in fact, Bandit's human. He'd had many human pets down through the millennia, and Emma was right up there, as one of the top seven or so on his 'B' list of humans, that he had come to appreciate, slightly more than most.

Bandit was the only Pegasus that Maya had ever encountered, although she strongly suspected that sometimes, he was just a little bit too aware of his own magnificence. His patented mane flick and whiney performance, being somewhat reminiscent of Emma's 'Dressing-up troll's' combined hair-flick and giggle routine.

Bandit, illustration by Maya age 10

Earlier that morning, Maya and Emma had flown together down the coast to Culzean castle. Bandit was every bit as fast as Blink. But Bandit was much more graceful in flight, than any other creature, that Maya had ever seen. She longed to ride him, but she knew that such a privilege was only granted to one pet, sorry rider, at a time.

Emma and Bandit had a special understanding, especially in flight. They swooped and turned, with a grace and an elegance, that Maya and her by comparison, rather cumbersome young dragon, could only dream of. Just watching them skim across the surface of the sea, hooves galloping across the water's surface, was a sight Maya would never tire of seeing. Bandit and Blink played together all morning, frolicking on the secluded beaches and plunging from the cliffs, not far from Culzean castle itself. In the afternoon they made their way to Cambusdoon, for a picnic and lots of girly chat and nonsense.

Now as midnight approached, Maya and Emma sat by a log fire, tired and contented, waiting for the moon to rise to its apex and with that, for the spectacle that was the Coven of Deeds to convene. Maya had promised Emma quite a show tonight and she was sure, that they wouldn't disappoint. They did things in style around here.

At the top of the long slope, above the River Doon, a slender figure, clad in long turquoise robes, stepped out from beneath the stone archway. This was the Deed's new High Priestess. In one hand she carried a long staff, with a bright turquoise crystal mounted on top. Slowly, she raised the staff above her head and pointed it towards the moon.

"I call upon the coven and all heirs," she cried, before bringing her staff down three times heavily onto the stone beneath.

"Heirs?" whispered Emma.

"Witches who would join their ranks," answered Maya, sounding more like her know-it-all cat with every Deed's related fact she imparted.

"Ah, we call them sprites, back home," Emma replied.

"Interested?" Maya asked hopefully. She would love it, if her big cousin decided to stick around.

Before Emma could answer her, the earth trembled beneath them with awesome power. Twelve huge pillars of glimmering turquoise crystal pushed their way effortlessly through the turf. On the

308

horizon the unmistakeable silhouettes of twelve dragons and their riders soared into view, arriving from the direction of the full moon.

"Wow!" Emma gasped. She couldn't help herself. Maya was the only dragon rider, she'd ever met. It was a rare gift indeed. Even in Wales! Someone had gone to a lot of trouble to put together such a coven. This might well be the most powerful coven ever assembled, Emma thought to herself.

Smaller pedestals of blue-green marble, now pushed their way up through the grass, in front of each of the larger pillars and glimmered in the moonlight. Emma was awestruck, she had never seen such a magnificent spectacle.

"Twelve seats for thirteen witches, yet everyone gets a seat," Maya muttered under her breath.

Emma smirked.

"I still don't understand it either. It gets me every time," she whispered with a smile.

Maya enjoyed watching the show, sharing the experience with Emma, as if it were her first time too. One by one, the witches arrived, mounted on the backs of their dragons, then dismounted. They were all dressed in matching flowing turquoise robes, with gold embroidery sewn around the seams. In gold lettering the word, 'Deeds' was emblazoned on each of their dragon's ebony-coloured saddles.

As the witches entered the coven, they raised their hoods up over their heads, as if to conceal their identity. Before taking their seats, each witch stooped and dropped what looked like a small pebble onto a golden tray, which sat atop a stone orb in the centre of the coven. Then in turn, thirteen dragons flapped up and perched obediently on top of each of the crystal pillars behind. The High

Priestess's impressive buck dragon taking the highest perch, behind her seat.

Now, very slowly, as if to emphasise her rank, the High Priestess entered the coven, dropping the final pebble onto the central stone. As it reached the tray, there was a blinding flash of blue light and both the orb and stones were transformed into translucent turquoise crystals, which matched the outer pillars. The crystals and pillars glowed and pulsed with a dazzling blue light. Lightning crackled between the pillars and to and from the crystal orb in the centre.

"The Deed's crystal ball," Maya explained.

Emma's jaw dropped. Maya had never seen Emma lost for words before. That had never happened!

Now, the High Priestess raised her staff once more and the coven was convened. A faint magical turquoise curtain, a protective shield, rose and enveloped the whole coven. No magic, nor witch, could pass through this impenetrable barrier now. Maya and Emma sat back to watch the show. There was to be an initiation ceremony tonight and that meant only one thing. Some serious magical skills would be on display.

Above them, the skies darkened and Maya shivered unexpectedly. There was a strange chill in the air. Dark shadows flickered across the moon. There was an eerie silence, followed by a piercing shrieking noise, which cut through the cold night air and pierced deep into Maya's chest. This unearthly wailing sound accompanied the first fireball. A ball of smoking black and violet flame which tumbled down through the night sky and passed straight through the coven's defensive shield. It plunged into the crystal ball, which burst into flames, scattering charred crystals to the floor in all directions. The coven's shield simply evaporated.

Panic and confusion broke out, as witches ran for cover, scattering in all directions. Dragons took to the air, spooked and frightened. Maya looked despairingly to the skies above, as a barrage of six and then seven more fireballs were unleashed. One for every witch in the coven.

Now mighty spells and firebolts were sent skywards by the Deeds, in retaliation. The Deeds was not a coven to be messed with. They fizzed through the air, much faster than the sluggish black fire weapons of their foes, and homed in on the dark shadows above. As they approached, they lit their quarry, revealing their unmistakeable forms. Dragons, black as the night sky, their bodies scarred from nose to tail. Evil looking beasts, which soared on tattered wings.

"No match for the Deeds," Maya whispered under her breath.

Above them in the starlit sky. All of the Deeds' spells found their targets. The attacking dragons made no attempt to evade them, but their spells and firebolts simply passed straight through these phantom-like enemies, as if they weren't there at all.

Below, the black fireballs closed in on the Deeds. Each one, adjusting its course, as though homing in on the source of the Deeds' firebolts. The High Priestess unleashed her own powerful incantation, then summoned her dragon, as the first of the deadly firebolts struck.

The coven was ablaze. Black flame leapt, from witch to witch and pillar to pillar, consuming them and devouring their magic. Witches dropped stricken and helpless to the floor. Panicked dragons circled the coven. Only the High Priestess escaped. Her dragon swooped in to cover her with its wings. Its scales reflected the dark fire. The High Priestess pulled herself onto its back, then instinctively, they took to the air.

311

Emma climbed onto Bandit. Wand drawn by her side. Bandit leapt into the night sky.

"Stay here!" Maya's big cousin ordered.

"No chance!" Maya scoffed. Launching Blink skywards, taking position on Emma's right wing. Maya was shaking with anger and fear.

"Cover the High Priestess," cried Emma, as the High Priestess swooped down on her dragon, to scoop up one of the younger witches, who staggered helplessly beneath her, trapped amongst the flames.

Emma sent up a flare and lit the sky above, as if to draw the attention of the attackers. It worked, too well. A dozen or more dark shadows, which circled above, now turned as one, to pursue her. Black dragon shapes, on torn and tattered wings and red piercing eyes, headed their way.

Bandit, in full flight was magnificent. He turned on a sixpence and swooped down elegantly, mane and tail flowing in the wind. Bandit now revealed his true speed. He was much faster than Blink and twice as manoeuvrable, as any dragon that Maya had ever seen. He drew the dragons' fire and evaded the incoming fireballs with ease.

"Enough of this," Maya resolved. "Down them Spell!" Maya commanded, holding up her living wand. Spell's roots gripped tightly onto her wrist. This was no ordinary spell, it crackled with power and Blink shook beneath her, as the powerful incantation left the little living wand.

"Whoa!" cried Emma. She had never seen Maya's living wand in action before. She could sense Spell's awesome power. It pulsed right through her, like she was standing in front of the speaker bank, at a heavy metal concert.

Their gaze followed Maya's fireball upwards, its brilliant white light, illuminating the whole night sky. It shot up vertically, before splitting into thirteen smaller fireballs, each of which now targeted one of the shapes above. With a fizz, like a giant firework, they homed in on their quarry, darting this way and that, tracking their attackers every move.

"Payback time," Maya whispered beneath her breath, as her firebolts closed in on the shadows above. They all found their targets. Then in a cataclysmic anti-climax, burst straight through these unearthly black dragons and out of the other side. It was as if they weren't even there.

"No," cried Maya in disbelief.

Suddenly though, the dark dragon shapes fell, one by one from the sky.

"Yes!" cried Emma. "Take that!"

"No!" cried Maya, again in disbelief.

Far from being shot down, they had turned, one by one and now homed in on the source of Maya's spell. Diving towards her with deadly intent. Maya turned in fright. She fled in the same direction as the High Priestess.

Blink was agile in the air, not like Bandit. But, by any 'normal' magical yardstick, he was formidable. Blink ducked and dived, eluding the incoming fire with ease. But Maya could see, that ahead of her, the High Priestess was much less manoeuvrable. Her dragon was heavily laden, carrying both her and the young witch she'd rescued. Maya knew that she had to draw the attackers fire, if they were to have any chance of escaping.

Piercing screeching noises cut through them from behind, announcing the release of another barrage of black firebolts, as the shadows closed in. Maya dug in her heels and Blink veered upwards in a steep ascent, then peeled off towards the blinding light of the moon. Eluding their fire, but still the dragons pursued with deadly intent.

Below, Maya caught a last glimpse of the High Priestess and her dragon, as they finally reached the cover of the trees. It gave Maya some hope. At least there would be two survivors tonight. Witnesses who could warn the other covens. Perhaps they could find a way to strike back, against this seemingly invincible foe.

Bandit followed Maya up into the sky and matched her every twist and turn, skilfully evading the demons, who relentlessly pursued them. Bandit was formidable, turning one way then another in response to Emma's slightest movement. They were as one, drawing the fire of the approaching dragons. It was as if Bandit could anticipate Emma's every thought and moved accordingly.

Bandit criss-crossed behind Maya and Blink. Emma's wand drawn and glowing in the night air, its magic attracting the attentions of the black firebolts, from their pursuit of Maya. Emma steered the fire bolts off course, before veering away at the last moment, as they closed to strike her down. Bolt after bolt hit the ground beneath. Emma and Bandit had Maya's back. Maya always appreciated having her big cousin around, but never more so, than now.

Maya was no slouch on Blink either, thanks to her dragon flying lessons from Evaline, when training for dragon combat. Maya looped the loop, spun out through a corkscrew, then turned to give her foes an entirely inappropriate hand gesture, before heading for the sanctuary of the trees. She knew that Blink was smaller and more manoeuvrable than any of these dragons. She was certain, they could lose them in the woods.

Maya entered the woods first and Bandit and Emma followed. They zig-zagged through the forest, cutting parallel paths through the trees. Checking anxiously over their shoulders, but they needn't have bothered. No dragons followed. They were clear.

"Thanks Emma!" Maya called.

Emma just grinned, as they wove their way through the forest.

It was like watching an Olympic skier's master class on a slalom course. Emma swooped past each branch, their leaves brushing against her shoulders, as she passed. She was clearly in her element here. Emma though, now had a strange grin on her face. Maya was suspicious. Emma was up to something. As she cleared an ancient oak tree, Maya was suddenly aware that Bandit was no longer beside her. She turned from side to side.

No sign? She'd vanished.

"That's impossible!" Maya heard herself gasp. Had Emma collided with that last tree, surely not?

There was a sharp tap on Maya's shoulder, causing her to jump half out of her saddle, in fright. Maya spun around and looked back.

Nothing?

"Eh?" she grunted.

There was a giggle from above. Maya knew that laugh instantly. She looked up. Sure enough, it was Emma. Flying Bandit upside down, following her every move, as she zig-zagged through the trees.

"Show off!" Maya laughed.

"If you've got it flaunt it, my mum always says!" Emma laughed, whilst adjusting her ample bust with both hands, in a most undignified manner. It brought a smile to Maya's previously panicked face.

They exited the trees at the foot of an old sandstone railway bridge, which spans over the River Doon. The girls stopped and hovered, to catch their breath by the water's edge. They both turned and looked back anxiously, to confirm once more, that they hadn't been followed. Much to their relief, it appeared they were alone.

Old Railway Bridge over The River Doon, viewed from Alloway

In the distance, they could still make out the fractured remains of the Coven of Deeds. Smoke hung heavily in the night air, marking its location and dark shadows still circled in the sky above, flickering across the full moon, but they had stopped firing. Neither was there any return of fire from the Deeds. All had fallen silent. The battle, if you could call it that, was over.

The Deeds hadn't stood a chance.

316

"What were they?" Maya panted.

"Death dragons, I think," Emma gasped. "Mum used to tell me stories about them at Halloween. I thought it was just a story that Mum had made up, just to scare me witless and to make my brother cry. I didn't ever dream they were real!"

"Death dragons?" Maya frowned. She'd never heard of them.

"My mum used to put the lights off and tell me about them. I listened from under the covers, but my brother just hid under his bed," Emma panted. "She can be spooky like that sometimes. She said that they were the spirits of dead dragons, dragons which had long since passed into the afterlife. Dragons which did terrible things in the past and now served Death himself, as their penance."

Emma and Maya shivered in unison.

"Nice bedtime story Aunty Helen!" Maya scoffed. "No wonder they called her Morticia at work!"

"Mum says that if your dad ever repeats that, I've just to call him Uncle Fester!" Emma responded, trying to make light of the situation.

"Did your mum say anything else?" Maya prompted.

"Oh yes... it's getting her to shut up, that's the difficult thing. Especially when it comes to the Munsters!" Emma explained.

"No! Not about the Munsters... anything about the death dragons? Remember? The scary black fire breathing efforts, that just tried to kill us!" Maya exclaimed, her exasperation at Emma's frivolity, finally laid bare.

"Oh yes. Hmm..., Mum said that long ago, they once rode with the Grim Reaper himself, as he waged a cruel and terrible war on man

317

and witchkind alike," Emma continued, with a strange morbid delight.

Maya leaned in closer, fascinated and eager for more.

"It was a dark time and many witches fell victim to his terrible cruelty," Emma continued. "Eventually the most powerful witches in all the land came together, laid a trap and banished him."

"How?" Maya demanded impatiently.

Emma hesitated, then possibly, even blushed a little. "I don't remember," she confessed. "I hid under the covers and didn't hear that bit."

Maya just glared in disbelief. After a very long pause, long enough to make her point and suitably shame her elder cousin. Maya finally broke the silence.

"So, who's this Reaper chap anyway?" Maya asked.

"You know, you must have heard of him?" replied Emma. "The Grim Reaper. He rounds up the dead. Wears a big black cloak, no face, carries a long scythe. Very scary!"

A chill ran up Maya's spine, like a frosted stoat had just taken up residence in her pyjama trouser leg.

"The Grim Reaper?" Maya repeated. It did sound familiar.

"You called?" a deep and gravelly voice rang out from behind them.

The girls spun around in their saddles. A huge back dragon loomed up behind them, its wingspan twice the size of both of their trusty steeds combined. On its back, a faceless hooded black-cloaked demon, cackled and raised a scythe above its head.

"No!" cried Emma. "It can't be!"

The hooded figure now pointed his scythe slowly towards Maya and a black fireball formed at its tip, then leapt straight at her. She had little time to react. Maya instinctively raised a magical shield. But the fireball passed straight through it. She was powerless against him. Blink too reacted on instinct alone, raising a wing to shield his rider, just as the fireball hit.

Maya and Blink tumbled towards the ground, dazed and hurt. But they had not taken the hit, not its full force, not by a long way. Blink, half stunned, started to flap his wings and Maya dug in her heels and pulled his neck back to halt their descent. They stopped, just above the tops of some prickly bushes, which grew below.

Instinctively they fled.

"What... where... Emma?" Maya called out, slowly regaining her wits.

Maya turned, looking frantically over her shoulder for her cousin. Just in time to see poor Bandit, as he tumbled head over tail, towards the ground. His magnificent wings, charred and ablaze with the Black fire. Emma's unconscious body tossing from side to side and slumped backwards across Bandit's back, as he fell to earth.

"No!" Maya cried despairingly. "That was meant for me!"

Maya, now coming to her senses, now realised what had just happened. Emma had taken the blast. She had put herself and Bandit between Maya and the Reaper. Emma had taken a direct hit, a blast from the Grim Reaper himself.

Maya dug in her heels, to signal Blink to turn around.

But Blink didn't obey her, he'd never done that before. He headed her towards the cover of the nearby trees. Maya struggled to turn him again, but Blink disobeyed once more.

319

Maya's frustration, outrage and anger started slowly to subside. She was in shock, but slowly logic had started to prevail. She knew, in her heart that Blink was right, she needed to survive. She had to run, she had to survive and raise the alarm.

"Run away, to live and fight another day," her dad often quoted, every time Mum was giving him a hard time. If not, her big cousin Emma, had just given her life for nothing.

Tears came flooding to Maya's eyes, as they fled. Maya cowered into Blink's neck for comfort. He grumbled reassuringly from deep inside his chest. The vibrations and reverberations, through her dragon's back were normally comforting, but nothing could dull the pain she felt now.

Blink kept a wary eye on his tail, but the mighty dragon, on which the Reaper sat, was too big to follow through the tree tops and made no attempt to do so. Instead, it descended slowly on powerful wings, carrying its master down towards Emma and Bandit, as they lay motionless on the ground beneath.

When Blink was sure they were clear, he stopped and perched on a high branch, of an ancient oak tree. They both turned their heads nervously, compelled to watch, helpless to intervene, as Grim landed and dismounted from his mighty dragon.

From the relative safety of their vantage point, they watched in horror, as the Reaper slowly approached Emma, where she lay. Just the sight of this figure sent sharp shivers up and down Maya's spine. Every nerve in her body jangled. It was about as pleasant as chewing on a tinfoil biscuit wrapper, with a mouthful of metal fillings (or for readers with a nice set of white teeth... it stung like a panicked scorpion trapped inside your underwear!)

The Reaper raised up his scythe and suddenly Emma's body convulsed on the muddy ground, where she lay.

"She's alive!" Maya gasped with relief.

But her relief was short lived. Emma's body dragged itself, as if possessed, from the floor and sat kneeling, facing towards the Reaper. An involuntary hand lurched towards his raised staff and twisted painfully, palm now facing upwards. A bony skeletal hand reached out from beneath his black cloak and touched Emma's palm, with a single outstretched digit. At his touch, Emma collapsed, lifeless to the floor.

"No!" Maya sobbed.

The dark figure laughed aloud, remounted his dragon, then took to the skies once more. The Reaper hovered briefly, then turned, as if to look straight at Maya. A chill like nothing she had ever felt before, stabbed through her, like an icicle piercing her heart.

Another evil chuckle was lost on the wind and with that, the Reaper's formidable dragon, carried him back to the North. A V-shape of death dragons flew in from the clouds, over what remained of the Coven of Deeds and followed him, squabbling, clawing and snapping at each other, as they flew.

When the hellish hoard had cleared the horizon. Maya and Blink made their way despondently, back across the tree tops to recover Emma's fallen body.

Maya knew in her heart, there was no hope. Emma had been touched by the hand of death, literally. Emma and Bandit lay dead and motionless in front of her. Bandit's wings singed and burnt back to their bones, which lay shattered by his side. Acrid wisps of smoke rose above them.

It was heart-breaking and Maya broke hers now. Maya knelt and wept. She felt cold, hollow and helpless. She needed her mum. She needed her big cousin back. Maya held out her hand to touch Emma, as if to comfort her, even in death.

321

Emma's hand twitched. Maya jumped out her skin, landing in a cowardly shivering one, two sizes too small.

Emma was still alive! Maya shuffled closer and cradled Emma's head in her arms.

"No!" Emma screamed, sitting up abruptly. Mad eyes stared up at Maya. Emma turned the palm of her hand up in front of her face.

"No, no... no!" Emma cried in horror.

Then she passed out, once again.

Bandit too, now started to stir.

"He's alive!" Maya let out a jubilant cry.

Bandit's head rose groggily from the floor. His front legs stretched out in front of him. His hooves clawed at the leaf litter beneath him, pulling him jerkily off his flank. Bandit stumbled unsteadily to his hooves. His eyes now red and bloodshot. The remnants of his broken wings hung lifelessly from his shoulders.

Maya laid Emma down gently and tried to approach him, but Bandit whinnied and reared up on his hind legs, to warn her off.

"It's okay boy," she said gently. But it wasn't. Nothing about this was okay.

Maya tried again to get closer, to calm him, to comfort him, but this time Bandit turned, whinnied once more and ran. He galloped for the cover of the trees. Maya watched in despair, as the last flash of his tail disappeared from sight.

Maya knew there was no time to waste. Emma needed help and she needed to raise the alarm. Maya struggled and heaved Emma onto the back of Blink for the journey home. She dared not use her magic, for fear of summoning one of those hellish beasts, or even the Reaper himself.

"Too many puddings Emma!" Maya puffed. With a final shove, Emma's surprisingly heavy and floppy body finally balanced precariously across Blink's back. Then slipped over the other side, crashing face first into the dirt.

Emma let out a groan, but she didn't awaken. After three more unsuccessful attempts and 'face plants', none of which were going to improve Emma's good looks any, Maya had her cousin balanced precariously onboard Blink and she dug in her heels, to signal their departure. Blink took to the air.

They skirted around Cambusdoon Park, then up over the hill with the old ruined archway. The once proud and magnificent crystal Coven of Deeds, lay in ruins beneath them. Black and charred coven pedestals still smouldered. Most were cracked and broken, some had completely crumbled away to ashes. Black smoke and embers glowing with a strange purple light, still filled the air.

There were none of the Deed's dragons left. Their scales littered the ground beneath, like glitter after a Glasgow hen-party. All had fled. Maya hoped that some of the witches had escaped, but she counted eleven grey shadows beneath. Most lay motionless, others cowered and wept openly. Some clawed at the ground with broken nails.

Two of the older witches, whom Maya knew well, crouched on the ground and wailed, staring in terror at their outstretched palms. One stumbled to her feet, staggering from side to side, as if dazed and half-blinded. She lurched from one charred pillar to the next, lost and disoriented. Only the High Priestess and that one young witch had escaped. It was like a scene from a post-apocalyptic movie or the morning after a New Year's Eve party in Edinburgh.

Maya landed briefly to see if she could help, but none of the Deed's witches responded to her at all. None of them answered, her repeated and ever more despairing offers of help. None could even meet her pitying gaze. They stared through ghoulish bloodshot eyes at their own outstretched palms or clenched their fists, as if hiding away some awful secret.

Maya felt empty inside, an emptiness she had not experienced here before. It normally crackled with magic and excitement. As a charred wand broke under Blink's talons, Maya realised with horror, that there was no magic left here. None! The black fire had consumed it all.

Maya felt so helpless. She needed to get help for these poor souls. She knew that she had to get Emma back home too and talk to her mum. Mum would know what to do.

The merciful few

The skies above the Prestwick Coven were filled with smoke from the black fire. As the remnants of green distress flares faded from view, the silhouettes of a few remaining witches appeared on the horizon. Drawn in silence and fear towards the sad spectacle which awaited them. Older witches, long retired from active magical duties, and those from nearby covens, descended from the skies to help.

Granny was amongst them. After landing close to the centre of the coven, she made a beeline for her favourite daughter. Nearly trampling on poor old Aunty Dot's wand hand in the process, as she ran straight past her to Anne's side. There were tears and snotters a plenty and a rather sickened Evaline, not known for her sentiment, went over to check on Dot and the others.

Those coven witches, those who had recovered consciousness, sat in an eerie silence. Some stared, with madness in their eyes, at their own outstretched palms. Others wept, holding clenched fists tightly against their chests. More and more witches arrived, sending further distress flares into the sky.

Dot awoke now and let out an anguished cry. Granny now looked slightly embarrassed. As she finally remembered her other daughter, then reluctantly, went to console her too. Anne tried to get to her feet, but stumbled to one side, still dazed and disoriented. Evaline caught her, just before she fell.

Evaline bundled Anne onto the back of her own dragon and mounted behind her. It was time they left this place. Evaline caught Granny's eye, who nodded her agreement. Then with a kick of her heels, Evaline's dragon took to the air. They headed towards Ayr.

Evaline knew that she had to get Maya's mother home. She had to warn Maya and alert the witches from all the other covens too. She wasn't looking forward to this. Not one bit.

***

Maya headed home, with tears in her eyes. She had to warn her mother. Her mum would know what to do next. How to help poor Emma? How to heal Bandit's injuries? But more than that, right now, Maya just needed her mum.

Maya was haunted by the day's events. How do you fight the Grim Reaper himself? How do you fight a foe on whom magic has no effect? Maybe her mum, Granny or Grandma would know?

As Maya neared home, she slowed Blink and hovered over the woods behind her house. She could see another dragon beneath her, landing in their back garden. It was Evaline's dragon and there were others there too. Quite a gathering. An impressive audience, for her terrible news.

"That's just reckless!" Maya announced, to her unconscious passenger. They never landed brushes, let alone dragons, in their own back garden... what if her dad was in? What if the neighbours saw? Not that they could see magical creatures, but non-magical objects, like cushions and lunch boxes levitating above the ground, could still arouse suspicions. Maya looked down at Emma, but there was still no response.

"Oh, so what?" Maya heard herself say. It really didn't seem to matter that much now, not after all that had happened. Besides, Maya knew her dad was away at some boring business conference all week.

Granny was there too. A floppy looking thing, that resembled her Aunty Dot, flung over her knee. She hovered on her old-fashioned broom, over the lawn. Granny looked tired, and dumped her second favourite daughter clumsily onto the grass beneath her, face first.

As Maya landed on Blink, she jumped out of the saddle in alarm. Panicked by the sight of her stricken mother, slumped over the back of Evaline's dragon. Poor Emma slipped silently and unseen from Blinks back, once more landing heavily, face first, in the dirt.

There were tears and snotters galore, as Evaline helped Maya carry her mother inside. They laid her down in the conservatory, on a sofa and propped her head up on a star shaped pillow, which Maya had fashioned as a child at sewing classes. Evaline carried Emma inside and dropped her rather clumsily in Maya's dad's beer seat. A couple of minutes of frantic fussing over the casualties followed.

As things finally calmed down, Maya got Granny a cup of tea and a biscuit. Eventually, Evaline remembered that Aunty Dot had been left outside, lying face down on the back grass. After a vote, a split decision and a third re-count. Evaline defied the result and brought her in too. Mischief, also joined them now, showing uncharacteristic concern and even compassion for his human counterparts.

Evaline and Maya took it in turn, to relay the grim events from earlier that night. The chilling similarity of their stories struck everyone. Maya's heart raced, as she contemplated how quickly and easily, their new foe had dealt with, two of the most powerful covens in the land.

Mischief's ears pricked up, as Evaline recounted how the dragons had parted for her and her dragon to pass. His distrustful glare cutting through her, especially as she recalled her brief exchange of glances with the Reaper himself. It was no secret that Mischief

327

didn't trust Evaline, not like Maya did. He never tired of reminding Maya that Evaline had, on more than one occasion, tried to kill her in the past and therefore could never be trusted again.

"Those days are gone!" Maya would scold him, and remind him of all the times Evaline had also saved her life. But Mischief remained ever wary of her.

"Can a leopard really change its spots?" he'd grumble to himself.

"What I really don't understand is, why didn't the Reaper just kill everyone, when he had the chance?" Maya asked curiously. "He had every single witch at his mercy. If he really is the Grim Reaper, then why did he spare them?"

"He didn't!" Granny answered. She was a tough old thing, wise with her years, but those words brought her close to tears. Now choked with emotion, she couldn't find the words to explain and just shook her head despairingly.

To Maya, it seemed strange that the Reaper, who did Death's bidding, had spared so many. But to Granny, his motives were all too horribly clear. She'd heard legends of how witch kind had banished the Reaper, but never took them to be true. Horror stories at Halloween, to frighten little witches, but now it seemed that they might in fact, be based on true events. Events that, over the years, had fallen into myth and legend.

Maya's mum nodded sadly in agreement with Granny. She was coming to her senses, once more. Now, she spoke quietly, her voice frail, shaky and barely recognisable.

"It's true," she whispered. "He's spared us nothing. We'd be better off dead!" Maya's mum announced tearfully.

"You can't mean that?" Maya rebuked her instantly.

"I can," Anne continued, after a husky cough. "I felt his thoughts, when he touched me. His name is Grim and he will punish all witch kind for what they have done to him. His revenge will be terrible!"

Maya held up a glass of water for her mum, which she sipped on gratefully.

Evaline took up the story.

"Survivors have no magic left. They all have a date and time burned into their palms. A date which cuts their life-line," Evaline explained sadly. She could not meet Maya's horrified eyes. She gulped down a breath of air, then dropped the bombshell:

"I think, I mean... I think it's the time of their death."

Maya stared, transfixed and horrified towards her mum, then down towards her mother's clenched fist. Her mum looked away. She couldn't meet her own daughter's eyes either. She simply nodded.

Silence. Stunned silence followed and lingered in the air like the smell of cabbage and steamed herring at Grandma's house.

Eventually, Anne spoke again, sobbing this time:

"That's not the worst of it."

"What? What could possibly be worse?" Maya demanded.

Maya's mum spoke now, with a fear in her voice, that Maya had never heard before.

"He has taken our magic and with his touch gifted us foresight of our own end. Premonitions of the gruesome way, that Grim has devised for each of us to meet our deaths."

Maya let out an involuntary gasp.

Anne took another sip of water from her glass, before continuing.

"All before the year is out. The youngest first, so that mothers will be forced to watch their own daughter's fate," Anne sobbed. "He's a monster!"

"How mum? How?" Maya demanded anxiously.

Anne shook her head.

"I would spare you that, little one, that is my burden, but they did not call him Grim for nothing," Anne sobbed.

"Not burning?" Maya demanded. "Tell me it's not burning!"

"No, little one. If only, that would be relatively quick. Burning at the stake isn't slow enough for Grim. He's spent the last 600 years plotting his revenge. He has something new and terrible in store for each and every one of us!" Anne confirmed, visibly shaking with fear.

"Knowing it...," she gulped. "Knowing our fate, I fear will drive us all to madness!" Anne announced, looked up suddenly with crazed eyes. Her face so fearful, that Maya could hardly even recognise her own mother's face.

Maya's mum took a cloth from the sewing box on the table in front of her and bandaged over her hand feverishly, so as no one else might know the date on her palm.

"Not a word!" she growled at Evaline. Then, her head fell back onto the pillow and she fell back into an uneasy, tormented unconsciousness.

Emma, Dot and Maya's mother, all lay unconscious now. But they did not rest, they did not sleep. Their heads tossed from side to side. Dot screamed, sat upright and slumped back into her cushion. Emma tossed and turned and fell face first, from her seat onto the cold laminate floor. She was definitely having a bad face day.

330

Two days passed. They were the slowest and most agonising days of Maya's life. Whenever her mum or Aunty Dot woke, they were close to madness. Neither could bear to look Maya in the eye. They shook relentlessly, whenever she hugged them for comfort. It frightened Maya. Shook her to her very core. Dot and Emma were silent, withdrawn, empty inside. They never spoke, not even once.

By night, distant howls pierced the still night air and green distress flares lit up the horizon. The few witches, who had escaped Grim, fled south or returned to the non-magic realm with no real hope of ever returning. Only Grim's victims and a few elderly witches, remained in the magic realm, to care for the stricken.

Granny had taken Aunty Dot home. She had taken to spending all day staring into a mirror and sobbing at the wrinkles and frizz that had returned, as her magic had failed. Her torture at the hands of Grim, had already started. Evaline stayed to help Maya look after her mum and Emma. They left the magic realm for now; in case their magic gave them away, to Grim's or his death dragons.

Maya had magical lineage on both sides of her family. At Granny's request, Maya's Grandma, her dad's mother, had also come to stay. She had taken charge now. With age comes wisdom, and Maya was in awe at how this seemingly frail old women, now took up the reins and bore the heavy burden of command.

In just a few days, she had gathered together quite a gathering. Old friends, retired witches, who no longer flew with their covens, and so for now, had been spared Grim's awful curse. A few coven elders too, the lucky few, who had escaped the attacks and still held their powers. At first, Maya thought that this was the start of the resistance, but gently Grandma took her to one side to explain. It was clearly one of the most difficult things that her grandmother had ever done.

This new gathering of witches, was no resistance. There was no grand plan to strike back. They were to be hidden away... the 'merciful few,' they would be known as.

"You don't mean?" Maya stared at Grandma, with tears in her eyes.

"Yes, my dear," Grandma confirmed. "I'm afraid so. As the date on their hands draws close. We will spare them the fate, which Grim has chosen for them. We will take them far away from here and cast a merciful spell."

"No..., not...?" but Maya already knew the answer.

"Yes, my dear, I'm afraid so," Grandma confirmed sadly.

"The death spell?" Maya whispered, her voice breaking, as too was her heart.

The old woman just smiled and tried to comfort Maya with a big hug. There was a long silence, as Maya tried to come to terms with what Grandma was saying.

"I'm going with her, you know, when it's time," Maya announced defiantly.

"No, I'm sorry little one, but you can't," Grandma apologised. "She must meet her fate without you, as casting such a spell will instantly bring the death dragons down upon us."

"But you'll...," Maya couldn't finish her sentence.

Grandma nodded:

"Yes, my dear. So, the merciful few will not just cast their spells for the witches, they will spare. They will cast it for themselves too."

Only Grandma, could deliver such news, with a kindly smile.

Maya just wept.

Run or hide?

Grandma looked deep into Maya's eyes once more, and spoke gently:

"You have a choice to make, Maya. You can stay in the non-magic realm, make a new life for yourself. There is no shame in choosing to live. If you decide to hide away from Grim and his beasts, you can still live a normal life."

"And abandon my mum and Emma? No!" Maya glared at her grandmother. "There must be another way!"

"Or you can return," Grandma continued. "But, if you do so, your magic will surely give you away. Sooner or later, he will find you."

Maya heard herself swallow loudly.

"If you return to the magic realm, you must leave immediately," Grandma whispered. "Flee south with that living wand of yours... somehow, somewhere, you must find a way to defeat him. And if you cannot? Well, then you must survive, because only through you and that precious living wand of yours, I fear, will magic itself be kept alive."

Maya knew she was right of course, but to abandon her mum at a time like this, it was more than she could bear.

"Take Emma with you," Grandma could see that Maya had already made up her mind. "She needs to be back with her own mother now, but tell them, if it comes to it... I'll be there for Emma, when she needs me. Granny will look after your mum."

Maya knew only too well, what the old woman meant. Grandma's words cut right through her chest and cleaved her heart in two.

334

"Take this," Grandma thrust a charm bracelet into Maya's hand. There were several small silver charms on it, but one stood out. It was a delicate looking silver door, with a tiny key on a chain.

"It's a beacon... if Emma opens the door, I'll be drawn to her, wherever she is and... well, there's no need to dwell on that now, is there," Grandma mumbled, close to tears. "Be away with you now and stop upsetting this old lady!"

Tears ran down Maya's face. She kissed Grandma on the cheek and gave her a long and crushing hug, as if this might be their final goodbye.

Maya said she'd sleep on it, but she knew that she wouldn't. She wouldn't sleep at all. Maya had already made her decision. She had to return to the magic realm. She couldn't just hide away and let this happen to all those, who she loved. There had to be a way.

Early next morning, at sunrise, Maya woke Evaline and Emma. She sat them down in the conservatory and explained what Grandma had said the night before. She couldn't bring herself to tell Emma about the 'merciful few' though. Not yet, she had already suffered enough.

"When do we leave?" asked Evaline, pre-empting Maya's forthcoming question.

Emma nodded too. She was strong and had 'slept' better than most of the stricken, but she had still not spoken since the night, when she'd encountered the Reaper and lost Bandit. And none of their subsequent searches of Cambusdoon, had shown any trace of him.

With a heavy heart, Maya tip-toed her way through to the bedroom and kissed her mother goodbye, as she slept. She chose not to wake her. Some goodbyes are just too painful. She left a pelican's foot shell, they'd found on the beach together, on her mum's pillow. So she'd know that Maya had been, to say her goodbyes. Then she left.

Maya composed herself, then led Evaline and Emma upstairs, to her mother's secret room.

Once on the landing, Maya used the key charm from her neckless to open the door. Slowly, as the cupboard rotated back into the wall, she led the way into the poorly lit chamber beyond. Evaline and Emma followed her in.

Mischief, lay curled up, asleep as always, on a comfortable red cushion in the corner. All was as it should be; an old chest sat in the corner with three triangular bottles placed on top. Next to it stood a full-length mirror and an old dressing table. Everything was covered in a thick layer of dust. Maya's leather-bound magical book, sat closed on top of the dressing table, next to her mother's.

Maya sat down at the dressing table and placed the neckless charm into the heart-shaped recess in the metal straps that bound her magic book. The metal straps sprung open and the book opened itself slowly and welcomed her, with a more sombre greeting that she was accustomed to:

"Hello little one, sorry to hear about your mum. She doesn't deserve that." Its words writing themselves in elegant prose across the blank parchment sheets, as it spoke.

Maya acknowledged its good wishes with a nod, wrote the book.

Mischief had just awoken from his slumbers. He jumped up onto the wooden chest and was now circling a potion bottle with a pendant necklace on it. It looked familiar, but Maya couldn't place it. He paused and sat down behind that bottle with purpose. Maya stroked him with one hand and picked up the bottle with the other.

336

Maya took a deep breath, looked around at Evaline and Emma, shrugged her shoulders and popped the cork. The room filled with all the colours of the rainbow. Light spun out, like silken threads unravelling from a Hawaiian shirt. It streamed out from the little bottle, illuminating everything it touched, in an ever-changing light show that filled every corner of the room. Then, the lights faded away, as quickly as they had started.

Maya's full-length mirror began to ripple in front of them. Maya reached out to touch it, her fingers tingled as they passed through and into the magic portal. Mischief leapt from behind her and through the mirror, leading the way as usual.

Maya stepped out of the other side of the mirror accompanied as always by a faint puff of white smoke. It usually made her smile, the whole magic smoke and mirrors thing, but not today. Today was not about laughter. Emma and Evaline followed.

On the other side, all in the room was as before, except that Mischief had already prized open a little door, or as Maya had christened it 'witch flap', behind the dressing table. Maya now led Emma by the hand and followed the impatient scamper of feline footsteps, down the dark passageway ahead. The way was lit by small silver glowing caterpillars, which hung from the ceiling and lit as they approached, then faded once they passed. But there were shadows here now. Shadows, where they had been none previously.

There was something else different too. A darkness that Maya hadn't felt before. Not since she'd been stalked by something or someone in the portal on the way to the snow leopard's cave. Mischief had often explained how impure thoughts and temptations could open up new passageways, in magical portals and Maya realised that she'd have to be careful. With all that had happened to her mum and Emma. She was full of hatred and

337

loathing for Grim and that was opening up new and darker paths for her to follow. Other passageways now ran off in all directions, tempting her to take a darker route, to seek her revenge. For the first time, Maya stopped. Unsure of which path to follow.

Evaline sensed her hesitation.

"Don't worry Maya. I get loads of these ... sometimes, I even have to lay down a string, just to find my way back," Evaline laughed.

Maya raised a smile too. Evaline must indeed have strayed from the right path in the past, when doing her tyrannical mum's bidding, back when she was a member of the Coven of Deeds.

"Just close your eyes and think of your mum or Spell. Back in happier times," Evaline advised. "They'll show you the way."

Maya chose Spell and Blink. Her mum's current plight made thinking of her, just too painful. Thinking of her dragon or her living wand, always brought a smile to her face. There, in front of her, the path she should follow lit up, as if to lead the way.

"Thanks, Evaline," Maya acknowledged.

Emma raised an impressed eyebrow. Like her mother before her, she had been known to stray from the righteous path, just occasionally. That little trick would come in handy, the next time she was visiting the magic realm, with no other purpose, than to nip back and torture her dad with lookalike trolls.

Maya opened the witch flap, on the other side and led Evaline and Emma into her log cabin in the woods. Mischief jumped up onto his favourite red cushion. After all, it had been over ten minutes since his last nap.

"Morning Spell," Maya turned and greeted her sapling wand, which grew in a terracotta pot on a small wooden table. Maya smiled, as she bent down and held out her hand. The young wand shook the soil from its roots and wrapped itself tightly around her wrist with a squeeze, as if to say hello. Emma looked on, in wonderment and delight.

Spell was getting larger now and ever more powerful, a second branch had recently started to grow from her main stalk and it was now in bud. Maya was glad her little wand was thriving, but it saddened her also. She knew that one day, as a living wand, Spell would outgrow her pot and join her mother as a magical tree. But for now, she was still portable enough to accompany Maya on her adventures, in the magic realm.

Maya showed the girls around. Normally, she would have relished the opportunity. Sharing this place with her friend and big cousin, but not under these circumstances. It felt darker and less welcoming here too, reflecting Maya's own mood. The skies were cloudy outside and rain fell just in time to disguise her tears, as she showed Emma and Evaline the stables, where she kept Blue. Maya cropped some fresh mint from a planter and fed it to her faithful brush, as she stroked his bristles affectionately with her other hand.

"Not today," Maya apologised to Blue, as she fed him. "I'm sorry, I can't risk using magic, not with all these death dragons around." Maya turned away again, leaving a rather dejected looking brush, for once still locked behind his stable door.

Maya gathered her thoughts and blinked three times. She needed her dragon now. Only a dragon could offer any protection from its own kind and fly undetected. Blink could take her where she needed to go, without her having to cast a spell.

Blink must have been sleeping close-by. Just a couple of minutes passed, before the silhouette of Maya's dragon appeared above the treetops. With a few powerful slowing beats of his wings, the purple dragon landed in front of Maya and nuzzled into her outstretched hand affectionately.

Evaline too, summoned her own dragon, using a whistle carved from a dragon's tooth, which she'd produced from her pocket at Maya's request. Evaline's larger dark green dragon arrived from the north and snapped towards Blink, as it came in to land. Blink returned its greeting with a snarl and a puff of sparks and black smoke, which sprayed forth from both nostrils. There was an uneasy standoff between the two creatures. This was Blink's territory and other dragons were not normally tolerated.

Maya climbed onto the back of Blink and pulled Emma up behind her. Emma held on tightly. It was as if their roles had now been reversed. Maya was behaving like Emma's big cousin and looking after her now. She owed Emma a lot. After all, that bolt from the Reaper, had been meant for her.

Evaline allowed Mischief to set up his comfortable red cushion on her dragon's back. He'd looked a bit put out, when Emma climbed aboard Blink. That was his position, but these were not ordinary times. So, for once, he decided not to complain.

Maya and Evaline kicked in their heels and their majestic creatures carried them together into the sky, with just a handful of powerful downbeats from their wings. They headed south, into increasingly dark and forbidding skies. Up over the Galloway Hills and the expansive pine forest beneath, skirting around Loch Doon and the picturesque Glen Ness. They flew over the sprawling metropolis of Carsphairn and on towards Castle Douglas, where finally the skies brightened a little, and started to lift their spirits. Unseen in the morning light, Evaline's pendant necklace glowed brighter with every mile that passed. By midday, they were approaching Gatehouse of Fleet and the Cardoness Estate, where Emma's parents had been staying in the family tin can, sorry caravan.

As they neared Cardoness, the thought of telling her mother was clawing at Emma. Tormenting her, as she ran through the horror of the moment to come, over and over again in her head. Maya could feel Emma shaking and just make out the sound of gently sobbing, over the noise of the wind, as they flew. Emma's grip around Maya's waist tightened, and she squeezed in closer.

"It'll be okay," Maya responded, trying to reassure her.

"No, no it won't! Nothing will ever be okay again!" Emma snapped.

Maya knew, however that this was a good sign, even if poor Emma did sound upset and rather grumpy. Those were her first words, since their encounter with the Reaper. It was a start. Maya should have predicted her next question though.

"Why does my face hurt so much?" asked Emma, rubbing her poor bruised features.

Maya blushed and chose not to answer.

Ahead in the distance, dark shadows circled in the sky. It was the first time they had seen death dragons during the daytime. They were getting bolder. They, not the witches, now ruled the skies. The little band of friends landed briefly, by the banks of the River Fleet, to rest and to hide from the unwanted gaze of their winged foes.

It had never occurred to them, that the death dragons would be this far south and from their position in the skies above Cardoness, Maya now feared the worst. Were they too late to save Aunty Helen?

It didn't look like an attack though. It was more like a patrol, like they were searching for something. Looking for more witches, as they criss-crossed the skies above. When the fearsome beasts had finally departed, the girls flew on nervously to investigate.

They flew in low over Cardoness House, spooking some horses in the fields below. Then out over the chapel and past the little island known as Cat Craig and along the golden beach towards the caravan. There was no sign of Emma's parents, no car outside the family tin can. Emma's brother Ross though, was walking on the beach below them, oblivious as all non-magic types, to their presence in the skies above.

Maya and Evaline landed their dragons, near a viewpoint on the nature trail, situated above the caravan. Maya and Emma continued on foot, whilst Evaline guarded the dragons, in case of prying eyes and in readiness should the death dragons return. Mischief decided to keep an eye on Evaline and curled up on his comfortable red cushion to rest. One eye open and trained on Evaline. Sleeping all the way since his morning nap, had completely worn him out.

Ross was still meandering on the beach, when they clambered down the path from the old nature trail and onto the rocky part of the shoreline. When they finally caught up with him, Ross, like most men, was about as much help as a chocolate fireguard. He confirmed that, he thought that, Uncle Kenny, but possibly not Aunty Helen and had:

"Definitely, probably, eh, gone somewhere. Either on foot or in the car and would probably be back sometime today, tomorrow or maybe, it was Saturday, they'd said?"

Maya didn't have a big brother, so was unaware of just how useless they could really be, especially when fitted with headphones. Emma explained that she shouldn't be too hard on him.

"Behind those rugged bad looks," she explained. "He has nearly as many hidden shallows, as your Aunty Dot!"

It was nice to see Ross again though, even if he was only a man, and to be honest, of little to no practical use whatsoever. They walked with him for a bit, on the beach. Ross even removed his headphones briefly. Long enough to confirm he had seen nothing unusual this week, but also that Emma had picked a good time to make herself scarce.

"I think mum was a bit upset earlier Emms," Ross confided. "She wasn't herself at all. Mad staring eyes and she's got a nasty burn on her hand too. She won't show it to anyone!"

His words cut right through the girls, who stopped in their tracks. They were too late!

Maya could tell that Emma was close to tears, as she called time on their walk. Ross wasn't suspicious though, after all Emma was allergic to all forms of physical exercise, unless it involved Bandit of course. Ross stayed on the beach, listening to weird punk electro cello jazz music or something through his headphones. Maya and Emma walked slowly up to the caravan, dreading what they might find. As they approached, a gaunt looking figure appeared in the window. Her face haunted and hands, one heavily bandaged, pressed up against the glass doors.

"Mum?" cried Emma.

It was not the homecoming that Emma had wanted. Aunty Helen was in shock. After a long hug, Emma sat her mum down. Aunty Helen just stared into space, rocking backwards and forwards gently in her chair. Wild tormented eyes darting this way and that. Then they stopped. Aunty Helen froze, her eyes now focussed on one thing, Emma's bandaged hand. She did not speak. That really was a first!

Again and again, the girls gently comforted poor Aunty Helen, but it was as if she could no longer hear them. They pressed her again

343

and again, to recall anything that she knew about the death dragons, but there was no response.

"It's like Ross, after a Saturday night out with his mates. The lights are on, but there's nobody home," Emma whispered sadly.

"We have to keep trying. You said, she used to scare you with stories about the death dragons. Maybe she knows how they were defeated in the past? She might know how to banish them again," Maya speculated, but couldn't muster any real hope.

"I need to stay with her," Emma replied, after a few minutes. "If she says anything, I'll find you."

Maya nodded. She knew a polite brush off, when she heard one. Emma needed to be alone with her mum right now. But there was one important thing left to do, before she departed. Maya pulled out the charm bracelet from her pocket. The one that Grandma had given to her, and passed it to Emma.

Explaining to Emma and her Aunty Helen, about Grandma and the 'merciful few' was one of the hardest things Maya had ever done. But when she'd finished, Emma looked strangely relieved. She smiled gently and thanked Maya with a big hug. Aunty Helen just rocked back and forth, still staring at Emma's hand. Maya wasn't at all sure, that she'd heard a word of what she'd said. But for now, Emma was here to look after her. That, seemed to have taken her mind off her own fate, for a while anyway.

Maya left them there. She made her way back up the nature trail. Faster and faster, she strode out. Gathering pace, anger and resolve, with every stomp. She was going to put a stop to this. She had to find a way!

An "air flume"

Maya relayed what had happened to poor Aunty Helen to Mischief and Evaline. It was a setback. They still had no idea how Grim had been stopped in the past, but Maya's resolve was stronger than ever. By the time that Maya, Mischief and Evaline took to the skies once more, the light was beginning to fade. Mischief, now proudly adopting his more accustomed position, behind Maya on Blink's back. Perched, as always, on top of a comfortable red cushion.

They flew east along the coast road, not really knowing where they were headed for. It felt important that they headed somewhere though. So, they'd agreed to that they should head somewhere specific. Maya weighed up a few options. She knew this part of the country well. The little town of Kirkcudbright was close, but Maya liked Castle Douglas. More interesting food and craft shops. Evaline agreed, it was as good a place as any, to start their search. A search for... well, that was another problem. Neither of them really knew what they were looking for, but regardless, it felt like they were on a quest anyway.

They didn't get far though. Dark shadows appeared on the horizon and the girls headed north, to avoid them. They had travelled barely a dozen miles though, when more dark shadows circled ahead and they were forced to cut back south, once more. As night closed in, Maya turned and looked over towards Evaline on the back of her impressive wild dragon. She was suddenly struck by a strange green glow, coming from beneath her friend's tunic. Evaline picked up on Maya's confused sideways glances and explained:

"It's a necklace, that my mother gave me. Don't worry, it was a long time ago. Long before she was turned to the dark side. I've had it as long as I can remember," Evaline explained. "It's a family 'air flume' or something?"

"Heir loom?" Mischief corrected, with a disdainful glare.

"No, I've never worn it in my hair, just around my neck," Evaline corrected him. "It glows when I head south, like a compass, but it's much handier, especially when I'm flying."

Mischief just groaned, deciding not to waste any more energy, explaining what an heir loom, actually was.

The weary travellers arrived back at the shore line, really not that far from where they'd started from. Choosing to ignore their obvious lack of progress, they followed the coastline east once more. Flying out over the sea, to avoid rivers and fresh running water which would drain their powers. It was more out of habit than necessity. Their dragons were unaffected by running water, but whenever witches were in the magical realm, they would always avoid it, whenever possible.

Soon, they crossed over the coastline once more, heading for Castle Douglas, which sits inland a few miles, quite close to the River Dee. They followed the river's banks upstream, crossing over the first footbridge they came to.

A furry paw tapped at Maya's back and pointed towards Evaline. Maya could see that her friend's neckless glowed once again. Maya raised a curious eyebrow in response.

"I thought you said that that pendant only lit up when you headed south?" Maya asked curiously.

"Yes, it does...," replied Evaline, then...

"Oh! It's never done that before. But then, I've never been this far south, not since I was too young to remember."

Maya caught a glimpse of Mischief shaking his head out of the corner of her eye. He didn't trust Evaline and made no secret of it. They weren't friends, but so far on this trip, they had declared an uneasy truce. If only for Maya's sake.

The further north they rode, the brighter Evaline's pendant glowed. Then, as the river meandered south or east it dimmed again. It felt like Evaline's pendant was guiding them somewhere, but where and why? Mischief grew increasingly agitated. He wasn't happy about it. Not one bit!

"Oh, great idea!" he ranted sarcastically. "Let's all follow the stone given to 'Evil in Deed' by her wicked mother."

Maya didn't answer. Evaline however, just glared at him and tapped her hunting knife, which she kept strapped to her thigh in a leather holster, just in case.

"I could do with a new pair of furry slippers," she grinned threateningly.

"Stop it you two!" Maya insisted, but Evaline's pendant was worrying Maya too. She was also concerned about what Evaline had told them before, about her escape from the Prestwick coven. The way her pendant had glowed then and how the death dragons had just parted and let her through. It didn't make sense. Why hadn't they attack her? They had shown Maya, no such mercy. Not when she'd confronted them, on the back of her own dragon. It felt like a trap, but what else could they do?

Eventually, Maya's tongue reasoned, that if Evaline or her evil mother did have something to do with this, then this pendant was really the only lead that they had. So, what other choice did they have, but to follow it?

By the time they detoured from the river bank, following a road sign to Castle Douglas, they were far too late to stop for ice cream or shopping. Everything had long been closed up for the day. Besides, their mission had changed now... from follow their noses, to follow the pendant.

They followed the guiding green glow of Eveline's pendant again and soon met up with the meandering river bank once more. This they followed for another half mile, until they came upon a small island. The pendant shone noticeably more brightly here and besides they were all getting tired. So, with no objections to Maya's suggestion, they decided it was as good a place as any, to stop and rest for the night.

Maya knew this place well. They could shelter here. On the west bank of the island, stood the ruined tower of Threave Castle. She had often visited it with her parents. They had viewed ospreys here and seen otters too. Dad said that he had even spotted a 'pair of green vulcans,' whatever they were? He claimed they were the fastest birds on the planet, but mum said they were just out of a nerdy TV show called Star Trek.

On the near riverbank, there was a wooden jetty and a bell, which tourists rang to summon the ferryman. A small wooden rowboat would then collect them and take them across the water, whenever they wanted to visit the castle. Being night time, the little rowboat was tied up on the opposite bank and bobbed gently in the current.

Maya and Blink led the way and they all landed on the riverbank, so as to avoid crossing the running waters of The Dee. Both of the dragons were now clearly exhausted, from the long flight. Maya patted Blink thankfully on the side of his neck and sneaked him a handful of marshmallows, as she dismounted. She was feeling a bit guilty for pushing him so hard today. He had earned a treat and a rest. They'd make their own way across the river.

"To the island Blink," Maya instructed, as the weary dragon spread his wings, jumped into the air and glided over the river and landed on the little island. Evaline's dragon followed.

Maya raised her wand hand and commanded:

"Bring the boat, Spell."

With a silvery glow from her wand, the little rowboat untied itself and steered out into the river, to collect them.

Evaline turned open mouthed and glared daggers at her.

Instinctively, Maya had used her magic. Used magic to bring over the rowing boat, so they could sail across to the island. No sooner had she done so, than she realised her mistake.

"How stupid of me!" Maya scolded herself. "Sorry!"

Evaline just glared. Fear betrayed in her staring eyes.

Almost that instant, black shapes appeared on the horizon. Like sharks, picking up a spot of blood, dropped into the water from miles off. They turned as one and headed towards the girls.

Maya, Mischief and Evaline clambered quickly into the little rowing boat and made for the island. Evaline took charge, she was an impressive rower. She was one of those annoying sporty types. Naturally good at just about everything.

Evaline's pendant shone ever more brightly now. It was only a short row to the other bank and the girls were soon reunited with their dragons. As the black shadows closed in on the island, Maya reflected on the wisdom of crossing onto an island surrounded by running water. An island which trapped witches with power sapping running water, but yet presumably presented no obstacle for the death dragons, which now pursued them.

"Stupid Maya... how could you be so stupid?" she cursed herself. She was tired and making mistakes. Mistakes which she knew, against a foe like this, could prove to be very costly for all of them.

"Just what I was wondering?" Mischief chipped in, just to add to Maya's misery.

Had they just rowed straight into a trap? Guided there by a pendant, gifted to Evaline, by the nightmare that was Cruellen. Death dragons, three of them, now dived with evil intent, from the clouds above, preparing to attack.

They were trapped. Imprisoned on an island, encircled by deep fresh running water. Facing a foe that they couldn't fight. It was starting to feel hopeless.

Evaline climbed back onto her trusty dragon. The girls exchanged respectful glances. Then with a nod of her head, Evaline said more than a thousand words could ever convey. Maya knew exactly what it meant. She knew her friend well. Evaline was a dragon rider and would choose to meet her fate on the wing. Maya decided to make her stand alongside her good friend. Mischief too, shook his head then clambered back onboard Maya's weary dragon.

As the death dragons approached the far bank, Maya and Evaline rose up on their own dragons to face them. Maya raised her living wand, maybe it would work this time. Evaline followed her lead, her pendant glowing like a beacon through the night sky ahead of her.

The death dragons reached the far bank, then veered right and started to circle the island. Much to everyone's surprise, they didn't attack. Two more shapes appeared on the horizon. Were they simply waiting for re-enforcements?

But, as the other dragons arrived, they simply joined with the others and circled around the tiny island and its castle. Maya and Evaline exchanged confused glances.

"Why didn't they attack?" Evaline asked.

Maya shrugged her shoulders.

"The pendant?" Mischief suggested.

As Evaline hovered on her dragon, her necklace pendant glowed brightly, regardless of which direction she faced.

"It's never done that before. I don't understand, why now?" Evaline asked out loud.

Maya's tongue was out again, gathering midges and her thoughts, in equal measure.

"Perhaps, it's because we're here!" Maya announced.

"Here, where's here?" Mischief asked.

"Here is exactly where the pendant wants us to be," Maya replied rather cryptically. "The real questions are; why are we here and who wants us to be here?"

Threave Castle

There was an uneasy stand-off. As the death dragons circled the island, still more came to join their siege. There could be no escape, but yet, neither did they attack. Something was holding them back. Dragons being untroubled by running water, could easily have crossed at any moment. But something stopped them from attacking and right now, they'd settle for that. Eventually the girls landed their weary dragons.

Threave Castle near Castle Douglas on an island in the River Dee

They felt safe to use their magic again. After all, what further harm could it do? Their foe already knew exactly where they were. They made camp within the outer walls of the castle.

This ruin offered no roof, as shelter from the elements, but it was a mild night and no rain fell. Maya made a fire and conjured up a roast chicken and choc ices. It was a strange combination and on reflection, might have been better served as two separate courses.

352

Evaline did suggest a vegetable might be nice for a change, but this was met by a very disapproving glare from Maya and Mischief alike.

Evaline was in charge of soft furnishings... the girls would not be slumming it this evening. It felt like it might be their last, so they didn't hold back. Enough pillows and fake fur to hide a grizzly bear and three cubs for the winter, were dully conjured, and the girls cosied in together, for the night.

Blink scorched the ground beneath him and curled up, like an asbestos cat, on a bed of hot ashes. Evaline's dragon fired a pile of rubble in the corner and scraped an indent into the ground with his talons. Then using the side of his tail, it fashioned the hot rocks into a fire pit, on which to bed down. Mischief bedded down on a comfortable red cushion, closest to the fire. The glow from the open fire and dragons' nests made the whole, open-air sleeping thing, feel rather cosy.

The girls took it in turns to sleep and stay up on guard duty and stoke the fire, but eventually, under the less than watchful gaze of their dragons and cat, both girls fell into deep haunted sleeps.

Morning broke, so Maya decided to fix it by conjuring sausages, pancakes and more wood for their fire. The death dragons were still there, although they no longer circled in the skies above. Dark shadows now perched motionless in the oak trees, on the opposite bank. They did not react to any of the girl's magic, cast from within the walls of their new castle home. One of the death dragons had roosted on the old osprey's nest upstream of their island. That might give the twitchers something to write home about, Maya thought to herself.

As the sun rose further into the sky. Maya and Evaline were keen to explore their new surroundings. The wandered around the little island on foot. Mischief too, padded reluctantly behind them. He didn't really do walkies. The chat from the night before, suggested

353

they had been brought here on purpose. Apparently guided by Evaline's pendant. They were all curious to find out why. What secrets did this place hold?

The island was about half a mile long. It was beautiful, surrounded on all sides, by fast-moving waters. Reed beds lined the island, providing sanctuary for herons and water fowl. The castle itself was a roost for a pesky pair of barn owls, that had kept Mischief awake half the night with their constant 'Twit-Twit-Twooo.' The occasional ring of bright water and intermittent splash from a wet tail, betrayed the presence of a shy family of otters.

Whether it was being in such idyllic surroundings, the hearty breakfast, camping out with her friend or being able to use her magic once more, she didn't know, but Maya felt more optimistic than she had done for some days. Evaline though appeared more distracted than ever.

"Penny for them?" Maya prompted, after a particularly long and thoughtful silence.

"What?" Evaline was clearly still miles away.

"Penny for your thoughts," Maya clarified.

"Oh, yes, sorry. It's just... I think, it's like I know this place," Evaline spoke quietly, looking rather puzzled herself.

"But I thought you'd never been this far south before?" Maya asked, looking rather surprised.

"I haven't, it's just. I mean, I'm not sure but, think I might...," Evaline stuttered.

"Be incapable of forming a sentence this morning?" Mischief interrupted.

"No!" Evaline snapped. Evaline cleared her throat and started over again.

"My mum used to tell me about the castle where she once lived, when she was first married. It was on an island, with a little boat. You had to ring a bell to be collected, you know, when you wanted to cross over."

"And the pendant!" Maya interjected excitedly. "It was like it brought us here. As if it knew the way!"

The girls exchanged excited glances.

"Hate to bring a touch of reality to these proceedings, but nobody has stayed in that ruin for hundreds of years," Mischief rebuked them scornfully.

"I know, it doesn't make any sense, but she lived on the second floor, above the main hall," Evaline insisted.

The more Evaline stared at the ruined tower in front of her, the more long-buried memories, she recalled. Stories that her mother had told her. Stories about a castle, but that wasn't it, not really. Her mother hadn't talked about it, as if describing any old castle. No, she was talking about her home.

Evaline led them back towards the castle. Her eyes fixed ahead, scanning the ruin with a strange combination of fascination, nostalgia and bafflement, as if gathering partial recollections from a long-buried past. Evaline led the way in silence. They crossed a draw-bridge over a moat and walked through the outer battlements. These thick outer walls, surrounded a long ruined inner grey stone medieval tower, which rose some thirty meters into the air. A more modern set of wooden steps, now led them up and into the inner castle tower.

The roof and floors of the ancient five storey tower had long since collapsed. Ancient fireplaces, built into the walls, betrayed the layout of the original castle. Evaline though, was somehow able to described it, in peculiar and personal detail.

"My mum said that the cellars had tall vaulted ceilings, sparrows used to nest in there and steal the grain out of the sacks. It drove our cat Alfie mad. At this level, was the entrance hall, which led through to where the kitchens were. That's where they prepared feasts for the master, the Laird. Archie, she called him. A cruel man, my mother said," Evaline explained, as if she could see it now, in all of its previous splendour.

Mischief nudged into Maya's leg. He'd been standing in front of a little white board. The sort, that only Maya's Grandma bothers to read. Underneath the Douglas Coat of Arms, it read:

Sir Archibald Douglas (of the Black Douglases) built the tall, forbidding tower that now dominates the island in 1369. He had recently become Lord of Galloway, but is better known as Archibald the Grim. By the time he died at Threave in 1400, he had become the 3rd Earl of Douglas, and was one of the most powerful magnates in southern Scotland.

Evaline continued, oblivious to their exchange of glances:

"On the floor above us, was the great hall. Mum said it was splendid, with its long oak table and impressive stone fireplace. A tapestry, my mother helped to embroider, hung from that wall. It had pictures of farm animals and her favourite hunting dogs."

Evaline turned to look towards a dark passageway in the corner, before recollecting further:

"A spiral stone staircase, in the corner of each floor, wound its way from one floor to another, up the tower."

Even Mischief was starting to look more convinced.

Evaline explained, that above the great hall were the apartments, where her mum once lived with Archie.

"Archie... was he your dad?" Maya asked.

"What?" Mischief objected. "We're talking ancient history here. How could he be?"

Evaline just shrugged. "I don't know, mum never said. She always just changed the subject and latterly she wasn't exactly an easy lady to talk to," Evaline replied.

"You can say that again!" scoffed Mischief.

"And latterly, she wasn't exactly an easy lady to talk to," Evaline replied with a smirk, but Maya could tell from her demeanour, that she was starting to find all this, a bit difficult. Instinctively, she held her friend's hand for reassurance.

Evaline had never mentioned Archie before. Maya hadn't heard her mention her mother recently either. Not since her mum had been banished from the Coven of Deeds. But there was a softer tone in her voice now, as Evaline recollected these stories from the past. These were stories, that her mother recalled in better times. From a time, before she had been turned to the dark side.

"And above that, the servants' quarters, was where...," Evaline fell silent. A sudden realisation, written large across her face.

"What is it?" Maya prompted.

"Of course. My mother's secret room!" Evaline whispered. Her mother had described a secret room here. A room where all the magic happened.

Evaline turned and looked towards the stairs in the corner of the stone tower. She stepped towards the spiral staircase and the light from her pendant glowed noticeably brighter.

"Your pendant Evaline. I think it's a keystone," Maya whispered excitedly. "It's led you home. Like my mum's charm, led me to her secret room!"

"To open my mother's magic room?" Evaline asked, her eyes ablaze with excitement.

Maya nodded and Evaline stepped forward expectantly, towards the bottom of the stone steps. She paused, took a deep breath, then started to ascend the remnants of the spiral stairwell. Her pendant lit the way, growing ever brighter with each step. It started to pulse, like a living heartbeat, matching time with each step that Evaline took towards, whatever it was they were being drawn towards.

The pendant led the way once more, up past the great hall, but it didn't stop them there. Evaline continued on further, upwards towards the servants' quarters, passing a slit window, built into the thick outer stone walls. They passed a small stone plaque carved into a stone block and some more 'modern' 21th century graffiti. This brought a "tut" from Mischief, as he panted his way up the stairs behind them.

The stairway grew darker again, now completely illuminated by the pale green light from Evaline's necklace. The pulse from her pendant quickened now, as if to match her rising heartbeat.

Evaline stopped just short of the next floor level. This floor, together with all those above, had long since collapsed. The spiral staircase simply stopped. It was barriered off, with a metal chain to protect the public, from a long drop with a sudden stop.

Evaline turned, she looked disappointed and confused. She gestured to Maya with open palms.

"What now?" she asked.

Maya's eyes though, were drawn to her friend's pendant. It was pulsing with green light, but in the centre of it, Maya could just make out three tiny silver stars. There was something strangely familiar about them. It reminded her of something she'd seen recently, but couldn't quite place.

Maya closed her eyes and her tongue came out. It traced her lips, like a slippery eel looking for something to eat amongst the creases, then retracted suddenly. She had it!

"The coat of arms!" Maya announced suddenly. "On the sign we saw earlier Mischief, the Douglas coat of arms."

"What sign?" Evaline asked, obviously rather confused.

Maya headed them back down the stairwell, towards the sign that she and Mischief had read earlier, but stopped suddenly, just before she reached the great hall. The light from the slit window now illuminated the small carved stone plaque she'd observed on the way up. It was this, that now caught Maya's eye and held her gaze.

The stone plaque had been carved with a coat of arms. The same coat of arms, as they'd seen earlier, printed on the white sign, on the floor beneath. Maya studied it closely. Lots of fancy bits, like feathers around the outside, a heart shape and three stars in the centre. Three stars, like Maya had noted earlier. They matched those on Evaline's pendant.

Maya stood aside and let Evaline past. They exchanged excited glances. Instinctively, Evaline removed the pendant from around her neck and held it out towards the stone plaque.

As she did so, the stone upon which the three stars were carved, started to move. It moved slowly upwards accompanied by a dull rasping sound, of stone on stone, which echoed around the spiral staircase. As the stone moved, it revealed a small silver receptacle, inset into the rock wall. It resembled a half egg-cup, but much smaller and more delicate. It too sported the same three stars as indents. A perfect match to those on the pendant. With an uncertain look back to Maya, for support and reassurance, Evaline placed the pendant stone into the receptacle.

"It fits!" Evaline called out, with mounting excitement.

As the pendant dropped snugly into position, a blue flash of light illuminated the staircase. The top steps started to sink slowly and surely, causing Mischief to jump clear in panic, or risk plunging to his doom. This sudden movement of stairs, was accompanied by a much louder noise, of stone grinding on stone. One by one, the steps dropped in front of their astonished eyes. Each of the stone steps, now lower than the preceding one, reversing the clockwise direction of the spiral stairway, so that the steps now led downwards, in an anti-clockwise direction.

"Here goes nothing!" Evaline announced, as she stepped gingerly onto the first step. It didn't collapse. She didn't fall to her death. A good start, Maya and Evaline agreed. Gaining in confidence, Evaline followed the new staircase, in an ever downwards spiral. As she neared the bottom, a stone arch came into view, leading to a small dark room beyond. The girls paused at this hand carved stone entrance and surveyed the scene ahead of them.

There was a very old dark wooden table in the centre. It was covered in a thick layer of dust. A large substantial leather-bound book sat open on top. They both knew what this meant. This was a magic room, presumably holding a portal to the magical realm, much like Maya's own room. Also, after hundreds of years, it was nearly as dusty as Maya's mother's room.

A witch's book, still open, lay on the desk. Whoever it belonged to, was clearly still in the magical realm. The book did not speak. It was not theirs after all, but they knew that they could still read its story.

In the corner, stood an old cracked mirror. Ancient, its glass clearly thicker at the bottom, than the top. Maya smiled. She knew her geeky dad, would have said something about:

"Glass actually being a liquid at room temperature, you know."

Potion bottles lay on a small bedside table and in the corner of the room. There were scattered fabric remnants, from what could once have been a comfortable cushion, stuffed with hay. Before the moths and mice had eaten it away.

Evaline stood transfixed at the sight of the book. There was a name on the spine.

"Ellen... that's my mother's name!" she gasped. "Or was."

"Was?" Maya prompted.

"Before she went over to the dark side," Evaline replied soulfully. "Only latterly, did they call her Cruellen."

Maya and Evaline approached the book. Cruellen's life story lay in front of them. Maya shivered at the thought of what horrors it might hold. But for Evaline, she viewed it with wonderment. She knew exactly what this meant for her... answers.

Answers; to who she really was and to all the questions that she had never been brave enough to ask her mother. Evaline was frozen to the spot. Exhilarated and terrified in equal measures.

Beside the magical book, on the table, sat a small hand-held mirror, cast in silver, with a simple oak handle. Maya and Evaline crowded together in front of the book. They started to read the last page, at which the mighty tome, lay open.

Cruellen was alive. Her magic too, was still intact. She was in hiding. Hidden away in a cave. It was cold and dark, with no home comforts. It matched her mood. She was alone and afraid, but still bitter and brooding over her defeat and banishment from the Coven of Deeds and especially bitter at its manner; at the hands of Maya and her own daughter.

Evaline looked away in disgust. This was going to be a hard read for her.

"What was it turned your mum to the dark side?" Maya couldn't help but ask. It was a question, that they'd both agonised over. What could ever have driven Cruellen to become the monster they both knew?

Evaline looked up with tears in her eyes.

"I don't know, I've never known," Evaline replied. "She wasn't always that way. She had a gentler side too, a long time ago. She wasn't always cold and manipulative. I do remember good times, her comforting me, holding me and telling me stories of her own childhood and much happier times. Good times, here in this castle, I think."

Evaline caught her breath.

"But ever since I was young, she was torn... her dark side called out to her. There was something in her past, some great secret or regret. Something that tormented her. It would not leave her in peace. Eventually, the darkness within her grew and that part of her won her over, completely. By the time I was about eight years old, there was little or no love left within her. Only greed and a lust for power and an obsession with... you know?" Evaline explained, looking down at Spell, as she clung to Maya's wrist. "The dark side consumed her totally. Her obsession with getting her hands on a living wand, it devoured her from within," Evaline replied rather shamefully.

Maya knew that part only too well. How Cruellen had used her own daughter to set a trap for Maya and Spell. How she had been so twisted in her pursuit of a living wand, that she was willing to watch poor Evaline, her own daughter, die to get her hands on it.

"But, why?" Maya asked. "That's the real question. Why was it so important?"

"Power, I guess... I don't really know why," Evaline replied.

"You know the answers are all in there, don't you?" Mischief added, with uncharacteristic compassion in his voice.

Evaline nodded nervously.

Evaline knew that the mighty tome, now laid in front of her, held her mother's life story. It would finally reveal who her father was. What had led her mum to turn to the dark side. She was fascinated and petrified at the same time.

Maya sensed the conflict in her friend. She knew, they both knew, that Evaline had to read it.

But first, Maya announced with a smile:

"We need to get comfortable!"

It started with a few scatter cushions, conjured from Maya's wand, but soon got rather silly. The girls taking it in turn to materialise increasingly ridiculous amounts of soft furnishings, cushions, cuddly toys and confectionary. A magical fire now burned in the corner of the room, complete with a marshmallow rotisserie and the obligatory chocolate fountain. It was, after all, a very large book.

Cruellen's story begins

The girls snuggled down together, holding one side of the weighty book each. They agreed, that this time, they should start at page one. This was something that Evaline had to do and they both knew that it wouldn't be easy for her.

Cruellen's story

Cruellen's story started with Ellen opening her magical book for the first time, in the very room, where the girls now sat. It was Ellen's mother, who had brought her here, as a young child, and gifted her the keystone necklace. The same pendant, which Evaline now wore around her own neck. Evaline was obviously relishing the opportunity to read her mother's story. Her face lit up with excitement, as impatient eyes darted from line to line.

Ellen's story was surprisingly happy, to start with anyway. The story of a pure-hearted and very young witch, exploring the magical realm, under the guidance of her grandmother and her cat guardian, Alfie. It sounded idyllic, much like Maya's first adventures with Mischief, but so unlike Evaline's own harsh upbringing in the Coven of Deeds.

The girls broke off at the end of each double page to discuss the revelations within. Maya felt very close to Evaline now, as they shared the story of her mother's younger days. It was good to see Evaline smiling again. She was revelling in this. How her mother found her first wand and struggled with unintentional spells in the magic realm.

They both giggled as Ellen accidentally paralysed poor Alfie by telling him to:

"Be still!" and how he lost one of his nine witch's cat's lives, when she used the very Scottish insult of:

"Awa 'n' boil yer heid!" to her impertinent cat. (That's; "go away and boil your head," for any remaining non-Scottish readers.)

"Ouch! Poor Alfie," the girls giggled. Mischief just tutted in disgust.

Ellen grew into a fine young witch and rode her first dragon at the age of just five.

"Five!" Maya interrupted aghast. Evaline grinned proudly.

She became an accomplished dragon rider and hunter. Something which definitely ran in the family. She won her first dragon riding competition aged just twelve.

Evaline was clearly engrossed in her mother's story. So, Maya conjured up a few more snacks, while Evaline read on transfixed and beguiled by her mother's adventures. Maya too could not help but like the young Ellen. Although, it made the thought of how she had turned out, all the more tragic.

"It tells how she met a young man Archie and how she fell in love," announced Evaline with a smile, but then, as she read on, her face saddened and Evaline's mood changed.

Maya put her arm around her friend, as Evaline relayed the next chapter in Ellen's tale.

"This young man of hers, it says he was the Laird. I think that's a Lord or something. Laird of all Galloway apparently," Evaline spoke, now with notable disdain in her voice.

"Archibald Douglas, from the sign downstairs?" Maya asked.

Evaline nodded and continued:

"They were wed, soon after they met. She wasn't much older than us!"

"Eww... yuk!" Maya gagged.

"He was a warlock too," Evaline announced. "But he grew greedy and obsessed by power. He started to treat her badly and Ellen began to suspect that he was falling under the influence of his own mother's dark magic. She was a witch too, but Ellen had never liked her. She was cruel and resented Ellen from the very start."

"My dad says that all mothers-in-law are evil!" Maya interjected, trying to lighten the moment.

"Archie was a powerful warlock and a formidable dragon rider too. Famed for his magical prowess and soon also feared for his dark magic," Evaline paused. Maya knew that there was something coming, from the way Evaline's voice was starting to break.

"He rode upon an enormous jet-black dragon, a huge dominant buck dragon, built like no other."

"You don't think...?" Maya started, but neither of them could quite bring themselves to say it.

The girls read on together, more anxiously now. They both knew that, whatever was coming, Evaline was going to find it difficult.

The girls waded through page after page. It was like getting to know Ellen, through her own eyes and thoughts. All Ellen's secrets were laid bare in front of them, through the chronicles of Ellen's magical journal. It was like Ellen was the heroine in a novel, but this was different. Ellen was Evaline's mother and they both already knew, that things would not turn out well for her, not in the end.

Ellen's book told of her increasing despair and unhappiness at her life with Archie. Archibald the Grim, as they now called him. He became invincible in battle, and he fought more than his share.

Grim being the name given to him by his foes, for his battle face, but also the fate that awaited anyone who dared to oppose his will. He delighted in their torture, becoming increasingly cruel and twisted, with every battle that he fought and with every new prisoner that he took.

Nothing was ever enough for him though. The more power and wealth he had, the more he craved. He became obsessed by something new too. It consumed him totally, the quest for the one magical power, which as yet, had so far eluded him... a living wand.

Maya and Evaline broke off from the story, looked each other in the eye and delved back in, without even a word.

A living wand, Ellen's book recalled. Born only once in a millennium, was long overdue in the magic realm. An object so powerful, that in the right hands, it could cast a spell like no other. A spell that could conquer death itself.

The girls broke off again for more silent eye contact, much to the exasperation of Mischief, who they were completely failing to keep up to speed.

They read on in captivated silence. For years he searched. Growing increasingly angry and frustrated by his own failure, but he never found any trace of it. For the growing evil inside him, prevented him from ever finding, that which he sought. Something with a soul so pure as a living wand, could never reveal itself to such a dark spirit. Maya glanced down at Spell, who squeezed her wrist gently with her roots.

They read on. Ellen avoided her husband as much as possible now. She took comfort in her magic and dragon flying and became ever more powerful, as a witch in her own right. She joined the local coven and moved swiftly through the ranks, to become their High Priestess. Maya could tell that Evaline read those chapters with some pride.

"Maybe my mum wasn't all that different to me, after all?" Evaline observed, out loud.

"No, that's what worries me!" Mischief butted in, with unwelcome sarcasm. But his point was well made and Evaline shrunk visibly, when she thought on it further.

As chapter after chapter of Ellen's harrowing early life was laid bare, Evaline and Maya could tell that there was trouble brewing. As Grim's powers and cruelty grew, he took increased pleasure in tormenting his subjects and in particular, persecuting the local witches. It was the witches, who he now blamed for his failure to locate the living wand and soon he grew to resent Ellen too. He became paranoid. Convinced that the witches were hiding the path to a living wand from him. Witches started to go missing. Stories and rumours of terrible torture and cruelty circulated throughout the magical world.

Eventually the local covens had no choice, but to intervene. Ellen as his wife, but also the High Priestess, was hopelessly torn. She still longed, for the man he once was. The dashing young man of old, the man she had once fallen for and married all those years ago.

Ellen had no choice though, she had to stand against him now. As High Priestess, she had also sworn to protect her coven. A great battle ensued and Ellen and her husband were on opposite sides. Grim mounted on his mighty black dragon, his hoard of dark witches, cruel followers, black dragons and warlocks on one side. On the other side, the witches from all the local covens, riding on brooms and dragons assembled to face him. A terrible magical battle was unleashed, where half of the witches and dragons were killed. It was carnage.

In a final showdown, Grim's hoards were well on top. A mighty firebolt from Archibald himself, finally unseated Ellen. Ellen was knocked from her dragon, her wand shattered into a thousand splinters. Archibald the Grim stood over his wife with madness, betrayal and revenge in his eyes.

Ellen knew, that she would not meet a good death at the hands of her own husband. Not after, she had betrayed him so publicly. He would show her no mercy. But Ellen had planned for this. Slowly she lifted her top, to reveal her now swollen belly. Ellen was with child.

"I have an older sister or brother?" Evaline gasped.

"Yes, six hundred years older!" scoffed Mischief.

Evaline ignored his taunts and continued with Ellen's book.

Grim hesitated.

"An heir!" he roared proudly, to his hoard of followers, raising both arms triumphantly above his head.

This was all the distraction that Ellen needed. Pulling a hidden wand, which she'd earlier concealed, inside her witch's britches, she fired.

A death spell, shot from his own wife's wand, at close range. Even the mighty Grim could not survive that and Archibald lay broken and dying in the dirt.

Maya let Evaline read the next bit on her own. This was all getting rather personal. Evaline read on impatiently, becoming increasingly agitated. She started to scan the pages, reading faster and faster. Evaline turned to the final page of the chapter. She read a few more lines, then sat bolt upright, her eyes now darting wildly from line to line. Her whole body starting to shake.

"No! Evaline cried out in despair, her eyes wide as saucers. It's me! I'm his daughter! He cursed me... and it's all coming true!"

Evaline passed the book to Maya. She was clearly, far to upset, to read it aloud herself.

"Don't be silly. You can't be… this, it's all ancient history!" Maya snapped back, trying to reassure her.

"What like her mum?" Mischief added, unhelpfully as ever.

Mischief had a point though. How old was Cruellen?

Maya read from the book for herself. Ellen watched, as Archie lay dying in front of her. Fatally wounded by her own hand. But as he looked up with hatred in his eyes, he cast his final curse.

Pointing to the bump in her belly, he vowed:

"This child will betray you, as you have me! She will be your only child. Her destiny will be to banish you and deliver me the living wand, over the body of my greatest foe!"

Then, just for good measure, with his dying breath, he cursed Ellen to:

"Go mad and turn to the dark side!"

Maya recoiled in horror.

"Only daughter!" cried Evaline in despair. "It has to be me! It's all coming true!"

They knew that Ellen had been driven over to the dark side and she was clearly unhinged. That Evaline had indeed been forced to betray her own mother and to banish Cruellen from the Coven of Deeds, in order to save Maya's life.

All that was left, to fulfil his curse, was for Evaline to deliver Grim the living wand, over the body of his greatest foe.

As the first custodian of a living wand in a thousand years, that part didn't sound particularly good for Maya either.

The girls stopped there for the night. Evaline could hardly look Maya in the eye. Maya took Mischief to one side, to bring him up to speed. Then it came, the inevitable:

"I told you so!" Mischief announced, almost gleefully. "I told you. You can't trust her!"

But Mischief's apparent satisfaction, was short lived, as the implications of the curse for Maya, finally hit home.

None of them slept a wink that night. They tossed and turned all night long. Evaline had always wanted to know who her dad was, but this hadn't been the result she'd been dreaming of, all these years. There were just a few unanswered questions too, that were praying on Evaline's mind.

Was she really the child that Ellen carried? If so, where had she and her mother been for the last six hundred years. Why couldn't she remember? Why hadn't she aged? Was Archibald the Grim, her father, the same Grim as the Grim Reaper himself? Was that why she'd felt such a connection, when he turned to look towards her, over the remains of the Prestwick Coven? Was she really destined to betray Maya and deliver Grim the living wand over the body of her own best friend? Would Maya ever trust her again? And the big one... was she, just like her mother and so destined to meet the same fate?

Maya's sleep was haunted too. Grim had been a mighty warlock and this dying curse of his was strong, very strong. Would Spell be powerful enough to break it? Could she trust Evaline now? If this all happened such a long time ago, why hadn't Evaline aged? Were Archibald the Grim and the Grim Reaper, one and the same? Why didn't the death dragons attack? It felt like a trap, but who had set it? Why had they set it and where were they?

Mischief tossed and turned all night too. If the Grim Reaper did achieve world domination... killing off Maya for her living wand in the process. Who would feed him? Recurring nightmares, about a shortage of his favourite dish, red herring, kept him and his empty belly awake, all night long.

Morning broke and stayed broken... neither of them had the appetite to face another sausage bun or pancake to fix it. Maya and Evaline had been the best of friends, just a few hours before, but now things had changed between them. There were awkward silences and suspicious looks.

Ellen's story was getting to them. It had already taken a heavy toll, but they needed to hear more. Maya knew that Evaline was going to find this next bit difficult. Too difficult, as it turned out. After just a couple of pages, Evaline could read no more. Maya had to take over and read Cruellen's book first, then relay Evaline the details.

Ellen's heart was broken. Forced into killing her own husband. Having herself and her unborn daughter cursed too. It was all too much. With every day that passed, she lost more of herself to dark side.

Slowly, but surely, she feared that she was losing her mind too. More and more passageways opened up, every time she went into the magic realm, and she had already started to resent her own unborn child. She was powerless to overturn Grim's curse. She knew, that she had started on an irreversible path over to the dark side and madness, just as her husband's curse had foretold.

After just one chapter, Maya too needed a break, but she and Evaline didn't speak. The burden of Grim's curse, now weighed heavily on them too.

It was all starting to make sense now. Why Evaline's mother had gone over to the dark side. Why she had lost her love for her own daughter. A daughter, who she'd always known, was destined to betray her. It was a cruel curse, set by a cruel warlock. Evaline's own father.

Maya made her way down the spiral staircase, to the ground floor and out into the courtyard. She needed to get some air and had also decided to conjure them both some drinks and snacks. Behind her another set of footsteps ran hurriedly down the spiral staircase and out into the castle grounds.

Maya couldn't find it in herself now, to go and comfort her friend. And besides, her curiosity was getting the better of her. Maya made her way back up to the magical room, which Evaline had left unlocked, in her frantic exit. A trail of small damp splashes, which Maya strongly suspected were tears, led the way, back up the staircase. Within the room, Ellen's book lay on the ground, as though suddenly dropped, still open at the next page.

Maya picked it up and read the last sentence aloud to Mischief, who for once, looked up from his comfortable red cushion in the corner.

Ellen cradled her new-born daughter in her arms, kissed her gently on the forehead and whispered;

"I love you Evaline, but how, oh how, I wish you'd never been born!"

Evaline returned, after a couple of hours alone with her thoughts. Maya was downstairs, tidying their makeshift camp. Instinctively the girls simply hugged. Sometimes there are just no words.

"Let's do this!" Evaline announced, breaking off and leading the way back up the spiral staircase.

Once back in the magical room, the girls snuggled down amongst the unnecessarily large pile of scatter cushions and began the next chapter of Ellen's book. For a time, it was more cheerful. Ellen bonded with Evaline and truly loved her new-born baby, caring for her just as lovingly as any new mother. For a few brief weeks, she was happy and Evaline seemed buoyed, as she read through the pages.

All too soon though, her mood was to change again. The girls read on, with increasing fascination and trepidation, as Ellen's story revealed itself. Archibald had died, but on the rise of the full moon, a year to the day after his death, a huge black dragon rose on the horizon once more. Ridden by a ghostly spectre, dressed from head to foot in black robes.

Maya and Evaline exchanged wide-eyed glances, nothing was said, but even Mischief rose from his cushion to look over their shoulders. They all cuddled in closer and read on.

Rumours spread like wildfire through the witching world, that Archibald the Grim had returned. That Grim had made a pact with Death himself; in exchange for his freedom, to return to the living realm by night, he had agreed to do Death's bidding. Archibald had struck a bargain. He offered Death the lives of every witch on the face of the earth, in exchange for his own passage back to the mortal realm. Grim was back from the dead. Back to seek a terrible revenge. His appearance striking terror into any poor unfortunate souls who beheld him. His putrid flesh decaying and falling from his bones with every day that passed.

He now carried with him Death's own scythe; a magical staff which granted him the power to return to the mortal realm and to take his awful revenge. Every night Death allowed Grim to cross over and he rounded up, not just the souls of the dying. No, Archibald the Grim, delighted in rounding up many poor souls, long, long before their time. He especially delighted in persecuting witches, whom he tormented and tortured first. After all, he was still obsessed, by the belief that they were still hiding the living wand from him. And he now held them responsible for his untimely demise too.

Death granted his warrior a terrible army. An army of dead dragons. Those whose riders had lost their way and turned to the dark side in the living realm. Dragons whos' hearts, like the witches to which they had bonded, had turned black. They were invincible in the mortal realm. Impervious to all magic, they shot forth a dark fire which consumed the very essence of magic itself.

"And now he's back," Evaline broke the silence. Finally stating, what they'd all long realised. Her quivering voice betraying her rising anguish. No-one bothered to reply, they were all too engrossed and worried.

Ellen's book went on to describe how Archibald the Grim became known as Grim the Reaper. Then later, simply as the Grim Reaper, on account of using his scythe, to cut down those in their prime, just like corn in a field. His trademark scythe struck fear into the hearts of all, as night fell. His nightmarish appearance destined to be passed down through time and strike fear into the hearts of all who gazed upon him. The legend of the Reaper was born.

377

It was a dark time indeed and coven after coven fell to this mighty army. They could not kill him, for he had already died and Death himself, was his closest ally. He waged war every night, on all of witch-kind and the witches who stood against him, were powerless against his powers. It took the power of all the covens to stop him.

"Whoa!" cried Evaline.

"How?" Mischief demanded impatiently. "Does it say how?"

They read on eagerly, their hearts pounding in their chests, like a pod of pigmy hippo, set loose inside a grand piano store.

Grim and his army returned every night. Grim sat proudly on the back of his terrible black dragon. It too had perished with its master, in that awful final showdown. Now invincible, in any dragon duel, no magic could ever knock them from the skies. Nothing and nobody, it appeared, was safe from his hellish hoard.

As Evaline turned over a new page, a fresh chapter of Ellen's book started, with her asking her witch's cat Alfie, the question on everyone's lips:

"How do you kill a man, who is already dead?"

Alfie just shook his head.

Ellen despaired:

"There's just no way. He has no weaknesses. He has no mercy!"

"Hmm... maybe not quite true," Alfie corrected her thoughtfully.

"What do you mean?" Ellen asked curiously. Was her furry side-kick onto something?

"He spares this place. He spares you and the child," Alfie replied.

Ellen knew it to be true. No death dragons, as they had become known, would ever dare to cross the waters of the River Dee, to attack Grim's own castle. Grim's legacy had to be protected. They were safe here for now, but Ellen knew that when Evaline was old enough to fulfil her destiny and complete his curse, then Grim would have a special fate in store for his treacherous wife.

This truth, above all others, tormented Ellen day and night and slowly, piece by piece, it consumed her. Just as her dying husband's curse had foretold. Slowly and surely, Ellen was falling into madness and was being drawn inevitably over to the dark side.

Ellen was acutely aware of her own fate, but she had not given up all hope. There was something in what Alfie had said and she had a daughter to protect. That above all other things gave her strength. She would find a way.

Inspiration came to her the very next day, as she collected water from the well. It was a cold and frosty morning. Ellen always did her best thinking in the morning. Very unusually, the well had frozen over. Time and time again, she dropped the bucket down on its rope. It seemed futile at first, but she persevered. Eventually, the bucket broke through the thin layer of ice. In that moment, Ellen knew what she had to do.

In a final desperate act, Ellen called together the last of the remaining witches. They had failed in battle against Grim, on every previous occasion. This time though, she had a new plan.

"Should we stop here for lunch?" Mischief interrupted sarcastically.

The girls' eyes were bulging. They now understood why the death dragons didn't attack the island and perhaps, now they were about to find out how Grim was defeated in the past. Perhaps how he could be again?

They read on fascinated and appalled in equal measure, by what they read. The next evening, Ellen kissed her daughter goodbye. Ellen was in floods of tears, as she held her daughter, as if, for the last time. Evaline was left in the care of her grandmother. Safe in their chambers within Threave Castle.

A single tear rolled down Evaline's cheek and hit the page, as she read.

The battle lines were drawn that night. Grim and his hoard flew in from the north. All witch-kind and friendly magical creatures lay in wait for them, in a do-or-die battle to the death. This time though, Ellen had decreed that the witches should not try to kill Grim. The witches' army was to draw off the death dragons and leave Grim to her.

Ellen raised her wand and cast a powerful spell. She summoned wind and torrential rain. A mighty storm blew, which seemed to befit the sombre mood of the occasion. Witches and dragons fought through thunder clouds and spun around tornados, casting spells and unleashing firebolts. The downpour providing some limited cover for the witches, who were hopelessly outgunned, right from the off.

Grim just laughed, as he tracked down one poor witch, after another. Fallen witches and dragons spiralled helplessly to the ground. Witch after witch, dropped from the sky. Black flames and soot billowing from their stricken brooms, as they fell. It was like target practice. The witches didn't stand a chance. Grim laughed aloud, as he spotted his treacherous wife, hiding by a waterfall, still mounted on her precious dragon. Now he would take his revenge, on the woman who had betrayed him so completely. By now, Grim knew, that his heir could survive without her mother's milk.

Grim turned in pursuit and Ellen fled for her life. Evading one, then two powerful fireballs, shot from Death's own scythe. Grim's mighty dragon pursued her. His dragon was much faster and stronger than her own. He was closing fast. She had no escape. In a last desperate act to evade him, Ellen plunged her dragon into the waterfall. A spectacular torrent of fresh running water, the "Grey Mare's Tail," as it was known locally.

The torrent was too much for any mortal dragon rider. She was helpless, thrown from her dragon's back. Her magical powers carried away on the fresh running waters. Ellen was swept away and carried under, by the power of the mighty waterfall, which plunged her into the pool beneath. Grim laughed heartily and followed on his death dragon. He closed in on his quarry and moved in for the kill. Neither he, nor his beast had any fear of running water. They were too powerful to be unseated by the waters or to be dragged to the depths below. This though, was Ellen's plan. She had been the bait.

Maya and Evaline exchanged wide-eyed glances, then read on impatiently.

Behind the falls, above the rocks and hidden from view, was a full coven. No ordinary coven. A new and powerful coven, like no other. The most powerful witches in all the land, had been assembled for this one task. Each one a dragon rider, they hovered on their magical beasts over the wet boulders beneath the falls and safe from the magic sapping running waters below. Their newly forged coven stone and High Priestess, lay in wait for the 'deed' to follow.

At the very moment Grim entered the waterfall in pursuit, they pulled all their powers, then focussed through a coven stone forged for the very purpose they froze the waterfall and pool beneath. Entombing both Grim and Ellen instantly, in solid ice.

Grim was trapped, frozen and motionless, imprisoned in solid ice and rendered powerless. With Grim and his powers frozen, the death dragons simply fell from the skies and faded back into the realm of the afterlife, where they belonged.

"Go Mum!" cried Evaline triumphantly.

Maya too sported a grin. This at last, was some hope. They knew now, that Grim could be defeated.

"Wow! My mother, she saved them. She saved everyone!" cried Evaline, fist pumping the air.

"Wow in *deed,*" Maya couldn't resist the awful pun. She had never thought of Evaline's mother as a heroine. Cruellen had turned out so badly. But she had warmed to Ellen. It would appear, that they all had Ellen to thank, for saving the world from Grim all those years before. Maya couldn't quite believe it.

"He won't fall for that one again though," cautioned Mischief.

Maya knew Mischief was right, but for now, she was just happy to know that Grim had been defeated once before.

"If your mum found a way, then so can we!" Maya announced, drawing an approving nod from Evaline and a disapproving, "Tut!" and shake of his head, from Mischief.

Maya and Evaline smiled and exchanged enlightened and hopeful glances. They read on eager for more.

So was born the mighty coven of the 'deed' or Coven of Deeds, as they soon became known. The Coven of Deeds was first convened close to running fresh water. A custom, they would continue to follow, down through the years. The first order of business was to decide what to do next. This part of Ellen's great plan, had not been discussed so thoroughly. Or in fact, at all.

The Deeds decided that Grim should remain frozen for all eternity. They could see no way to kill him, for he was already dead. So, frozen in ice, they banished his body to the icy glaciers and wastelands of the north. To the farthest most inaccessible ends of the earth. There, in the deepest glacier, they carved out an ice cave and left him frozen for all time.

"Question," Maya interrupted. "If Ellen's frozen too, how come her story's still writing?"

Mischief stroked his chin with his paw, as he often did, before imparting some of his great self-proclaimed wisdom, to his witchling friends.

"Although Ellen was frozen in ice. She was still alive," he explained. "So, her book has still recorded the events which most affected her."

"Oh," came the rather underwhelmed response from Evaline.

Maya though, didn't respond at all. She'd just realised that there was a problem, a big problem and read on in silence with some trepidation. She didn't have to wait much longer though, for an answer to her question.

The Deed's though had another decision to make, and this one was to prove much more difficult. Ellen too, lay frozen in ice.

Evaline gave Maya a confused look.

"What does that mean?" Evaline asked, once she'd caught up.

"I don't think you're going to like this," Mischief cautioned, meeting scowls of disapproval from Evaline.

The Coven of Deeds argued all night, but as the sun broke over the horizon, they had come to a decision. In spite of Ellen's great courage and her masterful plan. A plan that had saved them all and probably magic itself. To release Ellen was just too risky.

"What?" Evaline cried out in outrage.

The Deeds feared the curse laid down by Grim and the change they had seen in Ellen, since he'd cast it. They knew Ellen was turning to the dark side. Sadly, after a split vote, and with heavy hearts, they vowed to keep Ellen frozen in ice too.

"No!" Evaline cried out loud once more, tears of anger welling up into her bloodshot eyes.

But Maya had already read on, she like Mischief, had already deduced what was to come. Sadly, Maya read the words out loud:

"The Deeds feared Ellen's power, were she to become a dark witch, but more than that. Above all else, they feared her child."

"What?" Evaline couldn't believe it. "What had I done to them? I was just a baby!"

They read on. Evaline hardly able to contain her outrage. The Deeds feared Ellen's child would return to fulfil Grim's curse. To banish her own mother and deliver Grim the living wand, that he so craved. They feared that the child would finish his work. So, with great regret and much soul searching, they betrayed Ellen once more and sent for her daughter.

Baby Evaline was taken forcibly from her grandmother's arms, who's screams were heard for miles around. The original 'wailing banshee' as she became known. Driven to madness, she screamed and wailed through the night. Mourning the loss of her daughter and granddaughter from the highest tower of Threave Castle, from that day, until the day of her death.

"How could they?" Evaline sobbed.

The Deeds froze the child with her mother and sent them both to the frozen wastelands of the south. Evaline shook her head in despair, as she read on in disbelief.

And there, hidden away in an ice cave carved into an ancient glacier, they remained, as the centuries rolled past. Frozen solid in ice...

Evaline slammed the book shut and dissolved into tears. Maya put her arms around Evaline and comforted her friend, as she broke her heart.

Cruellen

The girls decided to take a break. Evaline needed to calm down and they all needed to reflect on what they'd read. There was nothing else for it, but to overdose on pancakes and chocolate sauce.

Ellen's story had answered a lot of their questions, but not perhaps, in the way that they'd hoped for. Ellen's story was disturbing, yet compelling reading, and it wasn't long before they found themselves back in the magic room again, picking up the mighty tome, ready for their next instalment.

As the years rolled by, the stories of the Grim Reaper passed into legend. As for Ellen's heroic deed, the very coven named after it, was so ashamed of her fate, that they banned all talk of it. Evaline, Ellen and Grim remained hidden from the world, safe in their deep-frozen prisons. Their whereabouts kept secret for centuries by the Coven of Deeds, and eventually long forgotten with the passing of successive High Priestesses. The stories of the Grim Reaper were passed down and changed from one generation to the next. Only occasionally spoken of, by admiring dark witches or for 'fun' at Halloween, by Emma's rather spooky mother.

But nothing lasts for ever. Mankind's destructive and selfish ways, were beginning to take their toll on the planet. Thanks to fossil fuels, global warming, was now out of control. Glaciers moved and melted, long before their time. Their once impregnable ice prisons, began to melt. First, Ellen was released from her frozen prison by the summer thaw.

Ellen bloodshot eyes opened slowly. Shaking uncontrollably with cold and pain at first. Then with rage. Unspeakable fury grew within her, as she surveyed her icy surroundings and came to terms with the treachery of her so-called friends, the Deeds. As her wrath grew and her powers returned, it was as if the earth quaked with fear, beneath her feet. Her rage grew further, at the sight of Evaline, entombed in ice and laid by her side.

With her first spell in over six hundred years, she defrosted her beloved daughter. Then she set her sights on the Coven of Deeds, and her revenge. Bitter at her betrayal, by the very witches whom she had saved, and incensed by the fate they had condemned her innocent daughter to. She plotted her vengeance. They would suffer for what they had done. She vowed that she too, could be as cruel as Grim himself. She had almost completed her journey to the dark side. Ellen was dead. Cruel Ellen or Cruellen, as she was now known, was now unleashed upon the world.

Cruellen was seething on her return to the Coven of Deeds. Death had long since spared the witches, who had actually betrayed her and nobody even knew who she was. The High Priestess greeted her demands for obedience and servitude, as a joke. But after the High Priestess found her insides on her outside and her twisted body coated in birdseed and hung from the nearest oak tree, for the crows. The rest of the coven soon fell into line.

"Yuk!" cried Maya.

"Mum always did have a bit of a temper," Evaline added rather sheepishly.

"A bit of a temper?" echoed Mischief.

Cruellen channelled her wrath in a new direction now. She reasoned; that if she had been released from her icy tomb, then it was just a matter of time, before Grim too would also return. Cruellen vowed to be prepared. She swore to become more powerful than any witch before her. She would be ready for him. She nurtured an elite coven, a ruthless coven of magical warriors. The Deeds. She ruled them with an iron fist and trained them in dragon combat. Only the strongest survived. They fought to the death.

There were long chapters about how Cruellen trained and bullied the Deeds and other 'less worthy' covens to do her bidding. The girls skipped past much of it. It wasn't very pleasant.

There were a few more tender moments though, when the softer side of Ellen showed through. Evaline snivelled shamelessly, as she read about the look of delight on her own face. The day her mum gave Evaline, her very first dragon, aged just six. It was a special moment. Her own dragon hatchling. A moment no young witchling could ever forget. Only partially spoiled by her mum telling her off, for naming him Smokey.

"Don't name him... he's not a pet. He's a dragon. He will lay his life down for you, and when the time comes, you must let him!" Cruellen scolded.

But, as Evaline reached her seventh year, these tender moments were few and far between. Evaline wept openly as the book recalled, how her mother had given her the necklace with the keystone pendant for her seventh birthday. It was the last real mother-daughter moment that they had shared. Except those on the battlefield or during dragon combat training.

"Someday my dear," Ellen spoke for the last time, passing Evaline the pendant which she now wore, "this will lead you home. It will show you who you really are and I suppose, who I really was too. Please forgive me," she whispered, planting a kiss on her daughter's forehead.

Strangely, a couple of pages had been ripped from Ellen's book here. This was worrying, what was she hiding? If she knew Evaline would return to read her book, what was it that she could not permit her own daughter to read?

The next page began with Evaline back in the magic realm, looking up into her mother's eyes, but the light in Ellen's eyes had faded. The last spark of compassion and love had left them for good. Cruellen now looked down on her own daughter, through cold manipulative and scheming eyes. Cruellen turned away from her daughter's gaze, then whispering to herself under her breath:

"This girl and her dragon will prove useful someday, with the right training."

Evaline could have written much of what followed herself. Evaline grew older and flew with the Coven of Deeds. A natural flyer, on her nameless dragon and soon, a fearsome warrior. First with bow and poison arrow, hunting wild boar and then with wand and firebolts. The other witches in the coven grew to fear her, especially when her mother named her as an heir to the Coven of Deeds. An heir, who earned her place by her mother's side with her first kill, aged just eight.

"Eight!" Maya gasped.

Evaline just nodded.

"You... you...?" Maya couldn't form the words. She was shocked. She knew that her friend had had a chequered past, but a first kill at eight! And they weren't talking about wild boar. The only way to claim a place in the Coven of Deed's, was to challenge one of their witches to dragon combat and the Deeds, as Maya knew only too well now, fought to the death.

There was more to Cruellen's plan, than a fearsome dragon riding army. She was clever, very clever indeed. She had proved that much, when she'd defeated Grim the first time. She knew exactly what she had to do now, to prepare for his inevitable return.

Cruellen knew that Grim would never fall for another trick, like the frozen waterfall again. So, she had hatched a new plan. Cruellen

389

too became obsessed with her husband's quest for a living wand. She researched it endlessly and sent out her spies to look for clues and to listen for rumours of its possible return.

Cruellen now understood, that a living wand was her only hope of banishing Grim for good. It was the only thing in this realm, which rivalled the power of Death's staff. A staff which Grim would wield once more, on his return. She swore to herself, that she would do whatever it takes, anything at all, to possess it.

"That's why she wanted your wand," Evaline gasped. "To stop Grim!" The pieces of the once jumbled jigsaw of Evaline's life, were at last starting to fall into place. Well, at least the corners and straight edges anyway.

Cruellen knew that her betrayal of Grim, not once but twice, would lead him to extract his most brutal revenge on her. She was desperate. She knew that Grim would return and that a living wand was only one thing that could stop him and save her skin.

Maya couldn't help but wonder; could the ends, really justify the means, when it came to stopping Grim? Was Cruellen right to do what she'd done? It was an uncomfortable thought.

It was all starting to make sense for Evaline now. The elaborate trap that her mother had laid for Maya and her living wand. Evaline had been so ashamed of her mother back then. She had never understood, how her mother had got to such a low point. At least now, she understood why.

Evaline could take some comfort now, from how her mother had once been a heroine and saved the world from Grim, at the height of his powers. She had liked the girl Ellen too, who wouldn't? She'd been so like Evaline herself, in so many ways. Reading her mother's life story, also had the added benefit of refreshing many of her earliest memories too. Memories from happier times, when she was very young and there was more of Ellen, and less of Cruellen.

But Cruellen? She was a monster. There was no love in Cruellen now, she was pure evil. She had betrayed her own daughter. A mother who had been happy to sacrifice her own daughter's life, just to get her grubby hands, on Maya's living wand. Had that been for the greater good or just to save her own skin?

Evaline read on alone now, how her mother researched the living wand. How she groomed Evaline and the Coven of Deeds, to do her bidding. Maya had no wish to relive the trap that Cruellen had laid for her and her own mother.

Maya couldn't listen to that story again, not right now. Not while her mother, was still in such jeopardy. Evaline too, chose to skip most of these pages. She had no wish to dwell on her part in Cruellen's elaborate plot to trick Maya out of her living wand. In particular Evaline had no desire, to hear of the betrayal that her mother must have felt, when Evaline eventually sided with Maya and broke her mother's wand. It had been bad enough living through that experience. She had no desire to relive it all again, especially not through her mother's eyes.

Evaline didn't know what had become of her mother. Not since the day, when she'd broken Cruellen's wand and left with Maya. After that she'd lost all contact with her.

Evaline found that part in her mother's book easily enough though, right towards the end... she simply flicked through the pages until she read:

"Betrayed! My own daughter... how could she?"

That sounded about right, so Evaline called Maya back, to read the next chapter together. She really didn't want to hear this next part alone.

Obligingly, Maya started to read it aloud, for all to hear:

"Cruellen was humiliated. Her own daughter had shown her, for the monster that she had become. The Coven of Deeds rounded on her too and banished her, never to return. Thrown out of her coven, rejected by her daughter and peers. No wand and her powers fading, she wandered aimlessly for days on end. Her plan had failed and one day soon, she knew that Grim would return and extract his cruel revenge. Cruellen had lost all hope."

Maya sensed that Evaline was upset and let her have a moment. Then she shared the book and let Evaline read on at her own pace. They read on together in silence.

Cruellen hid away from all other witches and eventually left the magic realm altogether. Her final words in the magic realm, recorded like a stark prophecy:

"Not 'till the time of reckoning, will I set foot in the magic realm again."

Then her story just stopped. True to her word, as the months rolled by, she had not returned... not that is, until just a few days ago. The very night, that the attacks from the north had started.

Evaline looked up at Maya, as she turned the next page... there was more. Just a couple of pages more, but Evaline and Maya realised with horror, exactly what that meant...

This must be the time of reckoning and Cruellen was back!

The trap

Their minds were racing. It was all too much of a coincidence; Cruellen returning to the magic realm, on the very night, that the attacks had started.

What was she up to? Could Evaline's mother really be behind all this? What if Cruellen had released Grim from his icy prison, in exchange for her own life? Could she have joined forces with Grim? Were they now working together, poised to take their revenge on all witches, who'd betrayed them both? What chance would any of them have, if Grim and Cruellen had joined forces?

It was a terrifying thought. It meant something else too, if they had joined forces... Maya and Evaline would be top of their most wanted list. Evaline passed Maya her mother's book. She couldn't face reading any more herself.

Maya took the book reluctantly, swallowed hard, then started to read. Paragraph by paragraph, she read slowly and carefully, relaying Cruellen's thoughts to her friend. She wanted to make light of it, but there was no sugar coating Cruellen.

"Cruellen opened her portal. She allowed herself a crooked satisfied smile, then replaced her keystone pendant, back around her neck. She stepped through the full-length mirror and walked into the dark passageway. Her path illuminated by the dim red light from the eyes of a thousand blood-eyed vampire bats. These hung from the ceiling and lit the way, as she approached. Then dulled again, as the larger bats feasted on their siblings, once she'd passed."

Maya shuffled uncomfortably in her seat, then continued to read aloud:

"Cruellen carried with her a new wand. A powerful wand. Her own mother's wand. A wand, which she'd prised remorselessly from the old witch's skeletal grasp, during a midnight grave-robbing excursion to the family crypt, the night before."

"Poor Granny!" Mischief scoffed unhelpfully.

Evaline glared daggers at him.

Maya shuddered, as if it were her own grave being violated, before she resumed reading, with renewed and morbid fascination:

"Fang, Cruellen's new albino Persian side-kick, following at heel. It reaching up a paw, to pluck a plump vampire bat from the ceiling, then bit off its head, as a juicy mid-morning snack. Blood dribbled down the cat's chin and splattered onto its thick furry coat. Then, out came the cat's tongue in response, to lap up the warm grizzly gravy, that still spurted from the bat's decapitated body."

"Yuk!" cried Maya.

"So, what's she doing here? Why has she returned to the magic realm now?" demanded Evaline impatiently.

Maya delved back in. The next part, however took her by surprise though. This wasn't at all what she'd expected or feared.

"It says, that now the time has finally arrived... she waits for her daughter in a cave," Maya relayed.

"Me, why's she waiting for me? And in a cave... my mum doesn't do caves?" Evaline insisted.

"A cave, miles from here, where her magical portal comes out apparently," Maya repeated, as she read onwards. "Nursing her wrath and her evil cat, just like the villain, in an old Bond movie."

Maya read on, paraphrasing the next rather uneventful paragraphs for her friends.

"She waits patiently, biding her time. Waiting for her daughter to come and if not, for her own inevitable and horrible death at the hands of Grim. Racking her brain for another way to defeat him. But she knows with certainty now, that there is only one way. She knows that the only chance to defeat Grim, lies with the living wand and she also now knows that... well I never! It just says; that she can never lay her hands on it," Maya blushed.

"Really?" Mischief asked scornfully.

Maya pursed her lips and scowled.

"Ok, it actually says; 'thanks to that interfering, goody-two-shoes, annoying little friend of her daughter's.' Well really! I think you can both guess, to who she's referring, for yourselves!" Maya added indignantly. "She now knows, that only a witch, who's pure of heart, can ever wield such a wand."

"So why is she waiting in a cave?" Mischief asked, looking rather puzzled.

Maya returned to Cruellen's book and read aloud.

"That pathetic little witch, with her living wand. I despise her more than any other, but unfortunately, Maya holds the key. Only through her and her wand, can I ever defeat Grim and be spared his cruel revenge."

"Pathetic little witch?" Maya chirped indignantly, in a disconcertingly high-pitched voice.

Mischief sniggered.

Evaline looked up, then asked the question nobody wanted to ask:

"Does that mean she's on our side now?"

There was a stunned silence.

"The enemy of your enemy, is your friend, as a wise cat once said," added Mischief.

"Are you sure it was a cat, who first said that?" Maya asked suspiciously.

"Why, don't I look like a cat to you?" Mischief grinned.

Maya had walked straight into that one. Maya just shook her head and returned to Cruellen's book. Which she read aloud, once more:

"That loathsome interfering little know-it-all, who thwarted my plans and turned my own daughter against me. Much as I hate to admit it, if there is any chance to defeat Grim. It lies with her," Maya read aloud, rather indignantly.

"What does she mean, loathsome interfering little know-it-all?" Maya demanded, with rising indignation.

Mischief sniggered loudly once more.

Maya chose to ignore him, and continued to read on regardless:

"So, here I'll wait. Wait for Evaline, it's just a matter of time, now that Grim has returned. When you read this my dear, you'll realise that you coming back home, was all my doing."

"What?" Maya interrupted herself, indignant and bemused by Cruellen's claim.

Maya read on with a mixture of trepidation and disbelief:

"The enchantment on that pendant, I gave you Evaline. It will draw you home, when the time comes. Grim's return will activate your keystone, as a homing beacon and you will be drawn home to read my story."

Maya looked up to meet Evaline's equally horrified eyes, staring right back at her.

"She's played us for fools all along, hasn't she?" Evaline gasped.

Maya just shook her head in disbelief and continued with Cruellen's book. Her thoughts betrayed her plans, but Maya had the uneasy feeling that Cruellen was still several steps ahead of them:

"Grim's dragons will not attack his own family, so Evaline, my dear, you will be spared. The pendant will guide you to Threave Castle, to our family home. You will be drawn home and the keystone will lead you to my magic room and then to read my story."

Cruellen knew that her daughter couldn't help herself, the book commented.

It was as if Cruellen herself, was there in the room, telling them exactly how she'd been manipulating them, all along. Maya reflected on how Cruellen, really was not a witch to be underestimated! Maya read on, aghast at Cruellen's cunning and shear audacity, while Mischief reached up a paw to close Evaline's gaping mouth, in case another fly should become trapped.

"She'll protest at first, but her objections will be futile," Maya read aloud. "Once Evaline has read Ellen's sad tale... her fate will be sealed. She'll be hooked. She'll realise, just how much like her, I once was. Then she'll come for me. She'll have no choice. She'll walk through my portal. She simply won't be able to resist; a chance to rescue her mother's pathetic 'better' half from my portal!"

Evaline's mouth was agape once more.

"Is it really possible?" she mumbled.

It was Cruellen's journal, that answered her question, with a spooky predictability, as Maya read:

"Oh yes my dear! Somewhere in my portal, what's left of her still lingers."

Maya looked up from Cruellen's book momentarily, her eyes wide as grapefruits. Then continued, compelled to read on:

"You won't be able to resist, my dear, you'll have to try. My Evaline will try anything to reunite me with that side of me that's been hopelessly lost, all these years. I know her, a chance for Ellen's redemption. Huh, the sap! Her courage and compassion will be her undoing! Oh, she's clever enough to know it's a trap, but still she'll come. She won't be able to help herself."

It was as if Cruellen was taunting them, goading Evaline to do her bidding. Mocking her, through the pages of her own life's story. Using her thoughts to dictate their every move. As apparently, she had done all along.

"You're not seriously considering doing what she said, are you?" winced Mischief.

"Of course, I am!" snapped Evaline. Evaline didn't know whether to feel anger, at the way Cruellen was pulling her strings, like a master puppeteer. Or elated at the prospect of redemption for Ellen. Was there really still hope for the mother she'd lost, all those years before?

Evaline grabbed her mother's book away from Maya, in an attempt to take charge of something, anything. But, as she read on, it was clear that Cruellen, was still very much in the driving seat.

"She'll pick up my hand mirror to talk to me. Won't you my dear?" Evaline's voice broke, as she read the words.

Evaline's eyes were drawn to the hand mirror. The family heirloom, that lay covered in dust on the table. Evaline resisted the temptation to grab the mirror, right there and then, to give her mother both barrels. Tell her exactly what she thought of Cruellen, but she knew that's exactly what her mother wanted. So, trying to compose herself, Evaline took a deep breath and read on:

"I won't even have to ask my Evaline, to seek out my other half and bring it to me. How could she not, after reading my sad tale? And that will be her undoing. She will come to me, one way or another. Either after losing her soul in my portal, as a dark witch and a powerful ally or with the ghost of my past self, in a futile attempt to save that part of me. But one way or the another, she will come."

Cruellen's thoughts, from her journal, taunted her daughter, at the turn of every page.

Evaline was outraged and perplexed:

"So, she knows I'm reading her story, right? Reading that it's a trap... so, why does she think I'm going to walk into it?

Mischief answered her first:

"Because she's your mother, and as she said, she knows that you won't be able to resist."

"Resist what? Walking into a trap?" Maya scoffed. "How do we even know, that there's anything left of her mother's better half anyway?"

"She's cunning alright," Mischief replied. "It does sound plausible."

Maya just glared at him to shut up. Evaline however, wanted to hear more:

"Really?"

Mischief took a long thoughtful deep breath and explained:

"They say, when you go over to the dark side. You lose a part of yourself. The good that's in all of us, it gets lost somehow. That part of you, which balances out your darker side. That side of Ellen, all the goodness, that once lived within her, is lost."

"Lost? Lost where?" Evaline demanded.

"That, I'm not entirely sure, but...," Mischief started.

"I think, her book said that we'd have to go through her portal to find Ellen, didn't it?" Maya interrupted.

Mischief cleared his throat and shuffled on his cushion in annoyance, as if ready to impart some more, of his self-proclaimed great wisdom, without any further interruptions.

"Remember, when we came through your portal earlier, Maya?" asked Mischief.

Maya nodded to confirm.

"There were dark shadows there. New passageways opened up in front of you. Tempting you to follow a darker path, vengeance for what Grim had done to Emma and your mum? You felt your dark side calling you, it pursued you, it stalked you and it will tempt you with your own deepest desires and fantasies. Follow the wrong path and give in to its temptations, then all that's good in you will be trapped there. Your dark side though, will not stick around, not in your fantasy world. There is nothing for it there. They say, your dark side continues on alone, devoid of all that is good in you. You lose your soul and with it, your reflection too."

"That explains the hair brushing then!" Evaline replied.

"What?" Maya demanded. Clearly bemused by her friend's, seemingly random response.

"Mum's hair… she always got me to do it," Evaline replied. She wouldn't have any mirrors around. Not except those hand mirrors and they didn't work, not that way."

Mischief just glared at Maya as if to say:

"Told you so!"

Maya gulped… Cruellen, yes that made sense, that she'd lost her reflection. But the revelation that these hand mirrors didn't work for Evaline too. That was worrying.

"So, the other side, the good side of my mum, what happened to it?" Evaline asked anxiously.

Mischief pondered, stroked his chin knowledgeably, then conceded:

"I'm not sure. Nobody really knows. Most think, it gets lost and stays trapped in the dream world of the portal. Others say it fades away and perishes completely."

"So, she might still be in there. There might actually be a way to save her?" Evaline probed anxiously.

Mischief shrugged his furry shoulders:

"I don't know, yes, maybe?"

"So, why does Cruellen think Evaline's going to risk everything and walk into her trap? Just to go looking for what may, or may not be left of Ellen. Especially after all this time?" Maya scoffed, but in her heart, she already knew the answer. Maya looked her friend in the eye.

"Please tell me, you're not considering...?" Maya started, but she knew it was useless.

"Well... I thought, I might?" Evaline winced.

"But, it's a trap!" Mischief objected.

"Of course, it's a trap!" Evaline snapped. "And she knows, that I know, it's a trap!"

"And she knows, that even though you know, that it's a trap and you know, that she knows, that you know, that it's a trap... you're still going to walk right into it, aren't you?" Mischief clarified 'helpfully' for everyone.

"What? Oh, never mind. Of course, I'm going!" Evaline snapped again.

Maya just nodded. She knew there was no point in trying to talk Evaline out of this.

"So where do we start, do you suppose?" asked Evaline.

"Pick up that mirror, like Cruellen suggested, and I think she'll tell you," Mischief replied.

"But that's exactly what she wants," cautioned Maya. "She's counting on it. It's why she gave you the keystone, in the first place, knowing it would lead you here. Tricking you into reading her book. It's all led up to this moment. All to get you to go after her other half in the portal or even to pick up that mirror and talk to her... it's a trap! It's all been her doing. She's played us all for fools, right from the start!"

"She's right you know. It's all playing out, just the way Cruellen's planned it," Mischief agreed.

"Okay, maybe, we should read on first. There are still a couple more sentences left?" suggested Evaline.

Maya shrugged her shoulders:

"Why not, surely it can't get any worse, can it?" regretting her words, as soon as they left her lips.

Evaline lifted her mother's book and braced herself, one last time. Evaline read aloud:

"Then, Evaline you will be mine again. Maya will do anything to save her friend. I believe she'd even...," Evaline stopped mid-sentence.

"What?" asked Maya.

"Too much," whispered Evaline. "No mother. You ask too much!"

Maya caught the book, just as it slipped from Evaline's grasp. She pulled it towards herself and scanned the lines, which her friend had been reading. Maya read the words aloud, slowly and deliberately, without conveying any emotion:

"I believe she'd even die for her friend. After all, only a spell from the great beyond, cast by a living wand, can send Grim back and restore the great balance. Only a pure soul, like her, can wield that wand."

Maya's words tailed off to a whisper by the end, followed by one of the longest and most awkward silences any of them had ever endured.

"Oh," was all Maya could find to sum up the situation.

"Don't listen to her Maya, she's... she's just playing with your mind. Trying to get inside your head?" Mischief advised, but the

403

hesitation in his voice, betrayed his inner fears and thoughts. After all, it did sound plausible.

"But what if she's right?" Maya asked, starting to shake. Her tongue was out. It whipped around her mouth, like an ant trapped on the end of a gecko's tongue. Could it be true?

"Ignore her Maya!" insisted Evaline. "It's just Cruellen plotting her cruel revenge on you. She's taunting you! She's never been a good loser and you outsmarted her, last time. Now, she wants you to suffer!"

Maya let out a forced laugh:

"You're right, I'm not falling for that, not from her, of all people."

But Maya wasn't fooling Mischief. He knew her too well. He could see the very real look of fear in Maya's eyes. Maybe Cruellen was right?

Maya's tongue had returned to home base with a disturbing thought. Maybe Cruellen was so desperate at the prospect of Grim's revenge, that she might actually be resorting to telling the truth. Shivers ran up and down Maya's spine, like a pair of frosty ferrets, dragging ice-cubes through a skin-tight leotard.

"What's this about a hand mirror?" Maya asked, trying nervously to change the subject.

"Oh yes, I remember that from when I was little," Evaline replied. "My mum used one, it had no reflection, but she used it to talk to her family and close friends."

Evaline made her way across the room towards the hand mirror, still sat on the dusty table top.

"They were the only things, which my mum owned, that had been handed down from her own mother's family. She loved them. A set of three old fashioned mirrors, set in silver, with oak handles. I only ever saw two though. This must be the missing one. She and her family could use them to communicate, wherever they were. No need to enchant a bird, to tweet a message," Evaline recalled fondly.

"What like facetime or skype?" Maya butted in, ruining any sense of nostalgia.

Evaline picked up the mirror in one hand.

"What harm can it do?" Evaline asked, as if trying to convince herself. "To talk to her a little, that's all. Just talk."

Mischief shook his head disapprovingly.

"I'm not saying, that I'm going to play her game, and go through her portal, just... just... just to talk, that's all!" Evaline insisted once more.

Maya stepped to one side, behind the full-length mirror. There was no need to confirm her presence to Cruellen, after all.

Evaline turned the mirror towards herself, and scraped off the eons of dust and cobwebs, with the side of her hand. Initially, the reflection was dark and gloomy. Then a faint image, foggy at first, swirling like a sink of dirty dishwater. Slowly, it started to clear. Cruellen's haggard face appeared. Evaline's jaw dropped, at the sight of the pitiful old woman, who now stared back at her. She had aged, aged horribly, since they'd last seen each other.

"Hello my dear, I've been expecting you," Cruellen cackled, with obvious smugness.

"So, I've just been reading," Evaline replied coldly.

"You've got older, I see," Cruellen remarked.

"You don't look a day over six hundred yourself mother," Evaline sneered in reply.

"Come to save my soul, have you?" Cruellen chortled.

"So, what makes you so sure, that I'm going to play your little game mother?" Evaline sneered back.

"Well, you see, that's the clever part, my dear. You see, not only do you find that prospect irresistible, but just for insurance, now that you've picked up the mirror. You simply have no other choice," Cruellen grinned back, through stained and crooked teeth.

"Oh really! And why is that, mother? If indeed, I still choose to call you that?" Evaline challenged the old crone.

"Well, now that you've picked up the mirror.... well, it's one of three, if you remember, my dear," Cruellen cackled.

"So?" Evaline interrupted, defiantly.

Cruellen grinned once more:

"One for you, one for me and..."

"One for Daddy!" bellowed a new voice, as a hooded skull suddenly appeared in the mirror, like a tablet switching to split-screen mode.

"Grim!" Evaline gasped in horror, nearly dropping the mirror in the process.

There, in front of a pair of fiery gates, Evaline presumed to be the actual gates to hell, stood Grim.

"Hello my dear. I see you're at home. I'll see you tonight then...," he bellowed, before breaking into cruel laughter. Clearly revelling in his evil villain role.

"Tonight, my dear. Tonight, you **will** fulfil your destiny!" he bellowed. "Tonight, **you** will deliver me the living wand!"

"Over my dead body!" Maya cried, breaking cover.

"That's the general idea," beamed Grim.

Maya had no words. There was simply no comeback to that one.

Evaline just froze with fear.

Cruellen spoke again, now with a threatening intensity, more reminiscent of the High Priestess, at the height of her powers.

"You see, now that you've announced to your father where his two favourite girls are. I'm sure, that when night falls, he'll be on his way. As soon as the clock strikes midnight in fact," Cruellen cackled.

"So, unless you want to face him on your own, I suggest you do exactly as I've asked you to, Evaline my dear," Cruellen taunted:

"Come to mummy!"

Cruellen's portal

Evaline slammed down the hand mirror. Tears tracked random paths, like drunken skiers, down her cheeks from bloodshot eyes.

"No, no, no!" Evaline wailed.

"And I thought your parents were hard work!" sighed Mischief, turning back towards Maya.

No humour though, could soften this moment for poor Evaline. Was it possible that her parents were in this together? Had they really just conspired to trap her? Would her father be coming, to extract his terrible revenge, this very night? One thing was certain though... Evaline was miffed!

"She's got us, right where she wants us, hasn't she? Grim too!" Evaline announced, as eventually she found the words to break, her stunned silence.

"No!" Maya puffed out her 'developing chest' and resolved there and then. "This stops now! From now on, we go our own way. Ellen we're coming for you!"

Mischief puffed out his under-developed chest with pride and nearly agreed, before coming to his senses and 'politely' demanding:

"Are you mad? That's exactly what she wants you to do, isn't it?"

"No!" Maya glared back, "That's exactly, what she doesn't want us to do! She wants us to come through the portal all right, to bring her daughter and the wand to her and for me..., well, you know, but I don't think she believes, that we'll actually be able to find Ellen in there."

"And how do you figure that out?" Evaline demanded.

"Because she says that's what she wants us to do!" Maya responded, with new found vigour and determination.

"So?" Evaline asked, still clearly puzzled.

 "Has she ever told us the truth before?" Maya explained.

It made sense, well sort of. Even Mischief didn't object... he was still trying to contemplate Maya's strange reverse logic.

Evaline nodded:

"Okay, let's do this thing!" she agreed.

Maya made her way over to the old wooden chest, which sat in the corner of Cruellen's magic room. Three small potion bottles lay on top. Maya picked up the first of them and wiped the dust from the label. A skull-and-crossbones greeted her, with a crooked grin. Underneath the words *'certain slow and agonising death'*. Maya shuddered visibly, as she read out the words. It sounded too much like a prophecy.

Evaline made her way across the room to join her friend and picked up the next bottle, then proceeded to wipe its label clean. A bottle with, *'hung, drawn and quartered (slowly!)'* scrawled on the label in red ink or possibly something much, much worse. Evaline too, shuddered at the thought.

"I vote for the third bottle!" joked Mischief.

Maya picked up the third bottle and wiped away the dust nervously. It read simply:

'Mother's revenge'

"Just a bundle of laughs your mother!" Mischief sneered.

"Can I see that?" Evaline asked, taking the little potion bottle from Maya.

Before anyone could say anything, Evaline had popped open the cork. Cruellen was Evaline's mother after all. So, if anyone was going to suffer Cruellen's revenge, Evaline reasoned, it should be her.

Green and purple smoke billowed out from the tiny bottle's open neck. Tendrils of smoke reached out, like hunting serpents, into every corner of the room. Wrapping themselves menacingly around Mischief and the girls. The room filled with a pungent acrid aroma, reminiscent of Grandma's kitchen after a meal of boiled cabbage and fried herring. The smoke cleared quickly, but the foul stench lingered and intensified.

"Yuk! Let's get out of here!" Evaline squeaked, through her finger pinched nose.

"Through the wibbly-wabbly-thingy?" Maya suggested, gesturing towards the full-length mirror in the corner, that now shimmered, like a pool of liquified silver.

Evaline just glared.

"It's a portal Maya," she responded, rather dismissively.

Maya felt herself blush with embarrassment.

Evaline led the way, stepping straight through the portal without any hesitation. Maya and Mischief followed, quickly on her heels. Although, why Maya, and in particular her cat Mischief, were wearing Evaline's high heels, the author never adequately explained.

Now inside, Maya observed, how Cruellen's portal was not at all like her own. It was dark. Its walls looked wet and slimy to the

410

touch, though no-one dared to touch them. The girls walked cautiously on through the dark passageway. It was lit by the dim red light of a thousand blood-eyed vampire bats, which hung from the ceiling above and lit the way as they approached. The light from their peering scarlet eyes dimmed again, once the girls had passed. Their long needle-like fangs glinted through the gloom. Maya could have sworn, that she saw some of them licking their lips and smiling hungrily as she passed.

"Give me glow worms any day!" Maya joked, but nobody was in the mood for laughter. They were all feeling spooked. Hundreds of tiny evil blood red eyes watched their every move. They tracked them hungrily, like miniature demons of the night.

As they ventured further into Cruellen's portal, Evaline slowed and then stopped. Ahead, the passageway split and split again and again. A labyrinth of possible choices opened up in front of them. Each as uninviting as the next.

"Which way?" Maya whispered.

"No idea... lucky left, I suppose?" Evaline suggested.

"What?" Maya and Mischief replied in unison.

"Lucky left, like my mum always used to say," Evaline reaffirmed.

"Oh, great idea. We trust everything your mum says now, do we?" scoffed Mischief. Suddenly deciding to take charge and deciding to lead them down the right-hand passageway. Then right and right again, just for good measure.

The passageway turned suddenly, narrowed and dropped down three shallow steps. It led them to a very sturdy looking old wooden door, studded with tarnished metal diamond shapes. Evaline pushed the heavy door open, accompanied by a long and piercing squeak, from its rusty hinges. Evaline stepped through the doorway cautiously and into the room beyond.

The room was less gloomy than the passageway. Lanterns hung from the wall and illuminated a collection of treasure, straight out of a Hollywood blockbuster. Jaws dropped (not the shark) at the bewildering spectacle of shiny stuff, laid out in front of them. Piles of gold, silver and jewels piled high, like a scene from Aladdin or a pirate movie.

"What?" Maya mouthed.

"Greed, riches, temptation?" Mischief suggested.

"We could just take a couple of pieces? You know for a rainy day?" Evaline grinned.

"Don't touch a single thing, it's a trap!" Maya ordered. Uncharacteristically, failing to see that Evaline was joking.

They retraced their steps, left the room piled high with shiny stuff and closed the door on unimaginable wealth and luxury. Maya led them back up the shallow steps, then stopped in her tracks. There was another door, off to the left now and yet another one to the right.

"Were these here before?" Maya asked aloud.

Mischief and Evaline both shook their heads.

"Lucky left?" suggested Evaline.

Maya and Mischief nodded to each other and Maya opened the door on the right. The next room was brighter still. A large golden throne sat within a long, pillar lined marble hall. A jewelled crown lay on an ermine pillow in front of them.

"Power?" Evaline suggested. "Come on mother, you're going to have to do a lot better than this, if you're going to tempt us!"

Maya nodded her agreement, as they backed out of the room via the door, through which they'd just entered.

Room after room of temptations were presented... a torture chamber of their very own, filled with annoying boys and maths teachers. Anyone who had crossed them before, appeared gagged and bound. Strapped into guillotines and racks and all manner of other contraptions.

"Revenge," Mischief commented, as they backed away.

"Could we just...?" Evaline started.

"No!" Maya interrupted. Much to the relief of Evaline's form-teacher, who lay sweating on a blooded wooden table, restrained beneath a huge pendulum axe. An axe set to lower fractionally with every swing.

Greed was next, but this time cakes and sweets proved much more difficult to resist. Evaline pulled Maya back from the brink, as she spotted the ice-cream sundae and pickled onion buffet.

After an hour of endless temptations, they were back where they started. Or were they? No, not quite, for now they were completely lost too.

A cold shiver ran up Evaline's spine. Maya and Mischief felt it too. Evaline turned to look behind them and froze.

"Do you believe in ghosts?" she whispered.

"No, of course not .... oh, oh... well...," Maya stuttered, as she turned to follow Evaline's gaze.

An apparition, ghostly, faint and only just visible presented itself, as a young woman and moved slowly towards them. The young lady walked down the corridor and passed straight through Maya, without any sign, that it had even seen her. Maya shuddered. The spirit made its way slowly along the passageway in front of them, as if searching for something.

Evaline stood motionless, transfixed, her mouth agape.

"Mum?" she whispered.

"What?" cried Mischief.

"Ellen?" asked Maya.

Evaline nodded.

"She didn't even see me," Evaline whispered, unable to hide the pain in her voice.

"Maybe we're too late? Maybe she's gone forever, just a ghost of her past self?" Mischief suggested, with typically undiplomatic flair.

Maya hit him with her most withering glare and obediently, he ceased his commentary.

They followed the spirit, as it made its way slowly through the passageways, turning left, then left again and lucky left, once more.

After a minute, Evaline raced past it, stopped and held out her hand flat in front of her own face, in a 'stop' gesture. But the spirit just carried on, passing straight through her.

Evaline crumpled visibly with disappointment.

"Ellen!" cried Maya, but there was no response.

"Hmm," uttered Mischief.

"Out with it pussy-cat!" Maya demanded. She knew the signs. He was on to something.

"Well, it might sound a bit corny," Mischief started then paused, looked a bit uncomfortable. "Perhaps only the love of her daughter can wake her?"

"But she didn't even see me?" Evaline sobbed.

"No, but if it comes from the heart, maybe you can still reach her," Mischief pondered out loud.

"How?" Evaline looked perplexed. Her heart was already breaking.

"Memories, especially shared ones, are powerful things," suggested the cat. "Especially in a place like this."

Maya was in shock. Empathy and compassion, from Mischief... had he lost himself in here too?

Evaline focussed. She closed her eyes. She knew just the memory. The day her mum gave her Smokey. Her very own dragon's egg, just on the point of hatching. Evaline smiled as she recollected the egg, as it rolled and cracked and a tiny smoking snout pushed its way, through a crack in the shell. The red-hot shell suddenly parted and the two halves, fell apart. A tiny green dragon then unfurled a perfect pair of gossamer wings, for the first time. Ellen gazed down gently at her daughter, with love and compassion in her eyes.

"Mum," Evaline whispered gently. Her words carried, as if floating on a gentle breeze, though the dimly lit passageway, towards the apparition. Ellen's ghost stopped, as if startled by a distant cry.

"Mum?" Evaline asked once more, this time barely audibly.

The apparition turned, smiled gently and beckoned her daughter with one hand, to follow her.

Evaline's eyes watered. Maya's eyes watered. Mischief wiped some dust from the corner of his eye. Dust, which he later insisted had been blown in on the gentle breeze. A breeze that nobody else noticed.

Ellen turned and changed direction, as if to lead the way.

"Follow that ghost!" snuffled Mischief.

"Where's she taking us?" asked Evaline. "Another room?"

"I hope it's not lust!" joked Mischief.

"Olowe!" Maya gagged at the thought.

Ellen's ghost made its way to another door, then simply passed straight through it. Evaline followed, pushing open the mighty door impatiently, then let out an involuntary gasp. Evaline's eyes were watering again, but this time with joy... it was her dream, the day her mother had given her, her dragon. The happiest day of Evaline's life.

Ellen's ghost was clearer now, more visible, as though partially awoken from its slumbers. It beckoned Evaline in, now adopting the position, that Evaline remembered her mother taking all those

416

years before. It was heart-breaking and heart-warming in equal measures.

Evaline watched transfixed by the spectacle unfolding in front of her. The hatchling dragon crawled free of its egg and spread its wings for the first time. The little puffling shivered and let out a cry and with it, a tiny puff of smoke. Evaline moved instinctively to pick up her tiny puffling friend. Maya grabbed hold of Evaline's arm, pulling her away suddenly.

"No, you can't," Maya insisted gently, but firmly. "You can't lose yourself in here too."

Her words stopped Evaline in her tracks.

"You know it's not real, don't you? None of this is," Mischief added softly. "This place, it's tempting you. Cruellen, it's her dark side, she's still tempting you. She'll do anything to trap you in here."

Evaline didn't answer. She backed away from the little creature with a heavy heart, hardly able to look away. Maya and Mischief turned and headed back through the door. They moved slowly back into the labyrinth of Cruellen's portal. Maya now led the way.

"Give them a minute," Maya suggested, sensing Mischief's nervousness, that Evaline and Ellen were now lagging behind them. Mischief looked nervously back along the corridor, just in time to catch a glimpse of Evaline, following her mother into yet another room to the left.

Maya and Mischief waited around the corner, until after a couple of minutes, Evaline returned.

"Sorry, my lace came undone," Evaline explained, as she brushed past them impatiently.

417

Maya and Mischief exchanged worried glances and Mischief gestured towards Evaline's boots.

"Wh...? Oh," Maya replied, spotting the buckled strap on the side of Evaline's boots.

"I don't trust her," whispered Mischief.

"She came back, didn't she?" Maya snapped back, rather defensively.

"Yes, but who exactly came back... Evaline or just her dark side?" Mischief queried.

Maya was unsettled by his comments. She knew Mischief had never trusted Evaline, not like she did, but now she too felt uneasy.

Maya shivered, as the Ghost of Ellen appeared through another door, just ahead of them.

Evaline led the way now, following her ghost mum.

"Come on then," Evaline called, beckoning Maya and Mischief to keep up.

They followed Ellen's spirit. It made another left turn and passed through yet another door. Reluctantly, Maya and Mischief followed Evaline through the door, but this time it wasn't a room into which they had entered.

This was new. A vast landscape opened up in front of them. Epic snow topped mountains, dropped down through broadleaf forest to a lake. A thatched cottage with white-washed walls perched on the banks.

"It's beautiful!" Maya gasped.

A stunning meadow of wildflowers, filled with pure white stallions, Shetland ponies and alpacas greeted them. There were stables for

418

Evaline's and Maya's brooms and a huge ancient oak with massive boughs, provided ideal landing perches for the girls' dragons. It was perfect.

Ellen had taken on a fully physical form now. As if, fully reanimated and whole once more. She led Evaline by the hand, across the meadow and on towards the cottage, with a big grin on her face. Anxious to share this place with her daughter.

Ellen led Evaline through the front door of the cottage and Maya followed them, rather more warily. It was stunning inside. Panoramic windows, lined with gnarled oak beams, framed the view of the lake and mountains. An aga, warmed a large open plan kitchen. A cosy lounge, crammed full of soft furnishings, scatter cushions and a shag-pile rug stretched out in front of an open wood fire. Ellen gestured for Evaline to light the fire, which she did with a flick of her wand. They could do magic here too and there were no death dragons outside. Best of all, Evaline had her mother back.

Maya made her way to the other side of the room. There were family photographs, displayed on top of an antique pine dresser. Her whole family... but how? Mum, Dad, Aunty Dot, Ollie and Finn and Emma on Bandit. Bandit stepped forward. His proud wings now restored. These were not just pictures though, these were miniature portals, like Ellen's mirrors, but for Maya's family; showing each of her loved ones. Maya eyes flashed back to her mother's picture, she too was happy, smiling and joking. There was no bandage on her hand.

"It's not real, is it?" Maya asked sadly, looking down to Mischief, as he brushed into her ankle.

"No little one, I think we should leave this place," Mischief replied gently.

"Can't we stay a bit longer?" Maya asked and Evaline nodded enthusiastically, whilst picking up a hunting bow from the top of an oak table.

"You both know it's a trap, don't you?" Mischief obviously had some experience to share. "Temptation, whatever you want, whatever you desire, it's right here, but it's not real. Dreams are lovely, but you cannot stay in a dream world... soon your other half, your dark side will leave. There is nothing here for it. That side of you, has with it, the courage you'll need to leave here and without it, you'll become trapped forever."

"Awe, just a bit longer. What harm could a few hours do?" pleaded Evaline. Maya grinned down towards her cat in agreement.

Mischief scowled back, his voice raised and stern:

"I don't want to think about what would happen to your friends and families out there, if Maya and you turned to the dark side and teamed up with Grim and Cruellen!"

That did the trick, Maya realised with horror, that this place had got to her.

"Get us out of here, now!" she insisted.

Maya grabbed Evaline's hand and led her quickly through the front door.

"You too!" she ordered, pushing Ellen rather roughly in the back.

Maya frog marched the little group, through the flower meadow and back to find the door. Through which they'd entered.

"Where is it?" Maya gasped with horror. Maya turned to Mischief. Her eyes now wide as two fried eggs, in alarm.

"Tell me, we're not too late?" Maya pleaded, her voice quivering with panic.

"No, don't worry my dear. Soon you'll not need a door at all, you'll just float through anything, like it's not even there," Ellen beamed encouragingly.

"Like a ghost!" Maya scolded. She was entering panic mode now.

"Calm down... there must be a way!" Mischief replied unconvincingly.

"Why don't you just wish for it... look," Evaline suggested, taking charge. "Doesn't this place grant your every wish?" she suggested, closing her eyes and concentrating hard.

As she did so, a door appeared, just to the right of them, straight in front of Evaline.

"See, told you!" Evaline gloated, smugly opening the door to reveal the portal beyond. "After you...," Evaline added, gesturing that Maya should lead the way.

"We owe you one," Maya sighed, stepping through the doorway with great relief. Only to reappear instantaneously again, as if coming from the other direction.

"Eh?" Maya exclaimed, confused and panicked.

"What?" Mischief added, then stepped into and straight back out of, the door himself.

"It's not real either!" Maya gasped.

"Mum?" Evaline cried, looking towards her mum for help.

"Don't worry my dear," Ellen replied, in a comforting voice. "Look, you're starting to fade too, just like me. Soon, you'll all be able to float right through, to the other side."

421

It was true. Evaline's right ear was missing. Maya looked down to where her hand should be. Mischief searched around for his tail and Evaline scanned the path behind... well, for her behind. None of them though, were where they should be anymore.

"No! Think Maya, think!" Maya scolded herself. The tip of her tongue came out, to help her focus. There was something not quite right here. Well, no, there were an awful lot of things that were not quite right now. But something else was bothering her.

"There's something...," Maya started. It was on the tip of her tongue. Which was rather unfortunate, as the tip of her tongue was now missing too!

"Think!" Maya scolded herself desperately, and Evaline too closed her remaining eye to concentrate.

"Brilliant Evaline!" Maya exclaimed. "This place, it's all an illusion, right?"

"We came in over here, didn't we? That door, it's in the wrong place? It's all just an illusion. Evaline wished it. It's no more real than the rest of this," Maya reasoned out loud.

"So?" the remaining parts of Mischief replied.

"So, close your eye and follow me!" Maya ordered, turning and walking straight into a tree.

"Ouch!" Maya screeched.

"Or here, ouch!" cried Evaline.

"Or here? Where our footprints came in maybe?" Maya grinned, with her three remaining teeth.

"If I still had lips and you humans weren't so damned ugly. I could kiss you!" Mischief's disembodied mouth replied, as he hobbled through the real, but invisible portal door, on all threes.

Parts of Maya and Evaline soon followed Mischief into the portal, then Ellen glided elegantly through the wall to join them... quite literally, as it turned out. She helped to join her daughter first.

Collecting the stray parts of Evaline and re-assembling them from head to foot. Then, she helped to disentangle the missing parts of Maya, that had finally decided to join them in the portal. Finally, Mischief was reunited with his front paw, tail and hind leg.

"I wish you'd pull yourself together Mischief!" Maya chortled.

Evaline was quiet though. Too quiet. No laughter... nothing. Not so much as a squeak.

"Evaline, what's wrong?" Maya asked, suddenly concerned for her friend. "Cat got your tongue?"

Evaline nodded.

"Oh, sorry!" replied Mischief, handing poor Evaline back her tongue, rather apologetically.

There was a final check around, for any further stray disembodied body parts. Which revealed, a pair of rather icky dangly things, which they all agreed were probably tonsils or an appendix or something and nobody was really going to miss them anyway. So, rather than risk installing an extra set of somethings, that might well belong to someone else, they resolved to leave them behind.

"Time to get out of here!" Maya announced.

"How, which way?" asked Mischief. After all, they were still hopelessly lost in Cruellen's portal. A myriad of tunnels greeted them in every direction.

"Follow Ellen!" Maya announced.

"What?" scoffed Mischief. "She's been lost in here for over six hundred years!"

"True, but this is her portal, so she's the only one, who can follow the right path, Maya announced. "Secondly, Evaline showed us how earlier, didn't you?"

"I did? Oh yes, I mean, no. I mean how?" Evaline stuttered.

"She has you. You're her happy thought. Hold her hand, tell her to close her eyes and think of you, back when she gave you the dragon's egg!" Maya suggested.

"No, that won't work. Not for my mum!" Evaline replied.

"Oh...," Maya looked a bit perplexed by Evaline's response.

Evaline smiled and turned to Ellen:

"Mum, close your eyes and remember when you took me on my first wild boar hunt. How it squealed, when I slit its..."

Maya covered her ears. This was a vision of a 'happy memory,' she knew, she could do without.

Evaline took Ellen by the hand, recounting blood curdling hunting tales, from her childhood. Ellen's ghost appeared less faint, stronger. It closed its eyes and smiled. Evaline stood aside and it was Ellen, who now led the way.

Left, left, left. At every branch, Ellen followed 'lucky left'. Every time that Ellen was confronted with a choice of passageways. After over six hundred years, Ellen finally knew the way out.

Evaline finally stopped recounting her hunting stories, but Ellen had her daughter now. She had a purpose again and now led the way with new found confidence. Maya though, kept her fingers in her ears. She could tell by the annoyingly smug look on Evaline's face, exactly what she was saying.

"Lucky left, lucky left... ooh and again, surprise, surprise... lucky left!" Evaline called, gloating at Maya and Mischief in turn.

One more lucky left and they came upon a 'witch-flap,' as Maya called them. Finally, the exit. Relief and elation though, were rapidly extinguished, by the realisation of what, or rather who, now awaited them, beyond this door.

Evaline pushed open the 'witch-flap' which screeched on rusty hinges. She led the way now, slowly, one small apprehensive step at a time, and the others followed her closely. Evaline stopped just a few steps in, to let her eyes adjust to the darkness that greeted them.

They were in a cave, cold and dank. Just like Evaline had seen through the hand mirror. Across the chamber a figure waited. She was unmistakeable.

Cruellen sat in the darkness of the cave, motionless and expressionless. Maya and her friends shuffled closer to each other for safety. Fang hissed towards Mischief, then crouched by Cruellen's side.

"Eveline my dear, I've been expecting you. Oh, but you do surprise me. I really didn't think there would be anything left of **that** pathetic creature left after all this time," Cruellen crackled.

"She's my mother, my real mother!" Evaline announced defiantly.

"It's too late for that feeble ghost," Cruellen taunted. "She's far too weak!"

425

Evaline squeezed Ellen's hand, but she feared Cruellen was right, Ellen was weak. She could feel it. This Ellen, was but a shadow, of the mother she'd once known.

"How can that wimp, ever help you fight Grim? You need my strength and power now, not her weakness! You might as well send her back to where she came from!" Cruellen scoffed.

"Okay mother!" Evaline agreed.

"What?" cried Maya.

But even as the words left Maya's lips, Evaline let go Ellen's hand and Ellen's ghost faded and was gone.

"I told you we couldn't trust her," sneered Mischief.

"No!" came a despairing cry from Cruellen. It echoed around the cave.

Ellen's spirit, all the good that was ever in her heart, was indeed gone forever. Just as Cruellen had predicted... gone back to where it belonged. Back, not into the maze of her portal, but back to where it really belonged...

"No!" another anguished cry reverberated around the cave, as Ellen's ghost plunged into Cruellen's cold broken heart. "What have you done? You fool, you've sealed your own friend's fate!"

Cruellen let out a final anguished cry, then Ellen and Cruellen were re-united once again.

A high price to pay

Ellen or Cruellen?

Who was it, that now confronted them? It was difficult to say. Cruellen looked no different. Evaline and her mother just exchanged suspicious glances. They were obviously still uneasy and distrustful in each-others company. Maybe there really wasn't enough of Ellen left, or maybe, as Evaline had often explained, Ellen had never been the most tender and maternal of mothers. Either way, there was certainly no soppy, tear-filled, mother-daughter reunion on display.

It was left to Maya, to break the long and uncomfortable silence:

"So, now you're re-united with your better half. Will you help us?"

Maya couldn't quite believe it herself. She was actually offering Cruellen a second chance. Asking for her help. Maya's mind took her back to the last time they'd met. Cruellen's haunting and venomous last words to her, all those months before:

"Mark my words, this is not the end! I did this for you, for all of you. **He** will come... and when that day comes, you will be the ones who come grovelling to me for help. You'll see!"

It had come true. Here they were, asking Cruellen for her help, just as she had foretold. Now at least they knew who "He" was. But would and could Cruellen help them now?

Cruellen nodded reluctantly.

"Okay mother, time to spill the beans. How do we beat him?" Evaline demanded, finally breaking her silence.

Cruellen cleared her throat. She really didn't sound like herself, she sounded exhausted and suddenly less certain of herself, as she spoke:

"Since we last crossed wands my dear, I've been studying the legends of Death's staff and the living wand. Grim made a deal with Death, now he carries Death's staff, in exchange for rounding up the living, long before their time."

"Go on, we know that much already," Evaline encouraged her mother cautiously.

"There's a balance to all things, my dear," Cruellen started to explain. "As we live, so must we die. Our food brings us life, but that same food, is only on our plate through the passing of another life force, whether animal or vegetable. So, it is with magic, there can be no good magic, without its darker side. Death's staff is a guardian of the dark side. Your friend's living wand, is a guardian of the light. A sapling, a seedling of the mother tree, mother nature herself. The bringer of life and renewal. Grim carries Death's scythe, the bringer of death and destruction."

"Very interesting," scoffed Mischief, "but how exactly does that help us defeat Grim?"

"The only magic that can match Death's staff, is that of the living wand and that's why I wanted it so badly," Cruellen explained. "I had to stop him... at any cost."

"Even your own daughter's life?" Maya challenged.

"Yes, even that! And I'd gladly do it again, to stop Grim," Cruellen confirmed unrepentantly, looking Evaline straight in the eye. "You've not yet seen the horrors he's capable of!"

"This is your mum with her tender side restored?" Mischief scoffed.

428

"You should catch her on a bad day!" Evaline replied coldly.

Cruellen continued undeterred:

"But I was wrong. Having chosen my path. I could never wield its great power. She was right about that, your little friend. Now, it can only be Maya."

"Good! I'm glad you've learned your lesson," Mischief rebuked her.

"Ha!" laughed Cruellen. "You may change your mind rather quickly, my furry friend!"

"Why?" Evaline asked suspiciously.

"There is a problem, a small technicality, you might say," Cruellen joked. "The price for returning Grim and his army to where they came from, is high indeed."

"Go on," Evaline encouraged Cruellen, apprehensively.

"Man has knocked the delicate balance of nature out. Greed for the world's resources has led to global warming and with that Grim's release from his prison in the icy wastes of the north. The scales have now been tipped to the dark side and Grim knows that he now has the edge," Cruellen paused for breath. She was old now, and clearly exhausted by the exertion of being re-united with her other half.

"He has released his dark forces, his dragon army into the living realm. But his dragons are dead, dead spirits of dark magic dragons long passed. That's why no magic from this realm, can touch them. They are not of this realm, they have crossed over and so they cannot be defeated from here," Cruellen explained, without showing any emotion.

"What? What's the point of all this then?" Maya cried in disbelief.

Cruellen laughed heartily and looked Maya straight in the eye, sounding much more like her old self:

"That's the rub. The price that must be paid, my dear. In order to defeat Grim, not only must the witch have great power and wield the living wand, as you do, but it can only be done from their realm."

"You don't mean...?" Mischief couldn't finish his sentence.

"Oh," Maya mumbled meekly. She had hoped that Cruellen's earlier assertion, that she must die, had just been to torment her. An act of revenge.

"Yes, I'm afraid so. She must die," Cruellen seemed to relish the misery that her words brought. "Only when facing death in that realm, can she cast a spell to return Grim and his army back to the spirit realm. Only then, can she restore the balance of nature once again."

"Oh, is that all?" Maya replied, her voice wavering. "I thought it might be tricky."

"No, my dear. I'm afraid, it's not that easy," Cruellen scoffed.

"Easy?" Maya whimpered.

"No, you see, for it to work, in order for you to send Grim back. When you cast the spell, you'll have to be in his presence when you die," Cruellen explained calmly.

"No!" cried Evaline. She knew only too well, what that meant.

Mischief opened his mouth, but he couldn't find the words.

"Oh, is that all," Maya quivered. "Face the Reaper, let him kill me, in whatever horrible way he sees fit. Face down Death himself, then cast the most powerful spell ever cast and then what?"

"Then, my dear, you can rest in peace. Happy in the knowledge that your untold suffering and sacrifice has saved my bacon!" Cruellen scoffed.

"Don't even think about trusting her! It's a trap!" Mischief exploded with venom. "She's... she's sold you out... to... to Grim, just to save her own skin!"

Mischief could hardly speak, he stuttered over his own words. Maya had never seen him so angry.

"She's played us all, right from the very start!" that's Cruellen not Ellen speaking. She's not changed. Her obedient daughter saw to that. She just let Ellen go. Released her other half back into the portal! Tell me you see that?" Mischief continued, glaring accusingly at Evaline. "I saw you go back into that room with Ellen, in that portal. You lied about your laces, why? Who really came out, Evaline or Evil-in-Deed? Mummy's little girl! She's in on this too!"

Evaline just glared.

"I wish I had a choice," Maya conceded sadly.

"What do you mean?" Mischief pleaded.

"How can I not do what she says? What else can I do? We have to stop Grim," Maya replied despairingly.

"Give Cruellen to Grim? Make a deal," Mischief pleaded, raising his paw to point towards Cruellen. "I don't know, there must be another way, surely?"

"You don't really think, that he's the type to stick to a bargain, do you?" Cruellen scoffed.

"No, you can't!" Mischief insisted. "Why you... why do you have to...?" But the poor cat was far too upset. He couldn't even finish his own sentence.

"Mum, Emma, Aunty Dot, Aunty Helen, Bandit, not to mention all my friends, the covens and perhaps even magic itself," Maya replied softly, with an air of resignation in her voice. "He'll never stop! He'll lay waste to the whole world!"

"He's right you know," Evaline intervened. "You can't trust her. She knows what Grim will do to her. She'll say or do anything, just to save her own skin!"

"Evaline my dear," Cruellen crowed, with a sarcastic smile. "How hurtful!"

"What choice do I have?" Maya whimpered. It was clearly getting to Maya now. Nobody had ever divulged the tortures, that Grim had in store for them. But the very thought of them, was enough to drive most of them out of their minds. How could she ever hope to cast the most powerful spell of her life, after Grim had taken out his gruesome revenge on her?" Tears ran down her cheeks and Maya's whole body started to shake visibly.

Mischief could see that Maya was losing the place.

"No!" Mischief insisted. "There's another way. There has to be and we're going to figure this out together. It's what we do!"

"What he said!" Evaline chipped in.

Maya managed a half smile, from somewhere.

Cruellen stood and shuffled her way slowly across the cave, towards her daughter. Maya needed time to herself and Mischief sensed an awkward, mother and daughter moment coming up. So, Mischief broke off, leading Maya away, as if to explore the cave, to give them time to gather their thoughts. Everyone needed some space right now. Mischief though, was very careful not to turn his back on Cruellen, nor on Evaline.

It was an unremarkable cave. Well, all except for the wibbly-wabbly magical portal, which glistened in the corner. The walls ran with water, which percolated through the sandstone roof. Moss grew up the walls from a sandy floor. The cave was warm enough, but cold shadows leapt out from every corner and crevice. Its confines, illuminated only by the dim orange light from the dying embers of Cruellen's fire. A couple of large church candles lit the far side and dripped into large wax accumulations, which rose like stalagmites, from the rocky cave floor.

"It's just the sort of place you'd expect her to keep a giant pet spider or arachnoscorpus," whispered Mischief, trying to lighten the mood.

"You're very perceptive," Cruellen replied. "He's over there in the shadows and very hungry, name's Fred and he likes cats!"

"Ears like a bat that one," scoffed Mischief.

They strongly suspected Cruellen was joking, but Mischief decided not to chance it. He could tell that Maya needed a few moments, to gather her thoughts. Maya took a deep breath, then asked the question that Mischief was dreading the most. Although he knew in his heart, it was coming:

"If it comes to it, you know, with Grim. Can I count on you to be 'merciful'?"

Mischief moved in for a cuddle, as Maya's tears came rolling down her cheeks.

"Promise me you won't let him take me alive," Maya snuffled. Hiding her face from Cruellen.

"I promise, little one," Mischief agreed reluctantly.

Cruellen now looked Evaline in the eye.

"I have to hand it to her, your friend has guts Evaline," Cruellen whispered to her daughter.

Evaline wasn't sure how to take this from her mother. Ellen or Cruellen, neither of them ever had any time for small talk, sentiment or even good manners, when she thought on it. Evaline wasn't even sure, that this was her mother speaking and not the shell of humanity, that Cruellen had become.

"Yes, she has!" Evaline replied proudly.

"Just make sure you're not in the way, when Grim spills them tonight!" Cruellen added coldly, as she turned away once more.

Evaline just glared at her mother, with horrified eyes. Even for Cruellen, that was brutal.

"You must go now, it's nearly time," Cruellen announced, suddenly raising her voice, for all to hear.

"Time for what?" Evaline asked. "We've only just got here!"

"He's coming for you on the stroke of midnight, and you'll need to be ready for him," Cruellen demanded coldly. She turned to face Evaline, as if she was a general, addressing her troops:

"Go now. Go and get ready, all of you. You know what must be done. Get your heads around it, go over your plan again and again, like true warriors going into battle. You must all be prepared. All know what part you have to play. You must be ready for him, when he comes. You'll only get one chance at this!"

It was like they were being put on a war footing by the enemy. She sounded convincing though, as if she'd been planning this for a very, very long time.

"You must travel back through my portal, so that the death dragons don't sense you," Cruellen continued.

434

Mischief looked up despairingly towards Maya, "Tell me you're not going along with this, please?"

"What choice do we have?" Maya snuffled back.

Cruellen was taking charge now. Dishing out the orders, like she was the High Priestess of her own coven again, and they were her latest reluctant recruits.

"I can't follow you that way, I must stay in the magic realm. You'll need my magic against Grim. I'll make my own way home, to our island and try my best to get past his dragons. Watch for me on the other side of the river and send the boat for me," Cruellen instructed.

"You're not really considering listening to a word that she says, are you?" Mischief pleaded once more.

"What's the alternative?" Maya found herself saying. She couldn't believe it. She was actually considering following Cruellen's plan.

Maya and Evaline looked at each other for reassurance.

"It has to be your call, Maya. Do we do what she says?" Evaline asked reluctantly.

Maya couldn't bring herself to answer. She paused, then looked down towards Mischief. Then, she looked Cruellen in the eye, then finally back, once more to Evaline. She thought on the sacrifice her own mother had made, trying to save Granny. On how the merciful few would sacrifice themselves, for their family and loved ones. She would be proud to be counted amongst their ranks.

Maya nodded.

"Good!" replied Cruellen, before clearing her throat, with a dry cough and continuing with her demands:

"You can return through my portal. It's not yours, so you'll still be in the magic realm on the other side, and believe me, the pair of you are going to need all the magic and courage you can muster tonight, when you face Grim!"

Maya, Evaline and Mischief started to make their way slowly and sombrely, towards the wibbly-wabbly portal, through which they had only just entered.

There was not so much as a goodbye or a good luck from Cruellen. Not even, as she watched her daughter leave to face Grim. Ellen or Cruellen? None of them were really sure, perhaps not even Cruellen herself. But one thing was certain, she had retained all of her previous lack of social skills and grace. She was a witch, who really didn't go in for small talk.

Evaline led the way through the portal. It was lighter and less intimidating than before. Maybe some of Ellen had got into Cruellen, after all?

Evaline had her happy memory, her hatchling dragon and she focussed on that. She knew the way now and walked confidently at first. Soon though, Evaline's stride lengthened. Suddenly, she picked up the pace once more, then broke into a panicked run. Maya and Mischief accelerated too, then started to run quickly behind her, as more and more dark passageways opened up, to each side of them. Each looked much darker and much more foreboding, than the one before.

Evaline was clearly losing focus on her happy memories and darker thoughts were taking hold. With a final gamble on 'lucky left,' Evaline burst through the full-length mirror and back into the magic room at Threave castle.

"What's wrong?" Maya panted, struggling to catch her breath and to keep up with her fleeing friend. Evaline didn't answer.

Maya was the one with the death sentence hanging over her, but right now, Evaline was the one who appeared more upset. She wasn't normally the emotional sort either, but Evaline just slumped to the floor, with both hands clasped tightly over her face. She was beside herself, shaking uncontrollably in fear and anguish. Evaline's world too, now seemingly collapsing all around her. Just when she thought she might have some hope, a chance for a little happiness in her life. A chance of redemption for her mother. A chance to get Ellen back and put Cruellen behind her. Now, the horror of Maya's impending fate, had brought with it, a realisation that she had been trying hopelessly to suppress.

"The prophecy, his curse... it's all coming true," Evaline whispered.

Maya and Mischief exchanged worried glances.

"It's my destiny, my fate; to *deliver Grim the living wand over the body of his greatest foe!*" Evaline cried with anguish.

"But...," but Maya had no words of comfort for her. She was right of course. Grim's curse was coming true.

"It means that I'll be the one to kill you!" Evaline delivered her cruel conclusion, whilst looking straight into the eyes of her friend. "I really will become Evil Indeed!"

Maya nodded and smiled. It was really not the reaction, that Evaline had anticipated.

"If it has to happen. I'd be honoured, if you would do it!" Maya replied.

Maya moved in for the inevitable hug.

"Besides, you'll be letting Mischief off the hook!" Maya snuffled through the tears. "He's not really the merciful type."

The girls hugged it out. There was nothing else for it. It went on for an age. It was difficult to let go, but eventually the tears subsided and a new emotion came to the fore.

Determination.

They all resolved, that they weren't going to take this lying down.

Instead, they sat! Mischief sat them down in a circle, like a furry general, ready to divulge his strategy and organise his troops.

"We can do this! All for one and one for all, as a wise cat once said!" the little cat announced, offering his paw up, for a fist pump.

Obediently, the girls leaned in and reciprocated. And so, their plotting and planning began.

"We could...," Mischief stuttered unconvincingly.

"Or... no, that won't work either," Mischief added after a few seconds. It wasn't an inspiring start.

Evaline just shrugged her shoulders. She had nothing either.

Mischief turned towards Maya. She looked distant, deep in thought, her tongue was poking through her lips, twitching like an earthworm, split in two by a garden spade. He recognised the signs. Was she onto something? Hopefully? Possibly?

They sat in silence. Seconds turned to minutes and, as the light faded, so did Evaline and Mischief's spirits. Still Maya said nothing. Her tongue continued to flicker between her lips, as if attached to every thought, which leapt randomly into her head.

Finally, it was Maya who broke the silence;

"We're going to need a mirror, a plant pot. Oh, and some soil!" Maya announced suddenly.

"What?" Mischief and Evaline asked in unison.

"If we're going to face the Grim Reaper tonight, then we need a mirror, a plant pot and some soil!" Maya repeated.

Evaline obliged, drawing her wand without further question. She conjured an old-fashioned, hand-crafted terracotta pot, filled with soil.

"This do?" Evaline enquired.

"Excellent, but we'll need some water too," Maya replied.

"Well, I do need to, you know? I could always...?" Mischief started.

"No, thank you, just water!" Maya rebuked him, before he could finish.

"And the mirror, what about the mirror?" Maya asked.

"That do?" suggested Evaline, pointing to the full-length mirror which concealed Cruellen's portal.

"Yes, but help me move it closer to the door. When Grim comes down those steps, I need to be able to see his reflection clearly," Maya explained.

Evaline helped Maya to drag the heavy wooden frame across the uneven stone floor towards the doorway, until Maya was nearly happy with its position.

"Left a little," Maya prompted.

"Lucky left, I hope!" Evaline added, as Maya gave her the thumbs up sign.

"Okay, spill the beans. A mirror, why a mirror?" Mischief announced.

439

"Why a mirror? Never mind the mirror... why a plant pot?" Evaline demanded.

Maya just grinned.

"I need to have a word with a very good friend of mine first, before I divulge that one, I'm afraid, but I will tell you about the mirror," Maya said softly.

"Grim will come tonight. But we **will** be ready for him. We need him to come here, right here, to this very spot," Maya announced, pointing to a spot at the bottom of the stairs directly in front of the mirror.

"What are you up to, little one?" asked Mischief curiously.

"Just like Cruellen, we know Grim's cunning too. He'll suspect a trap. He knows we have Spell. A living wand, the only thing powerful enough to send him back. So, he'll be wary."

"Go on," Mischief encouraged.

"So, when the time comes, if we believe what Cruellen said, about him needing to be present, when the spell is cast. We must know that it's really him. He still needs to be here when my spell is cast from beyond. Or it will all be for nothing," Maya explained, with a lump in her throat.

"He is pretty distinctive you know!" Mischief observed.

"True, but Grim was a powerful sorcerer, right?" Maya asked, without waiting for an answer. "So, he could disguise himself as anyone or anything. Even one of us or send someone else, disguised as himself, to do his dirty work. We have to be a hundred percent sure, that it's really him."

Evaline and Mischief nodded their agreement. It made sense.

"That means no splitting up either, not even for a second!" Maya warned.

However, Mischief was the one who now looked concerned.

"But, but I really do need to, you know... go!" Mischief protested with genuine alarm.

Evaline snorted in a rather undignified manner, at his expense, before she too realised that her back teeth were beginning to float.

"That's what the pot of soil's for, isn't it?" Mischief suggested, once more.

"No! You keep away from that!" Maya snapped. She was most insistent on that point, for some reason.

"We probably all need to go, but we can't take our eyes off each other, not for a second. So, I suggest we all... you know?" Maya blushed.

"What?" Evaline screwed up her face.

"I think she means, pick a window," Mischief suggested.

Maya didn't have to reply.

Nobody said anything else. They would never talk of this moment again, but as a dragon flew in silently and landed on the far bank. Its rider got a view of the castle, that it really wasn't expecting!

Necessary bodily functions attended to, they returned to their plotting. Maya lifted her living wand towards the strategically positioned mirror.

"Show the true nature of any who approach!" Maya commanded. A little blue light shone from the top of Spell, as the incantation was cast, upon Cruellen's portal mirror.

"Cunning!" Evaline acknowledged.

"She has a degree in cunning, from the University of Cunning, a BSc, I believe!" announced Mischief proudly.

"A BSc? What's that? A bachelorette of scheming?" Evaline jibed.

"I think it's more likely to be a bronze swimming certificate!" scoffed Mischief.

"And the plant pot?" Evaline enquired.

"Oh yes, give me a minute," Maya made her way to the corner of the room, with Spell cradled in her arms. Maya was clearly doing all the talking, as if starting her final goodbyes.

"Give them a moment," Mischief suggested.

"Oh, okay," Evaline replied, rather sheepishly.

"Bong!" the distinctive peel of the water taxi bell, rang out from across the river.

Hearts leapt into mouths.

"So soon?" Maya whispered under her breath. She knew now, only too well, for whom that bell tolled.

Maya took a few more moments to herself, then pulled Evaline to one side. She held Evaline at arms-length, by the shoulders and stared straight into her eyes.

"You know it's okay. I'm counting on you. Make it quick, don't linger, don't give him a chance to trick us. As soon as we know its him, I'll have one last spell, to say how I'll meet my fate... then, well, you know," Maya spoke firmly, yet reassuringly.

Mischief could tell that the girls needed a moment together, for a girly goodbye. Something that he really couldn't face. He knew that

442

Maya already knew how he felt. He couldn't stomach all that gushy stuff and anyway, he didn't have the words to express it.

There was a long exchange of barely audible snuffling noises and reassuring hugs, from which Maya suddenly broke off. Without another word, Maya led the way.

"Come on, stick together!" Maya ordered, as if they were heading out on a girl guides' field trip.

They made their way cautiously down the spiral staircase and out of the castle walls, onto the long-mown grass that carpeted the little island. It was a still night. The sky was clear and full of stars. Maya felt alive, very alive. All her senses heightened, every insect, every star, every blade of grass or tree she noticed every detail, as if it might be her last.

Maya led them slowly across the lawn and down a path to the jetty, where the little rowboat was tied up. On the far bank stood the unmistakeable figure of Cruellen, silhouetted against the rising moon. Her dragon had settled on a sturdy wooden post, to rest. Above her, perched in the trees, a pair of death dragons snoozed, with their heads tucked under tattered wings.

Maya untied the boat and with a swish of Spell and a flash of magical light, she sent the water taxi silently and speedily over to the other side, across the calm black waters. A tail slap in the water close-by, betrayed a mother otter, diving for fish in the open channel, just upstream.

"Are you sure about this little one?" Mischief asked, his voice clearly breaking with emotion.

"No!" Maya replied sheepishly. It felt like she was basting herself with turkey gravy and inviting a hungry wolf across for Christmas dinner.

The rowboat made it to the far bank, halting with a dull thud against the pier. Cruellen climbed carefully into the boat and waited for Maya to summon it back, not daring to use her own magic from this side of the river, for fear she might awaken Grim's sleeping beasties.

Maya raised Spell once more, her light blinding in the night sky. With that, the little boat, with Cruellen on board, slid silently through the waters again, back towards them. Maya and Mischief stood their ground, while Evaline went to help her mother from the small craft, as it made land.

Evaline held out her hand and Cruellen grasped it firmly, to steady herself, as she stepped back onto dry land.

"Thank you my dear," Cruellen spoke quietly. "Never did care for running water."

Evaline recoiled, like the touch of her own mother's hand, had sent a shiver up her spine.

"Welcome home," Mischief greeted her, through clenched teeth.

"Ready to die my dear?" Cruellen taunted, in Maya's direction.

"Are you?" Maya bit back, tightening her grasp on Spell.

Cruellen just laughed.

"This way," Mischief gestured.

"I know the way cat," Cruellen replied dismissively.

"Don't turn your back on her!" Mischief warned.

Maya moved aside and Cruellen led the way.

Time slowed for Maya now, as they walked back to the castle. She was aware of her own breath, her heartbeat, the faint flutter of bats on the hunt in the night air around them. It wasn't cold, but she couldn't stop shaking. She knew just how all those other poor witches felt, knowing the time of their fate. She could understand all too well, how it could drive them to madness. At least, if things went to plan tonight, she had chosen how she would meet her fate and Evaline would spare her, Grim's cruel torture.

Maya's heart missed a beat, as she entered the castle over the wooden bridge. Was that really the last time she would feel the grass beneath her feet? Was this really the last star-lit sky, that she would ever see? Her last glimpse of the stars, the moon? She turned briefly to look back at the moon. Big bright and more vivid in the night sky, than she had ever noticed before. Now, she appreciated how beautiful it was. Why now? Why only now?

Maya stopped herself. She was scared, who wouldn't be? But she had to focus now. Focus on her plan and have her wits about her, when Grim finally showed up. When he made an appearance, they all had to be ready for him. They had one chance. No mistakes.

Cruellen led the way up the spiral staircase and into the magic room. They passed the keystone glowing in its receptacle, just as they'd left it. Up Cruellen climbed, not even stopping to catch her breath. She was in surprisingly good shape for an old woman.

As they reached the top of the stairs, Maya's grip on Spell tightened. Spell's roots squeezed back comfortingly. Cruellen hesitated in front of the door, just shy of the mirror.

Maya closed the gap and looked past the old witch, for her reflection in the mirror. There was none.

Of course, there wasn't one... dark witches lose their reflection, whenever they lose their souls.

"How stupid of me!" Maya mumbled to herself. But there was something, an outline, a faint reflection... like Ellen's ghost.

445

Evaline was behind her and saw it too. Ellen's ghost even appeared to crack a smile. Maybe there was some hope for Cruellen after all?

Cruellen entered the room, scanning the new décor of scatter cushions and soft furnishings, that Maya and Evaline had introduced, with obvious disdain.

"Well, are you ready?" Cruellen asked.

Maya was about to answer, but Evaline beat her to it.

"Yes, I'm ready," she replied.

Mischief gave Maya a rather confused and suspicious glance, as Evaline suddenly moved to take up a position immediately behind Maya's back.

"How will you meet your fate?" demanded Cruellen.

"Really not one for small-talk, are you?" Mischief noted sarcastically. But the way his voice broke at the end, betrayed his anguish.

Maya raised Spell slowly, her eyes fixed lovingly on Mischief.

"If I'm going to die tonight, when Grim comes. When I go, to the afterlife. I think I'd like to be a cat! My spirit animal, my faithful guide in this life and into the next Mischief," Maya announced quietly.

With a final smile to Mischief, she closed her eyes and cast a transformation spell.

"Good choice," Mischief wept.

Evaline said nothing. She showed no emotion. She simply raised her wand and pointed it towards Maya's furry back.

"No! Not now!" cried Mischief in horror. "It's no use without Grim. You have to wait for Grim!"

But it was too late. Evaline's face had changed, there was only darkness in her eyes now. Mischief watched in terror as...

Evil Indeed cast the death spell:

"Mortify!"

Maya died instantly. Her crumpled furry feline body, fell to the floor lifeless. Spell too, burst into flames, for as a living wand, she too fell to the power of the death spell.

It was all over. Maya's final adventure had come to an end.

"No," whimpered Mischief. "How could I ever have trusted you?" cursed Mischief. "Like mother, like daughter! How could I have been so stupid?"

"Well done my daughter," Cruellen spoke with gloating pride, but it was not Cruellen's voice that spoke. Cruellen's face melted away slowly to darkness.

Her long turquoise robe, now transformed into a soot black cloak and her High Priestess's staff, unfolded slowly into a scythe. The Grim Reaper himself, now looked down at Maya's body, still holding the charred remnants of Spell.

The curse had come true. They'd all been duped. Grim's prophecy had been realised. First, Evaline had betrayed and banished her own mother. Now, the second half of his curse had come to pass as well. Evaline stood over the body of her best friend. Grim's greatest foe. Evil Indeed had delivered Grim the charred remains of the living wand. Grim was invincible now.

Grim had won!

For whom the bell tolls

The peel of the water taxi bell rang out once more, from the other bank of the river.

Grim laughed cruelly.

"That bell now tolls for your mother, Evaline my dear. She waits on the far bank for you, as we speak," Grim chuckled. "Fetch her to me, my obedient daughter. Then, you will behold my vengeance and it will be terrible!"

"How could you? Evil Indeed is right!" Mischief hissed, with fury in his voice. "You betrayed Maya. Your best friend! I knew you were up to something in that portal... you went back into that room, I saw you. You gave in to its temptations. You lost yourself in there, didn't you?"

Evil Indeed just smiled cruelly down at him and laughed.

"Just like your mother!" Mischief scolded.

"Your friend was lucky!" Grim now turned his attentions to Mischief. "A quick death! No witch or their cats will ever be that lucky again. They will all pay for their betrayal!"

"At least Maya was spared your torment," Mischief conceded sadly.

"Well not that lucky actually," Grim gloated.

"What do you mean? She's at rest now, even you can't touch her!" Mischief replied defiantly.

"No, she'll not get off that lightly, my furry little friend," Grim taunted. "She may be dead now, but let's just say Death owes me a few favours!"

448

"What have you done?" Mischief demanded, his eyes wild with rage and anxiety.

"She won't escape that easily, in fact, she'll never escape," Grim chuckled. "There may be a small clerical error on the other side, you see."

Mischief glared at Grim in horror.

"You see, at this moment, a seemingly kindly Death, in a fine white robe, smelling of rose and jasmine, will be escorting your friend with her fine not very living wand, gently through a beautiful inviting door. A door that, oops, because of some inexplicable error... now leads to eternal damnation. A door that will bring her and that wand of hers to my side, as weapons of the dark side!" gloated Grim.

"No, no, no," Mischief whimpered, burying his head in his paws.

Evil Indeed crossed the room towards the staircase, as if setting off to fetch her own mother, to meet the grizzly end which now awaited her. She stopped and paused by the window, overlooking the river. There on the other bank, the real Cruellen waited impatiently, beside the bell. Oblivious of the horrific fate which now awaited her.

A death dragon launched into the air, from its perch above her. Then another and another. They started to circle, as if called upon by Grim, to fly a victorious lap of honour.

Mischief turned to face Grim, his face had changed.

"Don't be so sure you've won," Mischief said defiantly. "Maya will stop you. She'll find a way!"

"What from beyond the grave?" Grim laughed heartily.

"Exactly!" Mischief barked back, in a very un-cat-like manner.

"No Mischief," Evil Indeed turned and spoke coldly. "Why should she even try? She had no idea that Grim was ever even here tonight. I saw to that."

Grim was obviously revelling in the moment, observing:

"She's very 'good' isn't she? I'm afraid that unless your pathetic little friend can rise from the dead, like a phoenix from the ashes, then she too, will soon bow down before me!"

Once more, Evil Indeed stared out the window expectantly, as if she was looking for something. Around the castle, the dark shadows of the death dragons circled through the night sky, like the harbingers of doom, announcing the dawn of a new and terrible age of terror.

There was a strange and eerie silence, then a dull thud, like a far-off explosion. Magic crackled through the air, as if unleashed by some unearthly and powerful spell. Without warning one of the death dragons fell from the sky. Its wings seemingly crumpled beneath it, then another, and another. Plunging earthward, then fading inexplicably from view, before they hit the ground.

"Not so much a phoenix father," Evil Indeed smirked. "But, perhaps a cat?"

"What?" Grim boomed.

"A witch's cat, you know, one with nine lives, that might just do the trick, don't you think?" Evaline smiled.

"What have you done child?" Grim boomed. His skeletal face turning in that moment from a cruel satisfied grin, to one of shock. Rage, terrible rage now took over, written large across his bony features.

"No!" he cried again, "What have you done?" as he too started to evaporate in front of their eyes. The horrified hooded figure, soon disappeared completely from view. Grim was gone.

"What?" gasped Mischief.

Eveline walked purposefully towards the body of the cat which lay in the middle of the room. She bent over Maya cat's furry body and stroked it gently on the flank. The cat's whiskers twitched and the fragile feline form convulsed suddenly and drew a fresh breath.

"Welcome back my frienemy!" Evaline laughed, extending Maya cat her hand. Maya cat raised her furry head from the floor. Slowly and unsteadily, she got up onto all fours. When upright, she transformed herself into human form once more and grasped Evaline's hand, to steady herself.

"What?" Mischief gasped again, clearly confused, delighted and outraged in equal measures. "But she killed you!"

"Sorry Mischief! We needed you to be convincing," Maya apologised, picking up her feline side-kick, for a long overdue cuddle.

"But...?" Mischief was speechless for once.

Maya reckoned, she owed poor Mischief an explanation. Not least, to save Evaline from his continuing suspicious dagger-like glances.

"If Cruellen's research was right, I had to die in the presence of Grim himself, so that I could send him back. So, we reckoned that he was never going to show up here, not in his own cowardly skin anyway, was he?" Maya explained.

"But what made you think you could ever trust Cruellen?" Mischief pleaded.

"Simple, her neck was on the line too!" Evaline replied. "My mother has very clear priorities!"

"Hmm," Mischief conceded, still casting suspicious looks in Evaline's direction. "But how did you know it wasn't really Cruellen?"

Evaline blushed visibly. Mischief still didn't trust her. Even now, he could tell that she was still hiding something.

Maya answered for her:

"You see... we knew Grim would set us a trap, he would try to deceive us somehow. Either in this realm or in his own. Most probably both!" Maya paused for breath.

"You heard me ask Evaline to make it quick, not to give Grim time to trick us. But what you didn't hear, was me asking her to play along with Grim's plan."

"Eh?" Mischief gasped, still clearly bemused by what had just happened.

"She had to pretend that she'd turned to the dark side and betrayed me. It was the only way, that she was ever going to gain his trust. He had to feel invincible." Maya explained proudly. "We had to keep him here, just long enough to give me time to cast the spell from the other side. So, you really had to be convincing too, I'm afraid."

"Sorry Mischief," Evaline smiled, in a way that he wasn't quite sure how to take.

"I may forgive you one day, I suppose," Mischief conceded. "But what a price to pay!"

"It wasn't that bad?" Maya replied thoughtfully. "Although that death spell of hers stung, like a jet-propelled porcupine in the butt!"

"Death, not that bad?" Mischief sounded bemused. "Grim said that Death himself was going to escort you to eternal damnation! How did you wriggle out of that one?"

"I didn't have to," Maya replied. "Maybe the Death you meet, depends on how you've lived your life? I'm not sure, but I felt only a deep and reassuring warmth, as my spirit animal greeted me on the other side. It gently suggested that it wasn't my time yet, nor Spell's. So, Spell helped me cast the most powerful incantation we have ever produced; one to return Grim and all his death dragons back to their own realm. To restore the balance of nature once more."

"Spell! Poor Spell!" Mischief gasped suddenly. "I forgot. She's burnt to a crisp! Spell didn't have nine witches' cats' lives up her sleeve, did she?"

Mischief stared despairingly down at the cinders still strewn on the floor, where the brave little wand had fallen.

"No," Maya said sadly, with a mischievous glint in her eye. "But then again, she didn't need them."

"Eh?" Mischief responded, looking even more confused than before.

"She had something better!" Maya beamed.

"What?" Mischief demanded, clearly getting sick of the intrigue.

"A plant pot, some soil and a good sprinkling of water! Just water!" Maya laughed, gesturing towards the windowsill.

Mischief pirouetted around, to see a rather smaller, but unmistakeable looking wand twig, planted in an old-fashioned terracotta plant pot. Spell (junior) was now proudly taking a bow and waving its only remaining leaf in Mischief's, rather gob-smacked direction.

"You took a cutting! Mischief beamed, with obvious delight. "Cunning as an honorary witch's cat!" I salute you all!"

Maya, Spell and Evaline took a spontaneous and well-earned bow.

"So, Grim and all his death dragons are back where they belong and can never return," Maya announced with a broad grin. "And I rather suspect, that now he's broken his bargain with Death. I don't think Death's going to be too pleased with poor old Archibald the Grim!"

But something was still bothering Mischief.

"Hmm… all very clever, but Evaline… when you fired, how did you know it was really Grim and not your mother? We all saw her partial reflection in the mirror. It showed her ghost, her good side, Ellen. How did you know that it was really Grim?" Mischief quizzed.

"Ah, I'm glad you asked that!" lied Evaline, her crimson face betraying her reluctance to be quizzed on the subject.

"Yes, Evaline… he had me fooled too," confessed Maya.

"Well, yes eh…," stuttered Evaline uncomfortably. "Grim was a powerful warlock. He'd have the power to disguise himself, so that we'd see only what we expected to see in Cruellen's reflection. He must have anticipated our plan, when he saw the mirror."

"Yes, we'd figured that out for ourselves, but how did **you** know at the time?" Mischief pressed once more. "You did choose to kill her after all… how could you have been that sure?"

454

"I'm really not sure you want to know," pleaded Evaline.

"No, no I think I really would like to know," Maya insisted with a growingly suspicious scowl.

"Well, it was when I helped Cruellen out of the boat," Evaline confessed rather sheepishly:

"She said thanks."

"So?" Mischief demanded after a long pause.

"So, well, em, er, well, that is to say," Evaline stumbled over every word, she really wasn't saying.

"Well?" Mischief pressed again.

"My mum. She was never that polite! Not even when she was just Ellen. She never said please, or thank you. Not like a well brought up Laird of Galloway, pretending to be someone else, might do. So... I kinda had a hunch, that possibly, maybe she might not be who she seemed."

"You gambled Maya's life and eternal damnation on a hunch?" Mischief cried in horror. "Remind me never to play you at poker!"

"Evaline!" Maya looked her square in the eye. "Don't you ever kill me again, please!"

"It's a deal!" Evaline replied, trying hard to muster a laugh.

***

They were all buzzing with excitement and adrenaline, so none of them slept a wink for the rest of the night. Not to mention that the opportunity to taunt Evaline mercilessly about her reckless gamble with Maya's life, or death, was just too good to miss.

Their sleepless night was sealed, when Evaline decided to retrieve her mother from the other bank. Nobody would dare to sleep, not when Cruellen was on the loose. But there was some progress. Maybe there was more of Ellen left, than they had all suspected. Evaline and Cruellen chatted away, all the way back across the river, in the little rowboat. It seemed civilised, almost normal. Unless they were mistaken, Cruellen even tried to smile at one point. Something, as Mischief was at pains to observe, her crooked teeth were never really designed for.

As they reached the island, Evaline put down the oars and hopped up onto the rickety wooden jetty. Evaline turned instinctively, to offer her mother a helping hand, up from the little row-boat, to steady the old woman.

"Why thank you my dear!" Cruellen responded graciously.

Maya and Mischief just glared.

"Evaline!!!" echoed through the fields, for miles in every direction. The earth shook and masonry crumbled from the highest tower of the castle.

"Oops!" cringed Evaline.

***

When morning finally broke, Maya fixed it with pancakes and chocolate spread. Then, rather reluctantly, she released Evaline from her bonds, in the torture chamber of her mother's portal. A facility which Cruellen had graciously allowed Maya and Mischief to confine Evaline in, the night before, after the now notorious 'row-boat' incident.

There was excitement too. At first light, they would all fly home. Maya couldn't wait to get back and check on her mum. Dad would be there too, she supposed. The girls mounted their dragons, on the grassy lawn outside the castle. The size of their grins reflected the anticipation and excitement they shared, at the prospect of returning home, once more.

At that moment though, all eyes were somehow drawn upwards. Out of the sun came a black winged shadow, silhouetted in the early morning light.

"No, no, no... not again!" cried Evaline despairingly. "It can't be!"

Closing at speed, incredible speed. Heading straight for them. On the shadow's back, a rider hunched forward, poised as if ready to attack. Hearts raced and wands were grasped quickly in defence. Suddenly, just short of the island, the dark figure reared up in front of them, spreading its terrifying and magnificent wings to halt its descent.

Evaline's drew her wand, the death spell ready on her lips once more, but this time not aimed at their attacker. If Grim had returned, she vowed there and then, that she would spare her friends his cruel revenge. She would do the merciful thing.

Maya raised her rather unimpressive twiglet wand, Spell junior, as threateningly as she could. But they were too slow, the rider's wand arm, was already raised high above her head.

457

"Whoa!" cried Emma, bringing Bandit in to an abrupt halt.

"Emma, Bandit, he's okay!" Maya cried, tears of joy and relief glistening in her eyes.

Above Emma's head, she waved her unbandaged wand hand back and forth jubilantly. No date, no time and a lifeline that stopped, only when Aunty Helen found out what she'd been up to last Thursday, with her new boyfriend. But that's another terrifying story altogether!

Emma beamed from ear to ear, as she addressed her little cousin:

"If Blink doesn't mind too much, Bandit would like you to ride him home!" she announced. Emma knew what a privilege it was, for a Pegasus to grant such a favour. Maya beamed from ear to ear. Unusually bashful and lost for words, she simply nodded enthusiastically.

There really was only one word for it, as Maya took to the skies on Bandit's back and headed home, to see her mum again:

"Whee!"

Epilogue: Cruellen's missing pages

The smoke from Cruellen's funeral pyre, still clung to Evaline's cloak, as she entered her mother's magic room. She had returned to Threave Castle, one last time, to collect her mother's book. It lay closed now, on top of the dusty table, where it had rested for the past 600 years.

Evaline and Cruellen had been reconciled latterly. Not exactly, a loving mother and daughter relationship, more a respectful and rather distant understanding. Neither able to drop their guard fully, in each other's company.

Evaline lifted the mighty tome from the desk with a sigh.

"What's this?" She asked herself aloud.

Beneath her mother's journal and framed by eons of dust, lay an envelope, addressed with her name, scrawled in her mother's hand. Evaline placed her mother's journal back on the table top and picked up the envelope. She ripped open the top impatiently and slid out a couple of folded sheets of ancient parchment.

Evaline gasped, as she unfolded them. These were the missing pages from Cruellen's journal. Those ripped from her magical book, just after Ellen had given her daughter the pendant keystone necklace.

Evaline took a deep breath and began to read. Ellen's words, leapt from the pages, as if spoken to her, in her own mother's voice:

Ellen knew exactly what must come to pass now. This pendant, now enchanted as a beacon, would lead her daughter home. It will activate on Grim's return. It would bring her daughter here, to read her sad story. A keystone from his castle, she knew, would keep her daughter safe, from Grim's evil hoards. Ellen would enter her portal

459

now, before she lost herself completely to the dark side. There, she would give herself willingly to temptation and split her soul in two. Her light side would wait in her portal for her daughter's inevitable return. Wait to be saved and trust the rest of her plan over to her dark side. A plan hatched in every detail, whilst frozen in ice, as the centuries rolled past.

Only that side of her, would be ruthless enough to make her plan work. No matter what the cost. Sadly, there was no choice. It would be her dark side, who would now raise Evaline, for one purpose only. To stop Grim.

There was only one way... a living wand, the only thing powerful enough to send Grim back and restore the balance of nature, once more. But to find one and wield its power. Only an innocent with pure motives, could do that. Her dark side must find such a child and set her trap.

Nedep's coven would make the perfect setting, to entrap someone dear to her, as bait. The child, if pure of heart and still untainted by the temptations of magic itself, could then summon a living wand. But only, if she truly believed it to be the only thing, which could save her loved one. Mother nature, Ellen knew, would answer such a call, with her greatest gift.

Evaline must be this child's friend. Lure her into joining the Deeds, where initiation, will afford the perfect opportunity to deprive her of the wand.

Then when Grim comes, Evaline will fulfil her destiny. She will read my journal and come to my rescue. She will bring the living wand through the portal, to find my better half. It's only that side of me, being itself pure of heart, which can ever wield the living wand. Evaline shall hold a duplicate for Grim's benefit. The real wand will be concealed upon my person, when I face Grim. As I must for Evaline's sake.

460

"Ellen had planned to face Grim herself! She planned to make the ultimate sacrifice... for me," Evaline mumbled to herself, in disbelief. Trying to take in and make sense of this latest revelation.

Evaline read on in shock and awe, tears blurring the book's final words:

His revenge will be terrible... but all things come to an end and when it does. Evaline will have fulfilled Grim's curse, having delivered him the living wand, over the body of his greatest foe. My body. Only then can Evaline be truly free. So, I will bear it and when death welcomes to me, so too, will the wand pass into the afterlife. Only then, can the balance of nature be restored. Only then, can the wand cast a spell to return Grim and his beasts, back to where they came from."

Evaline rocked back, still in shock. She took a moment to come to terms with what she'd just read. Then, another sudden realisation landed heavily, as she whispered to herself:

"It was my fault Maya had to face Grim. She was never meant to be there. Only once I'd put a spanner in the works and re-united Cruellen, with her better half. Was there no choice!"

Cruellen's haunting words, after Evaline had reunited her mother's halves, now came back to torment her:

"No, what have you done! You've sealed your own friend's fate!"

That had never been part of her mother's plan.

Mischief and Maya entered the room quietly, and closed to Evaline's side. Maya saw the tears and put her arm around her good friend.

"Is that Cruellen's book?" Mischief enquired.

"No, it's Ellen's… it's always been Ellen. The smartest, most courageous and noble witch, there's ever been. I'm proud, so very proud, to call her Mum."

***

If you enjoyed this story, please take the time to review us on Amazon and Goodreads. Thankyou and look out for the next instalment.

If you enjoyed this, but haven't read the original series upon which this book was based... What are you waiting for?

Maya's Magical Adventures

2017 Purple Dragonfly Winner available in paperback or e book from amazon.com or Amazon.co.uk (double click on book icon and follow look inside to get a **free preview)**.

Like nothing you've read before! A fast moving, laugh-out-loud imaginative comedy and fantasy adventure for young adults of all ages. Join Maya a young Scottish girl and her know-it-all talking cat Mischief, flying toothbrush (yes really) and dragon Blink on a series of magical adventures and mishaps as she discovers her magical powers and their hilarious pitfalls.

Find out what lies behind the forbidden door. Solve a series of strange riddles, journey across Ayrshire and eventually face her mystery foe. Slapstick, magic and mythical creatures with a generous helping of cheeky safe humour for the younger ones mixed with more advanced humour, intrigue, surprises and plot twists to keep older readers and adults captivated.

The book is based upon the bedtime stories and illustrations of Maya herself. How will each of her friends meet with their inevitable sticky end? Can she figure out who the mysterious shadow is and how to defeat it? Is Aunty Dot really that shallow and can she trust her? Or is she destined to live out the rest of her life in the strange nightmare of the mirror maze?

There's only one way to find out, read it! Failure to do so may lead to feelings of disappointment, delusions of sanity and the loss of a potentially right good giggle!

"Stop! Don't read this,

Give up now, It's Impossible!"

Maya's magical adventures continue... the quest for the magic bone.

If you're looking for answers... is Mischief really trapped in the book? Will Iona ever find her magic bone? Why am I reading this nonsense? Why does that goblin look like my dad? You need the sequel... take one chapter before bedtime. If symptoms persist consult a doctor!

Touching the Moon

"Magical mayhem, an emotional roller-coaster, hilarious and heart-warming!" Third in the 2017 Purple Dragonfly Young Adult Award winning series, Maya's Magical Adventures. If you like a plot twist or ten, real imagination, intrigue and a right good belly laugh, then this one's for you! If not check for a pulse.

Maya hates bullies. So how could she find herself on the wrong side as they rounded on her friends? With her mum missing, she must risk everything to join a powerful new coven and rescue her, but who can she trust? Can she ever master the art of dragon-back combat? Is middle-age spread something over 40's have on toast for breakfast? Was that relevant? Who writes this rubbish? Only one way to find out...

The Curse of Cardoness

More magical mayhem, giggles and suspense await you in this, the fourth instalment of the award-winning young adult series. A weekend visit to Cardoness with a good friend, turns into a dangerous and surprising quest to uncover the truth behind a curse which has haunted this place for generations. Was the surviving member of the McCulloch clan really responsible for the deaths of all her family or has there been a terrible injustice? Will Maya and her trusted friends survive long enough to uncover the truth or will they fall foul of one of the many traps set by their mysterious foe?

Murder in the Coven

When the High Priestess is murdered in front of the whole coven, there's only one suspect... Maya's good friend is caught red-wanded. But can things really be that simple? In a race against time, can Maya uncover the secret past of the coven and prove her friend's innocence or will she have to face up to the seemingly inevitable conclusion that she's guilty as sin? A light-hearted magical murder mystery with a difference, no in fact it's very different. This, the fifth book in the 2017 Purple Dragonfly award winning series for young adult fiction, is definitely one of the best since the fourth book. Warning: failure to read this book may result in delusions of normality.

They Came from the North

The magical world is thrown into chaos by the arrival of death dragons from the north. Coven after coven fall to this mysterious and seemingly invincible foe. The good witches of the world are rendered powerless and stricken by fear at the hands of the cruellest of enemies. Maya and Evaline are forced to flee for their lives, but there's more to Evaline's chequered past than first meets the eye. As the truth is finally revealed, have they walked willingly into a trap or can they find a way against seemingly impossible odds? This is the sixth book in the award-winning Young Adult series Maya's Magical Adventures, but don't worry each book stands alone. Hall of fame Amazon reviewer NN Light says of the series: "Looking for what to read after Harry Potter? Pick this up today! A must read for all fantasy readers, 5 stars.

Mischief and the Guardian Cats

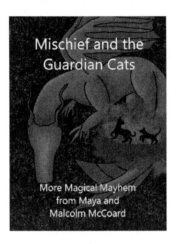

Follow Mischief a rather sarcastic witch's cat, as he trains up his rather dim-witted successor. As guardians of a great and ancient secret, the unlikely friends become entangled in an evil plot to steal the magic from every coven in the land.

The strange truth behind witchcraft and the true origins of magic is about to be revealed. If you've been waiting for answers to some of life's most perplexing questions:

Why do cats have 9 lives? Who really domesticated the first humans? Why are dogs no longer a cat's best friend? Is the author completely mad? Can I really resist reading this nonsense? Then the answer to the last question is, don't!

A spin off from the award-winning Young Adult series Maya's Magical Adventures, but a "cracking good stand-alone work in its own right!" Hall of fame Amazon reviewer NN Light says of the series: "Looking for what to read after

Harry Potter? Pick this up today! A must read for all fantasy readers, 5 stars."

Other Titles:

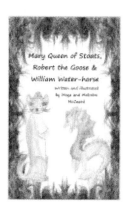

Mary Queen of Stoats

Humorous rhyming stories which parody the lives of great Scottish heroes of the past. Mary Queen of Stoats follows Mary from a troubled pup, crowned queen just one week old to her struggles against Liz the First, the weasel Queen of England. Though guaranteed historically inaccurate, it's a great light-hearted introduction to these historical figures which will bring a smile to the face of readers of any age. Robert the Goose chronicles the life and mis-adventures of a young gosling with spindly legs as he battles for the Scottish crown and to win the freedom of his native fowl against the tyrant drake King Edward the first. The final installment William Water-horse lifts the lid on the secrets and true nature of the Loch Ness monster. Also known as a kelpie or water-horse - the secrets of the identity and concealment of this practical joker across the ages are finally laid bare!

The Six Lives of Henry the Eighth

This charming and humorous rhyming picture book follows the mis-adventures of Henry, the accident-prone runt of a litter of eight black and white cats. As we all know cats have 9 lives. Henry though gets off to a difficult start in life and soon finds himself down to 6. After an unfortunate, but tasty incident with Aunt Dolly's parrot, our rather plump and lazy house cat finds himself cast out of the family home. The story follows our unlucky hero through a series of cunning plans, adventures and mishaps as he searches for shelter and something to eat. Each adventure ends unpredictably, but with inevitably disastrous consequences for poor Henry as he uses up each of his remaining lives. Will he ever make it back home? There's only one way to find out. Ideal bedtime reading that will keep mum and dad amused too! Suitable for and tested on kids of all ages 8 to 80

Follow Malcolm McCoard on Goodreads or Twitter.

Printed in Great Britain
by Amazon